WEST OF PREHISTORIC

ERIK 'TRACER' TESTERMAN

SEVERED PRESS
HOBART TASMANIA

WEST OF PREHISTORIC

WWW.SEVEREDPRESS.COM

ISBN: 978-1-922323-83-5

'For Meredith'

WEST OF PREHISTORIC

June 1885.

Circling buzzards made the killing field easy enough to find.

Soldiers' bodies lay scattered for a half mile across open prairie. Mangled, crushed, gnawed on. They'd made a running fight of it, but were slaughtered anyway.

A dozen men. Armed with the finest weapons and equipment since the War Between the States. Trained and experienced in fighting Indians, rustlers, and outlaws.

For all the good that did them.

All I could find were a couple of dead apes and a single wounded triceratops.

Sending the squad out had been the Lieutenant's decision. I didn't blame him. He didn't have a choice. But with the loss of these men, our low chances of survival dropped even further.

Turning my horse around, I touched heels to his flanks, leaving the weapons for the Indians to find. They were going to need them.

As for me?

My name is Jedidiah Huckleberry Smith.

And I'm probably going to die as well.

***

Two weeks earlier.
Smith Ranch, Wyoming Territory

The edge on the heavy axe burst through the wood with a satisfying thunk, sending splinters flying as the log split apart. Twin chunks toppled off the large stump. Picking one of the pieces, I set it to be split again, then rested on the axe handle.

With a gloved hand, I pushed a soaked mop of unruly black hair out of my eyes and blinked rapidly as a drop of sweat trickled into an eye. My shoulders ached, and my stomach growled.

My horse, Carbine, a beautiful dun mustang, stomped his hooves, impatient that he had to stay harnessed to the wagon while waiting for me to finish my work. Ignoring him, I stretched. As my back arched, I felt the familiar tugging from the large mass of decades old scar tissue.

The scars were a constant reminder of the singular day that changed the course of my life, and ultimately led me to where I am now. Living in isolation on a small cattle ranch, a fugitive from justice, a former outlaw… a damaged man. And somewhere out there, someone owed me a debt of blood for the scars. Someone who'd eluded me almost my entire life. Someone who may very well already be dead, but not by my hand. I wasn't sure which was worse, him still breathing, or someone else stealing the pleasure of taking his life.

Angry thoughts shifted my mood darker, and I quickly swung the axe over my shoulders and slammed the angular blade down with far more force than necessary. The explosion of splinters as the fractioned log burst apart did nothing to ease the hot anger that boiled up from within.

It was the sort of rage that made me want to stop this foolish charade of being a law-abiding citizen and go back to hunting him down. But that was pointless; there were no trails left to follow. They'd all gone cold years ago. Just like the bodies I'd left in my vengeful wake.

I swallowed hard and forced myself to take deep breaths. That wasn't me anymore. For two years now, I'd begun to put down roots, even if I wasn't much of a cattleman. And for once in my life, I was invested in something good and solid. Something that wouldn't shoot back at me.

Putting hands on my hips, I looked around the pasture, pleased with the amount of work I'd accomplished today. It was hard work, but rewarding. Felling trees, then sawing and chopping them into firewood was the hard part, the rewarding part was blowing the stumps up with dynamite. My ears still rang.

In the distance, storm clouds were gathering above the Granite Mountains and making their way towards me. It looked like a real doozy, but I was done for the day anyways. Tossing the axe and saws into the wagon, I threw a few more pieces of split wood into the back to top the load off.

Taking the gun belt down that rested on the seat of the wagon, I buckled it around my waist and climbed aboard. Call it a natural impulse, but I had a very rational fear of being unarmed. Without my Colt Peacemaker on one side, balanced by a nine-and-a-half-inch Bowie on the other, I may as well have been naked.

Carbine looked over his shoulder, and I could tell he was displeased. He'd been pulling double duty today as my mare, Misty, rested lame in the barn. Slapping the reins on his back, the tan horse leaned into his harness and the heavily laden wagon began to roll forward.

Relaxing as much as possible on the bumpy ride, I watched nearby cattle move into the trees to avoid the coming storm. My spread wasn't that big, but if my small herd kept growing, I'd need to hire some ranch hands on. That'd be a hassle all on its own. In the meantime, being alone suited me just fine.

Once we reached the house, I stopped my horse and lashed a canvas sheet over the firewood, before turning him loose in the fenced corral beside the barn.

As I bent over to lock the gate behind him, Carbine snatched the hat off my head and trotted off, the brown battered Stetson dangling from between his lips. He dropped it a dozen yards away and pranced in a circle around it, flipping his black mane and tail happily.

Swearing, I crawled through the creaking rails of the corral and picked the hat up. I considered smacking him with it, but he kept his distance, as if knowing my intentions. Instead, I slapped it against my leg a few times to knock the fresh dirt and slobber off.

It figures. I've two horses, one lame and the other an asshole.

I watched him happily trot into the pole shed built against the barn. He preferred that spot to stand in the shade and spend the night. Even with the big storm coming in, I wasn't concerned; the walled sides and thatched roof would protect him from the worst of it.

As a light rain began to fall and the distant rumble of thunder grew louder, I pulled the axe, saw, and leftover dynamite from the wagon and hauled them to the barn. The doors were closed, and as usual, stuck shut. I kicked, swore, jerked, and tugged on them before I finally got one open. They were wretched things, big and stout, as all things in the West needed to be. But they were a constant aggravation and would certainly be the death of me. One of these days, I'd split a gut forcing them open, and die writhing in the dirt as they towered over me, jammed shut in their mockery.

But the barn itself was a great big thing. A story and a half tall, with a wide opening down the center and several stalls along the side. Big enough to hold over a dozen cattle or horses with room to spare. Hay was kept in the loft, gradually added to during the short summer in preparation for keeping my critters alive in case of a long, hard winter.

Dropping the tools at the end of the barn by the small back door, I stopped by Misty's stall to feed her an apple. It'd only been two days since I noticed her favoring her right front leg. The swelling had gone down, but she still favored it and needed more rest.

Unlike Carbine, she was a good horse.

I gave her a good scratch on her withers before jogging through the rain and onto the porch of my one room ranch house. Once under cover, I turned and watched the swirling gray clouds grow nearer. It looked like we were in for a big one. The toe of my boot hit something as I opened the door. My saddle sat next to the rocking chair where I'd mended some stitching this morning. It needed to be put away still, but I wasn't about to lug it back through the rain to the barn now. It'd be fine here for the night.

Lightning split the distant sky, and moments later, the rolling boom of thunder reached me. Knocking mud clumps from my boots, I stepped inside to settle in for a stormy night.

***

The terrified scream of a horse jerked me awake and out of bed.

Two long strides and I peeked through the cross shaped firing port in the closed shutter.

With the storm blocking most of the moonlight, visibility was limited. I couldn't see much of anything, and heard nothing else except the drumming of rain and wind against the roof.

It was times like this when I was thankful that I didn't sleep naked.

I jerked boots on over bare feet and slung the thick leather gun belt around my cotton threaded drawers. From above the door, I took down a well-worn Winchester 1873 rifle and worked the lever, jacking a cartridge into the chamber. With weapon in hand, I felt the reassuring comfort that only ample amounts of firepower can give a man when he faces unknown things that go bump in the night.

I waited, standing still, listening for any noises past the sounds of the rain and wind. Nothing.

Lighting a lantern, I stepped into the storm.

The rain was falling at a slant, cutting underneath the roof on the porch and soaking me to the bone. I regretted not grabbing my slicker.

Rain plastered my hair to my scalp and I shuddered as cold water ran down my bare chest and back before soaking into my underwear. The lantern gave off a low glow, fighting to penetrate through the rain and darkness.

The open barn door squeaked on its hinges as I moved across the yard. Lightning flashed and moments later the rumbling thunder washed over me.

Holding the lantern out, I saw the top two rails of the corral lay splintered and broken on the ground.

I inspected the damage and area around it. No sign of blood or struggle, just a single set of hoof tracks leading away towards the forest at a run. Obviously, Carbine broke through the fence, but why? It wasn't like him to leave shelter and run into a storm.

Lightning flashed again, illuminating the empty corral and splitting a tree at the edge of the forest in a flash of sparks. The boom of thunder hit me a split second later followed by the heavy barn door thumping as it bounced against the board siding.

A couple of soft thuds came from inside the building and I took a few hesitant steps towards the barn, uncertain of what I'd heard. Another thud, followed by a crunching, like branches being stepped on. Then a snort and a tearing noise. More crunching.

I wasn't sure what I was hearing. It was hard to make out. Rain pounded my body, trees groaned and cracked in the heavy wind, and the rumble of thunder rolled over me again. Now I heard nothing but the noises of the storm and repeated thumping of the lone swinging door.

Puzzled, I figured I may as well check on Misty.

Rain poured heavily down from the angled roof, putting a sheet of falling water between myself and the inside of the barn. A hard wind gust hit me, and I staggered before leaning into it.

Frustrated with the pounding wind and cold rain, I raised the lantern and ducked through the sheet of water and into the barn. It covered me, soaking whatever tiny bits of my body that had remained dry so far.

I took two steps inside, blinking rapidly to clear the water from my eyes, and then I skidded to a sudden stop.

There was a monster in the barn.

Facing away from me, the giant beast swung its head over a shoulder and glared.

The creature had a thick, heavy head, almost reptilian in appearance. Something dangled from clenched teeth. Dark liquid dripped from jaws and onto the dirt floor. Black eyes reflected lantern light, giving off a sinister appearance. Two bony ridges started above the slanted nostrils, growing larger as they ran along its head and flared out above the eyes before ending at the top of its skull. Small bumps and ridges ran down the back of its neck along its spine, ending above the beast's shoulder blades.

A large, thick tail rose slightly into the air, tapering to a point, close enough I could have reached out and touched it. Muscular and powerful hind legs held the rear end up, while the front arms dug claws into Misty's body.

My sweet, injured horse lay ripped open, entrails and ribbons of torn flesh strewn among the shattered boards of her stall.

Shocked, I realized a hind leg dangled from the beast's mouth. Broken shards of bone glistened palely from the lantern light against the darkened flesh.

I couldn't move. I couldn't think. My mind couldn't comprehend what was in front of me.

The barn door thumped behind me in the wind.

The severed limb dropped with a sickly wet thud and the monster snorted softly, tilting its head to the side. It sniffed, as though trying to figure out what small creature would dare approach so boldly.

We stared at each other in the glow of the lantern, the moments stretching, then a strong gust of wind slammed the door shut behind me with a boom that shook the building.

That broke the magical moment.

I flinched as the monster roared, the noise assaulting my ears and revealing rows of large curved teeth coated with blood and bits of flesh. The stench was overpowering and nauseating. Droplets of blood and pieces of Misty flew from its mouth, splattering against my chest and face.

Forgetting the rifle in my hands, I turned and ran face first into the door.

It didn't budge. It was stuck. It was always stuck.

I shoved with a shoulder, throwing all my weight against the rough boards.

Nothing.

Screaming in rage, I stepped back and kicked in a last-ditch attempt to force it open.

It failed.

The creature turned in the confines of the hallway to face me, its tail slamming into the center beam with an audible crack.

The second-floor joists creaked and groaned as the heavy weight of hay shifted on the broken post.

I quickly looked for a way out. The large double doors were jammed shut. The windows in the stalls were too narrow to fit through. That left only the small door at the far end of the barn. But the beast stood between myself and escape.

The creature lunged, mouth agape and teeth bared.

Diving to the side, I dropped the lantern and it burst, spewing flaming oil as I rolled away.

The monster's mouth snapped shut where I'd been a moment before, then the creature jerked back, hissing, as it recoiled from the explosion of flames.

Kneeling, I gripped the rifle tighter.

It was time to fight back.

Jerking the smooth wood stock against my shoulder, I squeezed the trigger, sending a 200-grain bullet into the beast's chest.

Instinctively, I shucked the lever and fired again without waiting to see its reaction. Because I had ten rounds and I intended to use them all to send this creature back to the hell it came from. I worked the rifle quickly, peppering the beast with bullet after bullet.

Roaring in pain and anger, the creature lunged.

I flung myself aside, stumbling to avoid the spreading flames and slamming my face into the roughhewn boards of a stall.

Pain shot through my skull and tears welled as the rifle flew from my grasp.

Blinking, I rolled desperately as a clawed arm swiped at me. A sharp line of pain flashed hot across my chest. But the stall saved me by taking the brunt of the blow, sending shards of wood showering down on me.

I scrambled backwards, trying to put more distance between us. Blood trickled down my chest, but I ignored the wound. If I didn't die in the immediate future, I'd worry about it later.

The beast turned after me, its tail slashing through the smoke and slamming the stuck door open. Storm winds blew inside, fanning the flames higher.

The interior of the barn became a flickering smoke-filled haze as the fire spread, licking the sides of the stalls and along the door jamb.

Smoke wafted around the monster, illuminating it with dancing shadows. Dark fluid oozed from puckered holes where my bullets had found their target.

I stood carefully, bracing myself to move for another sudden attack.

The monster watched, eyes following my movements. It slowly rose on hind legs, the thick tail dropping to the floor, front arms spread with black claws extended. The gaping maw of bloodied jagged teeth opened.

I could taste its rotten breath in the air.

The beast reared back slightly, mouth opening impossibly wide as it prepared to strike.

This time, I was ready.

Drawing my pistol, I fired from the hip.

I emptied the Peacemaker. Each bullet hit a little higher than the last as I rode the recoil and worked my shots up its large body. The final bullet skimmed along the beast's snout, slicing open a flap of skin, exposing bone, and blowing out one of the creature's eye sockets.

The monster roared and thrashed its arms, pawing the wound that partially blinded it.

Damn thing just wouldn't die.

Turning to run, I tripped over Misty's remains. Blood, organs, and rendered flesh squished under my weight. My hand went into her stomach. Gagging, I slipped off her corpse into a stall.

The boards gave me a moment of concealment, but I had no illusion about their usefulness as protection. If I was found, the beast would make short work of my hiding spot.

Flipping the barrel of the revolver upwards, I rotated the cylinder and quickly dumped the empty shells. With gore covered fingers, I began to reload, carefully feeding cartridges into the chambers, one by one. Each turn of the cylinder made a quiet snick that I prayed the monster didn't hear.

Lightning struck nearby, temporarily overwhelming my senses with the painful crack of electricity.

I froze.

The barn was silent except for the crackle of growing flames and a low rhythmic hissing.

Smoke drifted into the stall, burning my eyes and lungs. I fought to stifle a cough.

Suddenly, black claws gripped the wood rail above me and I cringed lower as splinters trickled down. The beast leaned forward, searching the barn with its good eye. Blood dripped off the creature's pebbled hide and splattered onto my bare shoulders.

I only had two cartridges loaded. Fearful of making a noise, I eased the loading gate on the pistol shut over the cylinder, wincing at the tiny click it gave. Tilting the barrel upwards, I pointed it under the monster's jaw and began taking up the slack on the trigger.

The beast jerked back out of sight.

I gave a small sigh of relief.

Violently, I was catapulted forward onto my face as the damaged reptilian head slammed through the wall of the stall I'd been leaning against.

Teeth snapped shut as I scrambled away and rolled onto my back. The beast's head jutted through shattered boards, snarling and snapping as it strained to get through. Nails shrieked as the wall threatened to tear away from the posts at any moment.

Firmly gripping the pistol tightly with both hands, I raised my head and fired between my knees.

The bullet hit and skimmed along the thick skull like the last, gashing open another flap of thick skin and exposing bone. The monster jerked at the pain and my remaining shot missed.

Screaming in rage, I resisted the temptation to hurl my empty pistol at its bloodied face.

The beast wrenched its head back and forth, struggling to pull back through the jagged broken wall. Boards, bent inward from the creature's intrusion, pushed against the back of the monster's skull. They tightened and dug into flesh as it fought to free itself. The foul creature hissed and snapped.

I shoved my pistol into its holster and crawled into the open room and around Misty's mutilated remains.

The smoke was harsh and filling the barn. I coughed and hacked as it threatened to suffocate me. Looking past the thrashing beast's tail, I spied my rifle near the entrance with flames licking the barrel. Desperate for a loaded weapon, I slid across the packed dirt floor and scooped up the gun. The barrel was hot, the stock singed in places, but thankfully the rounds hadn't cooked off from the heat yet.

The beast roared, grabbing and ripping at the broken boards trapping its head with claws. Splayed feet dug into the ground as it leveraged its thick hind quarters to break through the wood. The tail thrashed back and forth, flinging tools and equipment across the floor and into the flames.

Bits of burning hay from the rafters fell between us as flames licked the ceiling.

The large front door was still open, but a raging inferno stood between me and my escape.

The only option was still the small door in the far end. And in my desperation for a loaded weapon, I foolishly made the horrible mistake of putting the monster back between me and my exit.

With a mighty jerk, the creature pulled itself free and backed into the cracked center post.

It broke.

The center of the barn crashed down, dropping burning debris, and stopping a mere handful of feet above the beast. Barely supported by broken and creaking joists, the barn threatened to collapse on us at any moment. Flames whooshed higher from air entering through the shattered roof, fanning them to towering heights as rain poured in and fought to quench them. The air cleared slightly as smoke billowed out above us.

Amidst the flames and smoke, I looked at the bloodied harbinger of death and terror before me.

Blood oozed from the monster's wounds, bits of splintered wood were embedded in its flesh, and one eye was a gaping ruin seeping blood from the mangled socket. A front arm hung low, damaged from one of my bullets.

I racked the lever and savored the snick of the action closing on a fresh round. I didn't know how many bullets were left in the tubular magazine. Four? Five?

Didn't matter. If I was going to be eaten, the beast would have to gnaw through my empty guns first.

The creature charged with a roar.

Adrenaline and fear gave speed to my hands. Jerking the barrel up, I stroked the action, firing faster than I ever had before.

My aim was true.

The monstrosity twitched and shuddered as it absorbed the rounds, slowing down as massive tissue damage and blood loss weakened the beast. But it still didn't stop coming with mouth and claws spread wide.

In desperation, I shoved the rifle in front of me and wedged it horizontally into the creature's open mouth. Large teeth clamped down, narrowly missing my hands. A gnarled, wet tongue slapped against the weapon as the stock splintered and broke beneath the pressure of its jaws. Even in a weakened state, its strength far surpassed my own.

Hot, rotten breath bathed me as the beast pushed me backwards towards the raging fire.

I screamed as the heat became unbearable and let go of the broken gun, diving aside before I was pushed into the blazing hot inferno.

The beast's head thrust into the flames. It sizzled and popped as skin and raw wounds burned. The creature roared in pain around the rifle jutting out from each side of its mouth. A flailing arm backhanded me and flung me like a rag doll.

I hit the ground with a heavy thud and slid against a shattered stall.

Forcing myself up, I ran around the struggling creature to the rear of the barn, dodging bundles of flaming hay raining down.

The monster thrashed, slamming into broken walls and beams as it tried dislodging the jammed rifle from its mouth.

The front of the barn shuddered under the impacts. It was a miracle the flaming structure still stood.

The barn had become a hellfire with a demon trapped inside, roaring in pain and anger. Smoke swirled around the beast, while rain dripped through the broken roof and fought spreading flames.

Reaching the back door, I paused as I noticed my tools from earlier. Next to the wedged head of the axe sat a small marked wooden chest with rope handles. Jerking the lid off, I saw the leftover paper-wrapped sticks of dynamite from earlier.

This was more like it.

I grabbed a blast cap and jammed it onto the explosive. Twisting the fuse around my fingers, I snapped it off short.

The partially blinded monster knocked the rifle out of its mouth and began stalking down the aisle. Blood and saliva dripped onto the floor, sizzling in the flames. It jerked its head aside as a bundle of burning hay fell in front of it. The wounded arm dangled lower now, and a hind leg dragged, giving it an uneven gait as it approached.

Rage seemed to be keeping the wretched thing alive.

Using a nearby flame, I ignited the fuse in a shower of sparks and burned quickly towards the blasting cap. Tossing the stick back in the crate, I kicked the box towards the beast before running out the back door into the rain.

Fire rose high into the air behind me as the barn was consumed in flames.

Slipping in the wet grass, I stumbled to my knees. Pushing up from the rain-soaked ground, I ran for the house. Shelter seemed so far away.

Behind me came a bestial roar followed by heavy thuds.

I dared a backwards look.

The monster ripped the small door off its hinges. Claws grabbed the frame and ripped pieces away as the creature fought to get through the narrow opening. The wall screeched and shuddered as siding snapped and broke.

Shoving its mangled head and shoulders through the opening, the monster roared at me.

The dynamite blew.

A chunk of flaming debris hit me like a train, driving air from my lungs and slamming me backwards against the ground.

For a moment, everything went dark.

Then I became acutely aware of pain. I blinked rapidly. Everything hurt. The gash across my chest stung. My lungs and throat felt like they were on fire. Dozens of small scrapes and cuts covered my singed body. My long underwear was in tatters.

I coughed.

Pain from the movement almost consumed me.

Bits of smoking debris were scattered throughout the yard. A pitchfork was embedded nearby, its broken handle on fire.

What remained of the barn shuddered and collapsed in a shower of sparks and flame.

The beast lay near me. Blood ran from its many wounds and mingled with the rain. The rear legs and tail were shredded and mangled from the explosion.

But still, it lived.

The hellish beast's single remaining dark orb glared. Snarling, it weakly stretched a forelimb towards me, sharp claws open and reaching.

My battered body responded sluggishly as I drew my Colt. I pointed the trembling barrel at the beast's face, and pulled the trigger.

Click.

The pistol was empty.

I dropped the useless gun and with thick, fumbling fingers grasped the handle of my Bowie.

The claws that reached for me suddenly clutched at the wet soil and with a violent spasm, the beast shuddered, before giving a final rattling breath and laying still.

Lightning danced across the sky as the storm raged on and closing my eyes, I embraced the pain and darkness.

***

I woke hacking and coughing, with a pounding headache and soaked to the bone as a light rain continued to fall. My empty pistol lay beside me, wet and gleaming in the early rays of the morning sun that peeked through retreating storm clouds.

The monster still stared at me, bloodied lips parted in a snarl, the single eye dulled and milky in death.

Beyond the creature, all that remained of my barn was a tumbled mass of burnt timbers and rubble amongst small residual flames that hissed in the rain. A thick gray smoke drifted across the yard.

Bits of smoldering wreckage and charred debris lay scattered around me.

Pushing myself up, I grabbed the gun and stumbled across the yard to the house. Slamming the door shut, I lowered the door bar and dropped to the floor with my back against the wall. If more monsters lurked outside, I didn't know if a barred door would stop them. But it was comforting, and right now, I felt like a kitten could finish me off with a single blow.

I dumped the spent brass from my pistol onto the floor. Pulling fresh cartridges from my belt, I reloaded. The gun, while smeared with the same sticky blood that coated me, would still function and that's all that mattered.

Stripping out of my boots and tattered underwear, I left them in a heap in the middle of the room and crawled naked into bed. My pistol I laid within reach on a small table.

Lying there, I stared at the exposed rafters in disbelief.

Misty was ripped apart, Carbine missing, and my barn burnt to the ground because of an ungodly creature. My mind tried to convince itself this wasn't happening, but the pain proved it was all too real.

I closed my eyes again.

***

When I woke hours later, I felt like I had been shot at, missed, shit at, and hit all over.

My joints were stiff. The cut across my chest was a congealed mass of blood and ash. Small nicks, cuts, and burns covered me. The stench of singed hair and blood filled my nostrils. Moving gingerly, I opened the shutters, squinting at the bright light as my eyes adjusted. The yard was just how I remembered it from last night. Full of burnt debris with a giant mangled corpse near the ruination that'd been my barn.

As for the inside of the house, it looked like someone had been murdered. Ash mingled with blood smeared along where I'd fumbled my way inside. The trail led inside the door, against the wall, and across the floor to the scattered pile of bloodied and shredded clothing.

Sighing, I pulled pants and boots on before stepping outside.

Carbine trotted around the side of the house, head and tail held high, as if proud that he'd survived. He snorted and pranced, keeping his distance from the smoldering remains of the barn and the monster's carcass.

Leaving him to wander around, I cleaned myself up in the creek.

The filthy and crusted scab over my chest was inspected and carefully washed first. The single claw that caught me ripped the flesh deep enough to warrant a few stitches. I'd gotten lucky; if all three claws had hit me with their full force, I'd be inside the creature's belly by now.

Then swallowing a couple slugs of whiskey, I bit down on a piece of folded leather before drizzling some of the harsh liquid across the wound. Tears rolled from my eyes at the burst of fresh pain. Then I stitched the gash shut, screaming through clenched teeth as the thread pulled torn flesh back together.

Once finished, the stitches looked horrible, but they'd hold.

Taking up the scrap of cloth again, I wiped away the rest of the grime and looked in a small shaving mirror. In addition to all my other ailments, I had two black eyes and a nice goose egg bump on my head from slamming into the stall.

I looked like hammered crap.

After cleaning myself up the best I could, I rocked back and forth on the porch, staring at the remains of the beast.

Even dead, it was frightening to behold.

Large and powerful, corded with muscle under pebbled tan hide. The undamaged eye that'd been so menacing last night was glazed over, but the teeth and claws still showed the creature's lethality. I'd never seen or even heard of anything like it.

Then there was the barn, which was destroyed.

Luckily my saddle survived. Leaving it on the porch last night had been a blessing. But the cost to replace the rest of my gear and tools lost in the fire would be staggering.

Not to mention Misty. She'd been a good horse.

And somewhere in the ashes were the remains of my rifle.

At least I had a spare, an old Spencer Repeater. Twenty years past its prime and fed by loading cartridges into a tube through the buttstock. It was something of an outdated oddity now. But it fired a hard-hitting round that could kill a buffalo.

It'd do if more beasts came calling, and right now, it lay fully loaded within arm's reach.

I whistled for Carbine and managed to harness and saddle him without too much swearing at the pain or his need to constantly side step away from me.

The Sheriff needed to know about this. More of these monsters might be lurking around and while I got lucky, anyone else caught in the open, unprepared, would be creature food. The hard part would be convincing him.

Luckily, I had a big corpse.

Taking a small axe that I used for splitting kindling from the house, I collected my proof.

Afterward, I slid the Spencer into the leather saddle scabbard. My vest pockets jingled with loose rounds for the rifle and the loops in my belt were filled with .45 cartridges for the Peacemaker. I wanted to be ready for anything. If I had more dynamite, I would've stuffed it into the saddlebags as well.

Easing myself up in the saddle, we rode the trail towards town.

I was edgy the entire way, watching for anything that might want to eat me. It was an uncomfortable ride. The pain from constantly shifting in the saddle coupled with my high level of alertness was exhausting.

But after several hours, we reached Granite Falls.

***

Cresting a hill, I slowed Carbine. The town lay exposed in the center of a vast valley below me. It was a beautiful place. Scenic, dotted with small stands of trees, lots of knee-high prairie grass and a gradual incline to the hills that surrounded it.

I always wondered why western towns never seemed to pick the high ground. It's as though town founders always desired someplace pretty instead of a nice hill with an elevation advantage in case of an Indian attack.

Regardless of the lack of a tactical advantage, the location was beautiful.

The town was laid out with the main street running north to south. A half mile to the west a wide river flowed. Cold and fresh, the river fed from melting snows and ice in the distant north and ran over a large waterfall on the edge of the valley that the town got its name from. Train tracks came from the west as well, running on thick log ties and steel rails across the river on a framed bridge to the southern end of town where the train station and corralled stockyards stood.

I hadn't been here in over a month, and the place had grown.

In addition to the church finally getting its steeple and bell installed, two more buildings had gone up since my last visit. All nice and neat beside each other in the center of town, with a few more outlying buildings in varying stages of construction.

The single, wide street between the buildings ran over a quarter mile past them, through rows of mismatched tents used for temporary housing and small businesses, and ending at the train station where a locomotive huffed steam and whistled as it prepared to depart with a load full of cattle and wool.

Probably five hundred people lived and worked in the town.

It was far too crowded for me.

Watching the busy town, I couldn't shake the feeling that this was a calm before the storm, and something terrible was headed this way. Pushing the dark thoughts away, I touched my heels to Carbine's flanks to urge him forward.

As I rode the rutted wagon trail into town and down the main street, I noticed peoples' questioning looks when they saw my battered face. I pulled my Stetson lower over my blackened eyes to avoid the attention.

Passing the church, the Reverend stepped from the shadows of its interior and gave a friendly wave. A tall, thin man, he wore a flat brimmed black hat, white shirt, and a dusty frock coat. As usual, he carried a dog-eared Bible tucked under an arm.

I gave him a wave in return, but kept moving. He was a good man of the cloth. I once found myself in his church one dark night, confessing to him about my past life. He was a good listener who gave even better advice, and was nice enough to not have me arrested. Ever since then, I'd become part of his flock.

As for the Sheriff, I wasn't overly concerned about him. I tried quitting outlawing once before and tried soldiering instead. It didn't take, but that's where I met our local Sheriff before he was a lawman. We'd fought together in the Nez Perce War and the strange twists of fate brought us to the same town years later. But just because we trusted each other with our lives, didn't mean I trusted him with my past. The less he knew, the better.

Tying Carbine to the hitching post in front of the Sheriff's Office, I dismounted and pulled a wrapped bundle from the saddlebags. Stepping onto the boardwalk, I noted the Mayor's Office with curtains pulled across the windows and a padlock on the door. Strange.

Walking past the locked building, I stepped through an open door. Sheriff Dan sat leaned back in his chair, feet propped on the desk, cup of coffee in hand. The polished silver star on his chest glinted from the light pouring through the open windows. A gun belt was strapped around his waist, and a Winchester repeating shotgun rested on hooks above his head. Old and stern, with a gray beard and bald head, he was the sort of man who would help a fellow out, or fill him full of lead.

He was a great Sheriff like that.

"Afternoon, Jed." Squinting, he took in my black eyes as I removed my Stetson. "Rough night?"

I waved off his concern with the hat and a small smile. "Don't worry. It was a fight against overwhelming odds, but I won."

He shrugged and gestured towards the coffee pot. "As long as I don't have to arrest you or anyone else. So far, it's been a pretty easy day."

Taking the battered tin cup beside the pot, I glanced inside. It looked clean, mostly. Ignoring the small dark spot in the bottom, I poured. "Actually... we may have something of a rather large problem." I took a sip and grimaced. The coffee was strong enough to float a horseshoe.

He raised an eyebrow. "Do tell."

"It's easier to show you." I tossed him the wrapped bundle.

Dan spilled coffee as he attempted a one-handed catch. "Dammit,

Jed!" He held up the oddly shaped bundle. "What's this?"

"A small part of a big problem. Go ahead and look. You wouldn't believe me otherwise." I dropped into the chair opposite him and tossed my hat on his desk.

He kicked his feet down and sat upright. Setting the cup on the cluttered desk, Dan began to unwrap the bundle. My eyes flicked to the board on the wall beside the cells with the Wanted Posters tacked haphazardly over each other. It was an old habit. I never knew if I might see myself or some old buddies on there.

I didn't see anyone I knew, but there were a couple of outlaws that I'd heard of before.

As he removed the canvas wrapping, a set of three large black claws and a short length of forearm lay exposed. The end was hacked off and bone jutted from the stump.

The lawman stared at the severed limb. His mouth twisted tight into a grim frown. "What in the hell is this from?"

"I don't know. But I need you to come out and look at the rest of it." I looked him in the eye. "If there are more of these... things... that those claws came from, and I suspect there are, folks are going to die."

I'd been worried he wouldn't believe me if I tried to describe what attacked my ranch. But the large clawed hand seemed to do the trick for piquing his curiosity.

He nodded, gently touching his finger to one of the black claw points. "I want to see this thing. Today. Where's the corpse?"

"Back at my place," I grimaced. "What's left of it that is."

"What do you mean, what's left of it?"

"Well... I used some dynamite to kill it. It's a long story." I took another sip of the strong brew.

He shook his head in disbelief. "Alright, fill me in on the way. But give me an hour or two to wrap a couple of things up and for the deputies to get back from their rounds." He jerked his thumb towards a man snoring softly in one of the twin cells behind him. "I've also got a drunk to kick out later. You weren't the only one who had an eventful night."

I snorted. The deputies were his nephews. "You still using those two buffoons?" I couldn't stand them. The feeling was mutual.

Dan glared. "Good help is hard to find. I offered you a badge before them, remember? You turned it down."

I did remember, and my concern was that I might burst into flames the moment I pinned it on. Standing, I downed the last mouthful of coffee and set the cup on his desk. "See you in a bit. I've got a couple errands to run."

"Jed? Try not to blow anything up while you're in town."

"I don't make promises I can't keep, Dan." I gave him a sly wink.

With a disapproving grunt, he wrapped the canvas back around the severed limb and tossed it to me.

***

Since I had time to kill, I put the severed claw back in the saddlebags and crossed the street to the Bucket O' Blood. The name was misleading. It wasn't that violent of a place, but the owner was something of a joker who figured the name would spur interest.

Personally, I thought people tended to stay away from establishments where they might get shot. But after last night, I could use a drink regardless of the time of day. Hopefully, it'd take away some of the dull aches throbbing through my body.

I pushed through the batwing doors and paused, blinking rapidly to allow my eyes to adjust to the dim interior. I hated this moment. It always seemed like a good time for a man with a grudge to plug you with a bullet.

After a few seconds and no gunshots, I could see well enough to make my way to the bar.

Being midday, there wasn't much going on. A trio of rough-looking characters at the end of the bar sized me up. One said something, and his friends laughed in response. They looked like miners blowing off some steam and probably wasting whatever gold they'd scraped out of a claim. At least one had a pistol tucked into his waistband that I could see. A sawed-off shotgun rested on the bar amongst their bottles.

A couple of working girls lounged by the piano, talking in low tones and most likely, nursing hangovers. One raven haired beauty smiled, showing me a wide gap between her front teeth.

Giving her a grin, I tipped my hat in return. I didn't partake in working girls, but I didn't disrespect them either. My southern, aristocrat mother raised me right like that.

In the far corner, a man sat with his back to the wall, idly shuffling cards. His tan flat-brimmed hat was tipped low, obscuring the top half of his face. An empty bottle and several glasses lay scattered on the table before him from a game long finished.

Other than that, it was dead in here.

For a moment, I considered telling them I'd been attacked by a giant beast. But I didn't want the reputation of being the local crazy who went around shouting about monsters in the darkness.

I'd let the Sheriff do that.

The bartender put down the glass he was cleaning with a rag and walked over as I gingerly leaned against the polished bar. He took in my face.

"You look like you could use some whiskey."

"Yeah, the cheap stuff." I didn't think I'd be able to afford anything

17

nice for a while. Not until I made the long ride to the loot I'd cached. Stupid monster.

Reaching under the bar, he pulled out a brown unmarked bottle and shot glass. He poured a slug and started to put the bottle away, before looking at my face again and appearing to think better of it. The bottle was lifted questioningly.

I knew I couldn't drink the entire thing and make the ride back home without falling out of the saddle. But I could always cork the bottle and take it home for later. I gave him a nod, and he pushed them both towards me.

I dug a couple coins out and slid them over.

Scooping them up, he gestured at my face. "That's pretty fresh. How does the other guy look?"

I decided to be vague instead of crazy. "A little rougher than me."

The bartender must have decided he didn't care to dig any deeper, and simply nodded. If I'd broken the law, my money was good up until the moment I was arrested. Why hurry things along with a paying customer?

"Where's Left Arm?" I asked.

Left Arm O'Malley was the jokester who owned the bar. A veteran of the War Between the States, his name came from his missing right arm. Rumor was a cannon ball took it off at the Siege of Vicksburg, but the man himself always came up with new amusing stories as to how it happened. Last one I heard involved him being shanghaied onto a ship and a mermaid gnawing it off after a copulation of sorts. He was kind of an odd fellow like that.

"He went to Rock Springs. Family troubles." He nodded at the bottle. "Let me know if you need another."

"Thanks, but I won't."

The far end of the room was getting noisy. A miner looked down the bar before turning back and thumbing over his shoulder towards me with a laugh. They looked like trouble, and weren't even trying to be subtle about it.

I picked up the bottle and glass and moved to a table where I could keep an eye on the door and the miners, but also look out the window at the scenery. Right now, that consisted of Carbine across the street, lifting his tail and dropping a pile of manure.

Dropping my hat on the table, I settled into a rickety chair that wobbled on uneven legs.

The gambler in the corner rose from his seat and walked over. "Mind some company?"

He wore a dark suit with silver vest and had a fair complexion and bright blue eyes. For such a well-dressed, casual-looking fellow, there was something about him that I couldn't put my finger on. But he gave off the impression that he was someone who shouldn't be trifled with.

Even though drinking in silence appealed to me, I figured I might get some local gossip out of him. With a short nod, I pointed towards the chair beside him. "Suit yourself."

He dropped the deck of cards on the table and shifted the seat slightly, moving to keep the door in view. As he sat, his coat flared open for a moment, revealing twin pistol butts sticking out of his vest.

Apparently, my impression was correct. He wasn't just a gambler. He was a gunman.

Waving a hand, he caught the bartender's attention and gestured at my bottle and glass and then himself. The bartender brought another pair over and wordlessly set them on the table. My new drinking companion peeled a bill off a tightly folded wad of cash, handed it to him, and accepted his change in return.

Looking at me, he smiled. Bright white, straight teeth flashed as he poured a shot, then downed it in a single swallow. He slapped the glass onto the table and picked up the deck. Idly shuffling the cards between his hands, he squinted at me from under the brim of his hat. "Care for some poker?"

"No thanks. I never was any good at cards."

He re-shuffled and pushed the stack to the side of the table, before straightening them into a neat stack with his fingers. "Me neither, but it passes the time."

I doubted that. I knew a hustle when I heard one.

"Maybe we both just need more practice," he offered, still trying.

"Oh, I've had enough practice losing to know when I should stop trying."

He chuckled. "No offense intended, but that's a touch funny coming from a man with two black eyes and a busted scalp."

"The only game I've won at so far is staying alive." I took a sip of the rotgut whiskey. It was awful. I fought to keep my face from pinching up at the taste. "But eventually, the house always wins."

"I'll certainly drink to that."

"Please do." We both topped off our glasses.

Loud, raucous laughter drifted over from the miners. One of them leaned back against the bar and stared in our direction. A big man with chubby red cheeks, he crossed his arms over a belly hanging over his belt. He looked like the sort of bully who'd always been big and became accustomed to getting their way out of fear and intimidation based on size alone.

I immediately disliked him.

He smirked. The other miners remained hunched over the bar, backs convulsing with laughter and occasionally glancing at our table.

My drinking companion watched them before meeting my eyes with his. "I think they're making fun of you."

"I believe you're right."

"It doesn't bother you?"

I shrugged. "Sure, it does. But I also don't feel like brawling. My face hurts, along with everything else."

"The lady by the piano seemed to think you were handsome enough all busted up. Women like scars. This might be a good chance for some more."

I laughed, a bit too loudly. If only he knew the scars I carried. There was such a thing as too many of them. "I'm even better-looking without these bruises," I joked as I reached across the table and introduced myself, "Jedidiah Smith."

He looked at my hand for a moment before shaking it firmly. "Jedidiah Smith..." he said the name slowly, as though suspecting it was fake. "I'm Wesley Clemmons."

"Pleasure to meet you, Wesley." I doubted that was his real name, but a lot of men change their names when they come west. Paired with the double guns, the man could very well be the sort to use a new name for every new town.

"Hey, YOU!" the yell came from one of the miners.

I sighed and turned towards the obnoxious group.

"Yeah, you. With the ugly face." The big man staggered away from his snickering companions, a malicious grin stretching across his reddened face. He was looking for trouble, and who better to pick on than someone already wounded. The bartender edged away from the miners as the working ladies turned to watch.

Wesley winked at me with a sideways grin. "Trouble seems to follow you."

Ignoring him, I took a heavy slug, this time straight from the bottle. If this went badly, I might as well dull the inevitable pain beforehand.

The drunk stopped in front of us, rocking back on his heels slightly as he swayed. He laughed harshly. Spit flecked out of his mouth and landed on the table. Wesley raised an eyebrow at him in disdain.

The drunk turned to me, his words slurring. "Yeah, you," he snorted. "With a face like that, you remind me of the last squaw I had."

Oh lovely, an abuser of Indian women. I sized him up.

He was an ugly, mean looking fellow. A front tooth was missing, others were yellowed and rotten. Black stubble decorated his large jowls. He outweighed me by a good thirty pounds and reeked of booze and stale sweat.

With his friends watching, I knew I wasn't getting out of this without a fight. And since making him angry might work out to my advantage, I figured I may as well go all in. "Was she blind or dumb?"

"Blind... what?" He looked baffled at my unexpected response and squinted, trying to focus on me then he swayed and staggered back a step, almost losing his balance. He grabbed the top of a chair to steady himself.

Wesley laughed and sipped his drink.

The drunk's confusion turned to anger at the confrontation not going the way he thought it would. "Listen here, you-"

I cut him off, my temper flaring at the man who was bothering me with the intent of impressing his obnoxious friends. "Because any woman who would willingly have a fat, nasty slug like you must be blind, dumb, or both."

His face flushed crimson, veins bulged at his temples as he reached for me.

I stood swiftly. A flash of surprise crossed his face as I knocked his arms aside, stepped close, and swung as hard and fast as I could. The uppercut connected beneath his chin with a meaty thud that sent a bolt of pain shooting down my wrist as my knuckles connected.

I'll give him credit.

I put everything I had behind that blow, and he didn't have a glass jaw.

Instead of dropping, he staggered back several paces, rubbed the stubble on his chin, and looked a whole lot angrier and soberer.

Well, shit.

Wesley chuckled and refilled his glass.

The miner lunged forward, his shoulder driving into my waist and pushing me backward as we fell together. Our combined weight shattered my rickety chair, broken boards dug and jabbed into my back as we grappled on the floor.

Gasping from the miner's heavy weight pressing down on my chest, I punched him in the side repeatedly with no noticeable effect as he drunkenly threw haymakers at my face. I took several glancing blows along the skull before he hit me solidly in the face. My nose bore the brunt of his fist. The pain was excruciating. My eyes watered. The next punch busted my lips, and the metallic taste of blood filled my mouth.

Anger burned through me. Giving up on striking him, I grabbed the sides of his head with both hands and dug my thumbs into his eyes. I was going to gouge them out of his skull for his transgressions.

He screamed and shoved himself backward, jerking his head out of my grip and rising unsteadily on his feet.

Scrambling to my feet, I spat blood on the floor.

He swayed drunkenly, rubbing his eyes and squinting through the tears.

Behind him, his friends straightened at the bar. One grabbed the shotgun off the bar. They didn't look happy.

I didn't care. I was too angry now to stop.

Closing in, I grabbed the big drunk by his collar and belt buckle. With a sharp pivot, I felt stitches tear as I hurled the heavier man over a hip onto the table. Wesley jerked his glass out of the way and the table shattered, scattering bottles and playing cards across the floor.

The drunk grunted on impact, gasping for breath, eyes wide with the sudden shock and pain.

My face and chest hurt something fierce. Dropping to a knee, I grabbed him by the front of his dirty shirt and jerked up as I slammed my fist down. His head snapped backwards as blood splattered from busted lips.

He gurgled something through shattered teeth that didn't sound like an apology.

I smashed my fist down again. His nose crunched beneath my knuckles, and his eyes rolled back into his skull. I dropped him on the shattered remains of the table and chair. My breath came in ragged gasps, and all my previous injuries hurt anew. But compared to last night's monster, this guy wasn't squat.

Reaching across his unconscious body, I grabbed a bottle that lay gurgling as it sloshed out cheap booze and took a healthy swig. The whiskey burned like a red-hot poker.

"Get offa him!"

His friends had reached us.

The two other miners stopped a handful of feet away and they weren't laughing anymore. One was young and wore a derby hat cocked at a foolish angle, exposing greasy hair underneath. He carried the shotgun, and had a wild, drunken look in his eyes. The other one appeared a little more sober and eyed me warily while shifting a hand onto the revolver stuffed down the front of his trousers.

"Look what that sumbitch did to Timmy!" the man with the shotgun shouted as he pointed the short barrels towards his friend on the floor.

I slowly pushed myself to my feet and looked for the bartender. O'Malley was adamant about stopping things just like this from going too far in his establishment. But his bartender wasn't in sight.

That was just peachy.

The ladies had disappeared as well. Fist fights were considered good, wholesome entertainment. Gunfights, not so much, and no one wanted to take a stray round from a shootout that didn't involve them.

The sober one looked me up and down before putting a hand on the hothead's shoulder. "Let it go, it was just a bar fight. He didn't start it and he took his licks."

The one with the shotgun shrugged off the hand. "Don't matter. He almost killed him!" Small beady eyes glared from underneath his ridiculous hat. "You'll pay for that."

My hands trembled from excitement, and my knuckles were skinned raw. Drawing would be difficult. But I couldn't help myself and shoved the semi-unconscious man with the toe of my boot. He moaned faintly. "Pay for this, huh? What's the sorry turd worth to you?" I grinned at my own joke painfully.

The wild eyed drunk jerked the shotgun up and shoved it in my face.

I stared down the large double barrels. The shotgun was a ten gauge by the looks of them. Big enough to put holes in a man you could put a fist through. Things were about to get very western in here.

"How about I blow you through that window?" he sneered.

None of my options were good, especially with a drunk wild card behind the trigger. The best I could hope for was his inebriated state would slow down his reflexes. I braced myself to slap the barrel away and draw. Maybe I'd get lucky. If I didn't, it'd be a quick, if messy, death.

"Easy gents. It's over. No need for this to get any uglier," Wesley's voice was calm and even. He hadn't moved from his chair. He gave an easy smile, before knocking back his drink without taking his eyes off the two men. Almost gently, he rested the empty shot glass on his thigh.

The shotgun hammer cocked loudly, as the hot-headed miner swung the barrels towards Wesley. "Try and stop me, you pretty boy dandy-"

The first shot caught the miner in the throat, a split-second before the second burst through the bridge of his nose and blew his derby hat along with a spray of blood, brains, and bits of bone a good six feet behind him. The shotgun clattered to the floor as the dead man collapsed in a heap.

If it hadn't been for the sudden appearance of two holes, I'd have sworn it was one shot. The Colt Lightning that magically appeared in Wesley's hand turned, unwavering, towards the last man standing.

The dead man's partner stood frozen in shock. Droplets of gore splattered his face and shirt. A wet patch spread from his thigh, running down a pant leg and into his boot. He slowly raised his hands, eyes large and frightened as he stammered, "No! No! No trouble."

"Keep your hands away from that pistol, and there won't be any," Wesley said, his voice suddenly hard and the easy-going attitude gone.

The miner jerked his hand away from the gun. "Just... Just let me get Timmy, and I'll go," his voice trembled and quavered.

"Go ahead. Then git." Wesley twitched his pistol barrel slightly towards the door in emphasis.

With my hands on my hips, I tried to breathe around the blood clogging my nose. Suddenly, I felt very tired and out of breath.

The man roused his friend enough to pull him to his feet. The drunk managed a couple of steps before a leg buckled and they both almost collapsed to the floor. The unwounded miner shot us a glare, before steadying his semi-conscious friend and half carrying him out the bat wing doors.

Wesley kept his pistol pointed at the double doors until they stopped swinging, then twirled the gun before smoothly sliding it into a holster hidden under his vest.

"It appears we made some enemies," I said flatly, probing my teeth with my tongue. None felt loose, thank goodness.

"Anyone worth a hoot has them. You just got to outlive them is all." He patted his concealed pistols to emphasize his point. "But you were right, Jed. You do seem to win the ones that matter, if only by a slight margin."

I nodded slowly and unbuttoned the top of my checkered shirt to look at my chest. Several stitches had torn through the skin, sending small droplets of blood trickling down my stomach. I was going to have to get myself sewn back up again. "This time, you were that slight margin. It might have gone differently without your help."

"I'd rather have kept out of it, but I do detest people shooting my drinking partner."

Leaning forward, he carefully shifted his boots to avoid the growing pool of blood while rifling through the dead man's pocket. He pulled out three gold eagles and several folded bank notes. Keeping one coin for himself with the paper money, he handed the other two shiny gold eagles to me with a conspiring wink. "This is for our emotional distress over this sad matter."

I shrugged and accepted the coins. Looting the dead was nothing new for me, and most likely they'd be snatched up by one of the working girls, or that cowardly bartender anyways.

The saloon girls cautiously peeked down the stairs to see the results of the shooting as I shook the gunman's hand.

"Really, Jed?" Wesley held his hand up to show that I'd smeared blood on it.

I laughed and rebuttoned my shirt.

Since Wesley wasn't interested in the shotgun, I scooped it off the floor on the way out. It was an old coach shotgun with exposed hammers. My guess on the gauge was correct, it was a big ten. The barrels were cut down and the stock shortened and carved into a rounded grip. A handy size, with a helluva kick and the ability to make big holes. And it was mine now. To the victors go the spoils.

I stepped into the sunlight just in time for the bartender to reach the boardwalk with the Sheriff a step behind him.

Dan took in my freshly bloodied face and grunted angrily as he shifted from one foot to the other. "Jed, what did I tell you?"

"I didn't blow anything up," I growled. "The other guys started it. We were minding our own business, sipping whiskey, and one of them started a brawl. After I knocked him out, another one threw down on us with this scatter gun." I raised my new shotgun for emphasis before jerking my head towards the bar. "The fellow in there shot him in self-defense." I didn't mention that I started the brawl by throwing the first punch. But I'm not the sort of man who gives anyone a free swing at me before I fight back.

Dan pointed at the shotgun. "You know that's evidence, right?"

I tried to look as innocent as I could manage.

"Fine, I know where you live anyways," he squinted at me. "Do I need to get one of my deputies to escort you around town? You seem like you're having a hard time staying out of trouble."

The last thing I wanted was one of those clowns following me around, and he knew it. I also knew it wasn't an idle threat. "I'll try harder. Promise."

Dan shook his head in disgust, and walked past me into the saloon with the unhappy looking bartender in tow.

I went to find the local Doc.

***

The town doctor was an old man with a thick southern accent and steady hands. He had me strip my shirt off, and there was a long, quiet moment as he took in the decades old scar tissue. Most doctors in the West were used to all sorts of scars and disfigurements, but I knew mine were… unusual. Thankfully, he didn't ask how I got them or the fresh wounds and that suited me fine. One of the best things out here is that people tended to mind their own damn business.

A foul-smelling medicinal oil was gingerly applied to small burned areas of my skin, then several neat stitches were put in my chest. He poked and prodded my nose painfully. I thought it was broken, but it was just bent a little. Luckily for me, the whiskey was kicking in and numbing some of the pain as he went over my various wounds.

With my collection of fresh bruises, cuts, and burns, it probably looked like I tried to cremate a mountain lion alive.

After paying the Doc for doing his best to extend my life, I wandered by the general store and bought some cartridges for the Sharps and a bundle of dynamite with plenty of fuse. Just in case.

The Reverend caught me leaving the store.

"Jedidiah," he said in greeting. That was one of his ways. He always used a man's formal name, never the shortened version. "Heard you had some trouble and a man was killed." He clasped his hands before him, the old Bible clutched tightly between them, as he took in my bruised and battered face. "Would you like to talk?"

I shrugged. "Nothing to talk about. The man deserved it and people dying around me is nothing new."

"I know." He half-turned away, and watched a carriage roll down the street behind a team of horses. "There's nothing wrong with killing bad people who are trying to kill you or others. But I know how difficult it is for a man to escape a troubled past. Trust me, I wasn't always a man of faith." He looked at my face, his eyes searching mine. "I just wanted to make sure your past hadn't followed you here."

I nodded, understanding his concern after the things I'd told him. You never knew when your past might catch up to you. That'd be an awful day of reckoning. But so far, I was free and clear of it. "No, sir. He was just an angry, foolish drunk with an itchy trigger finger."

"Good." He patted my shoulder. "Let me know if you need anything. In the meantime, I've a funeral to prepare for."

"Will do," I called after him as he walked away, his boots thumping on the boardwalk.

***

An hour later, the Sheriff wrapped up his errands, which included the bar shooting, and was ready to head out.

I was still jumpy. But with the Sheriff traveling with me, I'd some peace of mind in our combined firepower. Worst-case scenario, I only had to outrun Dan's horse drawn wagon. That's what he gets for choosing slow comfort over a fast saddle.

On the way, I kept the storytelling brief and simple.

He shook his head in disbelief when I described the beast and our fight to the death in the burning barn. He had a lot of questions, but I had few answers.

After he grew tired of my lack of information to give, he filled me in on the latest news around town. The biggest news was that the town Mayor died, which explained the padlock on his office. A large man, his heart gave out and he dropped dead in the middle of the street in front of a wagon hauling manure. The wheels rolled right over him before the driver could stop the mules. There was irony in that somewhere, I knew it.

Following the trail, we broke free of the forest around my ranch, and the creature's body lay in plain sight by the pile of burnt timbers and ash. Broken, charred bits and pieces of debris still lay strewn across the yard from the explosion. There was a lot of cleaning up to do.

Dan pulled back on the reins to stop the wagon and stared at the body. It took him a long moment to gather his thoughts enough to ask, "Just what is that thing?"

"No idea. Something big and mean."

"Looks like it." Dan cut his eyes at me sideways. "You know, by all rights, that thing should have killed you."

"It almost did." I tapped boot heels to the flanks of my horse and led us into the green field surrounding the house.

When we reached the remains of my barn, Dan pulled the brake on the wagon while I dismounted and tied Carbine to a corral post. He jerked his head side to side, unhappy at being tied up instead of turned loose to pasture.

Dan leapt down from the wagon and we walked to the dead beast. Its mouth lay open, exposing jagged blood-stained teeth. Other than the mangled rear legs and tail, and the arm I chopped off, the rest of its body was in reasonably good condition except for all the bullet holes. The corpse didn't even stink yet.

I kicked its head with the toe of my boot for good measure and was rewarded with a thud. "I doubt there's just one of these. And folks will need to know about it. I barely killed this one and the next man won't be so lucky."

"You're right. We've got to figure on there being more of them. But it's going to be hard to convince them that a creature like this exists, even with the claw."

That'd occurred to me as well, but I'd already thought of a solution. "We won't be able to fit the entire body in your wagon, but the head will. If that doesn't convince folks, nothing will."

Dan glanced at his wagon and shrugged with one shoulder. "Works for me." He pointed towards my ash heap of a barn. "You got any tools left?"

"Not really," I said, thinking of the small kindling axe and Bowie on my hip. "This is going to be messy."

"Yes…It is," he seemed distracted as he tugged on his beard thoughtfully and walked around the corpse. Reaching the mutilated and torched tail, he stopped and stared at it in silence.

Leaving him to his thoughts, I walked over to the pitchfork that almost impaled me. The handle was burnt away, leaving a charred end sticking out of the twisted metal fork. Pulling it loose from the ground, I tossed the ruined tool towards the remains of the barns where it landed with a soft thud amongst the wet ash.

"I've seen something like this before," the Sheriff called out as he cut a plug of tobacco with a pocket knife and began chewing.

That got my attention. "What? Where?" I looked at him in bewilderment. "Hell, how?"

"Newspaper. Someone wrote in it about digging up giant bones in Montana and Colorado. Said they were from dinosaurs."

"Dinosaurs?" I asked.

"Big extinct animals that've been dead so long their bones turned to rock. There was a sketch of what they looked like when they were alive. One of them was like this one. Except it had a bigger head, small worthless-looking arms, and walked on its back two legs. Yours kind of reminds me of it, but the head is smaller and the front arms are normal sized. Anyways, I remember thinking it was ridiculous."

I looked at him in surprise. "Seems it ain't so ridiculous. You know who wrote the article?"

"Not a clue, and I used the paper in the outhouse. But the Smithsonian Institute was mentioned, I recall that. They could probably tell us what we are dealing with," he spat a stream of tobacco juice. "I bet they'd be real interested to know they're wrong about them all being dead."

"Can you wire them? Ask them how worried we ought to be?"

The Sheriff squatted on his haunches beside the corpse and gently touched its blood-stained teeth with his fingertips. "I will. But I got a feeling we ought to be mighty concerned."

"Me too."

Dan ran his hands over the pebbled hide and peered into the beast's empty eye socket. I stared at the burnt remains of my barn, alone in my thoughts. Until one struck me.

"Hey, Dan?"

"Yeah?"

"After we cut this thing's head off… you want to stick around for some steaks before heading back to town?" I asked.

"Steaks?"

I nodded, grinning. "Big ones."

He looked puzzled, until the realization of what I implied sunk in. "You're teasin', right?"

"What better way to celebrate my defeat of this horrifying beast than to feast on its roasted flesh?"

He sighed and looked back at the dead monster before spitting again. "Okay."

It tasted like chicken.

***

The next morning, I woke stiff and sore. Today's plan was to take it easy and try to salvage anything of value from the ruins of my barn. I wasn't looking forward to digging through the knee-deep ash and debris for any little treasures that may have survived.

I slung the gun belt around my waist and glanced at the Spencer Carbine above the door. It tempted me, but I had my pistol, and I'd keep a careful watch as I worked. I decided to leave it. My new shotgun was freshly cleaned and oiled, laying on a small table beside the door with a box of shells. I left that gun as well. It was daylight and with the open fields around the ranch, I'd be able to see any strange beasts well before they reached me.

Pulling the door open, I stepped out into the bright morning sun and arched my back as I stretched.

It was going to be a nice day.

A spear whistled by me and slammed into the log wall next to the rocking chair. It stuck, driven deep, the thick wood shaft quivering.

Instinctively, I drew my pistol and spun to face whoever just tried to kill me.

There were four of them scattered before me.

Big hairy things, wrapped in hides around their waists, easily a foot taller than me, with long arms and hands big enough to beat a horse to death. Only their broad, ugly faces and muscular chests were hairless, the exposed black skin marked with colorful swirls and strange patterns.

They reminded me of jungle apes from my childhood picture books. But instead of carrying bananas, they held weapons and didn't have any tails.

The smallest of the four knelt beside the dead monster, a bow in hand and quiver of arrows at his waist. Two others stood by the pasture fence, watching Carbine run away again. Meanwhile, the biggest one who'd thrown the spear sprinted towards me in large strides, a stone axe held high overhead. He let out a ferocious roar as he quickly closed the distance.

Even as the iron sights of the Peacemaker lined up on his broad forehead and I squeezed the trigger, it felt like this was a dream. This couldn't be real. It was laughable. First a monster and now giant monkey-men.

It was loco.

The recoil from the gun blast shocked me out of my stupor as the bullet punched through his skull and he dropped at the edge of the porch as though his strings were cut.

Behind him, the others began to react. The small ape nocked an arrow and drew the bow back.

Ducking, I snapped a quick shot at him as he released. I caught a glimpse of him spinning away, grasping his side, as I dove into the house. The arrow zipped through the open doorway, narrowly missing me, and thunking into the far wall.

Slamming the door shut, I shoved my pistol into its holster. Heavy feet stomped across the porch as I grabbed the shotgun off the table. Gripping it tightly with both hands, I thumbed the double hammers back, just in time for the door to violently slam open.

It bashed into me, knocking me backward onto the floor, and sending the box of shotgun shells flying off the small table. The cardboard box burst on impact, thick cased shells rolling in every direction.

The giant ape's painted bulk filled the doorway, stone club held low. Pounding a clenched fist against his broad chest twice, he roared, revealing large yellowed canines.

I let the shotgun roar back.

The twin large bore barrels spewed a cloud of white smoke and double rounds of buckshot punched through the ape's painted lower chest and out his upper back. At this range, the mass of packed lead balls didn't spread, they simply blew a pair of holes in the big monkey large enough to put my boot through. The hairy bastard flew backward in a spray of blood and pulverized flesh. The stench of burning hair filled the air.

Breaking the shotgun open, I plucked out the empty shells as fast as I could, before grabbing a pair off the floor. Dropping them in, I snapped the gun shut, just in time for another ape to come through the door and swing its club.

The big stone on the end of the thick wood stick hit the floor as I dodged aside. Splinters stung my face as the rock smashed through the floorboards.

I struggled to maneuver the shortened shotgun for a shot and managed to thumb one of the hammers back.

The ape grasped the barrels and ripped the gun away, inadvertently making me discharge a round of buckshot past his head into the ceiling. A spray of splintered debris rained down on us. Roaring, he dropped the club to clutch his ear while flinging the shotgun across the room with his other hand.

From the ground, I drew my pistol, but lost it, as the ape grabbed me by the shirt and leg with an iron grip and hurled me across the room. Slamming into a pair of bookshelves near the wood stove, I let out a cry of pain and fell in a shower of books.

A colorfully painted Wyatt Earp glared at me from the cover of a fallen dime novel, his face stern under a tilted hat. Below in large blue words, it said, "CAN HE SURVIVE?"

Thanks for the vote of confidence, Wyatt.

Floorboards creaked in protest as the great ape lunged across the room after me. No gun was within reach, but a cast iron frying pan was. I grabbed it and swung hard at the ape's knee. He easily dodged the blow, and the heavy pan slipped and flew from my grip.

Screaming in anger, I kicked at him in desperation.

He smacked my boot aside effortlessly and grabbed me by the throat. Single handed, the ape lifted me off the floor. Fighting for air, I pounded at his hand and arm, kicking futilely, struggling to draw breath.

The monkey watched me twist and flail, a thin trickle of red dribbling from his ruptured ear drum. His face twisted in a snarl, exposing his large canines.

As my vision began to fade, I realized I still had a weapon. Drawing the large Bowie knife from the sheath on my belt, I began stabbing whatever I could reach. The blade drove deep into his soft belly below the rib cage, slicing through muscle and fat and into organs.

The ape screamed, dropping me before toppling onto his back, clutching the gaping wounds. The heavy knife fell and stuck point first in the floor as I crawled to my hands and knees, gasping.

My attacker said something in a rough, guttural language through clenched teeth while writhing back and forth. Bright red blood poured through his clasped hands and pooled underneath him.

I didn't understand what he said, and I didn't bother asking him to repeat it. Instead, I added insult to injury by angrily punching him in the face. It felt like punching a hair covered rock, but I was rewarded with a small spray of blood from his wide nostrils. That was for trashing my house.

The ape may have been dying, but it wasn't fast enough to please me. I jerked the Bowie knife from the floorboards. Wrapping both hands around the handle, I brought the blade down, again and again, with all the force and violence I could muster. Blood sprayed and splashed across the floor as his body shuddered under the vicious knifing. That was for him and his buddies trying to kill me for no reason.

Breathing hard from the exertion, I stared at the mangled bloodied mess I had made. Then I suddenly recalled there'd been four apes and the small one was unaccounted for. Diving across the floor, I grabbed the dropped pistol. Sliding against the doorway, I peeked cautiously, waiting for the fourth one to pop around the corner to plug me.

Instead, the small one with the bow lay motionless in the yard. I'd gotten lucky with that snapped shot and hit something vital. He'd made it several steps from the dinosaur before collapsing.

***

Doc had done a proper job on my stitches. Only one tore loose during the brawl and it looked like I'd survive without it. But I desperately needed a week or two without violence to heal up.

Satisfied that I'd survive this assault, I buttoned my shirt and inspected my latest kill.

The dead ape in my house lay gashed open from painted chest to throat with over a dozen wounds. I pulled the knife out of him, wiped it off on his fur, and slid it back into its sheath while looking the corpse over.

Simply put, he was large, hairy, and ugly.

His face was a bald patch of wrinkled black skin covering his mouth, lips, and wide flat nose. The rest of his head was covered with the same thick, dark brown hair as his body, leaving only his chest, palms, and bottoms of his feet hair-free.

His chest was thick with muscle and painted with red, green, and white swirls and strange patterns. I scraped off a little of the green paint with my fingers and rubbed it between them. It was clotted with small bits of plant fiber and what looked like smashed bugs.

What gave me the greatest concern was the skins he wore. I picked up an edge of the hides and ran the treated leather between my fingers. The pebbled hide was like nothing I had ever seen before. Except on the monster I killed last night.

So, there were more of them. Many more. Somewhere. And with them were these apes. But where? How had they never been discovered until now? Just what the hell was going on?

A small leather pouch was stitched into the hides he wore. I opened it hoping to find answers. Inside were thin strips of leather, a sharp chipped stone knife with leather-bound handle, what looked like flint and pyrite for making fires, and several bright purple fern leaves tightly rolled. More questions without answers. I fingered the purple ferns, they were still green and appeared to have been freshly picked. But from where? I'd never seen anything like them before either.

Disgusted, I pushed the contents into a pile on the floor and grabbed the ape by his hairy legs. His feet were huge and barefoot, covered in callouses, with long toes and huge black nails. Grunting, I pulled the body towards the door.

The corpse left a long smear of blood across the floor as I dragged him out of the house and rolled him off the side of the porch into a heap with his dead buddies.

Then I checked their weapons.

I knew the apes were strong. One of them lifted my entire body with a single hand and almost choked me to death. But as I picked up one of their clubs and struggled to swing it, I realized just how strong they really were. The club must have weighed around thirty pounds. The handle was smooth dark wood with a reddish tint and small grooves cut to help the bearer keep a grip. The large gray stone at the end had been chipped into shape and bound tightly in place with strips of leather. Getting hit with one of these would end a man's life quick, or leave him permanently crippled.

I tugged the arrow out of the wall. It was almost a foot longer than an Indian arrow and twice as thick. The fletching was made of long strange greenish-yellow feathers, and the point chipped obsidian. The bow carried by the small ape was six feet long and made from what seemed like a type of carved horn and finely braided gut string. I tried to draw the bow back and gave up after moving the string only half way.

The spear was sunk deep into the outside log wall, and using the axe I chopped the shaft off, leaving the tip embedded. Like the club, it was much larger than anything a human could easily wield. The shaft was almost nine feet long and several inches in diameter. Big enough that I could jab with it two handed, but impossible for me to throw. I found enough spears for each of the apes to have carried one, and their points were of the same glossy chipped obsidian as the arrows.

I dumped the weapons in a pile and stood on the porch with rifle in hand, looking around in bewilderment. Once again, I found myself confused and trying to wrap my head around the notion that not only had I killed a creature that should have been extinct, but also several giant monkey-men without tails.

Just what in the hell was going on?

The breeze ruffled the hair of the apes in the yard and sent small dust devils spinning. Buzzards noticed my new yard decorations and circled lazily overhead. A sure signal for miles around that something was dead. I'd provided quite the feast for them of late.

I looked at the forest edge and wondered what else was out there.

There was no telling anymore.

As I watched Carbine trot back towards the ranch, I knew one thing for certain: I needed to know where these apes came from. Wherever that was, based on the hides they wore, there were more of these dinosaurs. Going without help didn't appeal to me. But neither did spending most of a day fetching the Sheriff while the trail went cold.

I'd go alone and cautiously. If things went south, I'd ride like hell for town. I glanced at my saddle bags that lay on the floor by the door. Just in case, I'd bring the dynamite along.

***

I tracked the apes easily enough.

The hairy men had followed the dinosaur, which explained how they ended up in my front yard. And that big creature left an easy trail to follow as it stomped through everything, leaving deep clawed tracks, broken branches, and crushed foliage in its wake. Regretfully, the dinosaur's tracks did like most wild things, they meandered all over the place instead of in a convenient straight line. Eventually the markings broke free of the forest, and out into the open rolling hills of the plains.

I'd no idea why the apes would follow the beast. If they were hunting it, then they were more badass than I originally thought and that much more dangerous. But it appeared I was attacked by the apes simply because I had the bad luck of the beast ending up dead at my place.

After a couple hours, I came across the bloody, grisly carcass of one of my steers. All that remained was broken horns attached to a shattered skull, punctured by teeth, and some crunched-up bones amongst shredded scraps of meat and hide. The area was painted with blood and gore for a good ten feet. The monster had eaten well here.

Eventually, the beast's tracks led me to an area of the Granite Mountain range further than I'd ever wandered before. The tall prairie grass ended abruptly against the base of mountain cliffs jutting up from the plains. Before me, the cliff face rose fifty or sixty feet into the air, complete with tumbled rocks and debris at the bottom and a few scraggly pines striving to survive tucked into small cracks and crevices.

Both the ape and beast tracks led right through a massive tunnel that stretched almost forty feet wide at the bottom and at its highest point, arched twenty feet or so above me.

But, somehow, impossibly, the tunnel was only thirty feet long, and defied everything I knew was possible.

In a daze, I dismounted and squatted on my heels, staring at it, trying to understand how such a thing could exist.

Not only should the mountain range have been miles and miles deep, each end of the tunnel was... different.

My side was normal, the other side... not.

What I saw wasn't possible. It didn't just break the laws of nature, it shattered them.

There was a clear line of division inside near the center of the tunnel. A line that showed where my side ended and the other began. Nothing in nature is perfectly straight, but this was. The grass on my side, small and thin, ended abruptly where large thick blades of grass and big green and red tinged ferns suddenly began and continued down a small rise where my view ended, showing only a blue sky with several puffy white clouds.

The unseen line continued up edges of the tunnel and along the ceiling, splitting two different types of rock. On my side, it was gray and marbled granite, then it suddenly became limestone. Cracks that began in one side or the other, ended abruptly when they reached the line.

I couldn't explain it. There should have been a solid mountain right there. But there wasn't.

The only thing I knew for sure was that apes and the beast came from the other side. The dinosaur appeared to have walked right through it, and wandered off to find a rancher to terrorize. Then the apes, but their tracks were muddled together as they crossed through and wandered around the area, apparently as baffled as I was.

I gave up trying to figure it out. To hell with it. My head was starting to pound something fierce. It was simpler just to accept it.

Frustrated and disgusted, I stood and kicked a fist sized rock into the tunnel. As the rock bounced across the unseen line and into the other side, for a brief moment, the air shimmered and tiny ripples spread in every direction.

At that moment, I said a lot of things my mother wouldn't have wanted me to say. But, in my defense, I was really getting sick of all this strangeness.

Unsure of what I was dealing with, I did what everyone does when confronted with something so strange and bizarre that it challenges your belief in what is real.

I walked over and cautiously poked it with a finger.

Like before, small ripples spread outwards, sparkling like clear water in the sun, before quickly fading away. I pushed my hand through and watched the ripple, flexing my fingers and watching them through the brief shimmer. I clenched my fist and waited a minute to see if it would wither and fall off. It didn't and other than the faintest of tingles, I felt nothing.

I was sorely tempted to go through and see what awaited me on the other side. But light was fading and shadows growing longer, and I didn't feel safe wandering through such a strange place in the dark. Running my fingers across the air to make a trail of shimmers once more, I reluctantly turned away.

We rode away from the tracks and cliff for over a mile, before finding a small stand of trees that would provide shelter and concealment from any critters prone to violence that might be wandering around. Especially anything that may have come through the tunnel.

Staking Carbine nearby, I trusted him to alert me if anything came near. My bedroll was spread amongst some fallen logs that formed a natural fort of sorts and I stacked a few large rocks in the gaps. Just in case.

Lying under my blanket, I looked through the leaves at the stars in the night sky and tried to decide which was worse; the creatures I'd encountered, or the unknown things on the other side that I didn't know about yet. Before I drifted off to sleep, I settled on the unknown and kept my rifle close by my side while sleeping fitfully through the night.

***

The next morning, I woke to Carbine nudging me with his muzzle and stamping his hooves impatiently. It was annoying having a horse that could occasionally work a slip knot free. But at least he didn't leave me stranded. After I shoved his head away, he looked me in the eye, lifted his tail and let loose with a load of manure. Cursing the day he was born, I pulled my blanket and slicker aside before any droppings rolled onto them. Somehow, our morning routine always seemed to begin with me swearing at him. This wasn't the first time that I missed Misty. She'd been a good horse and lacked a single mischievous bone in her sweet body.

I broke down my simple camp by rolling up the bedding, letting Carbine drink his fill from a small nearby stream, filling my canteen, and cinching the saddle tight on his back. I was anxious to begin exploring the other side, and since I didn't pack any coffee, I skipped a fire and ate a few hardtack biscuits for breakfast. Without my caffeine, I'd just be a little more ornery than usual. Dinosaurs and apes beware.

By the time we reached the cliff face, the sun had burned off the low-lying mist.

As best as I could tell, everything appeared to be just as weird today as it did yesterday. Except there were more tracks, from what looked like a dozen or more four legged creatures with small hooves. Whatever they were, they appeared to be heading east, probably to kill more of my cattle. I decided to follow them later, but for now, I wanted to see what the other side held.

I tied Carbine's reins to a small pine tree beside the tunnel, this time making sure they were sufficiently tight. Then I slipped my hand into the mysterious opening again. It rippled as before, and like last time, there was only a barely noticeable tingle.

Satisfied I probably wouldn't die crossing through the strange shimmer, I drew my hand back. It was time to see what this mysterious other side was all about.

Walking back to Carbine, I pulled the Sharps repeater from its scabbard. Scratching his withers, I opened a saddle bag and took out a collapsible brass telescope and tucked it under my arm. If the apes were on the other side of this tunnel, I wanted to be able to look at them from a safe distance. Carbine snorted softly as if to wish me luck. Gripping the rifle tightly, I gathered my courage, closed my eyes, and blindly stepped across the invisible line.

A tingle ran over my entire body. I cracked my eyes open a sliver and saw I was still alive. Now that I was on the other side, I tried to shake loose the fear of the unknown from last night, but the feeling lingered. This was unfamiliar territory. The sort of place that defied the laws of everything I knew possible. It was downright scary.

I exited the tunnel and looked up. The limestone cliff rose high into the air around me. It appeared to be a normal mountain range, except for the short tunnel leading back to my side. Looking back through the opening, I could see the back half of Carbine peeking out from the rock side and the grassy plains beyond.

Carefully, I stalked forward to the small rise that had limited my vision of this side. Once I reached its peak, I stopped in shock. Whatever I expected to find; this surpassed my wildest dreams.

I stood at the top of a large valley with a wide river running lazily through the bottom of it. To the right, the open grassy hills gave way to a forest of giant trees arching over a hundred feet into the air. More of the green and red-tinged ferns dotted the landscape mixed amongst knee-high, thick bladed grasses and small stands of trees.

A gust of wind rustled the fern leaves and brought to me the faint scent of salt water. Which meant that wherever I was, it wasn't Wyoming Territory anymore. On my side of the tunnel, there wasn't a sea for probably over a thousand miles in any direction.

My surroundings were strange indeed, but over shadowed by the creatures below. I found myself staring with mouth hanging wide open. It was probably only a few minutes, but it felt like I stood frozen for an hour watching the odd shaped animals. Finally recovering from my stupor, I extended the telescope and kneeled, bracing the optic to get a better look.

A small group of massive gray beasts walked ponderously along the banks of the river. Some were thirty feet tall, with thick bodies on stumpy legs, and long graceful necks curving up into the sky, their small heads plucking at leaves on the trees growing in the edges of the river. A young pair, perhaps six or seven feet tall, chased each other around the adults, running and nipping at each other with a gracefulness I wouldn't have thought possible in such strangely formed beasts.

A pair of vastly different animals ate near the forest edge. Their wide, thick bodies moved on short legs, with exposed bone plating across their backs. As they walked and grazed, they moved in an odd side-to-side gait that reminded me of turtles. A large knot was formed on the end of their tails, and swung back and forth in rhythm with their step. If the club on the end of their tail was used for defensive means, it'd smash a man flat. Or an ape for that matter.

Since none of them looked a bit like anything I'd ever seen or heard of, I reckoned these were all supposedly extinct dinosaurs. I swallowed hard at the thought. How could such a place as this exist?

An ear-piercing screech came from above as a bird without feathers swooped over the valley. It had a small thin body, sleek, with a long neck and toothed beak, and was carried aloft by wide, leathery wings tipped with talons. It skimmed low over the water before alighting beside more of its kind in a tree by the long-necks. They squawked and screeched at each other and the dinosaurs nearby.

The tracks of the apes were vague in the grass, but deep clawed imprints from the beast that ate my horse were clear as they moved east, away from the ocean scented breeze, and towards the forest edge. I'd originally planned on just taking a quick peek. But curiosity got the best of me once again and I decided to keep following the tracks. This was too grand of a place to simply turn and leave after seeing so little of it.

Pulling myself away from the strange view, I crossed back through the tunnel that divided two worlds. With some gentle coaxing and a few muttered threats, I persuaded Carbine to enter the tunnel. After seeing the shimmer from myself stepping through, he hesitated and looked around suspiciously. I let the reins go slack, and when he cautiously pushed his muzzle towards me, I gave the leather straps a yank. Once his head jerked forward through the shimmer, he leapt through so quickly I had to jump aside or be trampled. As I walked him out of the tunnel, he watched me suspiciously, knowing that I tricked him. But once the breeze blew past us, filling his nostrils with strange odors, his ears pricked forward, and he began paying attention to our surroundings.

I let him stand a few minutes on the hill rise to let him get settled in our new surroundings before pulling myself into the saddle and resting my rifle across the pommel. Then I drew my Colt and dropped it back into the holster, checking that it was loose and ready to draw at a moment's notice. We were in a strange land filled with strange beasts. I wanted to be ready for anything that might need shooting before we tucked tail and ran away.

Then we followed the ape and beast tracks into the forest.

***

We worked our way through the underbrush amongst the tall trees, following the beast's old trail as it smashed through saplings and churned ground and ferns with its claws.

Fifty feet into the forest, the thick growth began to thin under the darkened interior of the forest, making it easier to move without the threat of being knocked out of the saddle by a low-lying branch or flayed open by large thorns that jutted out from thick vines drooping from the towering trees.

After a hundred yards or so, I discovered a jumble of tracks where the apes' footprints joined with the beast's. The apes' tracks were on top of each other, as if they'd walked around looking at the monster's prints before deciding to follow it.

Here I left the dinosaur tracks behind and continued to backtrack the apes. It seemed foolish to keep going, but after coming this far, the urge to see where the big monkeys came from was overpowering. We pressed on, but I promised myself that I'd only follow for another hour or so before turning back.

Carbine was skittish, his ears flicking back and forth as he tried to absorb our strange surroundings. I couldn't blame him. This place was making me nervous too. Overhead came the constant sharp shrieks of leathery birds winging above us and resting in the trees and amongst the vines, and echoing throughout the forest were distant bellows and screams of unknown creatures. Several times we stopped, listening, as something large and unseen crashed through the forest nearby.

Small, furry brown animals with long noses and black tails skittered over raised roots and through fallen leaves as we plodded along the ape's tracks. They were everywhere. I bet the local predators munched on them like candy. At first, Carbine didn't like them underfoot, but after a while he ignored them. From the noises I heard, I'm confident he squished several under steel shod hooves.

The apes' tracks broke apart, and came back together as they spread out and moved through the forest. It was apparent they were searching for something, and I shuddered to think that they chased after the monster from my barn with only stone age weapons. Tracking them became slow going once they spread out. The only thing that helped was that there was four of them leaving signs.

We rode through a recent forest fire area. The bottom trunks of trees were scorched ten feet up and fresh green growth was beginning to spring to life in the ash enriched soil. Then we found a clearing.

A field of ferns and tall grasses about three hundred yards across and maybe a quarter mile long full of sunshine and open sky. It was a nice break after the dark interior of the forest. I took a sip of water from my canteen and watched for anything that might eat us. The only critters I could see was a dozen small rodents scurrying about nearby. It appeared safe enough. The apes appeared to have crossed through the clearing, but I was in enemy territory and being in the open was a good way to get killed and eaten. It was going to be a long ride around, and I'd have to pick up the tracks again on the other side. Turning Carbine's head, we rode around the forest edge.

We made it a dozen steps before piercing calls reached our ears followed by the loud crashing noise of multiple somethings approaching through the trees. The rodents scampered away, ducking into small holes and quickly leaving the clearing silent and empty. Even the leathery birds in the trees stopped their infernal racket.

As the calls grew louder, we rode deeper into the thick underbrush that ringed the clearing, stopping before I lost sight of the clearing through the vegetation. The rapidly approaching sound of snapping branches and rustling leaves filled the forest and made Carbine side-step and tug at the reins uncomfortably. I shushed him and held the reins tight, hoping he wouldn't draw any unwanted attention. I wanted to see what was making the odd noises but I was having a hard time telling how close they were to us.

A flock of gigantic birds burst out of the trees a hundred yards away. Dodging thick ferns and leaping through the waist high grass, they charged nimbly through the clearing.

The birds were larger than any I'd ever seen. At least six feet tall, they had thick bodies covered in tan and brown feathers, with a small head on an outstretched neck, and ran in bounds on long legs. The squawks came from toothed beaks below beady eyes, and their wings, too small to offer flight, stuck out on each side to give them balance.

A second later, the forest exploded in a shower of branches and leaves as an enormous two-legged monstrosity broke through the foliage after them.

It made the beast I killed pale in comparison.

A good fourteen feet tall and over twenty feet long, the giant dinosaur ran leaning forward on thick muscular legs balanced with a long tail held low. Its head was massive and looked as though it could gulp down a man with little effort. The leathery hide was a light green with thin black stripes running down its sides and stopping before the pale-yellow underbelly. The small arms clawing helplessly in the air did little to take away from its fearsome appearance.

It looked like the dinosaur that Sheriff Dan had described. And it certainly wasn't a bunch of old bones buried in dirt.

Carbine understandably lost his shit.

He snorted and reared, kicking and bucking, as I simultaneously struggled to prevent him from fleeing and wondering if we should be. My weapons were as useless as a sling shot against such a creature.

Luckily for us, the monster was fixated on the fleeing birds and ran after them, oblivious to my fight against Carbine's survival instincts.

The big-headed beast lunged, mouth stretched wide, teeth snapping shut on empty air as one of the birds nimbly leaped to the side. The birds screeched and left the clearing, ducking amongst the low branches of the forest. Mere feet behind them, the giant dinosaur bashed through the screen of trees with a swing of its head. A rotten tree snapped off at the base and toppled to the side, crushing vegetation with a boom. Within moments, the chase was out of sight, and the noise began to fade away.

Realizing I was holding my breath, I let it out in a big whoosh as my pounding heart started to slow. Carbine was still panicked, foam dripped from his muzzle and eyes rolled as he searched for more danger. Leaning forward, rubbing his neck and with soothing words, I began to calm him.

Everything here was monstrous and dangerous. And heaven help us all if that absurdly big predator crossed to our side. I don't know how we could stop something that big without a barrage of cannon fire.

Dismounting, I poured water from my canteen into my hat with trembling hands. That monster really did a number on me, and the memory of the smaller beast I killed was all too fresh. My horse drank from my hat noisily, sloshing water onto my pants. I let him rest for a few minutes, running my hands down his neck and shoulders while waiting for the trembling to subside in both of us.

When we moved out, we went slower and more cautiously than before, continuing to circle around the clearing then finding the long strides of the apes. Pure stubbornness and curiosity on my part kept me pushing forward instead of returning the way we came. I promised myself another hour, then we'd turn back. But I knew I wouldn't be satisfied until I saw where these mysterious apes, who survived amongst such large and ferocious creatures, came from.

***

The temperature rose with the sun, and there was so much moisture in the air I felt like I could swim in it. My shirt and pants were soaked through and sweat rolled down my face. We stopped at a stream, and I let Carbine drink his fill while I topped off my canteen. The water was brackish, but tasted normal enough to risk drinking. And in this heat and humidity, we were drinking a lot.

A quarter mile past that, we came across a rotting corpse. The scent was nauseating. As we approached, small green dinosaurs with long tails bounced away through the brush before I could get a good look at them. Whatever the dead animal had been, it was chewed and gnawed on past the point of recognition. It had been big though, something with four legs and large flat boney plates sticking from its back, but all that was left now were small amounts of decaying, rotting flesh on thick bones.

We skirted around the dead animal and fifteen minutes later, reached the end of the forest and where it turned into rolling grass covered hills and a river flowing from the mouth of a canyon entrance.

***

I jerked back on Carbine's reins to bring him to a quick stop.

This strange place was full of surprises.

Several hundred yards away, a pair of apes rode giant three-horned beasts over the crest of a grassy knoll.

I pulled the telescope from my saddle bag, and extended it to study the strange horned mounts in detail. They had short legs under thick bodies, with two long black horns jutting out from above their eyes and a smaller one centered above slanted nostrils and a beaked mouth. A scooped shield rose behind its skull, covering the back of the neck, with small round bone protrusions sticking out of the top. The animals were a darkened brown that merged into a tan on their underbelly, with yellow stripes running from nose to shield and across their bodies horizontally.

With an obvious lack of creativity, the first name that came to mind for these beasts was trikes.

Mounted behind the bone shield, on the trikes' front shoulders, were the apes. They used an odd form of saddle, with their feet tucked underneath the scooped shield. The reins held by the apes, circled around the sides of the shield, before meeting a harness that looked eerily like my horse's. The first loop ran around the beak and lower horn and attached to a second loop that ran from the throat to behind the larger horns. There was no bit used, the creature's beak didn't look like one would fit.

The apes held bows, with full quivers of yellow-green fletched arrows and stone axes hanging from the saddle. On the sides of the trikes, strapped above large leather sacks, were several long spears bundled together.

Staying in the darkened shadows of the forest interior, I watched the trikes lumber down the hill and walk along the river's edge into the canyon. With the telescope, I looked around the narrow entrance. All along the river the ground was churned into a thick mud and the grass plastered flat. A lot of *somethings* were going in and out of there.

I had to see what was inside.

The forest circled along to my right for a half mile before reaching the canyon edge. That would allow us to get close unseen. Clicking my tongue, I turned Carbine and we skirted along the forest edge. I wanted the best vantage point for seeing into the gorge that I could safely find.

***

As we neared the canyon edge, I saw thin tendrils of smoke rising from inside and twisting above the trees. Figuring this was close enough, I took my rifle and telescope, tied Carbine's reins to a tree, and stalked forward the rest of the way on foot.

Once I was close enough to be sky lined, I dropped and crawled the rest of the way. The sun was at its pinnacle now. Scorching heat reflected off exposed rock beneath me. Sweat dripped and practically sizzled on stone as I peered over the edge.

It was a box canyon and much larger than I expected, a half mile across at the widest point and a mile long from the only entrance to a distant cliff face where a large waterfall toppled over to the canyon floor over a hundred feet below. The ground was covered with a lush green grass and giant ferns with scattered stands of trees. The river slowly twisted around the base of the cliff where I lay, gently flowing through large pools and out the canyon entrance. It was a beautiful and isolated place.

It was also full of apes.

There were over a hundred of the big monkeys scattered across the canyon floor, with more moving in and out of cave openings in the cliff face opposite me. Groups of apes sat around fires, eating and crafting weapons, while others practiced shooting bows and throwing spears at large bundles of tightly bound dried ferns. Most of the ape's fur were a mixture of black and brown, although some had white splotches. One, an albino by the looks of him, bounded forward several steps and hurled a spear over fifty yards before burying half its length into one of the bundles. Apart from the others, a large group of monkeys were swarming over great big slabs of meat, hacking them into thin strips and smoking them over smoldering fires. There didn't seem to be a difference between the work the females and males did, they were mixed amongst all the tasks.

They all wore hides and skins wrapped around their waist or over a shoulder.

Except for the ones fighting naked.

Dozens of them wrestled with each other in the grass beside the shallow streams below me. Picking each other up and slamming them down as they scrambled and fought to get the advantage. I watched one rise from beneath the water he'd been pushed into with a handful of muck and fling it at the face of another before punching the blinded ape in the face. Loud bellows and guttural calls echoed up to me. Others stood around, watching the wrestlers fight.

A large herd of trikes were further down the canyon, tearing up plants and chewing the vegetation. They appeared docile and several apes moved amongst them. Overlooking the herd on a small rise nearby, nestled amongst the tall grass, lay a monster of a trike. He blended into the grass so well that I noticed him only because his head swiveled back and forth as he watched over his herd. Through my telescope, I could tell one of his horns was shattered halfway up its length.

And then there were the carts.

Dozens of them with rough shaped chunks of wood for wheels and two thick poles jutting out the front. None of them had harnesses attached, and guessing from design and size, they appeared to be pulled by a single ape. They were strewn across the valley floor, some filled with ferns for the trikes, others with logs and sticks, stacked hides, even stones. Many of them were staged in rough rows near the back of the canyon.

It was a lot to take in.

Battle seemed to be a way of life for these apes. While the ratio of females to males appeared almost even, it was worrisome that I saw no baby or juvenile apes amongst them. And the number of carts were far more than needed for simple tasks in the canyon.

But of everything in the canyon, it was the unnatural rock formation in the center that disturbed me the most.

Eight chunks of granite had been worked into a rectangular shape and stood upright, a dozen feet tall, in a large circle. In their center lay a large rectangular chunk of glossy black obsidian raised high on a stone platform. The light of the sun shone darkly off the rock, giving it an ominous appearance.

If it was an altar, I wasn't sure I wanted to see what sort of rituals the hairy savages held.

A pair of apes on trikes caught the corner of my eye as they splashed through the river into the canyon.

I turned the telescope on them. Large birds, identical to the ones chased earlier by the big-headed dinosaur, were draped across the backs of the mounts. Brown feathered bodies bounced with the heavy steps of the trike until they stopped before the caves. Leaping down, a different pair of apes untied the birds and effortlessly hoisted them across their shoulders. Carrying the corpses, they moved towards a small stand of trees against the canyon edge.

A distant chirping drifted to me, intensifying as the apes entered the trees with their load. Peering through gaps of leaves and branches, I could make out an outcropping of rock jutting from the canyon wall, creating a natural overhang. Beneath it was a large cage woven from thick branches that reached from the ground to the bottom of the bulge, with a gate near the center. Small black claws reached through the gaps, grabbing and shaking the cage as the things inside tried to get out.

One of the apes leaned a makeshift ladder against the cliff and climbed to the top of the overhang, carefully avoiding grasping claws. He opened a portion of the cage as the other passed the dead birds up. The chirps hit a feverish pitch as the birds' bodies were shoved through.

Apparently, trikes weren't the only tamed creatures in the canyon.

I watched the apes feeding the unknown animals for a few moments longer before deciding I'd seen enough. I needed to get back to town and let the Sheriff know, and figure out just what in the hell we were going to do about the tunnel.

I began to push back away from the edge, then stopped as an odd thumping noise reached my ears. Unnoticed, a pair of apes had moved beside the large slab of obsidian rock and were beating their chests with a fist. Others noticed and stood, copying the motion while facing the rock formation, adding to the dull thumping. Within moments the entire canyon was reverberating with the rhythmic pounding as it spread through all the apes.

Once all the apes were repeating the motion, the two that started the beating stopped abruptly and walked out of the circle. The others followed suit and the canyon grew quiet.

All the apes began moving to the strange rock formation. The ones wrestling pulled tanned skins back over their nakedness, while others stacked spears and lay down bows, and the apes cooking pulled meat away from the fire.

More apes poured from the caves in a steady stream. There was well over two hundred of them now standing around the circle of stone. But not a single ape stood inside the towering slabs of granite, leaving the area around the raised rock platform clear. I watched them through the telescope, in awe at the sheer number of them. Far more than I would have expected, and more were coming from the cave still.

A giant black-haired ape stepped from one of the cave entrances. Sensing something different about this one, I turned my glass on him.

He stood a head taller than the scattering of apes that hurried around him. The right side of his face was hideously scarred. The wound ran from chin to temple and twisted the side of his face into a grimace that exposed a large canine in a half snarl. He wore a simple waist belt and loincloth with a black handled knife tucked into a sheath. As he stepped forward, apes quickly parted before him. They jerked away, as though fearful of the big monkey.

Reaching the stone platform below the altar, he motioned back towards the caves he just left.

I swore viciously as a pair of apes stepped out with an Indian held tightly between them.

The apes in the large crowd began hooting and calling in deep, rough voices.

The man's chest was bloodied. His long black hair stringy and hanging over his face. He was naked, but he still had fight in him. Kicking and struggling, he tried to pull away. One of his guards brutally slugged him in the stomach with a large fist. He convulsed and went slack between his captors. Vomit dribbled from his mouth as his feet dragged. Uncaring, the apes dragged him through the jeering crowd.

I felt my face flush hot in anger as the guards pulled their captive through the horde and into the circle of upright stones.

Then I watched, horrified, as the guards ascended the stone altar and dumped him on top of the obsidian slab. The crowd's hooting grew louder as he thrashed weakly against the two stronger apes. With an almost dispassionate interest, they stretched his arms apart and lashed him down on top of the rock with leather cords. Their task finished, the guards stepped off the stone platform and disappeared into the crowd.

The black scarred ape stepped before the Indian captive.

A guttural chant began, followed by single clenched fists once again beating in unison. I felt it within my chest, as my heart seemed to pound in rhythm. My senses seemed to clear. I could feel the dryness in my mouth, my skin burning beneath the burning sun, the heat radiating off the brass telescope.

Sweat dripped from my brow, and the glass was fogging. The blurring of my vision brought me back. Shaking my head, I quickly wiped the eye piece clear and looked back through the telescope.

Someone in the teeming mass was passing up a misshapen bowl. Green smoke wafted from whatever crazy stuff burned inside. The scar-faced ape accepted the bowl and laid it carefully beside the squirming man on the slab.

The ape drew the blade from the sheath at his waist. It was obsidian, with a dark handle. The Indian hocked a wad of spit at him in defiance. In return, the giant ape casually palmed the man's face and slammed his head backward against the stone. His body went limp.

My jaw clenched, and I ground my teeth so hard I thought they might crack.

I didn't know what to do.

I didn't know what I could do.

***

Laying the knife on the black altar, the scarred ape cupped his hands around the smoldering bowl and raised it into the air as the chanting and pounding ceased.

The canyon was eerily quiet as he brought the bowl to his face and breathed in the green smoke.

For a long moment, nothing happened.

Then the bowl dropped from the ape's hands, shattering on rock. The black ape shuddered and braced himself against the altar. He twitched, violently, jerking his head from side to side. Knees bent and wobbled, threatening to collapse underneath him.

Whatever was in that bowl wasn't your ordinary peyote.

Suddenly the giant ape threw himself upright, thrusting out his chest and raising clenched fists at the sky. He roared, an ugly, harsh, inhuman sound as the other apes joined in. The thumping noise of hammering fists against chests began again with a fevered violence. The pounding was louder and harsher this time. There was no rhythm. Just a mass of noise that echoed and assaulted my senses.

The Indian stirred. Bewildered and groggy, he twisted and turned on the black rock.

The scar-faced ape scooped up the knife and savagely plunged it into the man's belly.

I wasn't prepared for the sudden violence and almost dropped the telescope as a high-pitched scream of agony pierced the air. The chipped obsidian knife slid upwards easily and stopped once it reached his rib cage. The man kept screaming in horror, staring wide eyed at the gaping wound in his stomach. The scar-faced ape set the knife down and reached into the cut, amongst the vitals, and deep under the ribcage.

The shrieking ended with a twist and rip, as the ape pulled out the man's heart.

Raising the lump of muscle in his fist for all the apes to see, blood ran down the ape's black hairy arm and splattered onto the altar.

Hundreds of throats roared in satisfaction.

The scarred black ape savagely took a bite out of the heart. Blood oozed from his mouth. Swallowing, he hurled the remains into the crowd.

Apes pushed and shoved each other for the muscled organ. One hairy monkey began pummeling another to the ground with both fists as others kicked and fought to get the chunk of human flesh.

A hand suddenly held it aloft victoriously above the thrashing apes, a bloody chunk of raw meat coated with dirt. Roaring, he bit off a chunk and hurled it across the crowd where the scene was repeated, again and again, until there was nothing left but apes fighting each other around the circle of stones while the scarred ape leader watched on in satisfaction. Around them the others hooted and howled primordial cries in celebration.

Saying I was in shock was an understatement. Horrified was more like it. But furious.... absolutely.

Slamming the telescope shut, I slid my rifle before me and braced it into my shoulder. I found the black scarred ape at the altar and guessed the distance.

Common sense told me that my position would be given away once I fired, but I didn't care. Every single one of these hairy men-monkeys needed to die. But, for the moment, I'd satisfy myself with just taking their leader's life.

Carbine stamped softly from the tree line and the wind stirred around me, making leaves rustle in the trees. I tuned everything out and slowed my breathing. Concentrating on the gentle rise and fall of the sights, I began taking up the slack in the trigger.

I was about to smite a giant, evil monkey with 350 grains of cast lead and vengeance.

Hell yeah.

Carbine snorted loudly, interrupting my concentration.

Irritated, I rolled to the side to see what he was upset about.

A spear point shattered on the sweat soaked rock where I'd lain a moment before.

The ape stood towering over me. His large brow furrowed in frustration. Another monkey grabbed Carbine's reins and was rewarded a vicious bite to the shoulder by my horse. He screamed, and Carbine twisted around, kicking the ape in the chest and sending him sprawling.

I bet that hurt, but not as much as this would.

With my free hand, I drew the Colt and shot the ape standing over me. He didn't give in to the wound as the bullet punched through his belly, instead jerking the spear back and preparing to thrust again with its shattered tip.

This time, I shot him through the center of the chest where his heart should have been, and he collapsed in a twitching heap at my feet.

As the other ape painfully crawled onto all fours, I carefully put a bullet through his skull and dropped him.

So much for the element of surprise.

Flipping back over, I realized the canyon had gone quiet. The multitude of apes had stopped howling and celebrating, and were staring at my position. I felt hundreds of eyes upon me.

Surprise monkeys, I have weapons of fire, thunder and lead. Fear me.

Scar-face pointed a thick, blood coated finger in my direction and bellowed a command.

The crowd of apes went wild as they began pushing, shoving, and running in different directions. Some ran back into the caves, others towards stacks of weapons, and most rushed towards the cliff below me.

Swearing, I yanked the rifle up and quickly shot at the ape leader as he turned away. The bullet missed and hit the Indian's corpse instead. The evil black ape disappeared amongst the frantic swarming mass of his followers.

There went my chance at killing their leader. But at least the Indian was already dead. He probably would have forgiven me anyways, all things considered.

If there was any doubt as to where my position was before, the gun smoke from the Sharps that drifted over the canyon made it abundantly clear. But I figured I could slay a few more of them before I needed to get out of dodge.

Working the action on the rifle, I randomly selected an ape splashing through the stream in my direction and pulled the trigger. The rifle boomed again satisfyingly, and the ape pitched forward and thrashed in the water as another puff of gun smoke blew out to join the other.

I grinned evilly.

This was like shooting monkeys in a barrel.

Rising to a knee for a better field of fire, I fired into a small band of apes headed for the trikes. Another boom, and this time an ape dropped while the one behind it screamed and fell, clutching her side.

One bullet, two wounds. My sort of math.

The trikes, stirred up by gunfire and excitement, were proving hard for the apes to throw harnesses and saddles on. Dust stirred as the dinosaurs shuffled in confusion, making it harder for me to pick out targets. But the two trikes that rode in earlier were still harnessed and ready to go. As an ape began mounting one of them, I fired. The shot was low, and hit the trike. It bellowed in pain and side stepped, shaking its horns and knocking the would-be rider off.

Apes were running for the canyon entrance now, trying to circle around and catch me from the rear. I ignored them. I'd be long gone by the time they reached my location.

An arrow zipped by, fired from an ape standing in the stream, and landing somewhere in the forest behind me. My aim was off, and I put a bullet through his leg as a large, hairy hand slapped the top of the edge.

Shocked that one of the apes reached me so quickly, I frantically worked the outdated reloading mechanism of the Sharps.

With both arms over the rock edge, the big female monkey began pulling herself up. A black hand reached for me.

Cocking the hammer back, I fired from the hip with the muzzle of the barrel mere inches away from her face. Unsupported, the recoil of the rifle almost knocked it out of my hands. But I managed to hang on to the gun as the bullet punched through the ape's throat with a spray of blood.

At point blank range, her flat face was filled with sparks of residual burning powder. Blinded and wounded, the ape clawed at her face and throat before toppling backwards and falling, yellowed canines bared in a silent scream.

Peeking over the edge, I saw her body twisted and broken amongst the rocks and a multitude of others clinging to the rocks below. Some stopped and stared at the corpse, others climbed faster. None of them looked happy.

From the canyon floor, more arrows whistled past me, thudding into the trees and ground nearby. Several hit the rock I was on, shattering shafts and pelting me with splinters. It was time to go.

I ducked and scrambled away from the cliff edge. Reaching Carbine, I slammed the telescope shut and into the saddle bags before leaping into the saddle. From behind came grunts and hoots as apes began reaching the top of the cliff. Smacking his flanks with the barrel of my rifle, I let him lead as I twisted in the saddle and fired at the apes behind me. I managed to make one duck before losing sight of them as Carbine charged amongst the thick trees.

Within seconds, we were lost in the forest.

***

In my defense, it's hard to see which direction you're headed when the sun is directly overhead, flittering through leaves of giant trees towering above you, and you're worried about getting your beating heart ripped out by hundreds of giant ape-men.

I needed to find some open space, somewhere I could look for the edge of the mountain range where the cliff face and tunnel was located. The problem was, it was hard to find someplace open where we could see. I turned Carbine's head to what, best I could tell, was south. In this direction, I suspected we would eventually run into the large river and could follow it back to the valley below the opening in the mountains. It was possible that it was fed in part by the smaller river that ran through the apes' canyon. I wasn't sure, but it seemed like my best bet.

The humidity and heat were relentless. My clothes were soaked with sweat and the stitches across my chest itched. Carbine was showing signs of fatigue. We came across a small stream where I let him drink and filled my canteen. My stomach grumbled. I hadn't eaten since breakfast. I pulled out some hard tack from a saddle bag to gnaw on while my horse tried his luck with the thick bladed grass. He seemed to like it well enough. After fifteen minutes of resting while watching our surroundings for any surprises, I mounted up and we rode on. So far, we'd been lucky, no apes managed to catch up to us.

At one point we ran into a large flock of leathered birds. They filled an entire tree, every branch holding several of varying sizes and swaying with their weight as they flapped their wings to stay balanced. We rode a wide circle around them; the last thing I needed was to send them flying and giving away our position, or worse, attacking us. And there was no way I could kill them all before they ate us.

An hour and a half later, I was struggling to pull thick strands from a giant spider web off my face when Carbine stepped through leafy bushes and onto the bank of the wide river we'd been searching for. The muddied water was moving slowly and looked deep. Lush, bright green grass grew in patches amongst river rocks and sand, while water plants with large leaves were scattered along the edges.

One of the wide bodied, armored dinosaurs that I'd seen earlier in the valley walked the opposite side. Its clubbed tail swung back and forth with its waddling gait. For a moment, it studied me curiously before deciding I wasn't a threat and turning back to snap up mouthfuls of river grass.

Water splashed, followed by ripples sent across the slow flowing water. Something moved in the muddy brown depths of the river.

Something large.

I kept Carbine far away from the edge, and whatever dinosaurs or creatures lurked in the water.

From where we were, I could see the mountains where the cliff face was located, and we headed downstream in that direction.

***

Once we had our bearing, it didn't take long to reach the valley and ride to the shimmering tunnel.

I stopped my horse and dismounted, holding his reins tightly in my hand. In the shadow of the mountain, I looked over the valley below. There still wasn't any sign of pursuers and the only creatures in sight were the ponderous long-neck beasts by the river. But I was confident the big monkeys were tracking me. After the bloody noise I'd given them, they'd want me.

And there wasn't any way of hiding the tunnel. They'd find it.

It was inevitable.

They would come to my side again, bringing with them their barbarism and savagery. They were a warrior culture, and with their army, they'd want battle and conquest.

The sight of the apes' sacrifice was seared in my mind along with the Indian's agonizing death cries. I looked at the long-necked dinosaurs one more time, sadly, before turning back to the tunnel.

This was a strange and fascinating place, full of wonder and mystery. Worthy of grand adventure and exploration. A new frontier. A lost world.

Too bad.

Unbuckling one of the saddle bags, I pulled out the bundle of dynamite and hefted it in my hand and looked at the length of fuse wrapped around it.

The apes could have their side, but they couldn't have mine.

***

Scratching a pair of match heads along the side of my boot, I cupped the small bits of flame and touched them to the fuse. The gunpowder filled cord caught and sizzled as it burned towards the intertwining of other fuses that led to every boom stick I'd brought with me.

Shaking the matches out, I scrambled away as fast as I dared.

If I slipped, I'd fall over a hundred feet and if that didn't kill me, thousands of pounds of falling rock from the explosions certainly would.

But I managed to turn the corner around the mountainside, out of sight of the cliff face and the explosives planted in cracks and crevices above it. The mountain was less steep here, and I turned my careful jog into a sprint.

My hack job of timing the fuses went about like expected. But I made it further than I hoped when the nitroglycerin and clay mixed sticks exploded with thunderous booms, sending gouts of dirt and rock into the air behind me.

I cringed, dropping down and cupping my hands over my head protectively as bits of rock rained down.

The explosions were immediately followed with tremors shaking the ground as giant slabs of rock broke free, sliding down the mountain, off the cliff, and hopefully covering the tunnel entrance. Dust billowed out in a dense cloud, overwhelming me and stinging my eyes until I clenched them shut.

I fumbled for the bandana around my neck and pulled it over my mouth and nose. Even with the cloth filtering the air, I struggled to breathe without choking. Dust coated the inside of my mouth and nose. My mouth went dry and my tongue felt thick. Cracking my crusted eyelids, I stumbled my way out of the dust cloud and towards the small copse of trees where Carbine waited.

My ears still rang as I reached the trees. I was thankful I hadn't been on the same side of the mountain face as the cliff when the dynamite exploded. Leaning against the thick trunk of a cottonwood tree, I hacked up a wad of dirty filth from my lungs and spat it out, so I could swear.

Carbine wasn't here.

This was where I'd tied him off. I could see where he'd pawed at the ground, and a pile of manure from where he'd relieved himself. I stalked out of the trees to look for him, knocking dust off my clothing angrily.

He stood a hundred yards away, nonchalantly munching grass, with reins dragging on the ground.

Relieved but still angry, I stuck my fingers in my mouth and blew an ear-piercing whistle to get him to come to me. He looked up, whinnied a greeting, then resumed grazing without taking a step.

Sighing, I walked to him and reached out to grasp the leather straps. He snorted and quickly backed out of reach, looking at me with mischievous brown eyes.

Gritting my teeth, I stepped forward.

He jumped away again, prancing playfully and tossing the reins with a jerk of his head.

"Carbine. Don't," I warned.

This time I lunged quickly for the reins, my hands closing on the leather straps.

He yanked them from my grasp with a half spin of his body then trotted in a circle around me, snorting softly, tail held high, obviously pleased with being such an ass.

I drew my pistol and cocked the hammer for added effect.

Dropping his head, he reluctantly stopped. When I grabbed the reins this time, he pushed his head against my chest affectionately, and I stroked his tan muzzle.

"You know you're a real pain in the butt, right boy?"

He whinnied in what I assumed was agreement as I de-cocked the Peacemaker and put it away.

We rode around the mountainside to the cliff. The stink of pulverized granite still lingered. But the dust was settling and revealed my plan had been a success. Tens of thousands of pounds of boulders, rocks, and dirt covered the entrance. Small tree branches stuck out amongst the large pile that covered well beyond the top of the twenty-five-foot-tall opening.

Good luck getting through that, you filthy apes.

Looking at the destruction I'd wrought, I was pleased. Blowing open safes and stumps was the extent of my previous explosive use. Except for that railroad bridge that one time. But I managed to do this, survive, and stop an army of barbaric apes from crossing over.

I turned Carbine's head to take us home. All in all, not a bad day of work.

***

The next morning, I was ready to relax a little.

I'd been wondering how the town reacted to the Sheriff rolling in with my beast's head in the back of his wagon, and if there had been any more sightings or attacks from other creatures. But after everything I'd been through lately, I decided I'd just take it easy for a day before I worry about anyone or anything else.

Dunking my body in the stream felt wonderful and the frigid mountain water did wonders for waking me up. Still on edge from all the violence, my pistol lay within reach on a pile of clean clothes as I scrubbed with a chunk of soap and gingerly dabbed at the scabbed cut across my chest.

There was no sign of infection. It looked like I might live after all.

Shivering uncontrollably, I dressed quickly and pulled my boots on. Then I got to work cleaning up my yard.

I pulled my bandana over my face and dragged the dead apes into the field behind the house. They were beginning to stink something awful. Tossing a canvas tarp over the hairy bodies, I weighted down the corners with rocks. Unfortunately, the beheaded monster was still too large to move, even with Carbine and rope. It'd have to stay where it was for the time being. I shot several buzzards that were feasting on the corpse and hung them nearby to warn others away. If anyone responded to the Sheriff's telegrams for help, I wanted the corpses intact.

I dragged more charred debris into a pile by the remains of my barn. Some of the burnt lumber could be kept for firewood, while the rest would need to be torched again and burnt down to the smallest amount of ash as possible before being hauled away and used to fertilize my small garden.

The bookshelves I rebuilt with a few pieces of repurposed barn lumber and carefully restacked the books. The Wyatt Earp dime novel, whose namesake glared so accusingly at me from the cover before, was stuffed in the middle and out of sight. That'll teach him.

Overall, it was a boring, if sweaty, day. Nothing tried to kill me. It was wonderful. That night, I slept like a baby. A wounded, exhausted, monster and ape slaying baby.

***

The next morning found me standing across from the Sheriff and his two deputies, James and Tom, as they filled me in on the townsfolk's reaction to my beast's severed head being put on display.

Apparently, the head had done a good job of stirring up townsfolk and surrounding ranchers. Folks were shooting into the dark at all sorts of moving shadows and noises. The result was wounded wildlife, cattle, and one stupid drunk shot off his horse after riding into someone's garden in the middle of the night. But no hide nor hair of anything strange. Which suited me just fine.

As for the head itself, that was sitting outside the office and looked like someone had taken a sharp knife and made incisions all around the hide, exposing bits of bone and decaying muscle. Some of the local kids must have been playing doctor on it. I couldn't come up with any other explanation for the mutilations.

All of that was fine and well, but then I told the law officers of the apes, and my latest adventures.

After I finished, Dan rubbed his beard thoughtfully and looked down at his coffee cup. "It's a hell of a story, Jed."

"I know, but I've got four dead apes waiting to be planted in my back yard. Come out and look at them."

Deputy James nudged his younger brother with an elbow from their position leaning against the Sheriff's desk and smirked. "Look Jed, it's not that we don't believe you. It's just that, well, we don't believe you."

They laughed until their uncle shot them a look that could kill. "Shut it. Both of you."

Deputy Tom, barely past eighteen and with a slight lisp, ignored the warning and spoke up. "Oh, c'mon, Uncle Dan. We've been waving that big claw around and showing off the beast's head, warning people about scary monsters in the dark, and no one has seen nothing. They just laugh at us now. And now we have this ridiculous story about a magical tunnel, giant monsters, and big monkeys eating some Injun's heart?" He sneered at me, which was a mistake.

Angered, I got into the Deputy's face and stared into his blue eyes. "You want to step outside, *boy*?" I asked, putting as much menace in my voice as possible with the insult.

Tom stopped laughing abruptly and practically squealed in outrage, "You threatenin' me? I'm an officer of the law!"

James stepped beside him, instinctively backing his little brother.

I flexed my fingers and clenched my fist, while trying to figure out which one might be stupid enough to try something.

"Enough!" Dan shouted and slammed his hand down on the desk. "Both of you, sit your asses down. I've fought an Indian War with Jed. He's a man of sound reputation and capability, not one to give into fears and foolishness. And you two all but called him a liar. Do it again, and I'll do more than threaten you!"

The sound reputation part was a bit much. But what Dan didn't know would only help me.

Tom swallowed hard and eased himself back against the wall, glaring all the while. He smoothed out his shirt and pinching the shiny star shaped badge between trembling fingers, pretended to adjust it casually. The movement reminded me of a rooster who almost got plucked trying to preen his feathers in fake indifference.

Sighing, Dan rubbed his temples. "If it wasn't for your mother, you two jack-wagons would be cleaning spittoons and digging latrines."

James muttered something under his breath.

Dan looked at him sharply. "What was that?"

"Nothing... Sheriff," he said sourly.

Dan grunted, and turned back to me. "Alright Jed, I'll send these two to check out that cliff you blew up. In the meantime, there's some people at the hotel who are real interested in meeting you. One of them is a good friend of mine. So, don't make me look bad."

"Friend, huh? Who?" I was a little put off. I thought I was his only friend.

He smirked. "You may have heard of him. Fella goes by the name Wolverine Wade."

Of course, I knew the name. He was a western legend. A famed scout for the army, renowned buffalo hunter and Indian fighter, and if legend was correct, he killed an attacking wolverine with his bare hands to earn his nickname. Both deputies spun to face the Sheriff, knocking several new wanted posters off the desk. They caught my eye as they drifted to the floor. One of them looked a little familiar, but thankfully it wasn't me poorly sketched above the bounty price.

"Wolverine Wade?" James asked with surprise in his voice. Beside him, Tom's eyes were as wide as a kid who just found out he might meet, well, the famous Wolverine Wade Mackin.

"Damn right. Scouted with him for the Army a bit before he was famous. Didn't know that about me, did you? I would introduce you and your brother, except you're embarrassments," he half-joked.

I certainly didn't know that. Turns out the old Sheriff had some secrets as well. "Why's he looking for me?" I cut in before the deputies could start fawning and whining more.

"I asked him to come look at this monster you killed. He's well-travelled and connected, figured he may be interested. Also, he's wanting to start a show, some sort of theatrical thing about the west. So, he's trying to find any sort of talent or critters he can scrounge up. But since you blew up the tunnel, I reckon there won't be any more."

"There may be a few more things out there lurking around." We couldn't rule out that possibility.

"That'll please him. The rarer the better. He brought his business partner, who also happens to be a sharpshooter."

I nodded. "Who else?"

"The Smithsonian Institute sent a couple people out. They got excited when they saw the head and have been studying it and making notes and sketches. They confirmed it is... well was... a real living dinosaur. Congratulations on killing something supposedly extinct. Now they are pretty anxious to see the rest of its body and meet you."

That was a lot more attention than I hoped for or needed, but I didn't see any way out of it. "Well, great. Is there anyone you didn't send a telegram to?"

"President Cleveland," he joked, then got serious. "Also, Jim from the newspaper wants to take your picture with the head."

"Hell no." The last thing I needed was my picture in a paper. That was just asking for incarceration.

"Suit yourself. This may be your only chance for fame."

I rolled my eyes and stood. "No thanks. But I reckon I've some acquaintances to make."

Dan checked his pocket watch. "You've got time to catch them before they leave. Wade said they were planning on heading to your place about noon."

"Want us to go with him?" Deputy James asked. Tom looked hopeful. I bet they wanted the famed westerner to sign their rifles or some such.

Dan crushed their hopes with a shake of his head. "No. James, you've worked in a mine before. Since you've the most experience with earth moving and explosives, I want you to finish your rounds and go look at that cliff. Take some extra dynamite and make sure it's sealed for good. Nothing else is to come through, you understand?" He waited for his nephew to nod his head obediently before continuing, "Tom, you go with him." He pointed a finger at them with an added warning. "In the meantime, both of you stay away from Jed, Wolverine Wade, and especially the women."

The two deputies spoke over each other in a rush.

"Women?" "Are they pretty?" "Any short ones?"

Women were rare creatures out west. Most were as tough as a rented mule, and about as pretty, but occasionally you got a rose without too many thorns or wilted leaves. Every man in the area always got real excited whenever a new one showed up in town. I just gave a manly grunt and pulled my hat on before jerking the door open. Women made a man talk, and an outlaw in hiding talking leads to an outlaw hanging from a rope.

Dan called after me. From beneath his desk he pulled the severed forearm and tossed it.

I caught the arm with one hand and wagged goodbye with the claws before closing the door behind me.

Reverend was waiting on the boardwalk, his back leaning against the Sheriff's rough sawn log wall.

"Saw you ride into town, Jedidiah," he said. "I hear you killed this beast." He pointed at the large severed head with his tattered Bible.

"Yes, sir. I'm betting you got lots of theological questions about that." Heck, I had some. I just hadn't had time to ponder them yet.

He smiled, showing crooked teeth. "I did indeed. I put the answers together and made a rather lively sermon out of them. I rarely get the chance to speak on the Behemoth and Leviathan from the Book of Job. Great monsters have always existed before us and with us. Now they usually take the shape of man, as you well know."

That was a fact. The mass of scar tissue across my back was simple proof enough. I squinted my eyes at him, curious as to why he was waiting for me. "What can I do for you, Reverend?"

He shrugged one shoulder. "You've encountered a lot of death lately." He looked me up and down. "And taken a pretty solid beating from it all. I just wanted to make sure you were doing okay."

I glanced around us to make sure no one could overhear our conversation. The door to the Sheriff's Office was closed securely behind me. "Honestly, I'm fine..." I hesitated, trying to think of where to start and how much to tell him.

Sensing I was uncertain of what to say, he put a hand on my shoulder and leaned close to speak privately. "You've led a hard life, Jedidiah. One full of pain and violence. Your sins have been forgiven. Don't let your past life define your future. Find something, anything, that is good, and worth fighting for and hold onto it." He winked at me conspiringly. "Maybe a wife?"

I laughed. "Sure Reverend, I'll get right on that."

Grinning, he patted my shoulder. "I'll be praying for you Jedidiah." Winking, he walked away, whistling *Camptown Races* happily.

***

Leaving the framed buildings, I walked past haphazard rows of tents towards the rail station. This was the lively part of town, where small businesses sprouted up amongst temporary housing for families and migrant workers. It was a loud, boisterous area. A place filled with every sin imaginable mixed amongst good families, hard workers, and criminals.

It was a lot like the cities back east. Except with more blacks,

Mexicans, and a few Chinese thrown in the mix. So, it had much better food.

The rail station wasn't my goal, it was the small building nearby the stockyards filled with mooing cattle. The Government Land Office. A popular destination for miners, ranchers, and anyone else looking to claim open land. Normally, I avoided any government building like the plague. Good things rarely come from such places. But I had business to attend to that forced me to this wretched location. The sort of business that would keep people from getting eaten in the future.

The fat, black man in suspenders behind the desk didn't bother to get up as I walked in. He sat amongst a mess of ledgers and rolled maps. Flies buzzed around the windows, and a mangy three-legged mutt growled at me from the floor.

"Shuddup, Tripod!" the slovenly government worker shouted before snatching a half-eaten biscuit off his plate and throwing it at the dog. The misshapen lump of bread hit the wall with a thud and fell. The mutt lazily stretched out to snatch it in his jaws and chewed, still laying on the floor and eyeballing me.

The man glanced at me and frowned. "What do you want?"

I looked him over. He had grease and sweat stains on his shirt and crumbs in his mustache. I disliked him immediately. "That's an interesting name for a dog."

"It's on account of him having three legs. He got hit by a train. I said, what do you want? I'm busy."

As he talked, I looked around the room. It was a pigsty. There was barely walking room between the door and his desk. A narrow path, and two holes amongst the junk, one fat man sized and the other for the mutt. Papers littered the floor. The trash can was heaped full and more garbage lay on the ground next to it. The walls were covered with shelves full of rolled up maps and deed books. The man wasn't busy, just lazy and worthless.

"Granite Mountain. I staked out a chunk of land. Need to file the claim."

"Hmmm… Granite Mountain." He waded through the mess to a shelf and pulled down a ledger and pair of maps. "These are the most up to date we got. Most of the mountain isn't surveyed," he said curtly as he opened the ledger. It was blank except for a single entry at the top.

"Only one other claim out there. Some fella named J. Johnson," the slob read before wiping his mouth on his sleeve and burping. My nose wrinkled at the stench of his stomach contents. "Must be a filthy Injun lover to live out there by himself."

I'd never heard of him. But any man living on that mountain probably wanted to be left alone.

Unrolling the maps, he stretched them out over a mound of leather bound ledgers. The area where I found the tunnel was blank, with only a few noticeable landmarks that had been scribed on the map with vague distances. It was also on the opposite side of the other man's claim. Apparently, no one had ever surveyed near his area either. That wasn't a surprise, vast swaths of the western territories hadn't been surveyed properly yet. I jabbed a finger at it where I suspected the cliff was.

"Here." I pulled a scrap of paper from my pocket that listed the markers I'd used for boundary corners and the paced off distances between them. Just to be safe, I staked out a big chunk of the land around the tunnel and used land features that couldn't be argued over and wouldn't change. A small pile of stones was usually all that was needed, but those were easy to kick over and I didn't want anyone near that place, ever.

He took the piece of paper and read the list. "Sounds fine." He copied them below Mr. J. Johnson's claim. For such a messy unlikeable individual, he had very neat and orderly handwriting.

"Name?" he asked, not bothering to look up.

"Jedidiah Huckleberry Smith."

He snorted disdainfully. "Huckleberry. Silly name."

I glanced at the fly covered window and tried to figure out if I could throw him through it. He probably wouldn't fit. But there were plenty of thick ledgers in here to beat him to death with. The temptation was strong. Maybe just a single good whack would do.

"Done."

His voice shook me from my daydreams of violence. I compared his script carefully to my scrap of paper. The information was correct in every detail. I paid the man and left, eager to be away from the place. The dog growled again as I closed the door.

***

Now that I felt sufficiently sleazy for dealing with the government, I went to the trade store to place an order for posts and lumber for the new barn. Paying the bill was painful, it looked like I may need to make the long ride to fetch the last of my hidden loot soon.

Shaking my head at the cost, I mounted Carbine and we rode towards the hotel. It was high noon, but I wasn't concerned about missing Wolverine Wade's group. If I did, I'd catch up to them on the trail easily enough.

As I passed the saloon, ladies called out from the balcony and I tipped the brim of my hat at them. The dark-haired girl with the gap in her teeth recognized me from before and whistled sharply before shouting a discounted price followed by a giggle.

Unbidden, the Reverend's words of finding a wife drifted to the front of my mind. I laughed and waved, but kept going. Maybe this was who he had in mind. She was certainly pretty enough, if a little less than reputable. But who was I to talk about reputation? I killed a bunch of people and broke their stuff.

Under the balcony, I spied Wesley leaning against a hitching rail and smoking a thin black cigarillo.

Blowing a puff of white smoke out the side of his mouth, he gave me a friendly wave. Pulling on the reins, I stopped Carbine in front of him. The gambler's hat was tilted back, and I studied his face. He looked a little like the man on the wanted poster. That didn't matter much to me, I wouldn't turn a man in unless he crossed me or did something sufficiently immoral. Even then, I usually just shot them and avoided the lawmen altogether. Sometimes straying onto the wrong side of the law has its perks.

"Heard you killed that monster whose head is decorating the walk outside the Sheriff's Office. Is that how you came to be in the bar when we met, all busted up and ugly?"

"Yeah. Figured if I told you, you wouldn't believe me."

"On that, you are correct." He took another drag before flicking the gray ash off the end. "The story's made the rounds. I've heard a few different versions, but they all agree that you're lucky to have survived."

"All it took was luck, bullets, and dynamite."

"Those things will get a man through just about anything." He grinned then dropped the thin cigar onto the boardwalk and ground it with his heel. With a flick of his toe, he knocked the remains into the street. "I'd like to hear the story sometime over a bottle."

"It'll have to wait. I've got to run some people out to my ranch to see the rest of the beast. Some scientists from back East."

He looked at me slyly. "And Wolverine Wade?"

Carbine pawed the ground impatiently. He was ready to get moving. I gave Wesley a nod. "Word must get around quick."

"People love to gossip, and a man can hear most everything at the bar, if he pays attention. Makes sense why he's in town now. He's looking for attractions for the show he's trying to put together. If he offers you a job, you should take it. Much easier living than ranching."

"I'd make a terrible rodeo clown."

He snickered. "That wasn't what I meant."

I spied a mule-drawn wagon rolling down the street towards us. The famous westerner was easily recognizable from the papers I'd seen him in. He wore a fringed jacket over a tan shirt, with jeans and black leather riding boots, and a side of his Stetson hat was turned upwards fashionably.

But it was the woman riding next to him that caught my eye. She was the most beautiful girl I'd ever seen. With pale skin and long dark hair, her tan dress complemented her looks nicely. She saw me staring and smiled. I shifted my gaze away, embarrassed at being caught looking.

In the back of the wagon, another lady sat with a rifle leaned against her shoulder. When the Sheriff said Wade had a business partner who was also sharpshooter, I'd expected them to be a man. But since she was the only person other than Wade who appeared armed, she must be the one. She was cute, in your average woman sort of way. Tan and lithe, with a dirty blonde ponytail draped over a shoulder. She wore a plain brown outfit, wide brimmed hat tilted back, and black leather boots that went to her knees. She looked born and raised in the west.

But the red faced, plump man sitting across from her, wearing a stylish black suit, silver tie, complete with top hat and spectacles had easterner written all over him. There was something about him I immediately disliked. Maybe it was his out of place immaculate outfit, or the way he seemed to look down at those who walked along the streets around him through his small round glasses. Either way, he appeared to think little of our town and its inhabitants.

Wesley followed my gaze and saw the wagon approaching. He turned away, quickly stepping onto the boardwalk. "See you around, Jed." He disappeared into the darkened interior of the bar before I could reply.

I raised a hand as the wagon came closer, and Wolverine Wade slowed the team of dark brown mules to a stop. The pretty lady smiled, and I was suddenly very self-conscious about my battered appearance, raccoon eyes, and bruised throat.

"Ladies..." I tipped my hat, "and gentlemen. I'm Jedidiah Smith and I understand you're looking for me."

Wade reached from the wagon to shake my hand. He had a grip like a vise. Not the sort of finger squashing handshake a braggart would give to try and establish dominance, but the sort of easy strength that came from a lifetime of hard work. His entire face lit up when he smiled, his mustache corners raised and the crow's feet around his eyes deepened. "Jedidiah, I'm Wolverine Wade Mackin. Which is a mouthful, so just call me Wade."

"And just Jed will do for me." My eye's flicked to the long-barreled rifle leaning against the seat between him and the pretty lady. It looked like a Ballard. With the thick octagonal barrel and cleaning rod strapped underneath, I bet the big rifle weighed near 12 pounds.

Wade indicated the beautiful woman beside him with the pale skin and dark hair. "This is Ms. Skyla Stratten from the Smithsonian Institute. The lady with the rifle behind me is my business partner, Ms. Ashley James. She's also our show's future sharpshooter." Wade disdainfully jerked a thumb towards the large well-dressed man behind him who looked completely out of place sitting on the twined bale of hay. "This is Oscar Ellis, also from the Smithsonian."

I swept my hat off my head and bent forward slightly. "It's a pleasure to meet you all."

The fat man in the nice suit, his name was Oscar I reminded myself, spoke up. "What sort of condition can we expect the rest of the theropod to be in?"

I looked at him blankly. I expected to exchange more pleasantries before we got down to brass tacks and I'd no idea what he was talking about. "Theropod?"

He looked at me like I was an idiot. "The dinosaur you so crudely decapitated."

I raised an eyebrow. "Well... as for the condition... lots of bullet holes, some parts blown off, and scorched bits here and there."

Oscar sputtered, his voice rising in pitch with his agitation. "What? WHAT? What have you done? Do you understand the importance of this discovery? Quite possibly the greatest one in humankind! And parts are blown off?!"

Skyla cut in quietly. "Oscar, the man obviously did what he had to, to stay alive."

"I don't care!" he shouted angrily as a vein throbbed at his temple. Carbine shifted nervously at his outburst, and I rubbed his neck to calm him.

I appreciated the pretty lady sticking up for me, and was glad she understood, but I still felt the need to put the man in his place. "You know what I did? I filled it full of lead after it ate my horse. Then I blew my burning inferno of a barn up with the thero-whatever inside, because it wouldn't die. But don't worry. If one tries to eat you, I won't stop it for fear of damaging your precious discovery," I told him sarcastically.

He started to respond but Wade cut in and changed the direction of the conversation. "Do you think there are any more dinosaurs still around?"

"Possibly," I said.

"Where?" Skyla leaned forward with excitement.

Everyone turned and looked as I pointed to the looming mountain range to the north-west.

"That's where the dinosaurs are?"

"Sort of. It's a long story. They came from there, through a tunnel in the mountains. But I don't reckon there will be many more coming though." I braced myself for their response before continuing, knowing it wasn't what they'd want to hear. "Because I blew the opening shut."

"WHY?!?" Carbine whinnied at the outburst and jumped away as Oscar screamed in outrage. I fought the reins to get him to settle back down. Bystanders stopped to see what the fuss was about, before moving on, warily keeping an eye on the wagon.

Holding the reins firmly, I walked Carbine back to the wagon and glared at the angry fat man with my hand on the butt of my pistol. I spoke low and forcefully. "That's twice now. Don't you ever frighten my horse again."

He blinked rapidly, shocked at my harsh reaction.

I gave my veiled threat a moment to sink in before addressing his question. "And I blew the tunnel up because of the apes."

Everyone in the wagon looked confused.

"What apes?" Ashley shifted her rifle beside her uneasily.

"The ugly, hairy, seven-foot-tall kind that eats people."

Skyla looked at the others before speaking slowly. "Surely, you jest."

"Sadly, no."

Wade twisted the sides of his mustache before stroking his long goatee thoughtfully. "Sounds like you've a story to tell."

I looked around us. The street was filled with folks on foot and horseback, with a few wagons mixed in, and we were blocking half the street. "Let's get going. When we get to my ranch, I'll tell you the rest."

Wade nodded. "Lead the way."

"Not to worry any of you, but I'll ride a little ahead, in case there is another beast lurking about. If that happens, turn tail and run back here as fast as possible. I'll distract it in the meantime." I patted my horse's neck. "I think we can outrun it, but you can't in that wagon. Even with the mules."

Ashley nodded and racked a round into the chamber of her rifle. "Don't worry about Wade or myself; if there's a target, we'll be shooting." Wade grinned at her enthusiasm and adjusted his rifle into a position where he could grab it quicker. Skyla looked uncomfortable at the mention of danger. I gave her what I hoped was a reassuring smile that she returned slightly.

"I'd prefer there was no shooting of any dinosaurs," Oscar protested weakly.

"I don't care." Turning my back towards him, I pushed my hat down firmly and touched heels to Carbine. As Wolverine Wade's Party Wagon followed, we carefully threaded through the busy street, out of town, and onto the trail that led home.

***

When we reached my ranch, Wade slowed the team of mules to a stop and propped his foot on the front of the buckboard. Everyone was silent as they stared at the mangled and decapitated corpse. It seemed to have that effect on people.

Wade spoke first, ignoring the obvious to pay me a compliment. "Well... nice spread you got here, Jed."

"Needs a little work," Ashley stated simply.

That was an understatement. Where the barn had stood, now lay a tangle of fallen and burnt timbers. The headless dinosaur carcass was rotting in my front yard with several dead buzzards hanging from tall stakes nearby to keep the others away. Varmints had snuck in during the night, tearing chunks off and feasting, leaving scattered entrails and pieces of ripped flesh behind. The finishing touch on the ghastly sight was the relatively fresh ape corpses behind the house under a tarp. It was going to take a lot of work to clean up.

I peeked at Skyla out of the corner of my eye, trying to not be obvious. She looked excited to be so close to the rest of the dinosaur I killed. Honestly, if I'd known a pretty girl was coming out, I would have cleaned up more. I was a little ashamed of how rough the place looked, and told myself that, given the opportunity, I'd clean up the house before she stepped foot inside.

Oscar stood in the back of the wagon, hands cupped over his eyes, squinting against the sunlight. "First living dinosaur discovered in millions of years, and its remains have been violated and disfigured beyond recognition."

"What do you think happens to dead critters after nature has a go at it?" I asked him.

Ignoring me, he climbed down and began walking towards the beastly remains in a side to side waddle. Getting a closer look at the dinosaur's remains, he turned back. His face was one of disdain. "I need to get started on my study right away, before nature, or Jed, does any more damage to the corpse." He took a couple of steps before calling over his shoulder. "Skyla, fetch the bags."

"What?" Wade's voice was loud and hard.

Oscar twirled about, confused. Skyla froze, half risen from her seat, looking back and forth between Wade and Oscar. Confusion and uncertainty etched across her face.

Wade rested his elbow on a knee, and leaned forward to skewer him with a glare. "Have you forgotten your manhood, Oscar?"

Adjusting his spectacles on his thin nose, Oscar's face flushed red. He pointed at Skyla whose embarrassment was obvious. "She is my assistant. It is her job to assist me." Seeing we had no noticeable reaction to this information, he continued with his defense. "That includes note taking, writing correspondences, helping with experiments and studies, and," he paused to take a breath, "carrying my bags."

"Like hell," I said, as Carbine took a pair of steps closer to him. "You may get by without manners back east, but out here a lady doesn't serve a man anything unless it's supper." I shifted the reins in my hand, allowing more length to slip out, half-hoping I'd get the opportunity to smack him with them. This man was rapidly becoming the most unlikeable person I'd run across since moving to Granite Falls, including the slob at the Land Office.

He opened his mouth to argue and closed it as he took in our stern faces. Even Ashley's look was hard and unforgiving. Chivalry's not dead out west.

"Fine. I'll carry the bags. But I have back pain." He moved back towards the wagon, his waddle gone as he now exaggerated by pressing a hand on the small of his back.

"And soft hands, no doubt," I heard Ashley murmur. Wade tilted his hat, hiding a grin.

Swinging down from the saddle, I stepped to the wagon and offered my hand to Skyla. She hesitated for a heartbeat, flustered from the awkward confrontation, then accepted. Her hands were small and warm. A shiver ran through me and I quickly released her hand, afraid that she may have felt it. I was well and truly flustered now.

Oscar fumbled with a bag as he tried to lift it over the side of the wagon.

Getting a hold of myself, I reached around him and picked up the carpet bag he was fighting with, and shoved it against his chest. He grasped the bag with both hands and glared. Ignoring him, I followed Skyla to the corpse. The stench was awful and bloated flies buzzed as they gorged themselves on the decaying flesh.

As Oscar waddled over with the bag clutched to his chest, Skyla held a handkerchief to her mouth and dropped to a knee beside the body. Her face lit up with excitement as she ran a hand across its pebbled hide. "So, this is the rest of it," she said, while trying hopelessly to wave away the flies. Instead of fleeing, they buzzed louder and appeared to multiply in number as she stirred them up.

Oscar dropped the bag and leaned back as if to stretch his back as he stared at the body. "And I thought the damage to its head was bad. Could you have shot it a few more times?" he asked sarcastically.

"No, I was out of bullets and guns," I replied honestly.

Wade looked approvingly at me and patted his holstered pistol. "Gun's emptied… That's the way I'd choose to go out."

Ashley poked the body with the muzzle of her rifle. "How many times did you shoot it?"

I tried to recall, and gave the best guess I could. "I think eight times with the rifle, maybe six or seven times with my pistol."

She grimaced as she saw the smudge of blood smeared on the end of her barrel. "And that wasn't enough? Maybe you should start carrying two of those Colts."

"That's certainly an idea worth considering."

Wade squatted on his haunches and looked up at me. "You killed a real monster, Jed." Skyla reached out and ran her hand over the large claws, gently touching the point with the tip of her finger.

Oscar scoffed. "It is not a monster. It is a theropod."

The famed westerner rolled his eyes.

"You've been saying that since yesterday, as though it means something to us," Ashley said as Skyla pulled several thin knives and bone saws out of the bag.

"It's a scientific classification. Take caninae, or canine as most people call them. They are a class of carnivorous mammals that include wolves, dogs, foxes, and coyotes. They are all caninae. This is of the theropod genus," he looked at me. "Or in simpler terms, for you westerners, it's a type of animal."

I grunted, letting the insult slide for Skyla's sake. She didn't seem like the sort who would appreciate me pounding her boss into the ground.

Skyla pulled out two pairs of long leather gloves that looked like they would go all the way to a man's shoulder and continued where Oscar had stopped. "More specifically, this is an Allosaurus. A young one, maybe half to three quarters grown. We've found larger fossils, so I'm basing my assumption off them. They can get another five to ten feet long and four feet taller. Of course, like most animals, that all depends on its environment. But luckily for you Jed, these are solitary animals, which is why you only had one to deal with."

"A young one, huh? Well, that's just dandy." I would've hated to have met a fully grown one in that darkened interior of the barn.

Oscar looked at her approvingly and took his top hat off, carefully setting it on the ground. "My assistant is correct. When I first saw the head, I was thinking perhaps it was a Carnotaurus. But now that I see more than just the chopped off chunk of claw Jed so unkindly removed, it's clear. The forearms are much too large, the Carnotaurus' front were small feeble things." He wagged the long stump of an arm towards us as proof.

I glanced over my shoulder at Wade. "Sounds kind of like a big-headed dinosaur I saw. It was massive, with tiny little arms."

The two scientists stared at me, both their mouths open.

Ashley noticed their surprised reactions. "What? What's that? Is it one of these? Where was it?" She hefted her rifle in her arms and looked at the surrounding forest with renewed suspicion.

Skyla's eyes widened. "A Tyrannosaurus?"

"What's that?"

Oscar bounced up gleefully, his fake back ailment forgotten. "That's what you're describing, right? Huge dinosaur, massive head, long tail, big teeth, little wobbly arms." He pulled his back to his chest and flapped his hands, mimicking what I saw as though I were a child.

I gave him a nod. "Yup. That's it."

"That's probably the most ferocious dinosaur that we know of." Skyla stood slowly with one of the gloves pulled halfway to her elbow. She pulled it off quickly, dropping it into a pile with the others. "You're lucky to be alive."

"It was chasing some big birds, didn't even seem to notice me."

"Sounds like something worth hunting." Wade squatted by the Allosaurus remains and poked his finger into one of the bullet holes.

I pointed at his rifle. "You're gonna want a repeater."

"Oh this?" He lifted the giant single-shot Ballard rifle. "It's all about shot placement, Jed."

"True, but sometimes one bullet ain't enough."

Oscar moved closer to me. I smelled the rich scent of whatever pomade he'd greased his hair back with. It stank of something fruity. But he was about to invade what I considered to be my personal space reserved for lovin' and fightin'.

"Where did you see it?" he asked sharply.

I took a half step back to gain some breathing room and pointed towards the mountain range looming above us in the distance. "Like I said, over there. On the other side of the tunnel through the mountain." As one, everyone turned and looked. There wasn't a single peak to focus on, just a long ridge that formed high in the north and gradually faded out to the south.

Oscar kicked the ground savagely before shouting, "And you blew the tunnel shut! You stupid, foolish imbecile! Do you know what you've done?!" Spinning to face me, he found the barrel of my Colt was pointed at his spectacled face. His hot-headed anger turned to wide-eyed fear in a split second. I'd had enough of his attitude and I wasn't about to let it go any further.

Skyla gasped and from the corner of my eye, I saw her raise a hand to her mouth. So much for getting in her good graces, but insults shouldn't be allowed to go without a proper response. This was twice now, and there wouldn't be a third.

I glared at him over the sights. "I reckon it's bad hospitality to kill a guest, but I already shot four who pissed me off. Those big, ugly monkeys are in the field behind the house waiting to be buried under some rose bushes. Mind your manners or I'll dig the grave a little wider."

A bead of sweat trickled down and dripped onto his black suit as the scientist swallowed hard and stared at the muzzle end of my pistol.

"Jed..." Wade cautioned.

Maybe I'd over-reacted a little, but this fat, obnoxious easterner needed to learn some manners. Firmness hadn't worked, so fear was the next best thing, right before violence. Grunting, I holstered my pistol and gave him a final warning. "As you were told, this ain't the east. Out here, if you insult a man, you'd best be prepared to defend yourself."

Oscar coughed and adjusted his tie with a trembling hand. "My apologies, Jed. I shall refrain from stating my mind so bluntly," he said with fake sincerity. In other words, he'd still think I was an idiot, but he'd keep such thoughts to himself. That was fine. His opinion wasn't one I valued, just his knowledge of dinosaurs in case there were any more lurking on our side.

"About these monkeys you shot. They are the apes you spoke of?" Ashley said, attempting to defuse the heated moment.

Skyla looked away as I turned from Oscar to face the rest of the group. I mentally kicked myself; easterners are such a finicky bunch. Of course, she wouldn't understand. But out here, your reputation and your word could make or break you. No one was going to smear my currently good name with unanswered insults.

"Backyard," I stalked off without waiting to see who followed.

The apes' bodies lay in a row where I'd dragged and dumped them. A corner of the tarp had been pulled aside and strips of flesh and hair torn off an exposed leg, white bone was etched with tooth marks from where some varmint gnawed on it.

Wade stopped beside me and looked at the chewed leg. "Coyote most likely… maybe a large fox."

Pinching the top of her nose, Ashley stepped around her partner to get a better look. "They smell awful."

"Didn't smell too pleasant when they were alive either. Kind of like a wet dog."

Skyla and Oscar left their surgical equipment and gloves behind and caught up. I noted he gave me a wide berth and stood on the other side of the tarp. Good.

Oscar rolled a couple of rocks off the tarp corners with his polished boots, then grabbed the canvas sheet and jerked it away to expose the damaged bodies of the apes. Then he promptly bent over and retched in the long grass. Skyla held a hand to her mouth and Ashley just looked curious.

I didn't hold it against them. The apes were ugly and the wounds I caused were ghastly on such vaguely human looking things. But for a man of science, Oscar had a weak stomach compared to the girls.

Wade didn't have much of a reaction. But then, the man had a reputation for seeing and doing things no one else had. He just grunted and said, "Hideous things, ain't they?"

Wiping his mouth with the back of his hand, Oscar spat into the grass before collecting himself and preening his clothes smooth. Without a word, he stepped away from his puddle of vomit and looked down at the ape in front of him. Its head was deflated and blown open from the .45 slug punching through. It wasn't a pretty sight.

He sighed angrily, but this time he kept his thoughts to himself. Of which I was certain involved me killing rare things in ways that displeased him.

The ladies, having recovered from the surprise, moved closer for a better view. Skyla inspected the smeared painted swirls and patterns while Ashley pointed at the ape in the center with the gaping wound in its chest and singed hair. "You do that one in with a shotgun?"

I nodded. "Both barrels of double-ought buckshot from my bedside shotgun." After saving my life, I decided it deserved that place of honor in case I needed it again.

"Bedside shotgun, huh? That's a new one," Wade chuckled as he picked up one of the ape's hands and compared it to his own. It was at least a third bigger. He nodded at the remaining one, whose body was gashed open from groin to chest. "That from the Bowie on your hip?"

"It got a little wild and we went hand to hand for a few rounds, I was fresh out of weapons and options." I rubbed the tender bruise around my throat and glanced at our scientists. "Are these some sort of, dinosaur people? Or something?" Even as the words came out of my mouth, I realized how stupid that sounded. I tried to recover, "Or just big monkeys?"

Oscar moved to join Skyla, reaching down to touch the decorative paint that swirled across the ape's chest. He scraped a few flakes off with his fingers. "I am a paleontologist, but Skyla has some knowledge of archeology."

I didn't know exactly what those terms meant, but I assumed that paleontologist had something to do with dinosaurs and archeology dealt with giant monkeys.

She shrugged her shoulders apologetically. "Only a little. A few years ago, I did some studying at the Natural Museum of American History in that field. Archeology is the study of human history and culture based on whatever leftover evidence we can find, shards of pottery, ancient tools, fossilized remains. Anything that gives insight into the people who lived before us," she took a deep breath before continuing. "When it comes to fossils, they're usually vague and incomplete. We may find one partial, fragmented skeleton for every few million of them that existed. There are all sorts of creatures that we haven't discovered yet, and many we will probably never discover. It's entirely possible these ape men things lived at the same time as the dinosaurs. We just haven't, or may never, unearth the remains of whatever civilization they may have had. Even today, there

69

are vast unexplored regions in this world that have never been seen by white men. There is no telling what sorts of beasts or types of men inhabit them. These apes may be still lurking in the depths of Africa or South America."

"Most likely, this is just more proof of Darwinism," Oscar added.

I snorted, and the scientists looked at me. "The only part of that crazed coot's theories I believe is the part about survival of the fittest. I've lived that. But our ancestors being monkeys? That's absurd."

"It's just a theory, Jed." Skyla leaned over the closest ape corpse to get a good look at its mangled face. "It's not fact until proven true."

"And how do you prove something like that?" Ashley looked as skeptical as I felt.

Oscar jabbed a finger at the bodies. "This is how. Missing links between discovered species that existed at different points of time. Showing an evolutionary change over time as a species adapted. It's possible these apes were an evolutionary step that was left behind on the other side of your tunnel, maybe we moved on and changed."

I nudged one with the toe of my boot, its body twisted slightly before settling back. "Or maybe these are just something different all together."

"Leave the science to us, and concern yourself with your guns, horses, and violence," Oscar huffed.

"A few of my favorite things," I muttered.

"I don't know, Jed. It's just a theory, untested and unproven," Skyla sounded exasperated.

Wade cut into our banter. "I've seen all sorts of things in my travels here and in Europe. And I've never seen anything like these apes in zoos or circuses. They vaguely remind me of the gorillas of Africa, but much more… human. Judging from their hands, they weren't walking on their knuckles when they attacked you, were they?

"No, they stood upright like a man. From what I've seen, they're smart, capable, and fearfully strong."

Wade stared at the apes, stroking his goatee thoughtfully. "You wanted to wait and tell us the story after we got here, I get that. But we're here now, and we've so many questions that I think your account of what happened will give us some answers."

"Agreed. Let's put your team away, and get settled on the porch for story time."

It didn't take too long to unhook the mules from the wagon and put them into the pasture. Without a repaired corral, they would have more room to run about, but be more difficult to round up later. I turned Carbine loose with them and soon he was prancing around, trying to get the mules to play.

Afterwards, we all settled in on the porch as comfortably as possible.

Oscar was reluctant to put off his dissection of the Allosaurus, but curiosity appeared to get the better of him. The women took the two rocking chairs, while we men settled for sitting on the porch and stretching our feet onto the dirt and grass clods of my yard.

Then I began my tale with the night I met the Allosaurus.

"So, there I was, asleep, when...."

***

My story was interrupted with lots of questions that ranged from Oscar and Skyla asking for more details about the dinosaurs, to Ashley's curiosity about the apes' weapons. Wade seemed most curious about the apes' physical capabilities.

At first shock and disbelief were evident on their faces, but as the story progressed, they seem to grow more and more accustomed to the strangeness of my tale. Everyone was disturbed as I briefly spoke about the part of human sacrifice and heart eating. Oscar grew visibly angry as I told of how I collapsed the tunnel under thousands of pounds of mountainside.

Once I finished and answered what questions I could, everyone was quiet in their own thoughts.

The air was warm and dry, but the shade was just cool enough to prevent a sweat from beading on the skin. The sun had crossed its apex as we talked, and began the long travel to the western horizon.

Wade ran his fingers back and forth over the crease in his hat, a thoughtful look on his face as he paced back and forth on the porch. Ashley stared at the mangled dinosaur corpse, her rifle laying against the house beside her. Skyla rocked slowly back and forth, wringing her hands together in her lap, while Oscar stirred the end of a broken stick in the ground between his boots, tracing out what appeared to be badly drawn etchings of dinosaurs.

I watched a dozen of my distant cattle moving slowly towards the stream. It'd been a wild week, but things should be calming down now. Whatever other creatures may have crossed to this side would be discovered eventually and dealt with. I suspected that'd be done with lots and lots of bullets.

Oscar's voice cut through the quiet air. "Those 'trikes' sound like they are from the Ceratopsid dinosaur family. My esteemed colleague, Othniel Marsh, discovered their fossils in Colorado several years ago. Since then, we've been finding them everywhere. There's a handful of different sorts, but the most common type is Triceratops. It means, 'three horned face'," he sniffed disdainfully. "I suppose 'trike' will suffice."

"What do you think was being kept in the cage?" Ashley asked as she waved away a bloated fly buzzing around her face.

"Without a better description, there's no telling. Even then, there are still hundreds of thousands of species we know nothing about," Skyla answered.

"I reckon we'll never know now." Oscar angrily jabbed the stick into the ground.

Wade stopped, towering over the scientist with his arms crossed. "Jed made the right call. If that ape army crossed over to our side, it'd be worse than the Indian Wars." He spat into the dirt.

Oscar scoffed. "They are obviously intelligent, and have language and a social structure. It's possible they could have been reasoned with."

"I watched their leader rip a man's heart out and eat it. Their first reaction to seeing me step out on this porch, was to try and skewer me with a giant spear." I jabbed my finger at the broken shaft in the siding above Skyla's head. "There was no compassion from them, no attempt at communication, only the sort of violence that comes from something who believes it is dealing with something inferior."

"It may have just been an understanding, Jed. Not everything needs to resort to kill or be killed," he protested.

My anger flared. "Listen here, Oscar. As you've been told, this ain't the East and full of pampered dandies and comforts. The West is a harsh, brutal place that'll kill you if you can't take what it throws at you and remain standing afterwards. I didn't ask for a ten-foot-tall dinosaur to try and eat me. I didn't ask for a bunch of apes to try and kill me. But they tried. So, I killed them. And having seen their casual brutality of a captive Indian, I doubt they would've had any interest in communicating with me."

"I'm certain any chance of that has most likely passed anyways, especially after you shot up their camp," he spat back at me.

Skyla cut Oscar off before he could infuriate me further. "We're scientists. We aren't the sort that typically believes in fighting against or wiping out new species without trying to understand them first," she absently tucked a loose strand of black hair back, "or pre-existing species, like these dinosaurs, that we are rediscovering. It's just not who we are or what we do."

"Alright." I could understand that, but it didn't make me any less snarky. "But if we come across any more apes, Oscar can be the one to exchange beaded friendship bracelets with them."

She sighed at me in exasperation, then stopped rocking. "Was the tunnel the only way to the other side? Is it possible there's another?"

I'd already considered that possibility. "Maybe. I've no idea how or why the tunnel even existed. It just, is. For all I know, there could be twenty more of them out there, I just pray there aren't."

"I want to see it," Oscar said abruptly. "Or what remains of it."

Skyla looked at me hopefully.

"Not a bad idea, we can look for tracks on the way. See what else might have crossed over. Maybe something worth hunting or capturing? Ashley, how about you?" Wade said.

She looked at the decaying remains of the beast. "I can't let my partner get eaten by himself."

Everyone seemed in agreement and I supposed it was just as dangerous as it was coming to my ranch. Which meant it was an acceptable risk to make the scientists happy. "Alright. We'll stay here tonight and ride at dawn. Don't mind the mess inside the house, that's mostly from the apes."

"Good. Then we still have time to examine the Allosaurus today. Skyla, shall we?" Oscar announced as he tossed his stick out into the yard and erased the dirt sketches with the toe of his boot.

Skyla stood and stretched. Her tan dress tightened over her figure as she arched her back. I tried not to stare, but by the time I pulled my eyes away, I caught Ashley smirking at me. I looked at the ground quickly in embarrassment.

"I think, just in case, we should set up a watch. More apes or another dinosaur might show up. At least until we are secured in the house for the night," Wade said as he twirled the ends of his mustache upwards.

Ashley spoke up. "I don't mind doing that." She hefted her rifle. For the first time I noticed that her gun was more than the average repeater, its custom stock and finish showed a high degree of quality. Curious, I started to ask about it but was interrupted by Wade.

"Sounds good. Jed, unless you've got more pressing matters to attend, would you like some help cleaning up that mess?" He thumbed towards the burnt rubble.

I looked towards the mountain of burnt timbers and ash. "You're my guest. It doesn't seem right to have you doing dirty work for me."

"Consider it helping to earn our room and board for the night. You're feeding us in the morning, right?"

I chuckled. "Last guest I had was the Sheriff, and we dined on freshly killed Allosaurus steaks. I promise you, breakfast will be boring in comparison."

"That's nasty," Ashley wrinkled her nose with obvious disgust.

"You may have caught some sort of prehistoric disease," Skyla warned disdainfully.

Oscar was disgusted as well, but for an entirely different reason. "First living dinosaur mankind has ever seen, and you ate it."

Wade shrugged indifferently. As a former professional hunter and adventurer, he was used to eating things he killed. I heard they ate snails and slugs in Europe. The dinosaur seemed much cleaner in comparison to those slimy things.

"Maybe, but it tasted like chicken." I felt fine. But Skyla was right, there was no telling what sort of diseases it may have brought from the other side. I resigned myself to drinking a little whiskey tonight to clean anything bad out of my system.

Wade took off his leather jacket and placed it where he'd been sitting, then laid his hat on top. "Let's get to it." He smiled at the ladies and carrying his heavy rifle, headed towards the barn.

I tipped my hat and followed.

After leaning our rifles against the corral and hanging our gun belts off the posts, we pulled bandanas over our lower faces. With my fading black eyes, I looked like a down on his luck train robber. Which, in a way, I kind of was.

Dragging the burnt timbers out of the ash heap was hard and sweaty work. It didn't take long before our arms and gloves were coated in a thick layer of grime. We worked for several hours, moving partially burnt timbers and stacking them beside the house to be cut into firewood later. Wade managed to find a couple of tools that were salvageable once the handles were replaced, but everything else was melted or twisted by the heat beyond repair.

I peeked at Skyla out of the corner of my eye as she worked with Oscar. They sliced apart muscle and tissue as they inspected the carcass. A few times I caught her watching us, but mostly she was intent with taking notes in a small book and nodding to her boss as he pointed at things. At one point he cut open what must have been the stomach and a horrendous stench wafted over to us. Even through our ash covered bandanas we gagged at the scent of decaying flesh and aged stomach juices. The two scientists sprinted back to the porch with Ashley, safely upwind of the stench.

***

Shadows getting long, and I signaled to Wade that we were done. Leaning ourselves on the remaining corral rails, he passed me a canteen that Ashley had thoughtfully brought by earlier. Lowering my bandana, I took a sip.

Swirling the water in my mouth helped to clear out some of the dryness from my mouth and throat, but not the taste of ash. I spat it out and took another mouthful, swallowing this time before passing the canteen back to Wade. His face mirrored mine, smudged with gray and black about the eyes and forehead, clean from the nose down.

I looked down at my clothing then at our scientists as they packed their tools away. Skyla managed to keep clean except for a small smudge of blood on one cheek. Her shoulder length gloves, leather apron and cautious movements had spared her clothing. Oscar's suit was a rumpled mess, but with all things considered, it was surprisingly clean as well. They were neat and meticulous about their work.

"I appreciate the help, we made a sizeable dent," I told Wade sincerely. The famed wolverine killer worked harder than anyone I'd ever met, and I struggled to keep up without tearing my stitches.

He sipped water before responding. "You're welcome. Thanks for letting us stay tonight and taking us to the mountain tomorrow."

"Not a problem. It should be a nice day for a ride." I picked up my rifle and gun belt. "Let's get washed up."

***

We cleaned off with an open topped barrel beside the house set up to catch rain runoff from the roof. It was out of view from the porch, so we wouldn't be exposing ourselves to the ladies. While Wade cleaned himself, I fetched a couple more buckets of clean water to rinse off with from the stream. Ashley waved at me from her place on the front porch, her feet propped up and rifle laying across her lap. She seemed content while watching the tree line. I trusted her abilities, but I still had reservations about how she would shoot if confronted with imminent death or violence. Hopefully, I'd never find out.

After Wade finished, it was my turn. Tossing my filthy sweat and ash covered shirt aside, I splashed water on my face and body, cutting rivets through the grime on my chest and back. Using an old cloth, I scrubbed the sooty filth off, then combed my hair over the best I could. It was an unruly mop, but slicked over I could almost pass as presentable.

Looking at my reflection in the barrel, I noted that I still looked rough. But the dark black circles around my eyes were fading with the mottled collection of bruises. The cut across my chest was healing, and another few days and the stitches might be able to come out. That'd be fun.

Hearing a startled gasp, I spun around to see Skyla had come around the corner of the house. Her eyes were wide as I grabbed for my clean shirt. It was a pointless move; she'd already seen the mass of scar tissue that crossed my back.

Her face flushed a bright red. "I'm sorry... I didn't know you were still here," she stammered and looked at her feet uncomfortably.

Embarrassed, I threw the shirt on quickly and began buttoning. The beads of water on my skin soaked through it instantly. "It's okay, I'm finished," I said gruffly.

She asked the inevitable question quietly, without looking at me. "You were whipped, weren't you?"

Giving up on getting all the buttons finished quickly, I slung my gun belt over a wet shoulder and grunted an angry affirmative.

"I thought that was only done to slaves."

"I'm an unfortunate oddity."

In the silence, I already knew the question she wanted to ask but was afraid to hear the answer to.

"Don't worry, I didn't deserve it." I gave her what I hoped was a reassuring smile that I didn't feel like giving.

From her body language I could tell she wasn't convinced, but she relaxed slightly, probably relieved I wasn't some horrible person whose punishment fit a terrible crime. Although, considering my recent interactions with Oscar, she may have been thinking that anyways. But that was as far as I was willing to go for an explanation. Instead, I turned the attention away from me. "Discover anything interesting about the dinosaur?"

"Everything about it is interesting!" she gushed, her thoughts turning away from my scars and back to her passion. "Usually we just find partial fossilized remains, rarely are we lucky enough to find an intact skeleton. This is a goldmine of information. Did you know it has shortened jaw muscles, but with large neck muscles, which enables it to open its mouth to an extreme angle. Almost like a snake."

I thought back to it roaring at me, the way its mouth opened almost vertically as it covered me in hot moist breath and bloody saliva. I shuddered at the memory. "I recall something to that effect."

"Oh, yes, of course. Well, we also opened its stomach to look at the contents. We found all sorts of flesh, hide, bits of bone and some feathers. But since we don't know exactly what was on the other side, we don't know what it all came from."

"If you dig around in there, you'll find parts of one of my steers." I scuffed the toe of my boot against the ground as I tried to think of something else to say while I had her alone. I liked spending time with her, and hearing her voice. I also hoped if I kept talking, maybe I'd put her at ease with the horrid disfigurement of my back. "How's your trip been so far?"

"It's been everything I dreamed of and more." Walking past me, she dipped a handkerchief into the water, and neatly dabbed her face and neck. Looking in the mirror she saw the smudge of blood on her cheek and quickly wiped it away. "I still can't believe we are studying a real dinosaur and an undiscovered species of apes or man. But I was hoping to see some Indians."

"They're around. There's a small band of Shaynee not too far from here. We've also got some Cheyenne and Crow depending on which direction you go. They mostly stick to themselves, but problems flare up from time to time. Every so often, there's a disagreement, or some young buck stirs up trouble to prove himself. Then we shoot at each other until they learn their lesson and stop."

She gently wrung out the handkerchief and looked at her reflection in the water as I had earlier, wiping away another smudge and tucking stray hairs back in their place. A trickle of water ran down her neck and soaked into the white collar of her dress. "Is it always so violent out here?"

I looked at the ripples in the water and thought about it. A normal person wouldn't think so, but violence became part of my life at a young age. Since then I'd come to terms with the inevitableness of death and bloodshed. I tried to give her what would be considered a normal answer. "Not always. But it's a rough place. Sometimes it takes violence to make things better." I was no saint, but I believed that to my core.

She rinsed the soap off her hands with one of the clean buckets of water. Quietly, she asked. "Are you a man of violence, Jed?"

I shrugged nonchalantly. "Absolutely. I try not to go looking for it, but if it comes, I'd prefer to deal with it than leave it for someone else to suffer through. I don't want it, but I'll take it. Someone has to accept violence for what it is, and deal it back out in spades if necessary, to bring about peace, and to keep it." I believed strongly in peace, but I also believed in righting wrongs. That's how I'd ended up an outlaw, trying to do the right thing, even if it meant going further than others would.

She stopped, her hands clasped together with the small piece of soap between them.

I knew she wouldn't understand, being from the civilized East separated you from most of the harsh realities of life. But it was the truth. I learned it the day I was tied to a tree and whipped within an inch of my life. And a year later, I accepted the yoke of the responsibility of peace through the willingness to commit violence when I pulled the trigger on the man who did it. Thinking about it began to dredge up old memories, and I clenched my jaw in barely contained anger.

She asked in a low whisper, so soft and faint I could barely hear it.

"How many men have you killed?"

"Too many and not enough," I said bitterly, then spun and walked around the side of the house, leaving her alone with whatever thoughts she may have about me. Like the reminders on my back and shoulders, it wasn't a topic I cared to discuss nor was it something she'd understand. Few people understood the desire for vengeance until they've been wronged severely enough.

Coming around the corner quickly, grinding my teeth, I almost ran into Ashley. She'd left her chair and was leaning against the wall in a heated discussion with Wade. His large rifle was cradled in his arms. Oscar sat apart from them, going through the contents of the leather bags I'd cut off the apes' hides.

Seeing me, the sharpshooter drew me in to the conversation before I could go cool off alone. "Jed, what caliber do you think is best for something like that Tyrannosaurus critter you saw? Wade swears his twenty-pound rifle in .45-100 would be just the trick."

"Ha! It's only thirteen pounds. And only fat people complain about a few pounds on their rifle when they carry dozens of spare pounds around the waist," he swallowed when he realized what he insinuated. "Not that I'm saying you're carrying fat around your waist... because you're not... you're very lithe, Ashley..." he stammered.

She laughed him off and looked at me. "Are you okay?"

"Fine," I snapped before taking a deep breath to calm myself before answering. "The Allosaurus soaked up all the .45s and .44-40's I could put in it without much effect. Personally, if I see a Tyrannosaurus, I'm running as fast as possible."

Wade furrowed his brow. "Hmmm... Well, speaking of rifles, I haven't seen a Spencer repeater like yours in years."

"It was my uncle's from the war. I kept it as an heirloom."

"I understand the sentimentality, Jed. Ashley and I both have rifles we are particularly attached to. She has her magnificent *One of a Thousand* and I have my deadly Ballard."

"*One of Thousand?*" I whistled at the revered name, that explained why it was so pretty.

Wade scoffed and caressed his single-shot rifle. He spoke to it softly, "Beauty ain't everything, is it girl?"

"No, but function is." Ashley cut her eyes towards Wade. "Yours may be more powerful, but mine holds more than one cartridge at a time." As the famed westerner began to argue about the strength of his caliber, she handed hers to me and I took it reverently in both hands.

The fabled *One of a Thousand* rifles were made from high end barrels with above average accuracy, and fitted with a set trigger. The walnut stocks were intricately checkered, and the barrels were engraved with the numerical count of the rifle. The rarity of the rifle had created an almost mythological belief in its accuracy. The cost of such a gun was astronomical.

I rotated the rifle in my hands. Its receiver was beautifully case hardened, and the polished walnut stock was gorgeous. The octagonal barrel was engraved with *Fifteen of a Thousand* surrounded by intricate swirls. It was a magnificent weapon.

Throwing it to my shoulder, I attempted to look down the sights only to realize my face was awkwardly pressed against the stock and the sights were far too close to my eyes. Confused, I pulled it down.

Ashley laughed before explaining, "I had it shortened. I've short arms to go with my height. The stock maker thought it was borderline sacrilegious. But a gun I can't shoot is worthless, regardless of the price tag."

I agreed and handed it back to her. "It's a very nice rifle." Then I turned to Wade. "Okay, what's so great about your gun?"

He hefted it with both hands and rested the stock on his thigh. "This here is a Ballard number 5." He pulled a long cartridge from a loop in his belt and flipped it to me, I caught it with both hands. The brass casing was almost two and a half inches long, with the solid chunk of lead bullet sticking out another half inch. It was impressive. I hefted it in my hand before handing it back.

"Big bullet, Wade."

"The better to kill things with," he replied, looking at Ashley smugly.

"Not if you miss with your one big shot," the sharpshooter teased back.

"Miss? HA!" he roared. "Never!"

Skyla came around the corner, freshened up and looking sheepish. She paused at the edge of the porch. "Jed, care to show me around? I've never been on a ranch before."

Wade waved his hand at me to go on. "We can talk guns for hours, best go on now while you can."

Ashley nodded her agreement before adding, "We can argue without you."

Glancing at Oscar, I saw he was oblivious to our conversation and intently looking over the small purple fern leaves from the bag. He bit off a corner and chewed a moment before spitting it out, then he scribbled in his journal.

I looked back to Skyla and felt like a fool for snapping at her earlier. "Sure. I'd like that."

***

Skyla broke the awkward silence as we walked. "I'm sorry I asked how many men you'd killed. I overstepped my bounds."

"And I'm sorry I was blunt. But out here it's not a question we typically ask or like to be asked. The truth of the matter is, I've killed some and there's others out there who still need killing. But I won't let innocent people die. That's why I blew the tunnel shut. There was an army of apes over there. I wasn't about to leave them access to our side."

She carefully stepped over the small plank bridge that I'd built to cross the stream with. "You really think the apes would have been that big of a threat?"

I thought of the screams of the dying man on the altar. "Yes." Having her alone again, I decided to find out a little more about her. "You mentioned hoping to see Indians before, is this your first time out west?"

She nodded. "I've always wanted to come, but my studies prevented me. The telegram from the Sheriff was at a fortunate time. I'd just convinced my father to let me go to a fossil dig in Colorado as Oscar's assistant. I was going to finally get some field experience."

"Convinced your father?"

"He's one of the Regents." At my blank look, she explained. "The Smithsonian is run by a Board of Regents. They determine policy, budget, and priorities."

"So, you're Scientific Royalty, huh?"

She blushed. "No!" A moment later, she added, "Sort of. My family is a little famous within the Smithsonian. We come from a long line of scientists and learned men. I'm the odd one out in that I'm a woman. But what about you? Where are you from? Ever been east of the Mississippi River?" She teased me by flipping my traveling question around.

I chuckled. "I'm from South Carolina originally."

The surprise was evident on her face. "Really? I guess that explains the slight accent. I didn't think too much of it before though, everyone out here seems to have a hodgepodge of accents. But is that where you went to school? You seem more educated than most out here," she hastily added, "No offense."

"None taken. But you'd be surprised at the sorts of backgrounds and histories folks out here have. Some are running towards something, others are running away. Depends on the person. I've met physicians, lawyers, farmers, sailors, doing all sorts of work. All of them left their former lives behind for a reason."

"Which one are you, running towards or running away?" She tossed her dark hair playfully over a shoulder.

"A little of both. I haven't always been the fine, upstanding man you see before you." I gave her a cheesy grin.

She laughed. It was a beautiful sound. "I do sense a bit of rogue in you. It could be the black eyes though. Where did you go to school?"

I waved away a gnat that buzzed near my ear. "My father thought highly of education. But it was a mix of formal and informal. I liked to read, so we made sure to always pick up whatever books we could find." At her puzzled look, I shrugged. "We moved around a lot."

"And here you are."

"Here I am." It had been a long strange ride, but here I was. And looking at the rays of a setting sun caressing her beautiful face and gleaming off strands of long black hair, I wished I'd led a better life. One that I could have been proud of.

We watched Carbine playfully chasing after one of the mules. A thought occurred to me. "Do you know how to ride, Skyla?"

"Only English style. I've heard you westerners have your own way of riding."

"Sort of. Take English style and throw out the pretentiousness, add sweat, cursing and bouncing and there you have it. Western style."

Her laugh was intoxicating.

Carbine must have assumed we were talking about him and trotted over.

Refusing to allow him the opportunity to embarrass me, I took my hat off and held it behind my back. Displeased, he tossed his mane and flipped his tail before pushing his muzzle towards Skyla's chest.

She rubbed his big head and combed her hands through his black mane.

"He's beautiful, what's his name?"

"Carbine."

She repeated the name as she scratched his neck. "That's a great name for a horse. How long have you had him?"

"Couple of years." Moving closer to Skyla, I patted Carbine's neck. "I tried to raise him right, but he still turned out to be a trouble maker."

As if knowing that was his cue, he tried to reach around me to grab my hat and I shoved his muzzle away with a free hand. "He's also kind of an ass."

She laughed and scratched Carbine more, to his delight. "Oh, I don't believe that for a minute."

Leaving us, she took several steps further into the pasture before stopping and watching a small scattering of black and white Holsteins grazing in the distance. Behind them, the setting sun sent hues of red and purple streaks across the sky.

"It's beautiful out here," she said without looking back.

The colors of the setting sun outlined her still form, and I'd never seen a prettier picture. "Yes, it is," I said softly to myself.

Once the last rays of the sun disappeared over the Rocky Mountains, we made our way back to the house to settle in for the night.

***

Dew was still wet on the grass when we loaded up and moved out.

Last time I wandered all through the forest following tracks. But with the wagon limiting our available paths, we took a roundabout way which meant we rode the trail back towards town, then turned north across the open plains to skirt the forest towards the mountains.

I rode ahead of the wagon again, as I did yesterday.

If we were attacked, we had the same plan. I'd try to distract the threat while they rode like hell towards town. Just to be safe, I stuffed the sawed-off shotgun into the center of my bedroll tied behind the saddle. It'd be difficult to yank out if I was riding, but you never knew when another gun might be handy. Personally, I thought we could throw Oscar out if the wagon needed more speed, or to slow down any pursuers. But for the sake of playing nice, I didn't make it a suggestion.

Riding ahead gave me plenty of time to think in silence. It'd been over a week since the Allosaurus attacked. Before all this began, my biggest concern was raising cattle and staying on top of ranch repairs. Tilting my hat back on my head, I rubbed my eyes. My overall physical condition was improving nicely, but mentally I felt exhausted. A lot had happened, and I'd just been pushing through as hard as possible. But with the destruction of the tunnel, things should finally be calming down. After this little scenic trip, the scientists would be on their way and I could get back to ranching. Everything would be back to normal.

And I needed some normal, because I had a lot of work to do. In addition to replacing the barn and my tools, a lot of things were being left neglected. The cattle desperately needed checking on. Fences needed to be ridden, more trees were waiting to be cleared from the pasture and I still had a wagon load of firewood that needed to be unloaded and stacked.

I looked over my shoulder, and saw Skyla gesturing with her hands in an excited discussion with Oscar. I liked her. But there was no point in getting attached. A nice girl like her didn't need to be around a bad man like myself.

Carbine stepped around a stand of thick brush jutting from the forest edge and I yanked back on the reins. He obeyed and stopped, blowing through his nose and trying to get a scent on what we were seeing. As the wagon rounded the thicket behind us, Wade slowed the mules to a standstill while Ashley cautiously pulled her rifle into her shoulder, muzzle pointed towards the ground, but ready to fire in a moment.

There was at least twenty of them grazing in front of us.

Small and reminiscent of the trikes, they were slightly larger than a sheep and much more colorful. Their bodies were a mixture of red and white splotches, and bright blue spots dotted the misshapen frill that extended upwards from the back of their skull. Their heads slopped away from the protective bone shield, with a single small raised horn bump between their nostrils, and a sharp eagle-like beak. Their tails had a mane of thick white hairs sticking up vertically and were several feet long, slowly swaying from side to side almost as if they wagged in happiness while they browsed. Several stopped and watched us warily as we sat in silence, staring.

They were dreadfully cute.

I wanted one.

In the distance, several miles away, a train moved along its track, bound for Granite Falls. A sharp whistle blast from the locomotive reached us and the animals startled and broke into a shambling run only to stop a dozen yards further away from us. They looked around, uncertain of where the strange noise came from, but suspecting us.

Wade tilted his hat back on his head. I expected he was thinking how perfect they would be for his show. "Magnificent creatures. So colorful and unique."

Ashley squinted at them suspiciously. "They don't look dangerous."

"Probably not. They are herbivores, of the same family as the Triceratops. But they are beautiful. What do you think, Oscar?" Skyla leaned forward over the wagon edge to get a better look.

He chewed his lower lip thoughtfully as he stared at the creatures. "Definitely of the Ceratopia family. But as for what one, I've no idea." He adjusted his spectacles and shrugged. "Maybe Protoceratops?"

"But all the dinosaurs Jed described so far are North American dinosaurs, that makes sense for us to see them here. This was their home once. Protoceratops fossils have only been discovered in Asia," Skyla said skeptically. "It makes no sense for them to be Asiatic dinosaurs."

"I know it doesn't make any sense, Skyla," he snapped. "I'm just basing my guess off what I know has been discovered. Everything else in the Ceratopia family from this continent, that we know of, is much larger."

"We should probably throw out the notion of things making sense," Ashley spoke up as she lowered her rifle and rested its buttstock on the wagon floorboards. "You two are scientists. You're supposed to make sense of things. But look at what is going on. Dinosaurs dead for millions of years are suddenly discovered in the Wyoming Territory. Giant apes sacrificed an Indian and attacked Jed. And they came through a shimmering magical tunnel thing in the side of a mountain. These things don't make a lick of sense. We've got to just accept it and figure how to deal with it. Well, Jed dealt with the apes and tunnels. So, all you two have to worry about is the dinosaurs trapped on this side."

"You're right though, Ashley," Skyla threw both hands up to emphasize her point. "Things don't make sense at all. Even the dinosaurs Jed has described didn't live together at the same time. The Allosaurus is from the Jurassic period, while these Protoceratops, the Triceratops, and Tyrannosaur are all from the earlier Cretaceous period. We're talking about millions of years between the two periods. Of course, with as little as we know about the fossil record, maybe our fossil dating technique is wrong?"

I could follow most of this conversation, Skyla and I had spent over an hour or so last night discussing her work. I'd learned a great deal in that time about the dinosaurs I'd seen and how fossils are formed. It was rather interesting, and it certainly helped that my teacher was as beautiful as her.

"Impossible," Oscar said. "It is proven science."

I looked over at him, "How? Have you ever set something down, then picked it up exactly a million years later and tested it the same way to see if your form of measurement is correct?" I was being a bit snarky but genuinely curious.

"It..." he stammered, before recovering. "We don't need to. We look at the layers of rock around and above the fossil and date it by that," he scoffed as he adjusted his spectacles on the bridge of his nose.

"That doesn't seem real accurate and you still can't test it to be sure. You're assuming nothing changes since the dinosaur died except dirt and such packing on top of them and eventually turning into rock. It could be exposed again and again over time." None of this made a lick of sense to me, even when Skyla had explained it the previous night. It seemed like they were basically guessing and treating it as fact.

"You know what? Why don't you leave the science to us?" Oscar sneered.

I shrugged. "Sure, sounds like you're just making things up as you go anyways."

"Speaking of making sense," Wade cut into our bickering, "what do you make of them eating our prairie grass? What was the grass like on the other side?"

"Similar to ours, but broader and thicker. It seems these...." I hesitated, trying to recall the name, "Protops things are eating ours just fine."

"Protoceratops," Skyla corrected me.

Wade studied them carefully. "Good. Because they'd be perfect for my show. Too small for a man to ride though."

Skyla looked at him, "Sounds like you need one of the Triceratops that the apes ride."

"That's exactly what I need!" Wade rubbed his hands together in glee. "Say Jed, let's blow that mountain back open. I need a new mount."

I laughed. "Let's not give the man any ideas, Skyla. The last thing we need is Wade trying to catch one of those brutes,"

"There's a rope back here," Ashley offered from the back of the wagon.

"You may get your chance, Wade." Confused, I looked at Oscar and he grinned widely at me before continuing, "I'm certain the tunnel will be re-opened."

"Like hell." I stared at him, shocked at such a suggestion. "I blew it shut for a reason-"

"And it will be opened for a multitude of them," he cut my protest off by speaking louder and faster. "Take your pick. Science, exploration, discovery, natural resources, adventure," he ticked each of them off on a finger while meeting my eyes evenly, refusing to look away or back down.

"It's inevitable. When news of this discovery spreads, everyone will want a piece."

"That's not happening. I filed claim on the land the tunnel is on. It's mine. No one is opening it up."

Skyla turned back to face me, looking apologetic. "He's right... It won't matter, Jed. Even with all the dangers that will come from it. Powerful people will demand it be opened back up..." She hesitated. "I know my father will, and the rest of the Board of Regents at the Smithsonian. They carry a lot of clout with politicians in D.C."

"They're right unfortunately. The government will take your land and give you a nickel in return," Wade shook his head sadly. "They do it all the time. I've seen it in person. Look what they did to the Indians, and the other side of that tunnel is far more important than a pretty piece of land Indians hunt on."

I felt sick to my stomach. But I knew they were right. From the moment I showed the Sheriff the beast I killed; the exploration of the other side was unstoppable. Already the entire town knew. Word had been spreading since Dan warned them with the Allosaurus head. It was probably in the newspaper in Cheyenne already. Once word of the tunnel reached them, people would come by the thousands to see the other side and what they could exploit from it. It'd be worse than a gold rush, and instead of finding precious metals and their fortunes, they'd find blood and death, fang and claw.

Unsure of what to say, I silently tapped my heels against Carbine's flanks and steered him around the colorful small horned animals. Behind me I heard reins slap against the backs of mules, and the bumping of wheels as the wagon followed.

Damn it all.

I felt like a fool. I should have kept my mouth shut.

The feeling stayed with me for the next five miles, until it turned into a heavy stone in the bottom of my stomach as we reached the cliff face.

In the two days that had passed since I collapsed the mountain side, the apes had re-opened the tunnel.

***

I jerked my rifle from its scabbard, and swore under my breath as I twisted in the saddle to look for any threats. This explained the Protops. I figured they'd come through before I blew the tunnel. But now... there was no telling what had come through the opening, or what was about to.

Wade slowed the wagon to a stop.

"Jed...you said..." Ashley hesitated, clutching her rifle close to her chest.

"We need to go. Right now," I practically shouted it at them. If the apes caught us... I tried not to think of that.

"No!" Oscar stood up in the back of the wagon, trying to get a better view over Wade and Skyla's heads. "I need to see the other side!" he cried.

I was about to tell him that he was welcome to go get eaten, when I saw the apologetic look on Skyla's face. She clearly wanted to go see as well. But, too bad. Skyla's life wasn't worth the price of curiosity.

"Jed, is that a dead horse?" Wade pointed to a reddish lump near the giant piles of moved rubble and dirt.

I pulled out my telescope. It was. I'd recognize that red roan with the three white legs anywhere. Tom had been mighty proud of that horse. I swallowed hard as I remembered.

"Dan sent his deputies to check on the tunnel," I told the others. As tough as the Sheriff was on them, he loved his nephews. If they were dead, he'd take the news hard.

Wade thought the same thing. "No sign of any apes." He rubbed his goatee and shook his head sadly. "We've got to check. If there are bodies, we'll bring them back. If there aren't any..." He trailed off as we all recalled what happened to the man I saw sacrificed.

"Right... We've got to go look! Someone may be hurt," Oscar said with barely concealed glee.

I gritted my teeth. This was a stupid notion, but we needed to check. "Fine. Let's make it quick." I flicked the reins and pushed Carbine to a trot as the wagon followed closely behind.

Grass was heavily trampled and beaten down around the mysterious opening. Tracks were so badly mingled and stomped, it was almost impossible to make any clear reading on them. All I could say was that a lot of dinosaurs and apes had been here, and we could see trails of small groups moving away in different directions.

That was a bad sign.

Wade recognized it right away as he looked at the ground with concern etched across his face. "That's not good. Not good at all." His hefty single-shot rifle leaned against the seat between him and Skyla. If he was driving the wagon, he'd only have one shot. Reloading would be difficult with reins in his hands, and I doubted Skyla could work the mules if he needed to fight.

None of the parties were headed directly towards the town. But there was no doubt in my mind. "Scouting parties. Mounted on trikes."

"Yup," the famed westerner said simply.

"Scouting parties?" Oscar leaned over the edge of the wagon for a better look. "That implies tactics of an advanced culture and civilization."

"You and I have very different definitions of civilized," I told him sarcastically.

He shook his head. "Humans have eaten other humans for thousands of years. Are we not civilized now?"

"That's of no consolation to the ones who were eaten." I looked at him. "Personally, I've no qualms about shooting cannibals on sight. Not everyone is worthy of the gift of life."

I had Wade stop the wagon a short distance away from the opening. I didn't want them too close in case something came through suddenly. We could see through it but our visibility was limited to the rise on the other side, and if there was anything lurking around the edge of the far opening, we'd have little warning before an attack.

Wade turned the team of yoked mules, moving them in a circle until they faced the way we came. "Just in case we got to go quick," he explained.

Leaving them, I held my rifle in one hand and kept a wary eye on the entrance. The ground was churned from heavy footprints and large amounts of earth being cleared away. Some of the boulders that'd been moved had to have weighed several thousand pounds. Around them were left over pieces of thick leather braided rope, I assumed used by trikes to drag the rocks aside.

The horse's body was bloated, but fresh. Tom's harness, saddle and bags were still strapped on, but the rifle scabbard was empty. That was a promising sign. The beautiful horse's head was twisted at an abrupt angle and part of the spine jutted through the skin near the reddish mane. On the other side of the horse, out of earlier view, lay an ape riddled with half a dozen bullets. A stone axe was tossed aside and a bow and quiver leaned against a nearby rock. Judging by the powder burn on the ape's face, an unneeded coup de grace had been performed at close range.

Hanging on the pommel of my saddle, I leaned down to get a better view of the tracks. As the others watched and waited, I walked Carbine in quick circles, trying to find human or horse.

Returning to the others, I had good news. "Best I can cipher, both deputies are alive and riding double on James' horse. It doesn't look like anything followed them. I'm going to guess they startled an ape watching the tunnel, and it snapped Tom's horse's neck before they gunned the big monkey down."

"Thank goodness," Skyla declared.

"That's freakishly strong," Ashley added. "You weren't fooling about their strength, Jed."

"Those boys annoy the daylights out of me. But I'm glad they're alive," Wade looked over a shoulder at Oscar, then back to me. "Since we're here. I'm going to side with our companions. I think we should take a quick look."

I looked at Ashley for her opinion. She hesitated, then nodded quickly.

I gave in. It wasn't like I could fault them for their curiosity, after all, I was dumb enough to go through the tunnel alone the first time. "Alright. Let's do it before apes come looking for their dead buddy."

Dismounting, I tied Carbine's reins to the wagon with a firm slip knot. I didn't trust him to not run away and being left on foot out here with packs of apes running around didn't appeal to me any.

Skyla's hand trembled with excitement as I helped her to the ground. But I didn't hold on for a moment longer than necessary. As soon as her feet hit the ground, my rifle was pointed towards the tunnel. I wasn't about to get jumped unaware if I could help it. Behind us, I heard Oscar fumble his way to the ground.

Wade hopped down and helped Ashley out of the back of the wagon. She looked nervous now that we'd committed ourselves to crossing over. But she was brave, there was no denying that. She racked a round into her *One of a Thousand*, and I hoped she wouldn't need it.

I double checked my weapons as Wade adjusted his gun belt and rested the long-barreled rifle over a shoulder. "We're doing this quick," I warned. "No lingering."

"Agreed," he replied and tilted his hat to keep the sun out of his eyes. I looked at Oscar, he nodded back. The ladies I wasn't worried about, they both seemed like they'd be amicable enough when time came for us to leave.

With the unarmed scientists behind us, we approached the mountain opening beside me with guns at the ready. Fallen mountainside still covered portions of the tunnel on either side, and the ground was uneven beneath our feet from rock and hard packed dirt. The top of the cliff was broken and shattered from the dynamite, leaving a jagged edge above us. I eyed it warily, hoping no rocks were waiting to fall on unsuspecting heads.

More rubble and mountain debris had been dragged or carried to the other side as the big monkeys dug themselves through before widening the opening, leaving the floor inside with deep ruts in places.

I stopped my group several feet short of the unseen dividing line between the two sides. "Here's where it changes," I pointed at the rock walls around us.

Oscar stared at them, "Look at the sudden split, where the rock changes. Two different types... granite and limestone, divided by a perfectly straight line." He leaned back and looked up. "The change continues above us as well. Fascinating."

"It also happens below us, you just can't see it because the ground is beaten up and trampled so badly," I informed him.

"Is it just me, or does the sky on the other side look slightly different than ours?" Skyla looked back and forth between the two openings.

"I see it as well. Subtle, but it's there," Wade told her. "Appears to be brighter on our side."

"Can't see much from here," the sharpshooter warily eyed the end of the tunnel and the hill that rose in front of it, blocking off our view except for a strip of blue sky.

I pointed a finger towards the hill. "Once we get on that little knoll, you'll see it dips down into a large valley."

"Show us the ripple, Jed," Wade asked.

I obliged by scooping up a small rock and tossing it underhanded through the opening. The rippling shimmer circled outward then quickly faded.

"Interesting," Oscar leaned closer to the divide and tried to see what caused the ripple.

"Speaking about things that don't make any sense," Ashley muttered as she warily watched the far end of the tunnel. "How is that possible?"

"I haven't the faintest idea." Skyla reached out and slowly moved her hand forward until it connected with the unseen layer that separated the two sides. We watched ripples form and dissipate as she moved her hand through. She wriggled her fingers. "Feels a little tingly. But there's no pressure needed to pass through. I thought maybe it'd feel like entering water, but it doesn't. It's just... there."

"No matter what goes through it, it sends out those shimmery ripples. Rocks, twigs, people. Or apes and dinosaurs I guess," I told them.

Oscar ran his hand alongside the rough rock edge until the air shimmered as it slipped through. He grinned as he watched the strange effect. "Fascinating," he said as he repeated the motion.

Wade leaned towards Ashley and I heard him whisper, "I didn't think that sourpuss had the ability to smile." She snickered.

"Any scientific ideas, which would explain this, Skyla?" I asked her.

She shrugged her shoulders daintily. "Not a clue."

"Oscar?"

"Same," he shrugged, still grinning broadly. "I've no explanation for it, but it's mesmerizing. I thought the dinosaurs were impressive, but this may very well be the greatest scientific discovery of the century."

"I wonder what the apes thought when they ran into this?" Ashley asked.

"Don't know, but they don't scare easy. When I started shooting and their friends started dying, they didn't run away, they just kept coming. You'd figure the first time they saw someone killing them with a rifle, they'd consider it magic and worship me as a god." I kicked a rock through the opening and watched the small ripples as the rock clattered against another and stopped. "Instead they charged across a field, through a river, and climbed a cliff lickety-split to try and kill me, even though I was dropping apes left and right." I shook my head. And now they had free access to our side. We were in lots of trouble. We also needed to get going before they showed up.

"If we're going to look, we need to get moving." I made eye contact with Wade. "Let's go first and make sure the other side is clear. Ashley, you mind staying back for a moment?"

Ashley nodded slightly. "I'm perfectly fine with that. You gentlemen be safe."

I grasped my rifle in both hands, finger resting alongside the trigger. "Alright. If we come running, don't wait for us. Get to the wagon as fast as you can." Nodding to Wade, we stepped through together as the others watched the shimmering ripple form around our bodies and disappear.

Wade shivered as he took in our surroundings. "That's a creepy feeling. Like someone walked over your grave."

"Let's hope not," I told him dryly as we walked to the end of the tunnel

Dirt and rock had been dumped off both sides of the knoll in large piles. It was startling to see how much the apes had moved in such a short time span. From the beaten tracks that led away from the cliff and into the valley, there must have been at least a hundred of them.

He glanced up. "Sun's in the same position as the other side." He took his hat off and wiped his brow before putting it back on. "We should be inside a mountain right now, instead it's like we stepped through into a new world."

As we walked to the top of the knoll, the view into the valley was revealed. Wade dropped to a knee and stared in shock. Standing knee deep in the river, a single massive creature with its long neck and small head was pulling leaves from the top branches of a tree that leaned over the water. "That's... they're... giant..." A pair of the dinosaurs with wide armored backs and clubbed tails, waddled side to side a hundred yards away from us, ripping mouthfuls of grass from the ground. There were also some new critters in the valley. At least a dozen yellowish green dinosaurs, perhaps six feet tall, moved along the river bank toward the forest's edge. They walked on all fours, lifting their legs high off the ground in an almost prancing gait. "And... That's..." His voice faded off again as he tried to take it all in. Something large roared terribly from the depths of the forest. The noise echoed in the valley and Wade startled and swung his rifle towards the forest edge. "What the hell was that?"

"No telling, and I don't know how any of it is possible. But it is." There wasn't a single ape in sight and the dinosaurs were far enough away that they didn't pose an immediate threat. Satisfied we were safe for the moment, I waved at the others to come join us.

Oscar eagerly stepped through first. If the tingle bothered him, he didn't show it in his rush to reach where we stood. The ladies followed, shuddering as they moved through the rippling air.

"I don't like that feeling one bit," Ashley said as they caught up with the rest of us. Then she saw the dinosaurs. "Would you look at that…" She trailed off as her jaw dropped.

Skyla grabbed my arm, her cheeks flush with excitement as she looked in disbelief at the view before her. "Oh Jed, this is… prehistoric."

Oscar began talking quickly, words spilling out as he tried to label everything we were seeing. "That's a Brachiosaurus! We don't know much about them, but with the massive size, long neck and tail it must be! Amazing. Just amazing!"

"And look!" He pointed at the pair of club tailed dinosaurs, "Ankylosauruses. I wonder if they are a breeding pair… We don't know anything about their mating habits!" Ashley giggled, but Oscar didn't notice. He practically hopped from side to side, trying to take everything in as fast as possible. "Look at their tails, the way they sway side to side as they walk. We think it's a defensive mechanism. I'd love to see how they use them! And that herd moving to the forest, I've no idea what they are!"

A flock of spindly leather bird creatures suddenly dove screeching from the mountain face behind us. Clasping their wings tightly to their bodies, they shot towards us. We all ducked instinctively except for Ashley. She snapped the rifle into the pocket of her shoulder and fired in one fluid movement.

Any doubt I had regarding her shooting abilities under stress evaporated as the bullet hit the lead bird in the center of its chest with a spray of blood. The remaining flock opened their wings and peeled away over the valley, shrieking their displeasure as the dead bird twisted and silently plummeted directly towards us.

Wade pulled Ashley out of the way as I abruptly shoved Skyla aside. She yelped and fell to the ground with me landing awkwardly on top of her.

No one bothered to grab Oscar, and the scientist froze in place while letting out a blood-curdling scream as the bird hit the ground in front of him with a meaty thud. Blood and goo sprayed as the body smashed open. The sickly scent of fish and gut juices filled the air.

Oscar's face was pale and his eyes large as dinner plates behind blood splattered spectacles. He blanched and held a hand to his mouth as slimy loops of blueish-white intestines slipped from the burst corpse and came to rest against his dusty boots.

I smirked at Skyla under me before grinning wickedly. I couldn't help it, what were the chances of what just happened? She began laughing and I carefully rolled aside and gave her a hand up. She dusted herself off and didn't appear to hold any grudges against my tackling her.

"Good shootin'," Wolverine Wade said to his partner as he watched the surviving flock flying away over the forest.

Ashley ejected the spent brass shell, racked a fresh round into the chamber and winked at him. "It's what I do."

Oscar gathered himself and sniffed, wiping blood from his spectacles, "Next time I would appreciate a warning."

Our sharpshooter rolled her eyes. "The sound of a gunshot should have been warning enough for you to get out of the way."

I nudged the dead bird with my boot. Its head flopped over, and a long skinny tongue fell from the toothed beak. "Any idea what this thing is? I saw one scooping fish out of the river last time. Which explains that God awful smell." It was truly revolting. I pulled my bandana over my nose. Wade followed suit, but it didn't help the stench any.

Oscar grasped one of the talons and stretched a wing to expose its full length. The thin, veined wing ran from the creature's ankles, along its side and to its neck before jutting out along a clawed arm.

"Some sort of Pterosaur," Skyla said as she touched the flap of skin. "Their hands are in the middle of the wing because they walk on all fours on the ground." She bent the wing to demonstrate. "The pointy end of the wing folds and sticks up. No telling exactly which type this is, but it's a small one. Some can have a wingspan over thirty feet or more."

"Yes. And this one is not a threat to something our size, Ashley," Oscar chided her as he rolled the leathery corpse over to get a better look inside its beak.

Ashley shrugged and turned away to look at the forest lining the valley. "Maybe by itself, but a flock could be a different story, and they were coming right at us. At least now you can examine it."

"And it's not nearly as damaged as Jed's kills," Wade chuckled.

I adjusted my bandana slightly and took several steps away from the stinking corpse. "I don't play nice with things that want to kill me."

Skyla looked down into the valley as Oscar inspected the Pterosaur. "This strange tunnel opening will allow us to observe dinosaurs instead of guessing about their physiology and behaviors. And since these dinosaurs are spread out from different periods of time, there could be anything over here!"

That caught my attention, "So, things worse than that Tyrannosaurus thing I saw?"

She reached out to stroke a large green fern. "Probably. We've only begun to scratch the surface of what existed before us. There are all sorts of things we don't know about or don't understand. These ferns for instance, we think they were a major food source. We've found fossilized imprints of them, but we don't know for sure." She quickly pulled her hand back. "Or they could be poisonous."

Kneeling beside her, I took a closer look at the fern. Small green bugs moved on the underside of the leaves. "Maybe if you eat them, but I touched a lot of them when I was here last, and I'm still kicking. But that's a good point. What we don't know can easily kill us, and we don't know much about this side."

Wade was eying the opening in the mountain behind us, trying to size it up. "I don't think those Brachio-somethings, can fit through that cliff. But a lot of other things can."

I sent one of the small green bugs flying with a flick of my finger before responding. "Our side is woefully unprepared for the threats of this side."

"How far away is the canyon the apes are in, Jed? Could we sneak over there and observe them?" Skyla asked. Oscar looked up, hopefully, from where he crouched beside the splattered bird.

"No," Wade and I said at the same time. We looked at each other and the wolverine slayer shrugged. Cautious minds think alike.

I pointed towards the forest to our right. The club tailed dinosaurs were moving in that direction as well, watching us warily while lumbering along. I bet they were hard to kill with the chunks of bone that armored their backs. "Canyon's a few hours that way by horseback. Last time, I was able to sneak up on them because they didn't expect me. But that hive has been kicked over and I don't think it will settle back anytime soon. It'd be suicide to go there now."

That ended any discussion on that notion, but we lingered for a few more minutes.

Ashley was asking Skyla something about the Brachiosaurus that I couldn't make out. But I could see her drawing an imaginary outline of their necks in the air with her hands. Oscar was alternating his attention between studying the dead pterosaur and keeping an eye on the sky for more of them. Wade was watching the Anklyo's moving away, most likely thinking of how to incorporate them into a show.

I decided we'd pushed our luck long enough. It was time. "Alright, everyone. Let's go."

"But, I need this…" Oscar protested and turned the dead bird's limp head towards me. The beady little black eyes stared at me while its pink tongue wagged back and forth at the movement.

"What do you want us to do, Oscar? Scoop it up with a shovel?" Wade teased as he began moving towards the tunnel.

"It's a vital sample!" he pleaded weakly as he looked to Skyla for support. She turned and looked at me with one of those faces I was finding hard to say no to.

"Fine." I drew my Bowie and stalked forward. "We'll take the head."

"Stop! No! Why do you have to decapitate everything? It's not that big. Two of us can pick it up." Oscar began folding the broken wings alongside the bird's smooshed body to make it smaller.

I growled and shoved the large knife back in its sheath. "Whatever. But you pick up any guts that fall out."

Skyla interrupted us by pointing down the knoll and towards the distant tree line below. "Look!"

It was the same tall, brown feathered birds I kept coming across. At least two dozen of them moving out from the tree line and into the valley below. The flock darted through the tall grass, effortlessly leaping over a small stream that fed into the river. For such big birds, they were astonishingly graceful.

I grabbed the dinosaur bird by its back legs while watching them run. "Huh. Those things are everywhere."

Four mounted trikes bashed their way through the underbrush with a suddenness that made me startle. I heard Skyla gasp, but luckily, Ashley didn't start shooting. Once the trikes cleared the forest, their riders sat upright from behind the bone shield where they had ducked down. A moment later, a pair of small two-legged animals bounded from the trees and ran alongside the trikes.

I didn't bother trying to get a better look at them. Instead, I dropped Oscar's bird and grabbed Skyla by the hand, pulling her as she unconsciously resisted to watch the beasts. "Triceratops! And those small ones, some sort of raptor!"

"RUN!" I shouted. I didn't know what a raptor was, but the apes would kill us if they saw us. Ashley and Wade took off at a sprint for the tunnel.

Grabbing Skyla by both shoulders, I turned her and shoved her towards the opening. "Go! Go! Go!" Oscar was struggling to drag the bird by himself, refusing to leave the body behind. "Oscar, drop it or die!" At that, the man moved quicker than I would have suspected was possible as he dropped the corpse and ran after us.

The apes must have spotted us, because their mounts changed direction.

The giant monkeys charged up the hills towards us with the small dinosaurs weaving around and between the trikes. They were nimble creatures, near the size of a newborn calf, but I doubted they were as gentle natured. And I didn't want to know what they would do once they reached us.

There was nowhere to put up a fight except the giant mounds of dirt and rock, but the opening was too big to defend. Our only option was to run for it.

Several steps behind Skyla, I sprinted through the shimmering air and for the wagon.

Ashley jumped into the back at a dead run as Wade climbed into the front seat and grabbed the reins. Placing her rifle into her shoulder, the sharpshooter prepared to cover us as we ran towards them.

Skyla reached the wagon a step ahead of me. Grabbing her by the waist, I threw her onto the front seat of the wagon.

Shoving my rifle into its scabbard, I jerked Carbine's reins loose and leapt into the saddle. He snorted with displeasure at my sudden weight and nipped at me.

Oscar was the slowest, but he huffed and puffed his way to the wagon. I drew my Colt Peacemaker as he climbed in with all the lack of grace a short fat man in dress clothes could have and fell to the straw covered floor. Carbine trembled beneath me, sensing the urgency in my movements and the others around us.

I swatted the closest mule on Wade's team with my hat and shouted, "GET!" They leaned into the harnesses and the wagon began to roll forward with agonizing slowness. Wade cracked the reins above the harnessed team to spur them on. After a handful of steps, the mules began to gain momentum and broke into a trot, then run. Carbine kept pace easily. I could tell he wanted to take off, but I held him back alongside the wagon.

We made it a couple of hundred yards before the apes and their mounted trikes came running through the mountain opening. Behind them bounded the raptors, snapping at each other almost playfully.

If the shimmer and tingle, or the strangeness of our side bothered them, they didn't show it. I took that to mean they'd been on our side before.

***

The trikes were gaining ground on us rapidly.

I cocked my pistol. It was going to be a running fight we had to win. But even in our dire situation, I couldn't help but give our obnoxious scientist grief. "Hey Oscar!" I shouted. "Want to ask them to be friends?"

"NO! Kill them! Kill them!" Oscar screamed, his face pale and fearful, as he clutched his black top hat against his chest.

Ashley was trying to keep her rifle sights steady as the wagon lurched over the uneven plains. "Are we shooting?" she shouted.

In response, I fired a shot towards the lead trike. The bullet was unlikely to hit anything vital at this distance. But the trikes were big, so I hoped for the best.

Ashley started firing.

Her first round hit the bone shield of the lead trike. Behind it, the ape rider ducked down and out of sight. She worked the action rapidly, sending bullet after bullet into the trike's shield. Either the bullets didn't penetrate, or they missed the ape. The trike bellowed at the impacts, shaking its head, but kept charging after us.

Skyla held onto the wagon seat for dear life as Wade cracked the reins over the mule's backs and chanced a glance behind them at the attackers.

An arrow zipped by Oscar, and nearly pierced his hand as it slammed into the wagon. He yelped a very undignified swear word.

"Eyes! Shoot for their eyes!" I shouted with no other weakness readily coming to mind and I prayed she could pull the shot off.

Ashley aimed, her rifle rising and falling erratically with the wagon. A blossom of fire burst from the barrel.

It was a beautiful shot.

At the sharp crack of the rifle, the lead triceratops' head dropped and plowed across the grass. Furrows were cut in the ground from twin horns as it slid forward and toppled to the side in a small cloud of dust.

Its rider rose to his full height behind the bone shield, shaking his bow angrily. Blood splashed across his muscular chest as a second crack sounded from the wagon. He toppled over as his friends rode past him.

Turning back to the wagon, I gave Ashley a grin as she racked her rifle. She looked pleased with her shot.

Oscar cheered.

The wagon hit a hole.

Iron wrapped wheels lurched high into the air before crashing back down. Miraculously, nothing broke from the abuse. But its occupants took the hit hard. Ashley landed in a crumpled pile beside Oscar as the buttstock of her rifle smacked against her head. In the front of the wagon, Skyla screamed and was almost flung off the seat, but Wade managed to jerk her back before she fell.

Even with one hand jerking her back onto the seat, he didn't stop slapping the reins on the mule's backs. We couldn't afford to slow down any. Even with the wagon moving at such a dangerous speed, we were losing ground to the trikes.

An ape raised his spear over-head, shouting something incoherent, and pointing the obsidian tipped weapon at us.

From behind the trikes bounded the two smaller dinosaurs, raptors as Skyla called them, and I got a good look at them. I didn't like what I saw.

They were six feet long and three feet tall. Light tan, furry in the body but colorfully feathered along the arms and the lengthy tail. Bright red feathers ruffled on the tops of their sloping heads as the animals ran with long strides. Their snouts were blunt and reptilian, with mouths open and full of teeth. Long arms with black claws were held out from their bodies, giving the impression that they wanted a hug before they ate your face off.

They were frighteningly fast. Within moments they'd crossed half the distance between us. They chirped loudly, and I realized they were what had been in the canyon cage.

Figuring the ape was giving them orders, I fired a shot and winged him. His spear fell as he clutched his shoulder and ducked behind the trike's sloped shield.

That'd teach him.

Meanwhile, the little monsters had almost caught up with us.

Ashley pulled herself into a kneeling position. Her hat was gone, and blood trickled from a busted lip. She reached for her rifle.

I shot the raptor closest to the wagon. It fell, twisting and writhing on the ground, biting at its wounds, until a trike's heavy feet trampled the feathered beast to death.

The surviving one leapt onto the back panel of the wagon.

Oscar screamed in terror and began flailing at the dinosaur wildly with a small carpet bag.

Toe claws dug in as the feathered creature took the beating. Then, with a savage swipe of an arm, the bag was clawed from the scientist's hands and flung across the grass with a trail of small knives and equipment spraying from the shredded fabric.

Oscar scrambled backwards against the front of the wagon as the raptor raised its head and screamed victoriously, exposing sharp teeth and a small red tongue.

I swung Carbine closer to the wagon. Ashley worked the lever on her rifle and tried to fire. Nothing happened. She quickly worked the action again.

Crouching on its hind legs, the raptor prepared to pounce.

Petite, five-foot-nothing Ashley James, spun her beautifully engraved, extraordinarily rare, and ridiculously expensive *One of a Thousand* rifle around and butt stroked the raptor in its toothy snout. The beast snarled as the metal plated buttstock slammed into its face, knocking its head aside and breaking several sharp teeth.

She pulled back to hit the dinosaur again and the raptor swung an outstretched claw.

Crying out, our sharpshooter fell, dropping the rifle and grasping her arm.

Skyla twisted around in the front seat and grabbed Ashley, pulling her away from the feathered dinosaur's reach.

Wade jerked hard on the reins, forcing the mules into a sharp turn to try and dislodge the raptor. The girls held on tightly as the wagon rose on two wheels before landing with a loud crash of protesting steel and wood. Oscar fell over with a heavy thud and a cry. The raptor rode the bouncing turn easily with its claws dug deep into the back boards of the wagon.

The sudden movement of the wagon put Carbine close enough that I jammed my pistol against the little monster's head and fired. The cast lead bullet practically decapitated the raptor with a spray of brains, pieces of skull, and scattered feathers. The body tumbled off the back of the wagon like a lethal sack of potatoes.

Oscar was right. I seemed to have a thing for removing heads.

A trike and rider moved up the opposite side, placing the wagon between myself and them. A flung spear narrowly missed the women and slammed into the floorboards of the wagon.

My sights were swaying all over the place as I tried to line up a shot. Between the bouncing movements of Carbine, the wagon, and the trike, it was hell trying to get a clear shot.

And unless I miscounted, there was only one round left in my pistol.

The ape tugged another spear loose from the back of his horned mount and straightened to throw.

I fired.

Blood splashed. The ape tumbled onto the prairie in a crumpled heap. Our pursuers howled as they closed to spitting distance. Another arrow zipped through the space, slamming into the back of the seat below Wade.

Dropping my emptied pistol back in its holster, I yelled at Carbine to move faster. We were coming up on a wagon trail. It would be faster than cutting cross country, but we would lose mobility in the deep ruts of the beaten path.

We didn't have much time left.

I screamed at Wade to be heard over the thundering hooves and rattling wagon.

"Gun!"

"What?" he hollered back.

"GUN!" I repeated, mimicking with a finger gun pointing at him.

He drew a large revolver and tossed it underhanded towards me with barely a glance before turning his focus back to the racing team of mules.

I caught the pistol upside down, by its grip, barrel pointed backwards.

It was an old percussion revolver, heavy with a long barrel and fancy engraved ivory grips. The sort of gun you could pistol whip someone with and not worry about damaging the finish. It must have meant a lot to Wade for him to carry such an outdated weapon.

Sliding my finger into the trigger guard, I spun the pistol upright. Not an easy trick with such a heavy gun, but one I had practiced for countless hours. Ranch life gets boring when it's dark out.

Carbine stumbled, nearly going to his knees before recovering, and I watched, horrified, as the revolver tumbled into the grass beneath his hooves.

Wade glanced over as my horse staggered, saw my empty hand, and the shocked look on my face. "What have you done?"

"I'm sorry!"

He glared at me like I'd just tossed his baby down a well.

Now I was just mad. Mad at these stupid apes. Mad at the tunnel being re-opened. Mad at myself for dropping his gun. Mad at not being able to live a peaceful life in exclusion from most of society.

Tugging back on the reins, I turned Carbine aside. He slowed and spun in a circle as Wade bounced the wagon onto the trail, jostling its occupants and followed closely by the remaining two trikes.

Now I was behind them.

I drew the Spencer rifle from its scabbard and smacked Carbine on the flanks with the barrel. He surged in great bounds after the apes and my companions. As we came up behind the trikes, Carbine gave me everything he had. Foam sprayed from his mouth, coating my chest and legs.

Dropping the reins and using my knees to guide Carbine, I carefully lined up the rifle sights on the back of an ape notching an arrow in his bow. He twisted around, drew the bow, and loosened.

Carbine miraculously stepped to the side as the arrow zipped by close enough that I felt the breeze off the feathered shaft.

Acquiring the sights, I fired as he reached for another arrow from the quiver. A hit. The ape landed in a hairy heap on the prairie.

He stirred on the ground, pushing up on both hands.

Carbine put steel shod hooves across his back and pounded him into the ground under almost a thousand pounds of horse. I turned and shot behind us, putting another bullet in the twice wounded ape just to make sure he was dead.

The trampled ape's trike was a problem. It didn't slow or peel off like the others, instead it kept running after the wagon. The large body and raised shield blocked my shot at the last ape and I could feel Carbine beginning to slow as exhaustion sapped his strength.

The remaining ape jerked on his trike's reins, driving his mount's massive shield and shoulder into the wagon, lifting it into the air before crashing back down to the ground. Ashley pitched forward, slamming her head on the edge of the boards and dropping from sight. Skyla crawled into the back of the wagon after her. Shoving Oscar to the side, she cradled Ashley's head in her lap.

A back wheel began wobbling from the repeated abuse, but the steel axles held.

Dust kicked up from the beaten wagon; the trail was thick and choking as I moved Carbine to the side, leaping out of the trail's ruts, and angling to get a shot at the last ape. The trike moved as well, as if determined to prevent us from getting the final rider.

In desperation, I fired a shot into the rear end of the dinosaur.

A Texas heart shot is a cruel thing to do, but people were more important than the ass of an animal that ought to be extinct. The horned beast bellowed in pain and turned, finally running away from us.

The remaining ape slammed his trike into the wagon again and Skyla yelped as she bounced on the floorboards. Wade shouted at me to hurry up and kill it as he and the mules fought to pull the wagon out of the deep ruts on the trail.

The ape leapt off the trike with spear in hand and landed in the back of the wagon with a heavy thud.

Wade spun in surprise. Shocked, he dropped the reins and struggled to reach his rifle from where it had fallen underfoot. In the back, Oscar grabbed Ashley, and with Skyla they frantically pulled the unconscious sharpshooter away as the ape towered over them.

I racked the rifle and prayed for accuracy. If I missed, I'd hit one of my party. If I hit, the bullet could pass through the ape and still hit one of them. The only chance I had was a head shot. And it was a small target, growing smaller as Carbine tired and lost ground.

Roaring, the ape drew his spear back to thrust. Even as my sights bounced and wavered all over the place, including on my companions, I began to take up slack on the trigger.

There was a small pop and the ape staggered back half a step as I pulled the trigger. I missed, the bullet going high and over the monkey's head. In horror, I watched as the ape recovered and lunged, thrusting the stone tipped spear with both hands. Oscar screamed in mortal agony. Wrenching the shaft free, the ape raised it overhead to stab again.

There was another mysterious pop. The ape dropped to a knee, the long weapon falling from his hands.

Wade twisted in his seat, rifle in hand. "DUCK!" he cried as he maneuvered the long-barreled rifle. Skyla leaned over Oscar and Ashley, covering them with her body as the famed wolverine slayer pointed the muzzle at the mysteriously wounded ape.

I jerked Carbine's head and wheeled us out of the line of the fire.

There was a massive BOOM.

Blood, meat, and hair sprayed as the bullet punched through at an incredible velocity. The ape cartwheeled off the back of the wagon like a rag doll punted off a cliff.

Without Wade urging the mules on, the exhausted pair began to slow. Catching up to them, I grabbed and pulled back on their harnesses. The wagon wobbled to a stop.

Carbine trembled, his ribs flaring as he sucked in air. My pants were soaked with foam and our mingled sweat.

"Jed!"

Leaping off my horse, I sprinted to the side of the wagon. Skyla sat hunched over Oscar with tears cutting rivets through the dust on her face. The scientist lay on his back, face pale, whimpering in pain, hands clasped over the wound. An awful moan of agony came from him.

"Let me see," I demanded.

She pulled away and I jerked Oscar's hands away from the wound.

There wasn't much blood. Grasping the sides of his shirt, I ripped it open, bracing myself for the worst as buttons popped off. I stared at the damage the ape's spear had done to the man.

He looked into the sky fearfully, small beads of sweat appearing on his clammy forehead. "It's okay, it's okay. I'm ready to go. I've lived a good life, I'll be remembered," his lower lip trembled as he fought back sobs.

Reaching out, he grabbed me with surprising strength. "Whiskey? Please. It hurts." Skyla's shoulders shook as she began to cry beside her boss.

I knocked his hands off and he flinched in surprise. "It's a graze, you insufferable ass. You'll be fine."

Wade laughed so hard he fell over in the seat holding his belly. Skyla grabbed the shirt and looked at the shallow cut that ran along Oscar's side. "He's not dying?"

"Unfortunately, no. But he does need a few stitches. How's Ashley?" I was more concerned about the useful member of our party.

Wiping tears away, she checked on the sharpshooter beside her. "Out cold. She's breathing fine, but she'll have a horrid headache when she wakes. And she's a nasty cut on her arm from the raptor."

Oscar's face went through a change of emotions, from fear to surprise, and finally to indignation. "Well, it hurts terribly. And there's a lot of blood!" He held up a blood smeared hand as proof.

"I've passed more blood with a kidney stone than that," Wade snickered.

"We'll get you to town and patched up. You should be fine. Unless you get an infection, then you may die yet and there's no telling what might be on those ape's weapons. Probably smeared with trike manure or something," I warned.

He gasped then groaned as he gently pried apart the wound with his fingers, wincing as he inspected it for signs of dinosaur poop.

Wade stopped chuckling abruptly and fixed me with a stare. "Where the hell is my pistol, Jed?"

"Yeah, about that," I sighed and looked behind us at the trail of churned dirt, corpses, and trikes scattered across the plains. It was my turn to be embarrassed. "I'll fetch it for you," I offered shamefully.

"I'd appreciate that." He flipped the lever under his rifle down, ejecting the spent shell and slipping a fresh cartridge into the chamber.

"Remind me to never let you hold my rifle." He snapped the lever shut and rested the gun back against the seat.

I shook my head in shame. I couldn't believe I dropped another man's gun. Even worse was that it happened in the heat of battle when it was needed most. It was humiliating.

Wade climbed over the bench seat. Kneeling beside Skyla, he patted her on the back before gently moving Ashley's hair away from her face. The sharpshooter's eyes were closed, and her face pale with a small smear of blood from her busted lip. He pulled back the sleeve of her coat and inspected the raptor's claw wound.

"How is it?" I asked.

"Could probably use a few stitches, but she'll be fine. It'll leave a nice little scar though. She got lucky." He tied his bandana tightly around the wound. I passed him a canteen and he dabbed some of the water on her forehead and cheeks.

Her eyes fluttered open and she smiled faintly. "Just like the circus back in New Orleans." She started to sit up, but stopped, winced and pressed a hand against the knot rising on her forehead. "Ugh, that smarts. I guess we got away?"

"We killed them all. Now, you just lay there and rest," her partner cautioned her.

Oscar sniffed and held out his hand for the canteen, "But not before they got me."

Wade passed it over, "Oh yes. Oscar got nicked and is dying."

The sharpshooter closed her eyes and chuckled softly.

Skyla moved away to sit by herself. In all the excitement I didn't see the small, silver derringer laying on the floorboards. But she was staring at it.

So, that's where those two mysterious pops came from. This entire time, I'd assumed she was unarmed. I was pleased she wasn't, and that she used the little gun when needed. But now that the immediate concerns for others was over, she was beginning to realize her part in our running battle.

I reached over and picked up the little pistol. It was a double-barreled Remington, ornately engraved with pearl grips. The sort of gun a gambler might use as a hideout, or tucked up a sleeve. It was also a good size for a woman to tote around discretely. The gun felt tiny in my big hands. Flipping the lever forward, I tilted the barrels on their hinge and pried out two fired casings with a fingernail. "Do you have any more rounds?" I asked softly.

She shook her head. Tucking the pistol into my vest, I looked away. I never was much good at comforting people. In my youth and former life, I learned to shove emotions deep.

Giving it a try anyways, I patted her arm awkwardly. "It's okay. You did the right thing. We're safe now."

She buried her head in her hands, taking deep breaths as her body trembled. Tears ran through her fingers and fell into her lap.

I wanted to hold her, comfort her. Instead I walked away to give her a moment alone to collect herself. The first time you kill someone is not an insignificant moment. For some it was a heavier moral weight to bear than others. Then there were some who were born twisted inside, and became addicted to killing after their first. I'd run into one or two of them before. It hadn't been pleasant.

But I remembered my first time. The hatred in the man's eyes turning to fear. The begging from someone who'd never shown an ounce of mercy towards others. The pathetic whimpering ending abruptly with a gunshot and his blood and brains coating the inside of an outhouse.

It was certainly not an insignificant moment for me.

But justice had been served and my outlaw days began.

Ashley waved Wade away and pushed herself up, faltering for a moment, before bracing herself and straightening.

"Ashley, you really should rest more," he warned.

"I'm okay." She then wobbled a little and threw up the remains of her breakfast over the side. I jumped aside, but not quickly enough to keep from getting splashed.

Leaning over the edge of the wagon, she wiped her mouth with the back of her good sleeve. "Sorry, Jed."

I wiped my boots off in the grass, one after the other. It was no big deal, I'd stepped in worse. "It's alright, just take it easy for a little bit. That was some good shooting back there. You ought to talk Wade into putting a wagon chase just like this in your show."

"Now that is a lovely idea, Jed," the famed westerner gestured towards the trikes behind us. "I'd need some of those though, then the customers could get the true feel of the chase. And some reasonably friendly apes, if any such sort exist, to play the bad guys." Wade pulled Ashley's rifle out from the scattered straw and looked it over before leaning it next to Ashley. "Just a few scratches."

"What happened with your gun and that raptor?" I asked, puzzled.

She nodded weakly, still looking a little green around the gills. "I didn't count my shots. I always count them. This time... I didn't," she squeezed her eyes shut as a wave of nausea hit her, "and it almost got me killed."

"You did just fine. You butt stroking that wretched critter was one of the best things I've ever seen," I told her sincerely.

She grinned, clenched her eyes shut and burped sickly.

Drawing my pistol, I thumbed the gate open and began ejecting brass shells one by one. Empty casings fell to the ground as I walked back to Skyla. She'd gathered herself, and sat composed, back straight and shoulders firmly set. She had an inner strength that I doubted she realized.

She gave me a sad smile.

Leaning against the busted side boards of the wagon, I began loading the pistol. "You did the right thing. That rotten ape would have killed you all."

She looked at the hairy body in the ruts of the trail behind us. "You were right, Jed. The West is a much more violent place than I imagined. It's one thing to read about, another thing entirely to be a part of." Her eyes met mine. "I thought less of you at first, when you told me you accepted violence as something that simply had to be done. It seemed so uncivilized, so brutal. But I think I understand now. Sometimes you are the only one in that spot, in that moment, with the power to act. And if you don't, people will suffer for your inaction."

I spun the loaded cylinder before snapping the gate shut and holstering the gun. "Yup. That's how it goes. The world is full of evil that ignores laws and morality, and only fears righteous and violent retribution and I greatly believe in delivering that when needed." I kicked a grass clod with my boot. "It's never really bothered me. I just accept that the world is a mean nasty place and I try to do the right thing when possible. If that means I've got to kill people, apes, or dinosaurs, I'll do it every time."

I really did believe that. I just wished I'd been so firm in my convictions in my past. Instead, I found myself skirting the line between right and wrong, and others suffered because of it. I looked at my vomit and dirt coated boots, suddenly ashamed as old memories floated to the surface. Guilt is a hell of a burden to carry.

She touched my shoulder, "Thank you."

Suddenly uncomfortable with my little speech and her attention, I grabbed Carbine by the reins and heaved myself into the saddle. "Back in a minute," I told her.

I trotted Carbine back to the gap between the second and third ape bodies where I'd dropped Wade's revolver. In what had seemed like an eternity, we'd only moved a few miles from the mountain, leaving corpses scattered in our wake.

Dismounting, I warily watched a trike grazing nearby. It didn't look like the one I shot in the butt. The horned beast flared its nostrils and snorted before turning back to tearing up large amounts of prairie grass in its hooked beak. I mildly wondered if eating our vegetation would make the dinosaur sick before realizing I just didn't care.

Not my dinosaur, not my problem.

It took me a few minutes to locate the dropped pistol in the grass. Picking it up, I saw it was an old Remington New Model Army that still used black powder and percussion caps. The gun looked like it'd seen a lot of use, but had been well cared for. Thankfully, I didn't see any damage as I checked the barrel before wiping dirt off the gun with an edge of my shirt.

The trike raised its massive head and lumbered towards me.

Startled, I thumbed back the hammer on Wade's pistol with a loud click and watched the dinosaur approach. Carbine was a dozen yards away, and I wondered how quickly I could get to him. Getting gored by an extinct beast was not how I wanted to go out. Not that there was a preferred method.

The trike stopped a couple yards away. Its small dark eyes shined with intelligence, and the slanted nostrils flared as it sniffed my strange scent.

Keeping the pistol at the ready, I slowly reached out with my free hand. The dinosaur snorted and took a step back. I froze, my arm still outstretched, palm turned up in what I hoped was a calming manner.

The beast took a couple of cautious steps closer, raising its mouth to my hand and sniffing again. I slowly eased forward and touched the dinosaur's snout. The dark brown hide was pebbled and firm. Since the beast didn't seem to mind my touch, I ran my hands along the bright yellow streaks that ran from beak to shield, then over the short black horn. I'd seen an elephant tusk once in my youth and it reminded me of that now. Except instead of an ivory white, this was a dull solid black.

The beast shook its head and I ducked as the long horns slashed through the air. Reaching up, I brushed my fingers along one of the twin black horns. They were covered with nicks, deep gouges and scratches from fighting.

It was a magnificent creature.

I slowly stepped back, and the beast turned and strode away, stopping for a moment to sniff at one of the dead apes and nudge it with its beak before moving on.

The others had been watching, and were waiting when I came back.

"I can't believe it let you touch it!" Skyla said, her excitement of the dinosaur overcoming her distress. "You're the first man to touch a Triceratops, ever!"

"Surprisingly. I would have figured you've the scent of death on you after killing so many of its dinosaur brethren," Oscar huffed.

"Don't be jealous. After all, you were the first person to be splattered by a Pterosaur," I smirked, recalling his scream as the leathery bird slammed into the ground in front of him.

"Surprised you didn't try and ride it," Ashley teased me in turn, watching the trike lumber away. She looked recovered, but probably needed rest. Head wounds are a tricky thing, you never know what you're going to get with one.

"Didn't even cross my mind," I replied honestly. It was a tempting notion though.

Wade twirled the ends of his mustache thoughtfully. "I want one," he declared.

"Then we will have to get you one. But right now, we need to put some distance between us and that tunnel." I carefully flipped the pistol around in my hand and shamefully held it out to him, butt first. "Sorry about your pistol Wade, but you should really consider getting something with metallic cartridges."

Taking the revolver, he inspected it. Pulling back the loading lever, he removed the cylinder and swapped in a fresh one from his vest pocket. "No thanks. I've had this gun for a very long time, and she's never let me down." He dropped the black powder revolver back into its holster.

The animals needed water, but we needed to get moving. We could stop them at the next stream we crossed. "Wade, you ready to roll?"

"Let's do it." He kicked at an arrow that jutted from the wagon, snapping the feathered shaft off before climbing into the driver's seat.

"Finally," Oscar said, pressing a hand tightly over his flesh wound.

I glanced at the sky and noted the sun. "We may make it to town by midnight."

"Midnight? I'm wounded! Run the horses!" the scientist cried in outrage.

Wade spoke casually over his shoulder. "They're mules. And we can't run them on account of your scratch. If we get attacked again and they're worn out, we may get caught, killed or eaten. And if that wobbling wheel falls off, we are going to have a long walk ahead of us. So, man up."

Oscar grunted in response and lifted his blood smeared hand to peek at his wound.

I looked behind us. "Let's double back and grab a couple bodies for show and tell. Without an ape and raptor carcass as proof, they'll think we are loco."

"Velociraptor," Skyla said as she settled in beside Wade.

"What's that?" Ashley asked.

"There are two basic types of raptors: Deinonychus and Velociraptor. Deinonychus are about six feet tall and a couple hundred pounds while Velociraptor are the small ones that chased us. But we typically just call them all raptors."

"Six feet tall, huh?" Wade asked.

She nodded an affirmative.

"Let's hope we don't run into any of those," Ashley said, clutching her rifle close.

The wagon rumbled and wobbled as Wade turned the team of mules around. We tossed the ape Skyla shot in the back. Both raptors were in bad shape, one was missing most of its head while the other was churned into meat. I ended up grabbing the one I shot with the mangled upper skull. Oscar looked squeamish after we tossed the ape next to him, so I made sure when I flung the raptor in some gooey bits sprayed on him. The blanch on his face was worth the childish prank.

Wade unrolled a sheet of canvas from under the seat and covered the bodies. We kept a careful eye about as we journeyed on, but the trip was uneventful.

Until we ran into the natives.

***

Over twenty of them crested a ridge before us and stopped, watching stoically from the backs of their spotted ponies. They had a miscellaneous collection of weapons, lots of feathered spears, some rifles, mixed with bows and arrows. They lacked the paint of a war party, but they also didn't look very happy.

The wagon rumbled to a stop beside me as I pulled back on Carbine's reins.

"Indians," Skyla gasped, holding a hand to her mouth. Oscar rose and peered around her at them. "Oh my, we're all going to die," he half-whispered, as if fearful that his words might reach the natives and give them an idea.

"What tribe you figure?" Wade asked as he spat off to the side, using the movement to mask sliding his hand onto the butt of the old revolver strapped to his side.

"They're Shaynees," I slid out of the saddle and stretched. Carbine left me and moved closer to Skyla. She gave him a scratch while keeping her eyes on the line of warriors before us.

"Heard of 'em, but never seen them," he admitted.

"There ain't a lot of them around." I studied the band of Indians. There was one in particular I hoped wasn't with them, but considering how today was going, it wasn't a surprise when I saw him glaring at me with open hostility.

"Are there any problems with them that we need to worry about?" Ashley asked as she shifted in the wagon to get a better look.

I gave a sigh. "Only personal ones, I reckon." I removed my gun belt, hung it around the saddle pommel and placed my hat on top.

"We should be fine, but Indians are finnicky. If things go south, get out of here. Ashley, shoot them all. Skyla, keep your head down. Oscar, you just start screaming, it may distract them."

He shot me a nasty look while our sharpshooter adjusted her grip on her *One of a Thousand.*

"Don't worry about me. I'll be fine." I patted Carbine on the neck before turning my arms out to show the Indians empty hands. Slowly, I walked forward.

After a dozen paces, the Indians rushed down the hillside in a stampede of hooves with raucous calls and whoops. I stopped and waited. They moved themselves into a semi-circle with myself at the center. Their horses stomped impatiently as the Indians stared. I didn't move. I just waited to see what they would do. We were on friendly terms, but that didn't mean they wouldn't kill us all if they felt like it and hide the bodies in a ditch.

A lean, sinewy brave handed his rifle to another and leapt off his pony. His bare chest had ugly scarring that ran diagonally from shoulder to hip. He pulled a decorated tomahawk from his waist, waving it slowly back and forth as he approached. Other Indians whooped and yelled encouragement at him and more than a few shouted insults towards me and my skin color.

I watched the scarred Indian approach with a wary eye, knowing what was about to come next.

Without warning he rushed, screaming gibberish, tomahawk rising overhead to bring down on my skull.

I fought against the impulse to defend myself and tried to look as stoic as possible.

He swung diagonally. The cutting edge swept past my head, close enough that air parted my hair. I didn't give him the satisfaction of budging an inch.

He stepped back, eying me up and down, then spat. I gritted my teeth as the spray of saliva hit my shirt and pants. I could feel the rage building, pushing me to lash out and hit him. Which was exactly what he was trying to goad me into doing. Veins throbbing across his temple, he jerked the tomahawk back to swing again, a look of savagery and hatred spreading across his face.

A sudden crack of a rifle sounded behind me.

The tomahawk flew from his hand, landing several yards away as the sound of a gun blast echoed in the small valley.

Behind me I heard the beautiful sound of a *One of a Thousand* rifle racking another round into its chamber.

The Indian stood baffled, shaking his stinging hand. The other Indians laughed as he twisted around to look for the weapon. When he spotted the damaged tomahawk, his face contorted in rage. He began stalking towards the wagon and Ashley behind me.

Stepping in front of him, I placed a hand against his scarred chest and shoved, hard.

The smaller Indian stumbled backwards, caught his balance and glared.

I jabbed a finger at him. "You owe me a life, asshole. Touch my people and I'm going to take it." I'd play their stupid Indian games, but if any of them laid a hand on anyone I cared about, there'd be blood.

He drew a bone handled knife from his waist and grinned wickedly, thrilled that I'd finally been goaded into putting a hand on him. He dropped into a crouch with the blade held before him.

I drew the large Bowie from its sheath. Fine. Let's do this. I mentally prepared myself to be cut by the Indian. No one gets out of a knife fight unhurt. I just had to take the pain from his blade and keep pressing on, using my size and reach to my advantage, until I could slit his throat from ear to ear.

"Step aside, Jed, and I'll drop him," Wade called out.

"I'll take the others. You know, with my ten round *repeating rifle*." Ashley couldn't help but tease Wolverine Wade during a moment like this where his one shot rifle put him at a serious disadvantage. I would have chuckled, but I was about to go chest to chest with an Indian who was bound to be a better knife fighter than myself.

From the ring of ponies, one of the Indians shouted in a deep, gravelly voice.

The brave stood up from his fighting stance abruptly. Grunting angrily, he shoved the knife into his belt before whirling and stepped over to scoop up his damaged tomahawk. A neat hole had been punched through the center of the blade by Ashley's bullet. Sprinting to his pony, he leapt onto the back of it and snatched his rifle from the brave beside him. Jerking the horse's head around viciously, he kicked its sides with his heels and galloped away. Three others left their spot in the circle and followed him over the crest of the hill and out of sight. Apparently, he was attracting some followers. That wasn't good.

I slid the weapon back into its sheath, thrilled that I wasn't about to get stabbed to death. I'm far more of a gunman than knife fighter.

The Indian who shouted slid off his pony and sauntered forward. He was a short, older man with a barreled chest and a craggy face full of wrinkles. Eagle feathers dangled from braided hair, and a necklace of white beads circled his throat. A rifle was slung across his back, the sling decorated with small feathers, shiny brass beads and trinkets. Many notches were scratched in the stock. Tucked into his waist was an old single shot flintlock pistol.

Reaching out, he clasped my arm in his and looked at the fading bruises around my eyes, "Huck Berry, you look like shit."

I nodded in agreement and gave him a smile, "Chief." I hated my Indian name. But that's what I get for telling them my full name. They took the Huckleberry part and ran with it.

He smirked. "Otto still mad."

"Otto always mad."

He laughed, loudly. "One day, he kill you."

"No. One day, I kill him." As soon as I saw the Chief was with the band of Indians, I knew I had two choices. Either I asked for shelter and protection, or we moved at night and risked being attacked by apes or dinosaurs, and now we had Otto to contend with as well. I went with the former option and waved a hand at my group. "We humbly ask for shelter for the night. Bad things are near. We are few, and no one is more brave and fierce than the Shaynee led by great Chief Toko." It was true, but I laid the flattery on thick. Staying in their camp would also mean Otto was honor bound to not try and kill us.

The Chief's smile vanished, and he scowled, "Yes. Bad things. We find some of my people, stabbed, crushed. One eaten." To make sure I understood, he pretended to stab with a spear and stomped his feet on the ground. "We hunt what kill them." His English was pretty good, but he learned to mimic words with actions to make sure white men understood.

"Have you seen these things that killed them?"

He grimaced. "Only tracks."

"We killed some. Come, look." I made shooting motions with my hands before gesturing towards the wagon. I knew I looked ridiculous doing it, but when I talked to him, I always fell into his pattern of mimicking my words with my hands.

Scowling, he strode to the wagon. I followed while the other Indians waited in place on their ponies.

Ashley stood behind Wade and Skyla, her rifle was lowered, but the stock still firmly tucked in her shoulder. The bandage around her arm was seeping red through the cloth. Wade lounged nonchalantly on the seat with his rifle. Skyla shifted nervously as the Chief approached. I doubted she'd ever seen an Indian, other than ones in the shows back east. She met my eyes as I walked by. I got the impression she hoped I knew what I was doing.

"Nice shot, Ashley," I called out to her.

"Things looked like they were going south," she smirked, "Huck Berry."

I rolled my eyes. "Thanks."

Chief eyeballed Wade suspiciously, but looked approvingly at the mules and women before stopping when he reached the back of the wagon. He looked over Oscar's torn and blood-stained outfit.

If the scientist was attempting to hide his discomfort under the Chief's gaze, he was failing miserably. He raised his hand awkwardly, "How."

The Chief cut his eyes at me with obvious disgust.

I shrugged, "He's not from around here."

"What's that supposed to mean?" Oscar asked, hesitating a moment before lowering his hand.

"It means stop talking, Oscar," Wade warned.

I grabbed a corner of the canvas. Jerking it to the side, I exposed the bodies.

Chief muttered something in Shaynee I didn't understand, then ran his hand over the raptor, almost caressing its hide. He rubbed the feathers that stuck up along its back, looking at them intently. Grasping the remaining lower half of its face, the Indian pulled the lips back to inspect the razor-sharp teeth. Nodding to himself, he looked at the ape for several moments before reaching out and shoving it hard, as if to make certain it was dead. Walking around the wagon, he got to the feet of it and picked one up to look at the bottom pad and five large toes.

"Yes. These kill my people," he scowled.

I picked up the spear with both hands and passed it over to him. He looked at the tip and ran fingers along the decorative carvings along the shaft.

"There are many more of them."

"Where?"

I pointed at the mountain range behind us.

"There's an opening. A tunnel. You walk through the mountain to another side." It was the best description I could come up with limited dialogue. "Follow our tracks and you'll see. But many bad things are there. Entire army of these apes."

He perked up at this and waved his hand towards the group of braves. One rode over, his black spotted pony prancing sideways as he came to a stop beside us. The Chief talked faster than I could understand, but I caught the gist of it. He was sending men to check on the tunnel. The brave looked in the back of the wagon then wheeled his horse and raced back to the group. After some quick talking and gesturing, four of them turned and rode past us, each looking in the back of the wagon as they passed. Kicking heels to the horses, they galloped down the trail we'd left behind us.

"They go for look. You stay night with us," he pointed at Oscar. "We help weak white man."

Oscar looked offended, and I spoke up before he could complain and most likely, insult the Chief.

"Thank you," I shot a warning look at the fat scientist. "This is a great honor."

Abruptly the Chief tossed the spear into the wagon and walked back to his pony. Pausing before mounting, he turned and gestured for us to follow him.

"That went well. Who was your friend? The one with the scars?" Wade lifted his goateed chin to indicate the hillside that Otto and his followers left over.

"That's *Otoastis*," I uncaringly butchered the pronunciation of his name. "I don't know what it means, probably 'Perpetually Angry' or 'Wet Bag'. I saved his life once and, apparently, being saved by an inferior white man hurt his sacred honor or something. It doesn't help that I can't pronounce his name, and just call him Otto. He doesn't like that either."

"That's ridiculous," Skyla said, astonished. "And the way he swung that tomahawk at you! He almost smashed your head in!"

"He was trying to push me into hitting him, then he can try to kill me." I thought about how I had shoved him back. He'd be after my scalp now. "It's about regaining his honor. They're different folks than us, with a different culture. As hard as it is for us to understand them, they don't really get us either." I grinned and added cheerfully, "Anyways. Their camp isn't too far away unless they moved it again. We are going to sleep over with them tonight, and leave for town in the morning."

"What about me?" Oscar almost shouted. "I've been stabbed, remember?"

"I suspect they can patch you up as good or better than a town doctor," Wade said.

"Well, okay," the wounded scientist agreed, reluctantly. "I would like to see a real Indian camp."

"Me too," Skyla added.

Wade snickered, "They ain't as nice as you would think. Watch where you step."

"With the Chief's hospitality comes protection. But keep an eye out for Otto or his crew, and be careful what you say or do so you don't insult anyone. If unsure, ask Wade or myself first. It's only for one night. Ashley, try not to shoot anyone."

"You probably ask too much," Wolverine Wade teased his sharpshooter. She playfully shoved him from behind. Maybe it was just me, but there seemed to be a little more between the two than just a partnership for a planned western show.

Shrugging to myself, I mounted Carbine and moved forward to ride alongside the Chief as the wagon fell in with our Indian escort.

***

The Shaynee camp had moved a few miles since I'd last visited and was now sprawled across a large flat basin with a scattering of trees and a wide river flowing slowly along one side. It was made up of several dozen tipis and a handful of cooking fires. Indians moved through the camp, tanning hides, sewing, cooking, doing whatever it is that they do. Dogs and children ran between tipis causing mayhem amongst their elders. Ponies were kept in a makeshift corral on the edge of camp, grazing on the thick river grass. Several braves were racing horses past makeshift targets, practicing archery from horseback.

As we entered the village, a group of children were playing cowboys and Indians amongst the tipis. Of course, the Indians were winning. One of the little boys grasped a pretend-dead cowboy by his hair and mimicked scalping him while grinning at us. I fanned a finger gun at him, and grasping his chest, the little boy toppled over.

I gave him a playful wink as the kid pushed himself up and dusted off his bare knees before chasing after the others. The dead cowboy followed him, and the game started over.

With apes fresh in my mind, I looked at how the Shaynee were armed. Just like the party that escorted us in, they had a random collection of firearms, old black powder muzzle loaders, single shots, and some lever actions amidst their traditional weapons like spears, clubs, and bows. Almost all the guns were borderline rusted junk, others were cheap trade weapons sold by unscrupulous white traders. This village would have a hard time fighting off apes and trikes would run right over their tipis. I hoped we wouldn't get attacked tonight, because the best we could hope for was to use the river bank for a defensive position. Even then we'd still probably get wiped out.

"What's that smell?" Skyla wrinkled her nose, distracting me from morbid thoughts as she turned her head slightly as if to move away from the unseen source of the stench.

"Tanning hides and meat processing is a stinky affair," Wade smirked as he maneuvered the wagon along the edge of the river.

Villagers walked over as we rolled to a stop, followed by dozens of children and dogs. Everyone gathered around our wagon and escort, peering into the back and looking at us curiously. Dozens of them were openly hostile, but for the most part they seemed more puzzled than angry or fearful at our being led here by their men.

Chief dismounted and pulled the ape spear from the wagon. Resting the butt on the ground, he held it vertically and the nine-foot-tall obsidian tipped weapon towered over us all. He spoke to the crowd as they gathered around us, poking and prodding at the corpses in the wagon in awe and inspecting the damage done by the trike's horns to the wagon. I only understood about a third of what he said, and interpreted the best I could to my companions. Basically, we'd killed the things that killed their people, and that there were many more out there. Also, be on your guard, don't mess with us or our stuff, white people are terrible, but we'll be gone in the morning. Typical stuff.

During this, I noted appraising glances cast our way by most of the men when the Chief gestured towards the corpses. We'd killed things that they'd never seen before, and their people had been living on this land for a very long time now. They were impressed and baffled.

I also noted numerous eyes lingering on the ladies and our weapons. Including Otto who stood near the back of the ground with several other braves. He gestured towards Ashley while speaking to his friends. They didn't bother hiding their laughter or smirks as they walked away. He'd be wanting revenge on her now as well. She'd made him lose face in front of the others.

Just another reason to kill him as soon as possible now. I glanced at Ashley; if she saw their attention she didn't show it. At this point, our sharpshooter had proven she wasn't someone to be messed with. She just might kill him before I got the chance to.

An elderly Indian with long, gray hair hobbled to our wagon with the help of a twisted cane and stood quietly beside the Chief as he spoke to the Indians gathered around us. Once finished speaking, the Chief of the Shaynee led the old Indian to us. The villagers around us parted aside in reverence as he walked among them.

"He heal. Help wounded," Chief Toko looked at Oscar with thinly veiled disgust. Then he pointed towards the wrapped bandage on Ashley's arm, "Her too."

It took both Wade and myself to help Oscar out of the wagon. The man swore he was in terrible pain and clutched his side. The old Indian clucked his tongue disapprovingly and motioned for them to follow. Ashley gave me a disgusted look before reluctantly following them. Like the rest of us, she had grown weary of the paleontologist.

Wade unhooked the team of mules from the wagon while I stripped the saddle and tack from Carbine, then we turned the animals loose into the makeshift corral. There was plenty of grass and access to the river for water. I warned Carbine to play nice with the Indian ponies. He ignored me and immediately tried to playfully nip one. Several Indians stood nearby, keeping watch on the animals and eyeballing us as we waited to be told where to go next.

"You know these people well?" Skyla asked, watching Indians spearing fish downstream.

I kicked a rock into the river, scaring a trout in their direction. "Not really. I come by occasionally to trade and keep up relations. Except for Otto, they've been mostly friendly. But I've never stayed the night, so this is a new experience. Honestly, if we hadn't brought the bodies, Chief probably would've turned us away."

A high-pitched scream pierced the air.

"What was that?" Skyla spun towards the tipis.

Chief slapped his knee and began laughing. "White man cry like woman giving birth."

I sighed. Oscar was making us look bad. When you're dealing with people who value courage and strength in the face of adversity, being a wimp is a severe disadvantage.

Wade winced. "Getting stitched up hurts, but that man is as weak as a daffodil in a snowstorm."

"He's not so bad," Skyla protested weakly. I raised my eyebrows at her as another scream from her boss sounded from one of the tipis. She grimaced and turned back to watching the Indians fish. One lifted his spear from the water triumphantly, a fish flapping on the end of it.

"Follow," the Indian leader said and began walking towards the tipis. We moved quickly to keep up.

Except for weapons and bags, the rest of our gear remained in the wagon with the bodies. Chief assured me nothing would be taken. He even went so far as to post a rather imposing pair of braves as lookout. Still, I fully expected our belongings to have been thoroughly rifled through by dawn.

Chief guided us through the village, stepping around fires and through throngs of Indians. Even after our introduction by the Chief, there were still plenty of suspicious stares. Children shadowed us, hiding behind tipis and their elders, following until we reached a large painted tipi in the center of the village. Apparently, the tribe preferred to keep us somewhere they could keep an eye on us.

A small fire, ringed with rocks, smoldered in front of the hide covered tent. A stack of sticks and chopped branches was dumped to the side.

The Indian leader flung back the flap covering the opening, exposing a comfortable looking floor of buffalo hides and blankets. "Stay here tonight."

"Thank you," Skyla said, moving closer and inspecting the paintings on the stretched hide that covered the tipi poles. "These are fascinating," she gently touched the paint with her fingertips. "Wade, what's this one?" She pointed at stick drawings of men on horseback and a herd of buffalos.

"Buffalo jump. Back when these lands were covered up with them, they used to run groups off a cliff, sometimes hundreds of them, and feast on them for days afterwards. One brave disguised in a buffalo robe would act as a decoy and get in front of the herd. The other braves circle and start pushing closer while the lone Indian starts running towards the cliff. The other buffalo follow him as the Indians push harder at their flanks, next thing you know, the buffalo push each other off the cliff trying to get away."

"What happens to the Indian in front of them?" she asked.

"Move fast or get squished."

I slid my saddle bags and rifle inside the tipi before kneeling beside the fire. Gently blowing on the embers, I coaxed the flames back and fed it small sticks.

Chief left, and my companions joined me by the fire.

"This is fascinating," Skyla looked around at the camp. "I hoped to see Indians on this trip, but never dreamed I would get to see one of their villages. Jed, you said these are Shaynee? Except for Otto, they seem peaceful."

The small sticks began catching fire. "There aren't too many of them, just a handful of bands stretched out over the territory. I don't know their tribal history. Seems they've always been around here."

"I'm surprised they haven't been killed off or absorbed by other tribes." Wade leaned away as the smoke changed directions and blew in his face. He waved his wide brimmed hat at it, coughing.

"Don't let them fool you. The Shaynee have a reputation. Hurt one of theirs, they kill a few of yours. Kill one of them, they wipe out an entire village. For the most part, the others leave them alone unless they want total warfare. Don't let Chief Toko fool you. He's pleasant enough, but he didn't become their leader by being a weakling. I'm sure he's killed more than a few whites. If you haven't noticed yet, he's not a big fan of us."

Skyla's eyes widened with the realization that the village wasn't as peaceful as she thought. "Oh."

Wade pulled a wrapped bundle of jerky and hardtack from his bag, and passed it to Skyla. "Let's not cross him then."

"They speak pretty good English." She took several pieces before handing them across the fire to me. Daintily, she tore a piece of jerky off with her teeth and began to chew the dried meat.

Taking a few strips and a chunk of hard biscuit, I passed the bundle back to Wade. "As much disdain as they have for whites, they've had a few settle down with them for a while. They also deal with traders from time to time. All things considered, they aren't too bad of a people. Just different is all." I gnawed on the bread.

Chief walked over quietly and looked down at our group before his eyes rested on me. "Come, Huck Berry. We show you things."

I glanced at my companions and stood, while pushing a strip of jerky into my mouth. Skyla looked concerned, but Wade just pushed a few more sticks into the fire. "Go on, we'll be fine," he said without looking up.

Leaving them behind, I tried to keep up with the thick chested Indian as he moved quickly amongst the tipis. The village was starting to settle down for the evening. There was no sign of Otto or his minions. A mangy mutt dropped low and growled at me. The Chief sent it scurrying with a well-placed kick. "White men smell funny," he said in defense of the dog's behavior as we stopped at a wide and low-slung tent by the river.

The hut stood waist high and was covered with a mix of animal hides and colorful trade blankets. A buffalo skull, its bleached white bone contrasting with the black horns, was propped on a rock facing the entrance.

Runs With Dogs sat cross-legged on a rock beside the skull, looking bored and whittling on a stick. He was a short, squat man who always had a scowl on his face. He gave me a look of thinly veiled disgust as the Chief stripped down to his breech cloth. "No speak. Do what I do," he told me while laying his clothes and rifle in a neat pile and slipping into the tent. Following his lead, I removed everything but my pants. My gun belt was carefully rolled and left beside the Chief's gear on top of my shirt, with my hat sitting on top.

I crawled into the tent on hands and knees.

When the hide flap closed behind me, the inside was pitched into darkness except for a small circle of rocks resting on a bed of glowing red coals in a shallow depression in the center of the floor. The heat was intense, the air thick and humid. It was suffocating and sweat immediately began pouring from my body. The smell of burning plants and spices was strong. My senses felt both deprived and overwhelmed at the same time.

Chief sat opposite of me, with the tribe's Medicine Man between us to the side. The ancient, gnarled old man slowly poured water over the rocks with trembling hands and steam billowed, adding to the moist hot air.

I shifted into a sitting position and tried to recall everything I'd heard of sweat lodges rituals. It was a great honor, one rarely bestowed upon a white man. Going off what little I knew, I guessed there would be some chanting, lots of sweating, and maybe some stick shaking. Hopefully my ignorance wouldn't cause any dishonor.

The old man began speaking. His voice wavered in a sing song voice. Chief struggled to translate the words into English.

"There was great warrior. One day. Wife taken by..." Chief shrugged. "Don't know word... hairy man. Warrior go after him. Fight many things... beasts, fire and thunder, men of... metal. Strange things. Other things... He kill many hairy man. But wife dead."

I got the impression I was missing most of the story. The Chief was giving me a few sentences from what sounded like paragraphs. I struggled to understand why I was being told a bedtime story. The temperature and humidity were becoming unbearable. I felt sick to my stomach and resisted the urge to run from the lodge and out into the cool evening air. That would be showing weakness. I steeled my resolve and focused on the words instead of my agonizing misery.

"Heart full of sadness. He go. Fight. Try to die, but keep living. Then he go through mountain."

Through the mountain? I perked up and stared at the Medicine Man in disbelief at what I'd heard. Like my mountain?

"Opening made by great gods." Chief spread his arms out, palms up. "Great new world for warrior. Easy hunting. Easy life. He find new wife. Much prettier. Make him happy. Give him many sons. He forgets about opening in mountain.... no more care about old life and ugly wife."

The wizened old man coughed, and continued. Chief waited several sentences before speaking. I leaned forward, desperately wishing I was fluent in Shaynee.

"He take best hunting grounds. Probably kill many white men."

I rolled my eyes, annoyed.

He shrugged. "OK. Kill many red man. But my story better," he smirked at me through the smoke. "Hairy men, here now," he jabbed his finger towards the ground angrily. "From mountain. Come kill Shaynee. Take our land."

My mind swam as I sorted through everything I just heard. It aligned perfectly with the apes and the tunnel through the mountain. The beasts on the other side, I'd already seen with my own eyes. The Indian I saw being sacrificed...

There were people over there!

As I tried to absorb what I'd just learned the Medicine Man reverently picked up a decorative pipe. Raising it above the steam, he began praying. With what little of their language I understood, I caught something about their gods helping. Finishing, he carefully took a small coal from the base of the rocks between two flat carved sticks, and placed it into the pipe, puffing until the contents began to smoke. He puffed several times, then passed to the Chief who used it as well.

Then it was my turn.

I didn't want to breathe a bunch of unknown smoldering weeds in, but I wasn't about to disrespect the tribe who was sheltering us for the night.

The smoke filled my lungs, stinging my throat and lungs as I drew deeply on the pipe and exhaled slowly. Coughing slightly, I handed it back to the Medicine Man as my vision began to dance. The two Indians began to chant as the dim glow of the rocks began to shake, then blur. I felt my body swaying back and forth as I struggled to stay upright. Thin tendrils of steam danced as they rose above heated rocks. I lifted a hand and looked at it, it didn't feel like it was attached to me. It was as if I was looking at someone else's body part. The hot rocks began to throb with the chanting.

Something was wrong, terribly wrong.

Instinctively, I reached for the pistol and distantly realized I'd left it outside. My mind didn't seem to be working properly.

I rose halfway to my knees before toppling over onto the blankets. I couldn't move. Drool ran from the corner of my mouth. My hands wouldn't work. The desire to crawl from the lodge was great, but my body wouldn't respond. I could only lay there, helpless, as the Chief and Medicine Man continued chanting with eyes closed and the steam swirling into shifting shapes between us.

My vision dimmed, then went dark.

***

When I opened my eyes, I was in South Carolina again.

Large cypress trees dangled Spanish moss, giving shade to a beautiful, white, two story antebellum house that stood before me. Tall circular columns rose from the fenced porch to patio roof. Shutters were thrown open, allowing a cool breeze to circulate inside through the windows. Rocking chairs sat empty and large ferns gave color to the porch.

This was my home, and father was still away.

His last letter was over a year old. At the time of its writing, he was at a place called Cold Harbor awaiting an attack by Grant's Army. But he told us not to worry, and that he suspected the war would be over soon. At first, I didn't worry. He was the strongest and bravest man I knew, and I happily continued getting in trouble without fear of a whipping. But as seasons changed and the end of the war came with no more letters, I started to worry. Union soldiers and carpet baggers poured into the South as our defeated veterans, starving, mangled, and diseased, struggled to make their way home. Mother cried every night.

But today was a warm summer day. A fateful day that altered the course of my life for the worse. I remembered it well, and saw it now as I did then, through the eyes of a naïve ten-year-old boy.

My mother and sister had taken the buckboard into town, leaving me in charge of the house. I thought it was an honor and felt like a grown man. But there was nothing to oversee, we had no household help left, no workers in the fields, and little in the way of food or valuables to protect.

I was playing with Cato, an African boy around my age whose mother died on a slave ship. My father, passing through Charleston on business, happened by the slave auction block when he was put on it. He stood alone on the raised platform, crying, dressed in filthy rags, with chains too large clamped around his thin legs. The auctioneer, unable to get bids for a slave who wouldn't be of any use for several more years, was dragging him off the block to be discarded when my father bought him cheap.

We didn't keep slaves and when he was brought to our home, he'd been freed with papers to prove it. At first, the only word he spoke was

'Cato', and it became his name as he learned English. Our bedrooms were side by side and we were inseparable. He became the brother I'd always wanted, and we got in the sort of trouble brothers would. Whenever we had visitors who inquired about the little black boy who lived in our house and ate at our table, my father would simply say, "He's ours," in the sort of stern voice that you didn't dare challenge.

On this day, we were chasing each other around the house, pretending to be soldiers at war. I had a stick I was using as a rifle complete with bayonet, while he had a curved briar switch that took place of a sword. Like most boyish games, it quickly turned from soldierly behavior to scrabbling in the dirt, wrestling and name calling all in good wholesome fun.

We were so preoccupied in our play, we didn't notice the Union cavalry soldiers' approach until their officer pulled me off Cato and flung me onto my back.

He was a large man, thick at the waist with a neatly combed red beard. He laughed as he looked us over, but his eyes were hard and mean and they frightened me. His men were ordered to search the house and barns, and we stood with our shirt collars locked firmly in his grasp under a large oak tree while they ransacked our home.

I heard Mother's fine china breaking inside the house and the sound of furniture being overturned with heavy thuds. The men's calls were loud and gruff, swearing and cursing as they tore through our home and barns. The war that we played at, suddenly became all too real and terrifying.

Shouting came from inside the barn, followed by a loud gun shot. Panicked, I struggled, trying to run away. The bearded officer jerked me back so hard that I choked, then cuffed me across the back of the head. I wheezed and gasped for breath while he laughed coarsely at my discomfort.

Union soldiers pulled a man out of the barn in a torn and tattered Confederate uniform. Blood ran down his leg from a bullet wound. They half carried, half dragged him across the yard before dumping the injured man at the red-haired officer's feet in a heap.

I recognized him as Mr. Turbin.

A neighbor of ours, he lived a few miles away and used to visit occasionally before the war. Early on I'd noticed most people treated Cato different than me, but not Mr. Turbin. We always looked forward to his visits because he'd bring us treats and tell funny stories. He always had a nice smile and a belly rumbling laugh that we used to mimic when he wasn't around. But now his face was sunken, his body gaunt, the gray uniform filthy and hanging off him like a scarecrow. There was something to his eyes, as though he'd seen things that could never be unseen.

The officer asked who he was, where he was going, and where his friends were.

Our old neighbor said quietly that all Confederate soldiers had been pardoned and the war was over. This angered the officer, and letting go of us, he kicked Mr. Turbin in the chest with his mud splattered riding boots, knocking him to the ground in a cry of pain.

I stood still, frozen in fear at the sudden violence that had arrived at my home. Cato grabbed my hand in his and clenched it tightly, as if afraid we'd be parted.

Mr. Turbin pushed himself upright, then paused when he saw us under the tree. A look of recognition crossed his face. The officer noticed it as well and asked me if he was my father. Mr. Turbin told me to not tell them anything. For that he was butt stroked with a rifle across the face, blood splattered as his nose crumpled flat. He lay on the ground, wheezing through the broken nose.

He needn't have worried. I was so terrified that I couldn't speak.

Cato answered for me. He told the red-bearded man that Mr. Turbin wasn't my father, but a family friend. The officer asked more questions… where his house was and how far away. Had we seen any more Confederates. Where was my father? Where were the gold, silver, and valuables hidden?

My brother answered the questions honestly. He told them we'd seen dozens of confederates walking home, and that my father was gone still, and that the silver spoons and my mother's jewelry were hidden under a secret floorboard in the kitchen.

The officer seemed pleased and had one of his men take Cato to wait with the horses. Cato replied he wanted to stay with me and the officer back handed him across the face so hard his lip burst, and blood dribbled down his chin.

He was jerked away from me and I shook in fear as I watched him being led away. He looked over his shoulder at me, sadness in his eyes, and I wondered if we'd ever see each other again.

One of the men returned with the valuables and father's letters that were kept in the same hiding place. The officer flipped through them, checking the dates and stopping at the final one. He read the neatly written script, then wadded it up and tossed it aside.

A thin man with a large nose, was ordered to ready the ropes.

He smiled evilly and began whistling the Battle Hymn of the Republic while shaking out a pair of coiled ropes before throwing them over the oak tree's thick branches. Mr. Turbin rose and tried to fight as soldiers began tying my hands. He was kicked and stomped viciously. Bones snapped and broke beneath meaty thuds of boots on flesh and skull. I stared at the crumpled, faded letter laying in the dirt and prayed my father would appear with a company of his finest men.

It was a foolish daydream of a boy terrified and alone.

Gunshots rang out as soldiers began shooting our livestock. Others threw burning torches into the house and barns. Smoke billowed from windows.

Something in me broke as I watched my home being violated and destroyed. We were good people with family on both sides of the war, and now the war was over. These men were evil. The Union Army was evil. The North was evil to allow such filth to terrorize the defeated South.

I trembled as a dark, angry, vengeful thing welled up inside of me and burned away the fear that gripped me. Tears stopped. I clenched my tied hands into small fists and ground my teeth so hard I thought they'd shatter.

They settled the noose over Mr. Turbin's head first and lifted his broken and shattered body into the air. His legs kicked feebly beside me, but I kept my eyes on my burning childhood home, feeling my hatred feeding off the rising flames. After several long agonizing minutes, his body gave a last great shake, then swayed back and forth gently.

When the thin man stepped in front of me and leaned forward to put the noose over my head, I grasped his shirt tightly with my tied hands and bit down on his nose with all my might.

Blood filled my mouth as he screamed and fought to get away. Soldiers began pounding on my head and back with fists as they fought to pry me off. Someone grabbed my hair and I felt a chunk of it tear away with my scalp. I held on gamely and ground my teeth with the stubbornness of a mule. When the nose came off, I spit out the mouthful of raw flesh and directed every single swear word I knew, including the ones I didn't understand, at them.

Soldiers circled around me, kicking and beating me with rifle stocks until I curled into a ball, helpless as I muttered curses through smashed lips while praying for their deaths.

The red-bearded officer stepped in, stopped the soldiers, and saved me from their fury.

Instead of being hanged or beaten to death, my arms were tied around the oak tree with Mr. Turbin's body still hanging from one of the thick branches. The thin man with the mangled nose, cursed and swore as I was whipped by the officer himself. I screamed myself hoarse as flesh was flayed off my back and sides until I mercifully passed out.

My mother and sister found me that evening.

By then the soldiers had been gone for hours, moving on to loot and burn Mr. Turbin's home and hang his family next. I was still tied to the tree in front of the ashes of our home, my broken and lacerated body hanging from bloodied wrists still bound with rope. I was delirious and near death from blood loss and dehydration. My back was a crisscrossed mass of broken skin and open wounds.

I never saw Cato again.

***

Everything faded away again before coming back into sharp focus with almost painful clarity.

This time, I was in the Bucket o' Blood saloon.

The thought of the name made me smile painfully.

I was sitting on the floor, leaning back against the bar. The metallic tang of blood filled my mouth. Sweat dripped from my face onto my ripped and dirty shirt, mingling with the blood leaking from the broken shaft of an ape's arrow that jutted through. A smeared trail of red showed me where I had dragged myself to this spot.

The weariness of battle and exhaustion turned the pain into a dull throb.

My pistol lay beside me, its hammer dropped on an empty chamber. My rifle lay discarded somewhere in the street, the stock shattered from beating an ape to death with it. All I had left was my Bowie knife. I held it tightly, the handle and long blade slick with blood, its tip broken.

A woman's legs with dirty black riding boots stuck out from around the corner of the bar, unmoving and still. They were Skyla's. She lay amongst the broken bottles of whiskey where the ape had flung her like a rag doll after snapping her neck. I desperately wanted to crawl to her, but my strength was fading.

The ape that killed her lay dead before me. His dark fur was painted with colorful swirls and patterns mingled with bright red blood. I'd emptied my pistol into him, then stabbed him repeatedly until he stopped twitching, snapping the tip of my blade off as I jammed it into his eye socket.

But not before he killed Skyla and hurled a spear half way through Wade's back. The famed hunter's face was frozen in an agonized grimace, his hands clutching the bloodied shaft sticking through his chest. He'd fallen by Ashley, who lay draped through the saloon window, punctured with several arrows. Broken and shattered glass mingled with spent brass cartridge casings that sparkled around her from the flames. Even in death she clung to her beautiful rifle, its stock cracked from trying to block the heavy swing of a stone axe that killed Oscar in the streets.

We'd fought valiantly, but failed. The town had fallen and was burning.

Cries of men and horses suddenly ceased one by one with a final scream or gurgle as apes finished off the wounded. Soon it was silent except for the crackle of flames that licked the doorway and singed my friend's bodies. The scent of burning human flesh stung my nostrils.

I coughed up bloody froth from a punctured lung. It dribbled down my chin. I didn't have the energy to wipe it away.

The scar-faced leader of the apes ducked through the smoke-filled doorway. His hands were soaked with blood past his elbows and his massive painted chest was streaked with it. The glossy black club in his hand dripped gore that sizzled in the flames. His fangs were bared. I could feel the anger and hatred radiating from him. He stalked towards me, grabbing a bar stool in his way and shattering it against a far wall.

Reaching me, he glared down. I'd never been so close to him before. The scarring on his face was hideous and twisted as he scowled down at me with yellowed and broken canines. His eyes were black orbs filled with death.

This foul creature had won, and I was doomed to die at his hands.

I coughed painfully, and with great effort, raised my faithful Bowie before me, determined I wouldn't go without a fight.

He slapped it from my hand and my last weapon tumbled across the blood-soaked floorboards out of reach.

Resigning myself to an inglorious death, I rested my head back against the bar, and tried to spit at the ape leader but only managed to dribble a little down the black stubble on my chin. It was a pitiful attempt at defiance. Shrugging with my good shoulder, I stuck my tongue through broken teeth and blew him a raspberry.

The obsidian club rose and swung downward as my eyes flicked to where Skyla lay. I looked forward to seeing her again soon.

My skull shattered, and my spine was driven down into my chest.

The light that followed was sweet and rejoiceful.

***

I woke with a jerk and a gasp, grabbing at my skull where the final blow had fallen and feeling something wet on my face.

My blurry vision cleared. Skyla was leaning over me, pressing a cold damp cloth to my forehead.

"What... ugh." My mouth felt full of cotton, my tongue thick and worthless. She passed me a canteen. With effort, I pushed myself into a sitting position and gulped the cool liquid gratefully.

"Easy there, take a moment. You've been out for a while. Chief and some other angry looking Indian brought you back here. He said something about you saw the past and a maybe soon... whatever that meant. His accent is so thick that I can barely understand what he's saying," she explained.

I drank, slower this time, savoring the sensation of water trickling down my parched throat.

"I thought you were dead at first, you were barely breathing. Chief wouldn't say anything else, he just dumped you here and left. Wade said it looked like you went to a sweat lodge."

The famed westerner was sitting on the other side of me, rifle across his lap, peering outside through a narrow gap in the tipi entrance. He spoke without turning. "It's an honor to be part of one, but they'll wear you out."

I managed to croak out, "Yeah." Suddenly self-conscience I looked down. The movement made my head swim, but I managed to stay upright until the feeling passed. I was naked from the waist up. Thankfully, my pants were still on but soaked through with sweat.

Gingerly, I ran a finger along the stitches from the cut from the Allosaurus. It was almost healed enough for the thread to come out. Then it would be just another scar for the collection. "Where're my clothes?"

Wade lifted a bundle up. "Here." He passed them over with my rolled gun belt and holster.

I checked the Colt first. It was still loaded and didn't appear to have been tinkered with. I dumped the rounds out anyway and dry fired it a few times before reloading it with fresh cartridges. The Chief, I trusted. Runs With Dogs who watched my gear, not so much. He never liked me. Or any white man for that matter.

Sliding my arms through the shirt openings, I worked the buttons. My fingers felt thick and heavy, making the simple task difficult. "Wade, I take it you've done a lodge before?"

"A couple times. Never had a vision or anything, just sort of hung out and got hot and sweaty. But they get angry if you turn such an honor down. Looks like you got lucky though, usually they want you naked in there with them."

Skyla blushed a bright crimson as she pushed my fumbling hands aside and began buttoning my shirt. She changed the subject, "Who is Cato? You said his name several times while you were out."

"Childhood friend, he was like a brother. He's dead I think," I left it at that. There wasn't much else to say. Father made it home and after several years of searching for Cato, we never found him.

The tent flap moved, and Oscar crawled in, followed by Ashley. The rip in his shirt showed the puckered flesh stitched together with a greenish brown paste smeared around the wound. He moved across from us and lay on his good side, a pained look on his face.

"These people are utter savages," he half-whispered. "Do you know what they did to Ashley? They blew some smoke over her head and uttered a bunch of mumbo-jumbo while waving a stick with feathers around."

"That doesn't sound bad." Skyla said as she looked over Ashley's freshly bandaged arm.

"It wasn't. They were pretty nice about it and I do feel a little better," she admitted.

"But not to me! They wanted me to put some filthy stick in my mouth. It had teeth marks on it!" His voice rose as he became agitated. "I refused because it was disgusting. Then they stuck me with a bone needle and greasy gut string. I start screaming, and those Indians pinned me down and shoved that stick into my mouth anyway. I couldn't breathe around it, and it tasted like smoke and blood. That healer, if that's what he really is, seemed more like a butcher as he sewed me up. He laughed as he did it!" Oscar's face began to turn red as he relived the experience through his telling. "They all laughed! Even Ashley!" He glared accusingly at her. "And one of those Indians took my spectacles… and if all that wasn't bad enough, they wiped this gunk all over my wound. It smells like manure!"

Ashley was laughing so hard she had to lean against Skyla. "Oh goodness, you should have seen him. He was such a big baby about it all."

"It smells like that because it's probably buffalo dung mixed with some other stuff to make a poultice," Wade grinned broadly. "Don't worry, it's supposed to help."

I shook my head and pointed outside the tipi. "Oscar, you're embarrassing us. You know your Indian name is 'Weak White Man' now? I don't even know how to respond when they call you that. It's offensive to our entire race."

He harrumphed, opened his bag, and pulled out a small bottle. "Well, luckily for me, I have this," the paleontologist held it up for us to see. The glass bottle contained a yellowish liquid and was wrapped with a blue label that read "Clark Stanley's Snake Oil Liniment".

"It'll cure everything. Including infection by buffalo manure." He spun the top off the bottle and using his handkerchief began to confidently dab it around the Indian poultice on his wound. We gagged as an overpowering smell wafted through the tipi.

"That smells like horse urine!" Ashley shouted, pushing back against the hide walls to get further away from the stench filling the air.

Skyla scrambled out of the tipi on all fours, while Wade stuck his head out the entrance, gasping for air. I pulled my bandana over my nose and tried to breathe through my mouth.

"Nonsense! This is a famous cure all!" He held the bottle out towards me. "It may even cure your ornery, blood thirsty disposition, Jed." He shook the bottle, swirling the yellow liquid inside. "You'll probably need several bottles though."

I waved the stinking mystery fluid away and pinched my nose shut. "I'm good with my penchant for violence, but thanks."

After holding the entrance open and waving our hands for a while, we managed to make the tipi inhabitable enough for Skyla to come back in and settle down beside me. The closeness of her body to mine made me feel self-conscious about how I probably reeked of sweat now.

"To catch everyone up. Chief put Jed through a sweat lodge and showed him some visions," Wade pointed at me. "Now, what is this business about you seeing the past and a maybe soon? Chief made it sound rather ominous. But his English ain't good, so maybe he meant something else?"

"Visions? You can't possibly be serious," Oscar said disdainfully.

Wade began to say something, but Ashley put a hand on his arm to caution him with restraint. The wolverine killer settled for a glare at the portly scientist.

Oscar rolled his eyes, but was smart enough to keep his mouth shut.

"Right. Well, it's creepy how he knew what I would dream about. But the 'past' vision he mentioned, showed me when my house was torched by a rogue Union outfit that was raiding the South after the war ended." Thinking about it made the scar tissue itch and I absently scratched at my back, "I don't know what that has to do with anything, it's not a place or day I'll ever forget. But that was the past he mentioned."

Skyla asked quietly, "And your vision of the maybe soon?"

I coughed to clear my throat before telling them the truth. "Apes kill everyone and burn the town to the ground."

The tipi went quiet.

After a long silent moment, Wade spoke first, "He said a maybe soon. That doesn't mean it will happen," his eyes darted to me before continuing. "The past is over. It's done. There's no changing it. But the future isn't fixed."

"Still..." I paused and swallowed hard as I remembered our deaths in the bar. "When we return to town... You all need to leave."

Wade opened his mouth to protest and I held my hand up to stop him.

"Look. This is my town. I've led a miserable, shoddy life for a long time before finding somewhere I could settle in peace. I've a lot to atone for, and I'm not leaving those people to die without doing everything in my power to save them. They don't know what's coming towards them, but I do." I looked them each in the eye, except Oscar who turned his head and looked away. "This ain't your fight."

Wade stroked his mustache and goatee. "I know the Governor of the Territory, I think we can convince him to send some troops. But I'm staying. My reputation would be forever tarnished if I fled a fight." He looked to Ashley. "I want you to leave though."

She turned to the famed wolverine slayer, her jaw clenched with determination. "Like hell. I can't leave you alone, you'll get in trouble. And it sounds like you could use my help. I'll be staying as well, and don't you say another word about it, Wolverine Wade Mackin."

He blinked, before slowly nodding as he reluctantly gave in to her wishes. "Yes, ma'am."

Skyla looked at me, her voice soft. "I'm staying as well." She saw the look on my face and cut me off before I could speak. "If you send me away, I'll just come right back. Even if I have to buy a horse and ride back in your strange western manner with lots of swear words. And most of them will be directed at you."

I chuckled softly. "Okay," I relented after seeing the determination in her eyes and I was even more adamant now that we'd prevent what I saw in my vision from coming true. I was relieved to have them, but hated the risk they were taking. They all had their own strengths, and each would be of use in any fight to come. I looked at Oscar; of everyone here, I could do without him. But like Skyla, he had knowledge that could be of value.

He still looked away, picking at the hairs on one of the buffalo rugs. "I'm not a fighter, and I don't believe in these hallucinations of yours. I'm a civilized man who believes in science. When we return to town tomorrow, I'm going to Cheyenne and relaying what we've found to the Institute. Once these apes are no longer a threat, I'll be on the first train back to study the dinosaurs on the other side. But fighting is not in my nature."

"That's good, because you were the first to die in my vision anyway. So, this maybe soon vision is already changing by you not being there," I told him happily. "For all we know, you lost us the battle and we'll win handily now!"

"I have better things to do than die in battle. The world will long remember the name Oscar Ellis," he said proudly.

"I'm sure they will," Skyla replied, but it was easy to see she doubted his boast.

I looked around the tipi, this was a good bunch of people. Even Oscar, with all his numerous faults, had become one of us. But I still wasn't saddened to see the man go. "One more thing... The old Medicine Man in the sweat lodge told me the history of their people. It starts with a warrior walking through a mountain."

Skyla's eyes widened.

"The side he left had great beasts... and hairy men." I looked around as the realization of our hosts' origin dawned on everyone. "It seems the Shaynee are descendants from the other side."

***

The next morning found me standing with Chief, watching Wade hitch the mules to the wagon. The famed wolverine slayer was cursing as he fought a tangle in the harnesses.

I turned to the leader of the Shaynee, "How'd you know that I'd have a past and 'maybe soon' vision in the sweat lodge?"

"Didn't. I guess. What you see?"

I rolled my eyes. "I saw my home when I was little. Soldiers came and burned it. Then I saw apes... hairy men... slaughtering everyone in town. What was I supposed to get out of those?"

"Don't know. Not all visions have purpose. Some do."

"That's real useful," I said dryly. "Why'd you call it a 'maybe soon'?"

He wiggled a hand from side to side. "Maybe happen, maybe not. I have vision once when young. It show me white man leave, buffalo come back before my many sons are born. But here you are. Few buffalo left." He grimaced and pointed across the camp at two little girls playing with cornhusk dolls under the watchful eye of his wife. "And she only give me daughters." Sighing, he rested his crossed arms on the makeshift corral. "Was good maybe vision."

"These hairy men are many. What are you going to do with your people?"

He looked at the mountain range to the south behind us. "I sent braves last night to mountain. They saw hairy men on strange horn beasts riding cross plains. We go-" He swung his arms to the north-east, "that way. Gather all Shaynee. Wait fight out."

I looked the way he pointed. "It'll be slow moving with women and kids. Easy target for the apes."

"We go careful. And in dark."

"You could come with us. We fight together," I offered. He had dozens of braves, and many more women and children that needed protection. It would be a major pain to negotiate through all the prejudices and hatred with the whites in town. But nothing made people come together like the possibility of mutual destruction.

He laughed loudly and jabbed a finger at me. "No! You said all town die."

"You said it was a 'maybe soon'!"

"Maybe happen. You maybe ok," he smirked. "Maybe Otto get you."

"That'll be the day," I snorted.

For a moment I hesitated, tapping my fingers against the rails on the corral. I was confident of the answer, but wanted confirmation of my suspicions. "Chief... When I crossed to the other side of the mountain. The apes killed a red man. Cut his heart out." I made a slashing motion over my chest. "Was he one of yours?"

The Chief squinted, clearly puzzled. He shook his head slowly from side to side. "No."

That matched what I recalled about the tracks into the tunnel the first time I went over. Putting that with the Medicine Man's story, that meant our assumptions were correct, there were still people on the other side. I told him as much.

"Maybe," he said, indifferently. I supposed to him it was just another tribe, an unknown group, and any shared blood between them wasn't important after being separated for so many generations.

Wade finished hitching the team as Oscar and the ladies made their way through the camp towards us. The chubby scientist seemed to be in better spirits than last night. But he still held a hand to his stitched wound, wincing occasionally as thread pulled flesh with his waddling steps.

I held out my hand to Chief. "Thank you. The Shaynee are a great people. If you ever need me, I'll come running."

He clasped my arm firmly in his. "I would light smoke signal. But you can't read it." He laughed again as I scowled at him. The Indian Chief couldn't help but jab and poke at the white man. I was never certain if he meant his insults or just did it to get a rise out of me. Probably both.

As we rode away from the village, we saw Otto and his braves had returned and were passing out large slabs of meat to groups of Indians scattered around the cooking fires. From the size of the hind quarters strapped on his paint pony, it looked like several of my cattle were on the menu. Seeing my stare, the scarred brave bent over while flipping up the back of his breech cloth in our direction. The nearby Indians laughed as he mooned us.

I resisted the urge to put another hole in his rear.

Ashley swiveled her head away in the other direction, "Well, that's disgusting."

"What?" Skyla asked as she twisted to see what the sharpshooter was turning away from. "Oh my."

"He's going to be a problem," Wade stated flatly, as we crested the hill of the small river basin encampment.

Ashley wiped dust off her rifle and checked the action for a loaded round for the third or fourth time that morning. You could feel nervousness radiate off her as she watched the surrounding dips and hills around us. "I don't think me shooting that tomahawk out of his hand helped his attitude any."

I rested my hand on the butt of my Colt. Chief's protection ended when we left their camp and I was positive Otto would want revenge on Ashley as well. I didn't want to worry her more than she already was, but I also wasn't going to lie to her. "Probably not. Ultimately, it's my fault that he's alive. I should have left his half-chewed carcass for the wolves when I had the chance."

Skyla spoke up, "Is that what gave him those scars?"

"No. He made the mistake of getting between a mama grizzly and her cubs. She tore him wide open and flung him into a briar thicket. I came across him not too long after. I thought he was dead. Turns out, he's a tough Indian. I'd seen the Shaynee village before, but avoided it, so I knew where to haul him to. Their healer managed to piece him back together. Since then I try to keep up good relations. But he always tries to goad me into a fight." I shrugged, "I reckon next time I see him, I'll end his miserable existence."

"What if he kills you instead?" Oscar asked from the back of the wagon.

"Then I die," I clicked my teeth and pushed Carbine further ahead to stave off any more conversation. There were too many threats in the area for me to get distracted.

The ride back was uneventful.

But as we reached the valley ridge overlooking the town, we came across trike tracks. Leaving the wagon, I followed them. They circled the town in a wide arc, occasionally stopping and leaving giant mounds of trike manure and ape foot prints from where they'd watched over the town.

I quickly rode after the wagon as it rumbled down the trail into town.

**

We made sure both bodies were fully covered. The Indian guards had done a good job of keeping everyone away and the corpses weren't mangled any more than before. I'd half expected to see the ape missing toes and the raptor without feathers this morning. But the corpses were still intact, and we wanted to make it through town with as little fanfare as possible. Gawkers would make that difficult.

I figured it'd be up to the Sheriff and Wade to figure out the best way to break the news to the town.

The famed westerner dropped his partner and our scientists off at the hotel to get cleaned up and put some decent food in their bellies. Oscar loudly announced he'd be visiting the doctor for some real healing, then on the next train to Cheyenne. I tried to be polite and bid him farewell, but he walked away without a word and nary a glance at Skyla. He wasn't pleased that his assistant was staying behind, but didn't seem to be concerned about what her father might have to say to him about that.

Turning the wagon around in the street was near impossible, so Wade drove it through the alley between the buildings and turned around behind them. Several streets were laid out there, with wooden stakes and string marking off lots. A few foundations had started to be built, and a couple of large tents set up, but most of the lots were empty and still for sale. Before his untimely death the Mayor had been expecting a substantial amount of growth over the next year or so.

Wade pulled the brake on the wagon in front of the Sheriff's Office and I tied Carbine's reins to the rail and gave him a scratch. He'd done well the past couple of days, mostly. When we opened the door to the office, Dan's feet were propped on the desk and his hat pulled low over his face. He didn't so much as stir until Wade slammed the thick door shut behind us with a loud boom.

Dan's feet hit the floor as he jerked upright, grabbed the butt of his pistol and glared at us. "Most people know better than to startle a sleeping bear."

I snickered. "More like a hibernating bear. Don't you ever do any work?"

He glared from beneath the brim of his hat. "As little as possible, that's what deputies are for."

"I reckon they made it back, safe and sound?" I didn't like the two of them, but I didn't want them dead or hurt either. Unless they gave me cause to do it myself.

"They are. Tom's pretty upset about that horse of his. But they are both firm believers in your story now and ticked off that you didn't convince them before they were attacked," he shook his head in disgust. "The fools. Any chance you brought back his saddle and tack though?"

"Didn't get the chance," I said, settling into a chair as Wade dropped into the other.

He looked us over. "I reckon it didn't go so well for you either then?"

Wade answered as he leaned back in the chair to get comfortable. "We had the same sort of excitement as your deputies, but a lot more of it."

"Are the others...." Dan's voice drifted off as a look of concern crossed his face.

"We're all okay, except for a few minor injuries. Everyone is back at the hotel. But we had a run in with some more dinosaurs, some apes, and Jed's Indian friends," Wade rubbed his eyes wearily. "It's been a real fun couple of days."

Dan sighed and clasped his hands in his lap. "Jed, tell me you didn't stir the Shaynee up. That's the last thing we need to be dealing with."

"I didn't. They were mighty helpful." That was true enough, except for the visions. They didn't seem worth a hoot, especially considering how terrible the experience was getting them.

The Sheriff grunted and tilted his head back to stare down his nose at me. "You kill Otto yet?"

"Everyone seems to agree that I should, but no. Not yet," I leaned towards him, completely serious now. "Look Dan, we need to get everyone who isn't willing to fight out of here. And anyone outside of town needs to be pulled in. The apes are already on our side, and we came across tracks around town. They're scouting us. It's just a matter of time before they ride trikes down Main Street and start slaughtering us. We've got to get defenses in place. We need troops as well." I motioned towards Wade beside me, "He thinks he can get the Governor to send some."

Dan raised a hand. "Alright. First we need to-"

The door behind us slammed against the wall with a loud crash as it was violently kicked open.

In a flash, my chair was knocked backwards to the floor and my pistol pointed at the door. Dan's nephews came barging through, carrying Wesley between them. His feet dragged on the ground, his hands shackled in front of him. Blood trickled from a gash on his forehead and dripped small crimson splatters on the floor.

"We got him! We're gonna be famous!" Tom shouted triumphantly.

James waved a crumpled and stained Wanted poster with his free hand. "Two thousand dollars! Tom can get him a new horse! And I can get that shiny saddle I been wanting, with all the brass tacks and fancy stitching. We're gonna buy all kinds of shit. Hard candy and whiskey for everyone! What you gettin' with your cut, Uncle Dan?"

Then the pair noticed Wade and myself standing in front of the desk, and almost dropped my cuffed and beaten friend in surprise.

"Hey Mr. Wolverine, look who we caught!" Tom was wild-eyed and trembling with excitement, then he pointed a finger at me accusingly. "You can't use dynamite for nothin'! That tunnel was wide open and-"

"Shuddup! Both of you!" the Sheriff shouted and slammed his fist down on the desk.

The room went quiet.

Wesley raised his head and seeing me, he grinned weakly.

"Oh, hey Jed. How's it going?" he said painfully.

***

"What the hell?" I asked angrily while slamming my pistol back into the holster.

Wade crossed the room to look closely at Wesley's face. "Well... Look who it is."

"Who?" I seemed to be missing something that everyone else knew. The Wanted poster I saw a few days ago came to mind. Apparently, he was the poorly drawn man on the paper.

"John Wesley Gardner! He killed over fifty men!" Tom said excitedly, grinning from ear to ear. "And we got the sumbitch. That reward money is all ours!"

I recognized the name. I'd never had any personal dealings with the man, which explained why I didn't recognize him when we met. But I'd heard stories from those who had. As far as outlaws went, he wasn't a terrible human being. To an extent, he was even honorable, but he was a killer through and through. We had that in common.

"It was more like twenty men," Wesley sighed. "I'm not the boogeyman. Besides, they all deserved it. Mostly. A couple were accidents. Like that fellow snoring," he laughed darkly then winced in pain. "I shot through the hotel wall trying to scare him awake. If he hadn't been sleeping propped up, I wouldn't have killed him."

The deputies shoved him into the cell and tossed his hat in after him. Tom stepped back, covering Wesley with a pistol as James removed the shackles. They closed and locked the door, then turned back to Dan, looking very pleased with themselves.

Dan stayed in his chair the entire time, quietly watching. "Good job, boys. As satisfying as it is to remove this man from our town before he kills again, we have more pressing matters to discuss."

"Who said I was going to kill anyone?" Wesley protested as he lay down on the worn-out cell cot and gingerly touched his busted scalp.

"I figure it was only a matter of time. Now be quiet," Dan warned.

Wesley grunted in disagreement, but obliged.

***

It took an hour to get the Sheriff and his nephews up to snuff on the events of the past couple of days. By the time we wrapped it up, Dan was pacing back and forth across his office scowling.

"Well, this is bullshit," James said, kicking the wall. "If Jed had blown the tunnel up properly, we wouldn't have apes scouting town for an attack!"

Tom stood up. "And my horse wouldn't have had its neck snapped! That big monkey could have killed me!"

"Quiet!" Dan warned. "Both of you." He peered at his nephews from beneath a furrowed brow. "If I hear another word from you that ain't helping, I'm going to pistol whip you."

He spun back to Wade. "Do our friends from the Smithsonian have any answer as to why there is an opening in the mountain that goes to another prehistoric world?"

Wade shook his head. "They haven't a clue. It shouldn't be possible."

"Well, that's just lovely," he continued to pace, stepping around his sullen nephews as they leaned beside the cell with Wesley inside. "So not only do we need to warn the locals, but we also have to bring everyone in from the ranches and mines... Even with Jed's severed dinosaur head outside as proof, it's going to be difficult to convince everyone they are in danger," he grunted. "How are you two going to explain this to the Governor?"

"Same way as you, and if he doesn't believe us, we'll show him the bodies," Wade said casually as he stood and stretched his back.

Dan stopped pacing in front of the wall covered with Wanted posters and handwritten advertisements selling cattle and chickens. He stared, his face conveying a mixture of confusion and surprise. "Bodies? What bodies?"

Wade winked at me and I grinned back. We hadn't mentioned it yet on purpose. "Oh, just an ape and one of them raptor critters," I told him.

The deputies perked up, but fearful of their uncle's threat, remained silent.

"Now you tell me!" the Sheriff said accusingly. "I want to see them, where are they?"

"Outside in the wagon. I figured we'd need them to convince folks to take us seriously. Once we start showing the corpses off to people, the news ought to spread like wildfire after that. Wade can help with that since he's trying to start his own western show. It's good practice for him, just don't let him charge admission."

Wade stroked his mustache, chuckling. "That would stir up the excitement. But right now, keeping everyone alive is more important than profit. There'll be plenty of time for that later."

I kicked my feet down and stood, grabbing my hat off Dan's desk. "Any idea when the next train is leaving for Cheyenne? Sooner we get troops here the better."

"We'll also need to take the bodies with us. So, if we are going to play show and tell, now is the time," Wade added.

"Next train won't be until this evening. There should be plenty of time to catch a nap, some grub, and get cleaned up... after we scare the town silly." The Sheriff grabbed his hat before motioning towards his nephews. "C'mon boys, let's go look at these bodies."

The deputies followed us outside, muttering to each other. It sounded like they were talking about trying to buy the Bucket O' Blood saloon with the reward money for Wesley's capture. It was a shame, I genuinely liked the guy and most likely, he saved my life. We may have both been outlaws, but he had a reputation for killing men who didn't always deserve it while I only killed those who had it coming. His outlaw days were over, it was time to hang.

The wagon was a mess. The stable wasn't going to be happy when Wade returned it. But at least the mules survived unscathed. The rear wheel leaned outwards, a couple side boards were shattered, the back was torn from raptor's claws, and broken arrow shafts stuck out from where we'd snapped them off.

A little boy was clinging to the side and curiously poking the covered bodies with a crooked stick. Wade winked at him and jerked the canvas sheet back, revealing the bloodied ape and nearly decapitated dinosaur. The kid fell backwards off the cart, and I managed to grab him by the collar before he crashed to the ground. He shrugged free of my grasp and scampered away.

"Well, that's one way to spread the word," I muttered to myself as he sped off.

The deputies crowded in around us and I stepped out of the way, so they could see.

Dan whistled at the exposed bodies. "That is one big, ugly man-monkey."

"Told you, Uncle Dan! That's what killed Lucy!" Tom said. He reached out and shoved the hairy body. It didn't move.

"Lucy?" Wade asked.

"His horse," Dan explained, forgetting his pistol-whipping promise, and instead looking closer at the dinosaur. "That thing looks vicious as all get out. Where's the rest of its head?"

"I blew it off. But that's the raptor. Apes used them on us like attack dogs. Judging by the size of the cage I saw, they have a lot more of them."

I picked up one of its rear legs to show Dan the large claws. "Watch out for these critters. Skyla said they hunt in packs and they seem smart."

Dan grabbed the raptor's head by the feathers and raised it to inspect its jaws. "Ugly thing. What's with the feathers? Just seems wrong."

"Everything about the situation we are in is wrong," Wade chided.

Dan dropped the raptor's head and it landed with a wet, meaty thud.

I pulled the spear from the back of the wagon and handed it to him. He grunted as he took the weight. "You wouldn't believe how far they can throw these. In their valley, they were making piles of them. There was a big, solid white ape chucking them with unbelievable accuracy and distance. If you see him, kill him. He'd be an unholy terror in a fight."

The Sheriff hefted it up and down, judging the weight. "Strong indeed." He brought it closer to his face and peered at the tip. "Looks like that glassy volcanic rock out by the hot springs."

James took the spear from him, whistling. "Imagine this going through your belly. Dead man. Guaranteed."

"That's obsidian. They use it on their arrows as well." I pointed to one of the broken off arrow shafts sticking out of the wagon.

Dan stared at the bodies. "First things first, we tell the townsfolk then I'll send the deputies to warn those outside town to come in."

His nephews groaned at the assignment. "But… we might die," Tom protested. "Look at the size of that big monkey! And this!" He shook the spear at us with both hands.

"It's your duty. Do it. Or turn your badges in and get out of my sight," the Sheriff snapped at them while fixing them with a look that they cowered under. He may have seemed like an amicable fellow, but I'd seen him in war before. He wasn't someone to be trifled with and he wasn't about to let his nephews forget it.

"Yes, sir," James responded, tilting his head down in embarrassment.

"Tom?" Dan asked, taking a menacing step closer to the youngest of his nephews.

"Yes, sir," he copied his brother.

"Let the reward money be motivation for you to shoot fast and accurate. You can't spend it if you're dead," Wade suggested with a grin. "Besides, you two should be able to outrun any mounted apes on horseback."

Dan turned away from his nephews and back to me. "I'll wire the Governor tonight and tell him to expect you tomorrow. After we show these bodies off, we'll get them loaded on the train to go with you. I assume you are both going?"

I certainly didn't want to go to the Governor's Office as a wanted man. It was risky, even if unlikely anyone would recognize me. But I didn't see any way out of the situation without looking suspicious. "Yup," I said, trying to hide my reluctance. "But I think we should take Skyla with us, being from the Smithsonian, her word will carry weight." I glanced at Wade, hoping he wouldn't think this was a ploy to spend more time with the pretty scientist. It was, but I was also being truthful about how useful her connections could be. "What about Ashley?"

"I'll ask her to stay here. She's tough, but I think that knock on her head took a lot out of her," Wade replied thoughtfully. "I don't expect it will take us more than a day or two, and hopefully we will return with a trainload of soldiers."

The little boy from before turned the corner, tugging his mother down the street by the arm. He was jabbering excitedly while trying to pull her along as she protested.

"Looks like your audience has begun to arrive. I'll let the ladies know the plan and fetch some tickets for the train. Good luck with your show." I turned heel and walked away, leaving the four of them to deal with the coming crowd. I didn't envy their job of explaining what was going on and what was in the back of the wagon. There were going to be plenty of questions and concerns to answer for.

After buying our tickets, I visited the stables to let the hostler know I'd be back in a few days for my horse. I paid in advance to make sure Carbine was well taken care of and groomed daily. He deserved a few days off.

I stopped at the corral fence and he walked over to greet me. "I'll be gone for a couple days. Try to be good, boy." As I reached out to rub his muzzle, he snatched my hat and trotted away, triumphantly, before tossing it to the ground. Sometimes, I really didn't like my horse.

Slipping between the rails, I cautiously made my way to the hat, keeping a wary eye on the other horses. Last thing I needed was someone's ornery horse stomping me into the mud. The others eyed me suspiciously and gave me a wide berth. Carbine pranced around, tossing his head and mane in joy at pulling one over on me.

I dusted off my hat and tried to reshape where his teeth had smashed it. At least it didn't land in a mound of manure. Now I was looking forward to a few days without that ass of a horse.

Taking one more look at Carbine, I climbed out of the corral and walked quickly to the two-story hotel in the center of town.

***

Skyla was sitting at one of the tables with Ashley when I entered. The sharpshooter felt better, but thought the idea of rest sounded wonderful and she wished us a fine trip with minimal gunfire. Skyla said she would keep her company until we left for Cheyenne.

I figured both the bar and Sheriff's Office would be packed with fear, questions, rumors, and bold-faced lies. So instead I decided to lay low and out of sight in Wade's room. I managed to even get a few hours' sleep until light taps on the door woke me and it was time to go.

The train smoke was thick, and the station overflowing with nervous passengers and belongings. Word had spread quickly about the likelihood of an attack by an army of giant apes and extinct animals. Suddenly, a lot of folks decided they'd rather be someplace else. I spied the saloon girls, standing beside stacks of brightly colored luggage. The gap-toothed girl waved when she saw me, and I waved awkwardly back, hoping that Skyla wouldn't notice the association. The slob from the Government Land Office was there as well, but not his dog, Tripod.

Most of the people crowding onto the train were women and children, with a scattering of men mixed in. They were either family men, or the sort of man who had no skin in the game. Drifters, card players, and wanderers, they'd all move on to the next town with no care for what happens to this one. Local businessmen and ranchers weren't going to leave their livelihoods at risk without putting up a fight. The upside of this was that we could count on them to help defend the town.

The ape and dinosaur bodies had already been carefully wrapped and loaded on the train. We made our way to the last car, pushing through throngs of families saying goodbye to their husbands and fathers. We were traveling light, with only small bags and guns. All I had was my bedroll, with a clean shirt tucked into it, and a borrowed leather jacket from Wade. It was fringed, very fringed. For guns, I brought my rifle and pistol, leaving the sawed-off shotgun behind at the hotel with Ashley for safe keeping. Because you never knew when a gal might need a double-barreled shotgun. Wade brought his heavy Ballard rifle, old pistol, and one of the ape spears.

I was impressed that Skyla only brought one suitcase for herself. Being the gentleman that I was, I hauled the heavy case aboard while keeping my swearing to myself as I fought to get through the narrow doors to the passenger railcar.

Passenger cars this far west were the typical colonist sort. Spartan, usually with uncomfortable sleeping berths above wood bench seats. For this route, the sleeping holds had been removed to lighten the load on the train. Less weight meant less wasted coal and more cargo. Luckily for us commoners, cheap passenger cars meant cheap tickets. Even if it made the two-hundred-mile ride to Cheyenne less than comfortable.

Skyla found an empty seat and sat first, and I sat beside her. Wade joined a mother with her crying child in her lap in the bench in front of us. The long spear was wedged between the seat and the wall of the car.

After a moment, the little boy's sobbing stopped, and he pulled away from his mother and looked over the back of the seat. "Are the apes going to kill my daddy, mister?" he asked me, wiping tears from his face with a sleeve. The mother turned to see who he was addressing and gave me a sad, apologetic smile.

"Of course not." I pointed at Wade next to him and Skyla beside me. "We're getting soldiers to come help. Then we're going to kill all the apes." Tilting my head, I gave him a confident smile. "Tell you what, I'll get you a nice ape scalp. Just like what the Indians take from us."

"Really?" That excited him.

His mother glared and pulled him away from me. "You certainly will not! Johnny, don't you talk to that man again," she warned.

Skyla gave me a look of disgust. I winked at her so she'd know I was only fooling and hoping to distract the kid from his fears. Wade chuckled beside the kid.

Grinning mischievously, I leaned back in my seat. Skyla fidgeted beside me trying to get comfortable. Wade pulled his hat low and slid down in the seat to take a nap.

There was no chance at conversation as the locomotive's sharp whistle blasted steam while the engine was stoked, and smoke puffed from the stack. Large metal wheels spun, caught, then slipped, shrieking in protest before catching and slowly inching the train forward. At the front of the train someone was shoveling coal from the tender into the locomotive's firebox at a furious pace as we began to pull away from the train station. Small black cinders drifted around the cars as smoke billowed from the top of the engine's chimney. The train gained speed, and soon the steam engine settled into a steady chugging as we sped across the river, up the valley, and out onto the open plains.

Skyla looked outside the window and watched the scenery pass by.

Being near her always made me feel like the ugly boy in school sitting next to the prettiest girl in class. There was a mixture of excitement and nervousness that I tried not to show.

She noticed me looking at her and leaned over so we could talk somewhat privately. "Do you think I could learn to shoot? I mean, really shoot. When I shot that ape," she paused for a moment, swallowing hard as emotions threatened to boil up again, "that was the first time I ever fired that gun. I bought it on a whim before we left. I figured, you go west, you need a gun, and it was an awfully cute one."

My heart fluttered inside my chest. Everyone loves a girl who can shoot. "Of course." I pulled her empty derringer from my pocket. The mother dragged her little boy back as he leaned over to get a better look at it, glaring at me once more. I ignored them, and turned the nickel-plated gun over in my hands. With the pearl grips, it was a pretty gun, just not terribly useful.

"You did well with this, but it's a short-range kind of pistol. Good for up close work, but you want to have as much distance between you and an ape as possible." I tucked the small gun away. We would need to find more cartridges for it before the pistol would be of use to anyone. "Still, it's easy to conceal and carry, and every lady should have one. But since you are insisting on coming back to town after this trip, you'll need something more powerful. I'll see what we can scrounge up in Cheyenne."

"Thank you! But, if you don't mind me asking, how come you only carry one pistol? You seem like the sort who would wear two."

I laughed, "That's either for show, dime novels, or gunslingers. I've practiced with my left hand in case my right is ever disabled, but I've never felt a need for two before, so I just carry the one."

"Are you saying that you're no dime novel hero?" she teased with a sly smile.

Shaking my head, I pointed at my hat resting on my knee. "Nope, and that's why I don't wear a white hat."

She took my beat up brown hat and flipped it over, studying the sweat band where I'd written my name. Grinning, she put the hat on and tilted it low over her eyes. She was dreadfully cute. "If heroes wear white hats and villains wear black hats, what does it mean when a man wears brown?"

"Reckon it means they are of dubious morals." Which was certainly the truth when it came to me.

She laughed and handed it back before patting her hair for any strays to tuck back in place. Smiling, I ran my hands along the braided cord of the hat band and tried not to think of my past. Dubious was the right word for it. I leaned heavily to the good side, but I'd also crossed the line between legal and illegal if I felt it was necessary. Sometimes people just needed to be shot, regardless of what the law had to say about it.

We were quiet for a while as the train steamed across the prairie. Both of us stared silently at the endless grass dotted with small stands of trees, shrubs, and occasional outcroppings of rocks that sprung from the ground. The little boy in front of us had fallen asleep, a thin stream of drool trickled onto his mother's shoulder. Occasionally I heard her sniffle, no doubt from leaving a husband and home behind.

Skyla touched my knee gently to get my attention.

"Can I ask you something? You don't have to answer if you don't want to," she said in a quiet voice, so low I almost didn't hear her.

"You want to know about the scars," I stated simply. It was a question I'd been expecting.

"Only if you want to tell me."

The vision in the sweat lodge had brought the memory back to me with startling clarity, some details I had forgotten, while others were burned in the depths of my soul forever. I'd only told a handful of people what happened to me, and there were even fewer of them who were still alive.

I told her though, after reliving the terror, anger, and pain of that distant night, it felt cleansing. She listened without question, and I watched her reaction as I spoke. Her eyes reddened as she blinked back tears, and her face paled when I told of the hanging and my whipping. It felt good to share, as though a weight was being lifted from my soul. But watching her dab a handkerchief against the tears brimming in her eyes, I felt guilty for making her upset.

She sniffed and sat quietly for a moment, collecting herself before asking, "Did they ever catch the men who did it?"

I hesitated, not wanting to say too much. "No. The carpet baggers that came from the north treated us like second rate citizens. Anyone sympathetic to us wasn't about to go searching for rogue Union soldiers when the streets were covered with them just itching to punish former Confederates. The Yankees…" I glanced at her, "No offense." She nodded for me to continue. "Well, they bought up everything cheap from those the war ruined, kicked out our elected officials and appointed their own kind. If anyone had been caught, it would have been brushed aside and a court would have ruled in favor of the Union. Winners write the rules and losers knuckle under them."

That was a half lie. I found most of them, then I killed them. All except their leader. No one knew his name. He only went by his rank the entire time he led them.

"Did you ever find out what happened to your friend, Cato?"

"Never saw him again." I swallowed hard, remembering his dark face and bright smile. He'd been a happy kid and good friend. There was no telling what happened to him. Blacks were treated with scorn before the war, afterwards there was a lot of animosity towards newly freed slaves. With the rise of the Ku Klux Klan, things became even worse for them. Most likely, like the officer I never found, he was long dead.

We were quiet for a while and Skyla began to nod off. I watched with amusement as her head dipped then jerk back upright as she fought off sleep, only to nod again. After several minutes, she gave in and her breathing deepened.

I closed my eyes and thought of the red-bearded Union Officer who had me whipped within an inch of my life. It was hard to feel at peace with my past when he may still be out there. I fell asleep and dreamt of his death at my hands.

***

It was dark when the train whistled its arrival to the station in Cheyenne and woke the slumbering passengers and refugees. I stretched and braced myself as the train car slowed, then jostled suddenly as brakes clamped onto the steel wheels and the high shrill of steel rubbing on steel split the air.

Skyla sat up, brushing her hair back and straightening her clothes. The mother whisked her son away without a word but giving me the stink eye as they stepped past Wade. Our wolverine slayer yawned and wiped the corners of his mouth before straightening his hat and reaching to untangle the spear from where it lay jammed against the car wall. It took both of us to work the nine-foot-long weapon free.

Boarding the train had been bad enough, but disembarking in the dead of night was far worse. It was chaos around us as the other passengers disembarked. Parents herded children while struggling to carry bags and sacks off the platform. Men swore and pushed, trying to keep their families together or pushing to get through the crowd. Kids cried, as they always do. It was an awful commotion.

We carried our belongings through the throngs of people packed along the station boardwalk, attempting to stay together as best we could. Having broad shoulders helped as I led the way through the crowd. On the far side of the platform I caught a glimpse of Oscar shoving his way through, our eyes locked for a moment before he turned away and disappeared.

Skyla left with Wade to secure lodging at the Elmont Hotel, a personal favorite of the famed westerner to stay at when he was in town. Meanwhile, I fought through the crowd to reach the station office. After throwing a few less elbows than needed, and a few carefully calculated stomps on people's toes to get them to move, I managed to work my way to the attendant. With lots of shouting to be overheard over the confusion, we finally came to an agreement on the bodies being stored overnight and brought to the Governor's Office in the morning. The conversation moved along nicely once I mentioned the Governor would be footing the bill. It was an assumption that might bite me later, but it certainly helped speed things along.

As I made my way to the hotel, attempting to follow the directions given to me by the attendant, I passed a gun store and promised myself to go back in the morning. Money needed to be saved to rebuild the barn. But with an army of apes coming through the tunnel, survival took priority. That meant I needed a better rifle. My Sharps was hard-hitting, but the rate of fire was painfully slow. Dying because I couldn't shoot fast enough would be an embarrassing way to go.

The Elmont Hotel was located on the corner where Main Street intersected Second Street. Beautifully built, two stories tall, with a wraparound porch and balcony. The rails were painted a dark red to match the brick that covered the sides while the name was painted in large white letters below the roof edge.

Wade was leaning against the brick wall, nonchalantly waiting, and I followed him inside as he held the door open.

The hotel was modest in decoration, but far nicer than anything I'd ever stayed in. A bar ran along the far wall with a few scattered tables, and a clerk's desk was to our immediate right. In the center of the room were wide stairs that rose to the second floor. Gas lamps lit the room, and plush red chairs were placed around a large fireplace that had wood stacked in it, but no flame. A low murmur came from the few people still nursing beers and eating at this hour. A soft melody I didn't recognize drifted across the room from a neatly dressed piano player in the corner.

I'd have to mind my manners. I suspected this wasn't the sort of place that appreciated violence in their establishment.

"Managed to get us a pair of rooms. We're sharing one. Skyla is in the room beside us... 104, in case you need to know," Wade watched for a reaction.

I narrowed my eyes at him, "Why would I need to know that?"

"Just a thought. I've seen the way you look at her and she looks at you. But don't worry, I know she's a proper lady, while you are something of a gentleman."

"It's not like that," I protested weakly.

"Of course it is," he said sarcastically as he dangled one of our room keys in front of me. "Now if you will excuse me, I think I'll hang around the bar for a bit and try to catch up on the latest gossip. Unless you care to join me?"

"Not tonight. I'm beat." I took the key and read the wooden carved tag. Room 105. "I'm going to get some shut eye."

"See you in the morning," Wade said over a shoulder as he worked his way towards the bar.

I climbed the stairs and walked along the halls, noting the numbered doors and searching for our room. I finally found it at the end, beside a glass window that overlooked the lamp lit street below.

I looked at the door beside ours. Carefully painted in white stenciled letters, Room 104. I shoved the key in my room's lock before looking at Skyla's door again. The temptation to knock on her door was strong. Resisting the urge, I opened the door to my room and stepped inside, quickly closing the door behind me.

Stripping down, I placed my boots beside the bed and slipped the Colt Peacemaker beneath my pillow. There was something about Skyla. Something that drew me towards her. She was beautiful, but it wasn't just that. There was an indescribable quality to her that I found irresistible no matter how much my brain tried to tell me I shouldn't get attached. She was an educated paleontologist from the east, I was a former outlaw turned small time rancher.

For a long time, I stared at the ceiling and thought about what an idiot I was.

***

The next morning, armed with Wade's knowledge of the town, we followed the famed wolverine slayer to the Governor's residence. Being polite, we left our rifles in the hotel room. Being smart, we wore our pistols. The spear came along as well.

I'd never been to Cheyenne before, and in the light of day I realized just how big the territorial capital was. The city was a major hub for commerce and railroads in the west, sending trains full of goods and people in each direction. Where Granite Falls had hundreds of citizens, Cheyenne had thousands. Our small group of refugees was nothing. The city soaked them up and scattered them amongst its own inhabitants without batting an eye.

Per my arrangement with the train station attendant, a wagon loaded with the wrapped bodies was waiting for us in front of the two-story building that made up the Governor's Office and residence. The driver sitting behind the team of horses was eyeing the mounds in the back suspiciously.

"You sneak a peek yet?" I asked as we walked up beside him.

He spun about, surprised, and twitched slightly. "No, sir! Of course not." His eyes darted to Skyla then away. He took his hat off and looked at his boots resting on the front board. With a voice so low we could barely hear him, he spoke, "Morning, miss."

"Good morning!" she said cheerfully and gave him a bright smile. He nodded bashfully, but refused to make eye contact.

I knew the feeling. Pretty girls make me uneasy also. But I was starting to get comfortable around this one.

"Right. Well, don't. You'll find out soon enough." Wade laid a few coins on the seat next to him. "This is for your trouble, and we would appreciate it greatly if you would keep folks away from the cargo until the Governor has a look at it first."

The driver bobbed his head up and down as he placed a hand over the currency and dragged it to him. "Yes, sir. Thank you, sir."

We stepped onto the walk and Wade slammed the brass door knocker against the thick wooden door several times. He carefully groomed his mustache as we waited for a response. Skyla fidgeted nervously, and I tried to act like I was comfortable. I've never been a fan of politicians. As I learned decades ago with the Union raiders, anyone with power over you should never be trusted. After a few moments, a butler in an immaculate black suit and tie opened the door.

"Yes?"

"I'm Wolverine Wade Mackin, my associates here are Skyla Stratten from the Smithsonian Institute, and Jedidiah Smith. He's…" Wade hesitated, unsure of how to introduce me, "a rancher. The Governor should be expecting us."

Wolverine shrugged at me apologetically and I gave him a sideways grin; it wasn't a bad title by any means and I'd been called far worse.

"Yes, Mr. Mackin. If you and your companions would please follow me." He stepped back with a white gloved hand extended to allow us entry into the foyer. Wade carefully maneuvered the spear through the doorway without scraping it against anything, and if the butler was bothered by us being armed, he didn't voice any concern. I suspect it had to do with Wade's reputation more than acceptance of armed citizens in an elected official's office. They usually frowned on that sort of thing.

The butler led us up a set of stairs and down a hallway filled with plaques, western paintings, and several mounted buffalo skulls. Stopping before a set of double doors, the butler knocked, waited for a muffled reply from inside, then pushed them open.

The doors opened into a large room with a large desk in the center covered in clutter and a side by side shotgun casually leaned against it. Behind the desk was a bleached white elk skull mounted on the wall with large forked antlers rising above. Off to the side was a long table in front of a row of windows. Maps of Wyoming and neighboring territories were scattered across the table amidst sheet papers covered in notes and sketches. A grizzly hide rug was spread on the floor with plush chairs staged around it. Bright blue drapes were pulled back from the tall glass windows, exposing the room to morning sunlight. Beside us, on either side of the doorway were large bookshelves filled with leather bound volumes and decorated with the occasional photograph and oddity. I recognized a Cheyenne bow and arrows and a small intricately carved wooden model train like the one we rode in on last night.

The Governor stood as the butler stepped out of the room and gently closed the door behind us. Tall and slender, with a white mustache that matched his neatly combed over hair, he wore a dark suit and gray tie. He looked exhausted and there were dark bags under his eyes.

"Wolverine Wade! What in the blue blazes is going on? A train load of refugees from Granite Falls comes in last night, spreading rumors of savage monkeys and big feathered lizards eating children while they sleep. Of course, a bunch of them came straight here and began hammering on my door, demanding that I do something about it. If it hadn't been for the Sheriff's telegram, I'd have no idea what they were talking about." He took a deep breath and with a calmer voice asked, "So, how have you been?"

Wade laughed and leaned the spear against a bookshelf before crossing the room to shake the Governor's hand. "None too shabby, William! Been an eventful past few days, but the rumors have been only slightly exaggerated. But first, I have to ask, how's the progress towards statehood?"

"A rather long and tiring process, I'm afraid. I've been corresponding with the new President Cleveland, and so far, it still doesn't look promising," he shrugged. "But I'll keep at it."

"Well I hope it happens; the United States of America could use a state of Wyoming. If anything, for the men of stout body and mind it produces. Speaking of which, I heard of your recent exploits."

"Oh that. Yes. Montana thought they could claim Yellowstone. HA!" He laughed harshly, and picking up a map off the table, shook it towards us. "Those northern fools tried and failed. I personally went and staked it for us. Yellowstone is Wyoming Territories and always will be. Old Faithful is faithful because we are," he paused, "and there is my next campaign slogan." He chuckled at his own cleverness. "Who is this young lady?" he asked, turning to Skyla.

Wade introduced her. "Governor Hardy, I'd like you to meet Ms. Skyla Stratten. She's a paleontologist from the Smithsonian Institute. She's here to help us figure out what we are dealing with."

"Good gracious, what is a true lady... especially an educated one, doing out here with this ruffian?" He took her hand and gently caressed his lips over her knuckles.

"Apparently making a true mistake, Governor," she smiled coyly and played along.

"Understandable, we all make them. But it is an honor, my dear!" He turned towards me. "And who is this gentleman?"

Wade spoke before I could introduce myself. "This is Jedidiah Smith. He's the rancher outside of Granite Falls who first came across these creatures. Of everyone, he's got the most experience with the apes and the dinosaurs."

"Only because they tried to eat me first," I explained.

"Good, I'm sick of wild rumors. I want to hear firsthand accounts of what we are dealing with. Each rumor I heard last night was more ridiculous than the last, but it appears there may be a kernel of truth amongst them." He shook my hand firmly while looking me in the eye before turning back to the others. "Where do we start?"

Skyla surprised me by speaking up first. "Out of curiosity, how do you and Wade know each other?"

Wade looked a bit put off. "Well, I'm rather famous, Skyla."

Governor Hardy laughed. "He teases, Ms. Stratten. Before he was Wolverine Wade Mackin, he was Wet Behind the Ears Mackin and we hunted buffalo together for a time."

Wade harrumphed and crossed his arms. "Wet behind the ears, eh? As I recall, I saved you from an Indian attack, two days after you met me, old timer."

"Saved is stretching the truth a bit... and old timer?" he scoffed. "Why I see more than a few grays in your hair. And don't think for a moment that choking a wolverine to death with your bare hands as a young man means you can take this old geezer!" the Governor raised his voice, pretending to be offended.

I watched the entire exchange humorously as Skyla, having gotten more than she asked for, tried to direct the conversation back towards the deadly threat at hand. "Gentlemen, please," she waited as the old acquaintances finally quieted down and listened to her. "Mr. Hardy, what do you know about dinosaurs?"

"Hmm. Not much. There have been a few dig sites popping up. Out of curiosity, I visited one to see what the fuss was about once," he scowled. "It was just a bunch of rocks, with a few giant bones mixed in."

Skyla nodded at his description of fossils. "Mr. Hardy-"

"Please, Skyla, call me William."

"William. I can assure you the rumors are correct. Dinosaurs aren't extinct. We've seen them."

The Governor leaned back against his desk and crossed his arms. "Not extinct. Okay. But what sort of dinosaurs are they?"

"All sorts it seems, carnivores and herbivores alike," Skyla said as she settled into a large armchair draped with a gray wolf pelt. "First one Jed killed was an Allosaurus. That was a big predator," she looked at me, "maybe... 12 feet long and nine feet tall?" I nodded an affirmation.

The Governor gave me a look that showed he was suitably impressed.

I figured it was my turn to speak and describe everything I'd seen so far. "Since then we've seen others, ranging in size from some with long tall necks, probably thirty feet tall, down to these little colorful ones about the size of a sheep. But dinosaurs aren't the only threat we have to contend with; there are giant apes also. Big, hairy, mean, strong as an ox, and smart too. They ride horned dinosaurs that are twice as large as a wagon, and use the feathered lizards you heard about like attack dogs." I gestured towards the spear. "Technologically speaking, they are about the same as Indians. Stone age level. Clubs, axes, spears, bows. But there are hundreds of apes, all warriors. A lot of females amongst them, but no little ones… it was an army and now they have scouts watching our town."

I watched the Governor for his reaction, it was a lot of details to take in all at once. He appeared to be a smart fellow, and behind his scowling face, you could see wheels turning as he weighed the implications of what I said. Picking up the spear, he rotated the shaft while staring at the lashing work on the chipped obsidian point. He lay the spear across his desk before gesturing towards the seats around the grizzly rug. "Please, have a seat."

As we did, he lifted a small wooden box from his desk and brought it over. Flipping the lid open, he asked, "After what you said, I think I could use a cigar while we get down to brass tacks on how to handle this situation." He held the box out towards us.

Wade and I both accepted while Skyla politely declined. I rolled the thick round cigar in my fingers; it'd been a long time since I'd smoked one. Holding it under my nose I sniffed the rich tobacco. These were the good ones.

Dropping the box onto the desk, Governor William Hardy took one for himself and flipped the lid shut. Scooping up a small trash bin from under his desk, we bit the ends off the cigars and spat them into the container.

After copying us, the slender, silver haired leader of the Wyoming Territory sat in one of the chairs across from us. Pulling out a box of matches, the Governor struck one and touched it to the tip of the cigar, gently puffing as the dried tobacco caught and smoldered into a large red ember.

Blowing a thick mouthful of smoke towards the ceiling, he leaned forward and passed the matches over before ordering us, "Tell me everything."

***

By the time each of us finished putting the story together, the Governor looked both astonished and worried. He sucked the cigar down

148

to a nub at a rapid pace as he grew more agitated. As I savored mine, he ground his out and thumped it into the trash bin. Then he lit another and was now pacing across the room with the smoldering tobacco forgotten in his hand.

He stopped in front of the windows, with his back to us as he surveyed the street below. "I'll send troops to Granite Falls to bolster the defenses. But with only three Regiments to cover the entire territory, they're stretched thin and chasing outlaws and Indian renegades all over," he sighed and turned back to us. "That means there is good news and bad news. The good news is I have a single platoon I can send. The bad news is that will only give you about forty men."

Wade began to protest, and William held a hand up to stop him. "I know it's not enough. Especially facing several hundred monkeys on the backs of these giant trikes. But truth of the matter is, we're lucky to have this platoon available and the only reason you're getting them is because their officer is currently confined to the brig for the next week. Otherwise they'd be somewhere else as well. But we'll let him out and dispatch them to your town today."

I raised an eyebrow at that. A drunk or fool in the heat of battle would not be helpful to our cause.

He noticed our questioning looks. "Don't worry, he's a pretty good fellow, just Irish. He got drunk, got in a brawl, and kicked another officer in the groin. From what I gather, the Colonel deserved it. So, you're getting a scrapper. It will take a while to recall more men from the field and send your way. You'll just have to hold out as long as possible. Wade, would you mind holding up the civilian end of this in Granite Falls?"

"Yes, sir. I know the Sheriff there well. But we lack firepower, sir. These apes are nothing to scoff at, but the trikes soak up a lot of lead before stopping. I'm not sure how many men will stay to help defend the town, we'll find out when we return. But without some heavy weapons and more troops, we won't be able to stave off a heavy attack."

"And we can't just abandon the town either. Very well." William set his burnt-out cigar in an ash tray, bent over his desk, quickly wrote on a piece of paper and handed it to me. "Use this at Carson's store, he may be able to scrounge some useful weapons for you. As for troops, I'll send for the Lieutenant and get them moving."

"Where's this Carson's place?" I asked.

"Carson's the owner, he named it 'Liberty Arms', but we tend to refer to it by his name."

That was the name of the gun store I saw last night. I looked at the neatly lettered script on his offices letterhead that he gave me.

"His story sounds outrageous, but I assure you it is not. Give this man what he needs and bill me."

The Governor's name was signed in a scribble at the bottom.

Oh, hell yes. A blank check.

"I know Carson well. Tell him hello for me," Wade said as he blew a puff of smoke towards the ceiling and looked sadly at the short nub that remained of his cigar.

Skyla wrinkled her brow thoughtfully as she leaned forward in the wolf pelt draped chair. "Is there anyone else, Governor, who can help?"

"You're welcome to ask around for any volunteers, I'll send the word out also that I'll pay well, maybe we'll get lucky." He looked hard at us. "But we need to end this as quickly as possible, with as little bloodshed and destruction possible. The last Indian War nearly bankrupted this territory and killed hundreds of Indians and whites; we don't need another," he paused. "Come to think of it, I may know a man who would be interested in joining you. He's a powerful and influential man of strict morals, well-traveled, educated, and a renowned big game hunter. And I'd be willing to bet my bottom dollar that he'd jump at the chance to join you."

"Who?" Skyla asked.

The Governor gave her a sly smile. "Come back tomorrow morning; if he's willing, he'll be here." The smile turned into a frown. "One more thing; the owner of the East-West Railroad is in town to keep an eye on the unrest in Rock Springs. The Chinese are protesting pay and conditions again. His name is Rayden White. I'll see if he will meet with us in the morning as well. He's not a very pleasant man, but he won't be happy if we lose Granite Falls and all of the import and exports it gives his business." He rubbed his hands together quickly. "Now, how about we walk downstairs and take a look at these bodies you brought?"

I spoke up, "You all go ahead. I'm going to head over to Carson's and see what he can do for us. I'll meet you back at the hotel when I'm done." The blank check was burning a hole in my pocket. And Skyla and Wade could talk about the corpses in the wagon as easily as I could.

"That's fine with me," Skyla said. Wade agreed and after shaking hands with the Governor, I left.

***

After getting directions from the Governor's butler, it took me twenty minutes and several wrong turns to find Carson's store. It was a large building, two stories tall, with wrought iron bars over the windows. If it hadn't been for 'Liberty Arms - Purveyors of Fine Arms and Ammunitions' in large white lettering over the thick slap board siding, I'd have thought this building was a jail.

The door was open, so I stepped out of the heat and into the cool shade of the store.

Guns lined the far wall behind a counter, between us were racks of leather gear and clothing. It wasn't quite a trading store, more like a gun store that offered some odds and ends for added income. The walls along the side of the room were decorated with stuffed mounts of deer, elk, antelope, and a lone bighorn sheep. A large grizzly bear rose on hind feet next to the door, greeting visitors with paws raised and fangs bared in a silent roar. A moose skull with massive antlers stretched across the wall, and beneath it was racks of rifles.

Behind the counter stood a tall, well-built man with dark hair that was graying and receding. He had high cheekbones with a mustache that ran into his neatly trimmed goatee. Dressed in a black suit with a dark gray vest underneath, he wore a holstered pistol on his right side, the butt turned forward for a cavalry draw. Altogether, he cut a rather imposing figure.

I only glanced at the jeans and shirts as I made my way along the low shelves. My clothing had been taking a beating lately, but the only thing on my mind was firepower.

The counter was cluttered with several disassembled guns, opened boxes of ammo, and bottles of gun oil. An old lightly rusted Beaumont-Adams revolver lay stripped apart on a rag with the cylinder missing and a set of small files beside it. The imposing man spoke in greeting, "I'm Carson Skinner, owner and operator of Liberty Arms. What can I do for you?"

He didn't offer to shake hands, and his voice carried a southern twang that reminded me of my youth in South Carolina. He also spoke with a sense of authority from someone who was used to giving orders and being listened to.

"Mr. Skinner, I'm Jed Smith. Governor Hardy sent me here to procure some weaponry." As I slipped the note out of my vest, I saw his eye twitch as he watched the movements of my hand closely. Apparently, he was not a trusting man. Moving slower, I put the folded note on the counter and slid it to him.

Carson unfolded the paper and read it. Then he frowned at me. "I've done some business with the Governor before. He always pays."

"Good to hear. I was also told to tell you that Wolverine Wade Mackin sends his regards."

His frown turned into a crooked grin and his cold demeanor was immediately friendlier. "Wolverine Wade! How is that rascal? I hear he's working on starting his own show now?"

"He is indeed, and he is well." I drummed my fingers on the countertop, dreading telling my story again. I felt like every day I was repeating it to someone and trying to convince them I wasn't loco. Taking a deep breath, I pushed forward nonetheless, "Mr. Skinner, we have something of a unique problem in Granite Falls."

The tall man adjusted the pistol at his waist, leaned forward against the counter, and spoke in a low conspiring tone. "Yes, you do. Because, if the rumors are accurate, I hear it involves giant apes and prehistoric monsters."

***

Once again, for the second time in the same day, I told the story in abbreviated fashion from beginning to end. Carson listened, his fingers steepled beneath his chin, forehead burrowed in concentration. He had a few questions, often on details I forgot to expand upon.

"It sounds as if you are in for a hell of a battle. I believe I have a few things that may be of service and it sounds like you could use all the firepower you can get. I'll also send a couple crates of surplus army rifles. Nothing fancy. I just happen to have a bunch of old Trapdoor Springfields I need to get rid of," he chuckled. "I'll send them on the train with you and make a nice profit from what I charge the Governor. So, let's get you set up. Is there anything in particular you need?"

I pulled Skyla's derringer from my pocket and slid it over the counter to him.

"How about we start with a dozen rounds for this?"

Picking the diminutive pistol up, he guffawed and opened the hinged barrels to inspect the empty chambers. "It's a lovely little gun. But you'll need something a mite bigger for what you are up against."

"It's for our scientist from the Smithsonian. She used it on an ape to good effect, but didn't have any extra rounds."

"She sounds like a keeper. I'll get you a box of cartridges for the pea shooter. But I'd suggest something a little more powerful for her."

"Agreed. Any recommendations?"

Carson walked to the far end of the counter and rummaged around under it. I could hear him muttering to himself as he searched, along with the sound of boxes being shuffled about. After a moment, he straightened and carried over a small wooden box stamped Merwin-Hulbert across the top in black ink.

He folded the lid back on its hinge. The box was lined with red velvet. Inside was a short barrel, nickel plated revolver with checkered black grips, and a second, longer barrel lying beside it.

"This is the latest model Pocket Revolver. The extra barrel is for when you aren't worried about concealment and want a little more uumpff." He plucked the pistol out of the box and spun it around in his large hands. "A unique pistol. One that is easily concealable for a lady who likes to stay discrete but well-armed."

"That should do just the trick, thank you."

Wiping any oils from his hands off the gun with a cloth, Carson placed the pistol back inside the box and pushed it aside. Leaning across the counter, he looked down at my gun belt. "You're wearing a Colt Peacemaker. What's the chambering?"

".45 Colt."

"May I see it?"

Drawing the pistol, I passed it to him, butt first.

He turned it around, inspecting the blued gun. Half-cocking the hammer, he opened the cylinder gate. Tilting the barrel upwards, he rotated the cylinder, carefully dumping cartridges onto the counter.

I stopped a couple from rolling onto the floor with the edge of my hand and pushed them together into a small pile.

He spun the cylinder gently making sure all the chambers were empty. Closing the gate, he thumbed the hammer back and dry fired it towards the floor. He did this several times.

"Hmmm..." He stroked the ends of his mustache. "I think we can do better."

"Well, I like mine," I protested weakly, but he ignored me. Mine had some sentential value to it and I wasn't keen on parting with the pistol. But I followed him down the counter, and we stopped in front of a large display case. It contained a dozen pistols, from Colts and Remington's to Smith and Wesson's. He sat my pistol on the counter and pulled out an identical Colt Peacemaker.

"Give this one a try."

I looked at the matching gun suspiciously. "Why? Is there something wrong with mine?"

"Other than needing a little tuning, no. But I was in the cavalry during the war, and the fastest reload is a second gun."

I didn't ask which side he fought for; out here that was considered socially unacceptable. A lot of veterans from both sides headed west after the war to start over. The common saying was you couldn't shake a juniper tree without at least a couple veterans falling out.

Picking up the gun and carefully dry firing it, I thought back to the wagon chase and borrowing Wade's revolver. The trigger on this pistol also broke cleaner than mine. "There've been a few times I could have used another one," I admitted.

"Then it's yours. I've got a holster back here for it." He ducked below the counter and rummaged around again, this time coming up with a dark tan leather holster. "This one won't match your other, but let's see your belt and give it a try."

I unbuckled my gun belt and laid it on the counter. He slid the bowie knife sheath towards the back, then slipped the holster onto the left side. I wrapped it back around my waist and he handed both guns to me. I dropped them into their mismatched holsters and they balanced each other nicely.

Drawing the left-handed pistol several times, I tried to get a feel for it. My left-hand draw was significantly slower than the right from lack of familiarity. But I had at least regularly practiced firing left-handed, so I could hit what I aimed at. Mostly.

"Practice that enough and you'll pick up speed. But it will take a lot of trigger pulling to make you accurate with it." He sucked his teeth as he looked me over. "What are you using for a long gun?"

"Sharps repeater, my Winchester burned in the barn." I watched his face for a reaction. The Sharps was a Union issued rifle and most likely had slayed some Confederates at some point in the past. I wasn't sure if he was a gray hat or not, because even with his southern twang, Carson Skinner could have fought on the other side. But while the War Between the States ended twenty years ago, bad blood ran deep, and some grudges never end. The scars on my back were a constant reminder of that.

Carson didn't bat an eye. "Good rifle, but outdated and slow. You need something newer, better." He walked along the racks of rifles hanging on the wall, stopping occasionally to look at one before shaking his head and moving past it.

There were plenty of perfectly good rifles I could see: Winchesters, Sharps, even a Ballard rifle like Wade's. Any of them would work fine for me, so long as it was a repeater.

Apparently, none of them pleased Carson.

Reaching the end of the rack, he turned around with a thoughtful look on his face. "Back in a minute." He disappeared into the back room, and returned with a long wooden box and a bulging sack of what I assumed was ammunition.

He managed to move aside enough gun parts that he could fit the box and sack on the counter. The case was rifle length, unadorned and plain, with no markings or stampings, only a brass lock and hinges. It was a very unassuming wooden box.

"What's in it?"

"Something special," Carson gave me a wink.

Well, that was interesting. "Do tell," I could feel myself getting excited.

"The new, unreleased, Winchester Model 1886."

"Model 1886?" I was shocked. "Where'd you get it?"

"Friend of mine named John Moses Browning. He sold his designs patent to Winchester, and they built several prototypes for John to inspect before it went into production. One of them," he tapped the case, "he sent to me. Let's just say, based off this gun, I bought a lot of stock in Winchester." Grinning widely, he handed me a small metal ring with a single brass key. "You're going to love it."

I unlocked the case and flipped the top back, revealing the latest design of the most renowned gun inventor in the world.

Winchester must have gone all out on these samples. This one had a stock and forearm carved from two matching pieces of black walnut heartwood. The gun's action and lever were case hardened, and the barrel and full-length magazine tube were a deep blue. It had a Lyman's tang rear sight folded down and an ivory beaded front sight. Imprinted on the lower tang was the serial number, 00002. This was more than a gun, it was a work of art.

"John kept number one, but gave me number two. Which I am now passing to you."

"I can't... this is..." I stammered in protest.

"No. Take it, you need it more than I do. Especially in the caliber it's chambered in."

Rotating the rifle, I looked at the stamping on the barrel. I squinted to make sure I was seeing it right. ".45-70!" I exclaimed, unbelieving. That was a mighty big powerful bullet for a lever action.

"Yes, sir. It's been a goal of Winchester for a long time to get that cartridge into a solid repeating rifle, and Browning delivered. He sent along a few thousand rounds for testing and I've plenty left over," he gestured towards the heavy lumpy sack he had lain on the counter. "This rifle has surpassed all my expectations. It's perfect for you. It will give you a heavy, hard hitting round, at high velocity, with eight rounds in the tube. And it's stout enough to take down a grizzly or moose. I figure it's the best we can do with your giant ape problem."

I racked the action several times, and practiced bringing it up to my shoulder quickly. It was heavier than my old rifle, by two pounds I guessed. The straight grip, crescent stock fit snug into my shoulder and the sights aligned perfectly. I squeezed the trigger. It was clean and crisp.

"Thank you, Carson. I don't know how I could ever repay you," I told him sincerely. Without a doubt, this was the nicest thing anyone had ever given me or I'd taken off a corpse.

He waved a hand dismissively. "Just don't get killed and we'll consider the debt paid." He tossed several boxes of pistol ammo into the heavy sack of rifle cartridges and hefted it over his shoulder. "Now, what do you say we get my buckboard, and get out of town for a bit to try them out?"

I felt a large grin stretch across my face.

***

The sun was setting by the time we came back to town and I walked to the hotel.

After half a day of shooting, I reeked of burnt gun powder, sweat, and manliness. My entire body felt like it had taken a pounding and my hands were sore from working the doubled pistols. My old Colt was left behind at the store with its holster for a trigger adjustment and the new rifle to be fitted to a scabbard. Carson mustn't sleep, as he promised to have both finished by tomorrow morning. The cased Merwin-Hulbert pistol stayed as well, and I promised to bring Skyla in to try it out before we left.

Wade was at the hotel lobby bar, drink in hand, talking to a pair of men. One of them, short and thin in a striped suit, carried a folded newspaper under his arm while the other wore a long black duster and hat even though he was inside. Noticing me entering the building, Wade waved me over.

"Gentlemen, may I introduce Jedidiah Huckleberry Smith. The famed slayer of the Allosaurus."

The man in the suit shook my hand excitedly. The newspaper was pulled from under his arm and waved in my face. On the cover was a picture of the Allosaurus head in front of the Sheriff's Office under the caption, "RANCHER SLAYS PREHISTORIC BEAST!"

"It sure is a pleasure to meet you, Mr. Smith! I'm Cheyenne's Mayor, John Teehorn." His face was a ruddy red color, and he had the look and slur of an alcoholic who was well into his cups already. He motioned to the man in the slicker, distaste apparent as he introduced his companion. "This is the local Sheriff. Beauford Johnson."

The Sheriff flicked back his duster to expose the tin star and holstered pistol while frowning at me, his black mustache dropping with the ends of his thin lips. His eyes were hard and cruel. A large wad of tobacco shifted in his cheek as he spoke. "You look familiar."

"Reckon I just have one of those faces," I told him, putting a carefree smile on my face that I didn't feel. It was never good when law enforcement thought you looked familiar, especially when you're guilty as hell of dozens of crimes stretching almost two decades.

"Uh-huh," he spat a stream of the brown dip spit onto the polished floorboards of the hotel. The bartender glared across the room and a lady in an evening dress seated nearby wrinkled her nose in disgust. "I'll be keeping an eye on you," he growled.

I felt my fingers twitch towards my pistol. If this man dug into my past, I'd have to kill him. That was okay with me, he made my skin crawl, and I doubted he'd be missed or mourned.

Casually, I turned to the Mayor while trying to keep the Sheriff in my sight. "Mr. Teehorn, what can I do for you, sir?"

"I'd like you to join me on the campaign trail for my re-election. That's assuming you and your town survive the attack of the apes, of course. Then you'll be a hero. Otherwise, you won't be any good to me."

The Mayor looked at the bar puzzled, then reached over and took Wade's drink, downing it in a single gulp.

Wade rolled his eyes.

"Well, I'll have to think about that Mr. Mayor. I'm not much of a politics sort." I was being polite, because the answer was a firm no. After a couple years of easy, peaceful living, I'd suddenly found myself thrust into the spotlight in every direction I seemed to turn. That didn't bode well for my future as an outlaw-in-hiding.

"You do that, Jebiah," his words slurred slightly as he mispronounced my name. "But from what I hear, your town needs a Mayor since your last one got run over by that manure wagon," he chuckled and burped. A scowl crossed Johnson's sour face. "We could help each other out. Think about it." Swaying slightly, he turned to the Sheriff beside him. "Shall we Booford?"

The dark clothed Sheriff Beauford Johnson grunted and walked away, leaving the Mayor to chase after him on short legs.

I watched the pair leave the building before speaking, "Mayor seems like an interesting fella. I don't think the Sheriff likes me though." I pulled out a stool and gingerly sat.

"Watch out for him. People have been known to cross that evil looking sumbitch and wind up mysteriously dead."

"I'm sure it's a real mystery alright," I said sarcastically. "You have any luck finding anyone willing to come fight with us?"

"None. Seems the railroad is also hiring anyone who is willing to sell their gun. Like the Governor said, the Chinese rail workers are getting pretty antsy over towards Rock Springs. Can't blame them, they get treated worse than dogs. If there's any shooting, it'll mostly be from the railroad side, and a massacre on the other. But between the two options, apes and beasts or Chinese, everyone would rather deal with the Chinese."

"I reckon it's just us and whoever the Governor is able to scrounge up. Maybe we'll get lucky and the railroad will send some of their gunmen. It won't look good for them in the papers if they let the town at the end of their rail be destroyed." This was the single moment in my reformed life where I thought about reaching out to my old gang. They'd come running, with guns blazing at me and anyone else in their way. Granite Falls had enough problems already without turning a dozen cut throats loose on them. Without thinking I rubbed my sore shoulder.

Noticing the motion, Wade slapped me on the back playfully and watched me wince from the pain. He laughed at my discomfort. "Every time I've bought a new gun from Carson, he's taken me to that range of his and wore me out. I've just about reached the point where I'm going to send someone else in there to buy for me, but then I wouldn't get my usual discount."

I stretched my back and rolled my shoulders to loosen them up. "I feel like I got stampeded. Everything hurts. But he's an interesting fellow, and he knows guns."

"Carson's a good man, with a wealth of knowledge." Wade eyeballed his empty glass that the Mayor had left him with disgust.

"How did you come to know him?"

"Met him years ago and talked him into moving out west to get away from the aftermath of the war. Being on the losing side was a heavy burden, and he didn't appreciate the lengths people went to to ruin his good name. After a while, he gave up on trying to salvage his reputation. His conscience was clear, but victors write the history books."

True enough. I'd witnessed the wrath of the Northerners first hand as they poured into the south. For most, the war didn't end when the surrender was made.

"What did he set you up with?" Wade asked, as he motioned for two fresh glasses from the barkeeper.

"A second Colt Peacemaker. Reckon I'm a gun slinger now so I'd better start practicing more. He also set me up with a new rifle. A Winchester Model 1886." I watched for his reaction and excitement to mirror mine from earlier.

"Surely you jest! An 1886? Is it a Browning design?" he said, obviously impressed.

"Yes, sir! In .45-70," I grinned at him.

"This I shall need to see... and try out."

The bartender dropped off the glasses, and walked quickly to the next customer waving a bill at him.

"You'll have to wait, Carson's fitting a scabbard for it tonight." I rotated the brown bottle of what he was drinking and read the orange wrapped label. It was Old Grand-Dad, bottled in Kentucky. Fancy stuff. "He's got a big store. Place is built like a fortress."

"He's still got enemies from the war. On both sides."

I watched Wade pour a finger of whiskey into both glasses. "I've never heard of Carson Skinner."

Wade shrugged and set the bottle aside.

It wasn't unusual for a man to change his name once he came west. I was certain Wade knew his true name, but it was none of my business. Some men just want a fresh start. That's how I ended up out here.

"He wanted me to come back tomorrow and pick up the guns and some more weapons. I get the impression he wants to take full advantage of the Governor's blank check generosity. He's also sending a couple crates of surplus rifles back with us."

"He's a clever and resourceful man, you never know what he might come up with. I'm going to hope for some railroad mounted artillery pieces." He slid a glass in front of me.

I sipped the whiskey. It was strong and smooth. "This must be the good stuff."

Wade held the bottle up and peeked through the amber liquid that sloshed inside it. "No, this is the okay stuff. I only drink the good stuff on special occasions."

"This isn't a special occasion?"

"Not until the battle is won, my friend!"

He finished his glass with a big gulp and picked his hat up. "The rest of the bottle is yours. I am going to retire for the evening. Tomorrow we will meet the Governor's man and see what he brings to the battle as well as this railroad tycoon."

"See you in the morning, Wade."

I watched him walk up the stairs. Back straight and proud. He was a good, solid man. I was glad to have him with us. I saw him tip his hat towards someone before stepping out of sight. A split-second later, Skyla rounded the corner of the hallway and came down the stairs.

She was wearing a white cotton dress, laced around the throat. Her black hair had been put up, with a few wisps falling on bare shoulders. The woman was naturally beautiful, but the dress accented her features in ways that would have made my knees go weak if I had been standing. Instead, I suddenly felt very dry mouthed and in desperate need of a glass of water.

I felt nervousness building within me as she crossed the room. Standing, I took her hand as she sat on the stool Wade vacated. She crossed her legs and spun around, resting her arms on the bar, and tilting her head towards me playfully with a smile.

"You look... beautiful." That was an understatement.

She blushed, and looked at the empty glass beside my half full one.

"Drinking alone?"

"Wade's too old to stay up late."

She laughed. It was a wonderful sound. I couldn't take my eyes off her.

"Well then," she picked up the bottle and read the label. "Mind if I join you?"

I tried to play it smooth and hide my shock, because I didn't expect the fancy eastern girl to drink whiskey. "Please do."

The bartender passed by us as he paced the opposite side of the bar and I asked for a clean glass. After giving an appraising look at Skyla, he pulled one from under the bar and carefully wiped any smudges off before setting it before her. With a flourish he took Wade's away, wrapped in his rag to be cleaned.

She poured a little whiskey in her glass and handed mine to me. "To our future victory over the savage apes!" she said with her glass raised.

We clinked them together then knocked the burning whiskey back. She grimaced from the burning of the whiskey, but recovered quickly. "Not quite what I'm used to." She daintily wiped the corners of her mouth. "How was the gun store?"

"Phenomenal. I need to sell my ranch and open my own. Play with guns all day, shoot them all afternoon, and take people's money. That's the dream. Speaking of guns..." I pulled her derringer from my pocket and slid it over with a box of cartridges. "It's loaded."

She tucked both items away into a pocket in the folds of her dress. "Now I'm armed like a proper western lady."

"Yes, you are. By the way, Carson would like you to come with me to the store tomorrow. He has a surprise for you."

"Oh, I can't wait! I have something for you too," she said excitedly and pulling out a paper and string wrapped bundle, she set it in front of me.

"What's this?" I said, surprised at the gesture.

"It's for luck. Open and see."

Untying the string, I pulled the paper back. It contained a braided leather necklace. Attached on the end was one of the Allosaurus claws with a small hole drilled in the top for the braid to run through.

"The claws are pretty big. So, I used the smallest one on that severed forearm you had. I hope you don't mind," she said shyly, as if unsure whether I'd like the gift or not.

Holding it up to the light, I watched the black claw spin back and forth on the cord. I could have kissed her right then and there. "Skyla, this is... thank you."

She beamed.

I pulled the looped braid over my head and let the claw drop to my chest before tucking it inside my shirt. "I will never take this off."

"You'd better not," she teased happily.

Chuckling, I picked my drink up and sipped. "Having seen them up close and personal, what do you think about dinosaurs now?"

"Amazing and terrifying at the same time. This is an archeologist's dream, to not only study extinct animal's remains but to see if our theories are correct! Oscar, wherever he is, took his journals. But I've been working on my own set today from memory. I've got sketches and notes on everything we've observed so far on both the dinosaurs and apes. Sometimes all of this feels like a dream, but then I remember how scared I was when they attacked the wagon." She gently rolled her glass between her fingers, staring at it with a frown. "And I remember how it felt when I killed that ape. I don't know if I'll ever forget it."

"If you hadn't, it would have killed you. Ashley was knocked out,

Wade was driving, Oscar was worthless, and I had no shot. You saved them both, and yourself." I raised my glass towards her. "That makes you a heroine." I set the glass back down. "But I know what you mean. One day I was working on my ranch, cussing at Carbine, then that night I'm blowing up my barn to kill a dinosaur that was supposed to have been dead for millions of years. Since then, I've been shoved into the thick of this mess."

"I guess that makes you a hero as well." She pushed a wisp of loose hair to the side and the frown turned to a playful smile. "Not bad for a man in a brown hat with dubious morals. You certainly know how to impress a girl."

"Speaking of that, did I mention I own a slightly successful small ranch?"

Laughing, she placed her hand on my arm. "It's a very nice ranch too."

I felt tingles shoot through my body at her touch.

She poured two more glasses for us. "If we only have a couple more days left before we die a horrific death at the hands of savage apes or non-extinct dinosaurs, let's make the most of it."

"I'll drink to that."

And we did, long into the night.

She spoke of her home in the east, growing up with a father of one of the most prestigious historical societies in America and I told her of meeting Dan while fighting the Nez Perce, and how I ended up in Granite Falls, all while keeping the darker secrets to myself. We laughed and drank too much.

Well after midnight, as well-dressed gamblers and hustlers spread cards and tossed their chips, I helped Skyla up to her room. She was full of giggles as she staggered up the stairs, bumping into me. She fell halfway down the hall. Her face was bright red with laughter as I helped her back onto unsteady feet.

Outside of her room, she fumbled the key into the lock and paused, looking at me. "You know I almost knocked on your door last night," her words slurred slightly.

I grinned and leaned against the wall, recalling how badly I wanted to knock on her door as well. "Me too."

Skyla lurched forward awkwardly and kissed me passionately. Her lips tasted sweet and her breath like whiskey. It was wonderful.

Pushing me away abruptly, she grinned, then quickly opened her door and ducked inside. It slammed shut behind her and the lock was thrown. I waited as I heard her fumble her way into bed, before pulling the key she'd left in the lock out and sliding it under her door into her room.

I floated into my room and made entirely too much noise as I kicked my boots off, happier than I'd ever been before.

With the sound of Wade's snoring in the bed beside me, I fell asleep thinking of Skyla's lips on mine and the feeling of her body pressed against mine.

***

I was at the hotel dining room, sitting in front of the remains of my breakfast, nursing a hangover and a cup of coffee when Wade dropped into the chair across from me. "Long night?" He smiled knowingly.

"Uh-huh," I saw the grin spread across his face. "No! Not like that. I was the gentleman you presumed me to be and she was a lady. But we certainly didn't drink like we were." I sipped the hot bitter brew. "We got a little soaked."

"I'm sorry she has to drink to be around you. You finished?"

At my nod, he snagged a left-over piece of bacon off my plate and popped it into his mouth.

The waiter walked over to our table and recognized Wade. "Back again for a second breakfast? Can I get you anything?"

"Just coffee, please. But tell the cook the eggs were delicious."

"He'll be pleased to hear that, Mr. Mackin." The waiter bobbed his head and moved to fetch him a cup of joe.

Once he walked away, Wade slipped a slip of paper in front of me. All the mischievous jokes were gone, and his face hardened. "Dan sent a telegram. The apes hit Hammdon's ranch. No survivors."

Startled, I grabbed the telegram, read it quickly, and shoved it away from me angrily. I hadn't lived there long when Jim Hammdon raised a barn. I went to meet the other locals and get established in the area. People came from all over, and after a couple long days of sweat and sawdust, they held a big shindig when it was finished. I danced with his eldest daughter, a sweet girl of nineteen with a clubbed foot. Now she was dead with the rest of them. "They were good people, honest, and hardworking. They even managed to save enough to send their oldest son away for schooling. He was going to be a lawyer. Now he's an orphan."

Putting my head in my hands, I closed my eyes and took a deep breath. If I'd shot that scar-faced bastard and collapsed the tunnel properly, they would still be alive. That was my fault. Next time, I'd make sure to kill him and salt the outhouse with his ashes.

I swallowed hard and took another deep breath, trying to calm myself down. After a moment, I felt good enough to raise my head back up and sip the coffee with a trembling hand.

Wade watched me solemnly. "With that single platoon of soldiers, whatever Carson has up his sleeve, and ourselves, we should be able to protect the town until the Governor gets enough reinforcements in to go after the apes. The Hammdons will be avenged. Not today, or tomorrow, nor the day after, but soon."

He folded the telegram and tucked it in a vest pocket before nodding towards the staircase. "There's the belle of the ball. Let's not worry her with such things as revenge."

Turning, I saw Skyla stepping down with a hand on the banister. Even with her hair a little messy, her clothes disheveled, and squinting at the bright morning light coming through the large glass windows, she was every bit as beautiful as last night.

She smiled shyly, and I grinned broadly back. Her cheeks reddened, and she looked away quickly.

"Well then, I'll leave you two to it." Wade winked at me before picking up his hat and adjusting his gun belt. "See you two at the Governor's." He tipped his hat at Skyla and left.

I stood. "Good morning, sleep well?"

"Yes, but I'm never drinking again."

"Even with me?"

Her faced reddened again. "Maybe with you," she admitted.

I pulled her chair out. "Well, Miss Skyla Stratten," I laid the southern drawl on thick, "would you care to join me for breakfast?"

"I would indeed!"

***

The Governor wasn't alone when we were ushered in.

A large man with wide shoulders in a dark gray suit was leaning over the large desk, his back to us as he pointed a finger at some parchment papers and talked with the Governor. Against the desk rested a polished black cane with an ivory handle. I suspected this was the rail tycoon.

To their right side stood a black man, tall and clean shaven. He watched us but offered no greeting. He carried two guns in black holsters embossed with silver. The bottoms of the holsters were tied around his thighs with a rawhide thong to keep them in place when he drew. He had all the looks of a hired gun hand. An expensive one, according to his attire, which meant he was good at what he did. He didn't look like the sort of man the Governor spoke of yesterday. If the other man was the tycoon, then this was his security.

Beside the tall windows with blue drapes, Oscar sat in a chair, wiping his new pair of glasses with a piece of folded cloth and ignoring us. His presence was a mystery.

And finally, a brown-haired gentleman dressed in leather breeches and fringed shirt with a pair of delicate round spectacles balanced across his nose above a thick mustache. A bright red bandana was slung around his neck. He was the most perfectly dressed westerner I had ever seen. A bit too much so. I suspected this was the big game hunter that the Governor had spoken so well of.

"Greetings!" The spectacled man's voice boomed as he strode forward to shake each of our hands. He had a vigorous handshake with the grip of a bear.

The businessman in the gray suit didn't turn around, still deep in conversation with the Governor, and the black gunman stood stoically, watching us warily.

The hunter paused when he shook Wade's hand, clasping him about the shoulder. "Mr. Wolverine Wade Mackin, I've heard of your exploits and how you strangled a skunk bear to death with your bare hands. How I've always wanted to meet you! You're the very epitome of an adventurer. We need to swap stories, you and I."

I gently shook feeling back into my fingers, trying to be subtle. I sized him up. He may have dressed like something of a dandy, but he appeared tanned and strong. I got the impression he was a very capable individual.

He stepped back, hands on hips as he peered through his small round lenses at us with light blue eyes. "My name is Fredrick von Holsak."

It was a famous name; one I knew well from the newspapers. He'd spent some time in politics and ranching, but most of his fame came from his big game hunting exploits in Europe and Africa. If only a third of the stories about him were true, he was just the sort of man we needed right now.

Wade grinned warmly at the man. "Mr. Holsak, I've read your book on African safaris. It's nice to finally meet you as well."

The hunter waved his hand dismissively. "Call me Fredrick! What did you think of it?"

"Outstanding," Wade said. "If it were with me, I'd dare ask for an autograph."

Fredrick chuckled.

Skyla gestured towards Oscar, who was still pointedly ignoring us. "We know him already, although I'm surprised to see him here. But who are these other two gentlemen?" she asked curiously as she eyed the intimidating black gunman.

The Governor must have been half listening to our conversation because he looked up from his desk towards her. "My apologies, Ms. Stratten," he waved a hand towards the suited man across from him. "This is Mr. Rayden White, owner of the East-West Railroad."

The tycoon turned to face us with an easy smile.

I drew my pistol and thumbed the hammer back in one swift move. Anger burst through me. The scars on my back burned like a branding iron.

The man before me was the very same Union Officer who'd burned my home, hanged my neighbor, and had me whipped to the edge of death. It was a face I'd never forget.

He looked puzzled as he stood defenseless, clutching the head of his cane tightly. The Colt's trigger reached the cusp of breaking and dropping the hammer on a bullet to send him to join his raider companions in the depths of hell.

An ounce of pressure separated me from the justice I'd desired for so long.

I savored the moment.

Vengeance was mine.

A loud pair of clicks to my right gave my trigger finger pause. Flicking my eyes over, I saw the black gunman, forgotten in the heat of the moment, had both his pistols pointed at my chest.

"Hey!" the Governor cried as he stepped around the desk. A vein pulsed across his forehead in anger. "What the hell is this?" he shouted in outrage.

"Jed, please calm down," Skyla said in a voice so low I could barely hear her over the pounding of blood in my ears.

"What's this all about?" Fredrick looked bewildered at the suddenly and vastly different situation than the one of greeting and pleasantries we had a moment ago.

Wade shifted his feet slightly, edging his hand towards his revolver. I didn't know who he meant to point it at, but hoped he'd back me. The black gunman shook his head slightly, both guns still aimed at me. Behind him, Oscar's face had gone white and he clutched the glasses against his chest protectively.

The railroad tycoon's hard, dark eyes stared curiously at me. He'd aged. His hair was silver and receding from his forehead. The neatly trimmed red beard was now almost completely gray, with a few surviving colored streaks left in it. A once large and powerful man, he seemed shorter now, weaker.

Or maybe I'd just grown up.

He chuckled softly, a jovial smile spreading across his face, but his eyes remained hard. Still holding his cane, he leaned back against the desk. "Easy, friend. I'm unarmed."

"I don't care," I growled. My mouth felt dry, my tongue thick and clumsy, as if anger had sucked all the moisture from my body and left only a husk of barely contained rage.

"If you shoot me, my friend will kill you. If, for some unfathomable reason, he fails, you'll be hanged for the murder of an unarmed man." He peered at me. "I've made a few enemies over the years. The railroad business is often necessarily and regrettably difficult. But I don't recollect you."

My pistol remained firmly aimed at his face, but I lessened the pressure on the trigger. "That's because it was twenty years ago in South Carolina."

Skyla's mouth dropped open in shock, her eyes darting back and forth between me and the tycoon as the pieces of the puzzle fell into place for her.

Reydan's left eye twitched and his smile twisted into a snarl before disappearing as quickly as it appeared. Then he was smiling again with straight white teeth.

"Twenty years ago... that'd be during the war. I'm not sure who you have mistaken me for, but I was a logistics officer stationed in Virginia. I never so much as saw combat, and if I commandeered any livestock or property of yours, I sincerely apologize. War is a nasty business for all."

His lies didn't fool me. I began squeezing the trigger again. Damn the consequences. I'd take him with me.

The silent gunman must have realized my intentions because Skyla suddenly gasped and took a staggered step back as he shifted one of the pistols away from my chest and pointed it at her instead.

I didn't move. The rage was burning so hot I felt it would consume me. I didn't know what to do. I couldn't kill them both before the gunman killed her. But I'd be damned if the murderous raider was leaving this room alive.

With a gun pointing at Skyla's chest, Wade had enough. He drew his revolver and aimed it at the black gunman. When he spoke, his voice was firm and loud in the quiet room, "I don't know what this is all about. But you'll not be threatening a lady in my presence. Adjust your aim, sir. Now."

The gunman ignored him, his pistol barrels still unwaveringly aimed at the two of us.

Things were about to get very western in here.

The Governor pulled the double-barreled shotgun from under his desk, thumbed back both hammers, and pointed it at my belly button. "Mr. Smith. This started with you. Holster your gun, or I will cut you down. Wade, this is double ought buckshot and you're a mite close. Take two steps to the right please."

Wade grunted and reluctantly lowered his pistol, but didn't move. He looked at me. "This isn't one you can win, Jed. Put it down."

The gunman shifted both barrels back to me. Skyla gasped in relief. Staggering, Fredrick caught her and quickly pulled her out of the line of fire.

With startling clarity, I suddenly realized how close I was to getting Skyla and Wade killed. No matter how evil the tycoon was, my friends' lives were worth twenty of his. Swallowing hard, I pushed the anger back down and gently uncocked my pistol before easing it into the holster.

The gunman twirled both pistols and deftly holstered them while keeping his eyes fixed on me.

The shotgun was slowly lowered as well, but the Governor didn't put it down. "Jed, I don't know who you think Mr. White is, but he's a gentleman of good family and standing. You must be mistaken."

I glanced at the black gunman, his face a stoic mask. His eyes were emotionless. He could have been an ebony statute. There was something about him that tugged at the edge of my memory and I wondered if I'd run into him during my outlaw days.

"I'm not mistaken. This shit bird may have friends in high places who can vouch for him, but twenty years ago he was leading raiding parties through South Carolina. Looting, pillaging, and burning farms and homes." I locked eyes with Reydan. "He was also executing pardoned Confederates and torturing their wives and children."

The predatory look was back as his lips curled in a snarl. Slamming his fist down on the desk, spittle flew as he screamed, "This is a LIE! How dare you! You come in here, putting a pistol in my face, threatening me, making false accusations, and slandering my good name! Governor, I demand you arrest this man!" His face was a mottled purple and red, veins throbbed across his neck and temple.

"How about a duel than? At noon, on Main Street. We'll give everyone a show of it," I offered. With his reputation on the line, I hoped to take advantage of his rage. Then I could kill him.

The Governor spoke sharply. "Silence, Jed! There'll be no dueling!" He sighed. "Mr. White, this man must be mistaken, but until he has broken the law, he cannot be arrested. I believe we have finished our discussion for now, so it would be wise if you and your," he cut his eyes toward Oscar and the gunman, "associates, leave us to tend to other matters."

Reydan ground his teeth as he recovered his composure and offered another fake smile. The mask of civility was back in place. "My apologies. You are correct, Governor. Mr. Smith, I do not know of, nor am I, this wretched raider you speak of. I can assure you, it is not me. However," he gestured with the cane towards Oscar, "before we go, I hope we can move past this unfortunate moment, and come to amicable terms. Mr. Ellis has informed me that you have filed claim on the land that this... tunnel... is on. I'd like to purchase it from you."

I skewered Oscar with a glare. He shifted uncomfortably in the seat. How he ended up in the tycoon's pocket, I didn't know. But I wondered what he was getting out of all of this.

My eyes flicked back to Mr. White. "No."

He grasped the edge of his suit with his free hand, tugging it forward around his chest. "Well, Jed. May I call you Jed?" He was smooth and polished again, acting the amicable businessman.

"No."

The tycoon's knuckles went white as his grip on the ivory head of his cane clenched tighter. "Fine. Let me be blunt, Mr. Smith. You can either sell me the property for far more than it is worth, or the full might of the U.S. Government will come down on you and take it, forcibly if necessary. Then they will give it to me and I will run a train directly through that mystical tunnel you are protecting."

The Governor cut in. "Easy, Mr. White. There is no need for threats," he looked pointedly at me. "I'm sure given time, and the resolution of our differences, we will be able to work out a solution that will benefit everyone."

"We shall see," he said angrily. I knew it wasn't an idle threat; the man had immense power and was no doubt well connected with people who could easily ruin me. But I wasn't afraid to kill people when necessary, so I had that going for me. And they can only hang you once.

"Oscar, why are you here?" Wade interrupted. His pistol was still unholstered, and he tapped it against his thigh thoughtfully.

"Mr. White offered me the opportunity of a lifetime, to lead a research team on the other side, fully funded. No more squabbling with Skyla's father and his board of penny-pinchers for funds to dig up old bones," he sneered. "Now I'll get all the knowledge and glory I deserve for my efforts and Mr. White will regain his investment from whatever profitable discoveries we make. It's that simple." He glared at me. "It also means I'll have whoever the hell I want carrying my baggage without some yokel cowboy shoving a pistol in my face. Or," a malicious smirk crossed his face, "is the proper term, an imbecile?"

The barely controlled anger boiled back up. "Bold talk for a coward. I should have pulled the trigger on you when I had the chance, you yellow-bellied weasel."

Oscar harrumphed as he stood and shoved hands into his trouser pockets with false bravado. "You don't scare me. I'm protected by powerful men now. Men who have a vested interest in my future studies in this lost world you found."

I took a quick step towards Skyla's former boss and he jumped back as the black man's hands flashed to the butts of his guns at my movement. I gave a tight-lipped smile to Oscar. "Protect you, huh? Are they going to stand between you and an ape spear through your chest?"

The little man paled and swallowed hard before trying to recover. "I'll have an escort," he stammered.

"Enough. We're done here," Reydan tucked the cane under an arm and crossed the room, passing me in large strides. He called over a shoulder, "Cato, let's go."

I stared in shock at my boyhood friend. The room spun as I realized the happy boy from my youth was now the silent gunman standing before me. The same gunman who almost killed me a few minutes ago.

"Cato..." I whispered to myself.

He locked eyes with me for the briefest of moments, then stalked out of the room without saying a word. Not a single emotion was shown. But he had to have known who I was when I called his employer out as having whipped me.

Oscar waddled quickly after them, head held haughtily in the air, avoiding eye contact. The butler quietly closed the door behind them. If he'd heard any of our conversation from outside the room, he didn't show it.

The Governor slammed the shotgun down on the desk. "Are you out of your bloomin' mind?"

I was still stunned and searched for words as I struggled to grasp the notion that after all these years, Cato was still alive. "He did it," I said softly.

"And what judge would believe your word against his? Dammit, Jed! You can't go around threatening people, especially railroad owners! Their trains are our lifeblood. Without them, we are doomed out here." He dropped into the chair behind his desk and rubbed his eyes.

I looked at my friends. Skyla had sat down in one of the chairs, carefully studying the floor and not meeting my gaze. Wade holstered his pistol and paced back and forth across the room.

Fredrick strode to a window and looked at the street below. "There they go. With that Mr. Ellis fellow trailing behind like a puppy." He turned back to me. "Jed, do you have any proof of your claim?"

"Only scars and ashes."

The Governor sighed. "He's a powerful man, with many wealthy friends and numerous high-ranking politicians backing him. His family comes from a long line of politicians. His father is a senator for God's sake! You want justice, but the law has no chance of trying or convicting him of any war crimes. Unless he torched a church full of nuns or something equally reprehensible, he'd be given a pardon before anything ever went to trial."

The fact that the Union raider was the son of a Senator who turned into a railroad tycoon was an interesting twist of fate. But, it didn't matter. I could never take him to court, there would be too much publicity, and my past would become known. That was fine, I didn't care if he hanged, just that he died. I'd make that happen myself.

As for Cato, his presence was a shock. I didn't know how to feel about that. We'd been brothers once. But we weren't innocent little boys anymore. He'd turned into a gun hand for his captor and my torturer, while I turned into a vengeful outlaw. I didn't want to kill him, even though he appeared perfectly content with killing me and Skyla a few minutes ago.

I hoped he'd stay the hell out of my way.

Wade stopped pacing. "Governor, did the Lieutenant and his men leave last night?"

"They did. I received word this morning that they'd arrived and were scouting the area around town. We were able to scrounge up a cannon to send as well."

"Excellent! I can't wait to see what a giant lead ball does when it hits a trike on the snout," Wade exclaimed before turning to address the famed hunter. "Fredrick, I hear you might be interested in giving us a hand."

"I am indeed," he replied. "The Governor has filled me in on everything he knows, and I'd like to join your little endeavor."

"Then I feel compelled to tell you, the soldiers sent are a boon, but with Jed's outburst, we probably just lost support of the railroad and their men. If William has fully informed you on our venture, you'll have an idea of what we are up against. Yesterday, they killed a rancher and his family. You may very well die."

Fredrick thrust his chest out and looked Wade in the eye evenly. "No adventure worth going on is without its risks."

I stuck my hand out. "Welcome aboard. We leave this evening."

Fredrick shook my hand with his crushing grip and leaned forward with a slight bow. "I shall see you all on the train." He gave the Governor and Skyla a quick nod, before striding briskly out of the room, slamming the doors shut as he moved past the butler who still waited outside.

"Wade, Skyla and I need to run by Carson's. Then we'll meet you back at the hotel afterwards?"

"Sounds good. I'm going to stay and talk with the Governor about a few things." Wade looked to Skyla as she rose from her chair. "Do you mind if I speak with Jed alone?"

She nodded her head slightly. "I'll be waiting downstairs," she gave me a sad smile before leaving the room.

Wade waited until the door closed behind her before he stepped in front of me. His jaw flexed as he spat the words at me, "You almost got us all killed. And if you don't learn to control that rage of yours, it will."

"Wade-" I started to protest.

"Don't. I saw that look on your face. You were going to drop the hammer on Reydan, even if it meant killing Skyla. If he's the man that burned your house and tortured you, save your revenge for another time. Right now, your town needs you, and we need you. Focus." He stepped back from me, shaking his head in disgust. "You're better than this."

I swallowed the lump in my throat; he was right. There'd only been a few ounces of trigger pressure that stopped me from screwing everything up and killing my friends. I didn't have any words. Embarrassed, I nodded and quietly left the room.

Skyla and I walked towards Liberty Arms in silence. Occasionally, she'd glance at me, as if she wanted to say something, then a moment later, turning away. It was an awkward silence, and I didn't know how to break it. What do you say to someone you almost let die out of selfish pride and revenge?

We paused on the edge of a street as a wagon rolled by. Stern faced women stood in the back, struggling to maintain their balance as the wheels bumped in the road, holding a large banner that read Women's Temperance Society with the painting of a white tied ribbon centered in a black circle.

I'd heard of them before.

They were the women who seemed to hate every vice known to man, even good ones like punching and shooting people who deserved it. If they got their way, all men would be as miserable as their husbands must be.

I shuddered at the thought as they passed by. From the disgusted looks of men nearby, they had the same notion. Some of the women around us watched the wagon approvingly, but not Skyla, thank goodness. She seemed indifferent to their movement and our manly disgust.

We made it two steps into the graveled street before I finally couldn't take the silence anymore.

"I'm sorry... I let my anger control me. I risked everyone's lives over it. And put you in harm's way," I said shamefully. There was a mixture of emotions bottled inside me. Part anger towards finally finding my torturer who destroyed my life and an overwhelming guilt at risking so much because of him. I almost threw away everything good I'd managed to build over the past two years. Including the lovely girl beside me, who deserved far better than me.

Grabbing my arm, she stopped me. "What you did was profoundly stupid," then she surprised me by hugging me tight. "Please don't be stupid again. I want to live, and I want you to live. There's a time and place for everything. Including justice for what was done to you. But that certainly wasn't it."

I looked in her brown eyes, feeling a rush of relief that she didn't hate me. Suddenly, I felt very self-conscience embracing a woman in the middle of the street. Feeling much better, I winked and grinned at her. "You're right. I'll kill him later."

She shoved me playfully and began to walk away. I jogged to catch up, and when I did, she shook her head. "That's not what I meant."

"I know."

She cleared her throat. "But I don't like Mr. White, and I don't appreciate your old friend pointing a gun at me."

"Me neither."

***

When we reached the store, the door was open, and a customer was leaving with a shotgun tucked under his arm. He bid us a good morning and tipped his hat towards Skyla with a smile as he passed by.

Seeing us enter, Carson gave us a friendly wave. Our weapons were already laid out on a colored blanket across the countertop. The wooden box containing Skyla's pistol rested beside my old Colt Peacemaker. My new rifle was tucked into a beautiful tooled leather scabbard with intricate swirls and patterns hammered into the top edge. It was a true piece of work, and it was almost a shame to strap something like it on a horse like Carbine.

The lanky store owner smiled warmly at Skyla. "I take it you're the young lady who used the derringer on an ape?"

Skyla looked at me skeptically, then back to Carson. "Yes, sir. That was me."

"I found you something a little more potent." With a flourish, he lifted the top off the wooden box and revealed the nickel-plated revolver with its spare long barrel.

Skyla almost squealed with delight. "It's beautiful," she exclaimed while running her fingertips over the checkered black grips. "What is the other barrel for?"

"For when concealment doesn't matter. Or a sense of preference, some people like the added weight. But the short barrel that's installed now should serve you just fine." Plucking the gun from the box, he handed it to her. "This will serve you much better should you need to kill something large and hairy, be it man or beast."

As she looked over the gun excitedly, Carson began walking towards the entrance. "Jed, your old Colt isn't quite as good as your new one. But it should be a substantial improvement over that crunchy trigger it had."

Picking up my old Peacemaker, I dry fired several times, and felt the smoothness of the trigger as it broke. I emptied the one I'd been carrying of cartridges and dry fired them both, side by side. I couldn't feel any difference between the two.

"Well, look who's carrying two guns now. Time to buy a white hat, Jed. You're one heroic deed away from being a true dime novel hero," Skyla teased as she watched me work the pistols.

"As I proved earlier, I'm not exactly good guy material. But if you need rescuing, I'll come running," I grinned at her while setting the pistols down and she blushed. Carson came back, after shutting the front door and locking it. "Thank you," I told him sincerely.

"Thank the Governor. He's footing a rather hefty bill, but you are welcome just the same." He pointed towards the back door. "Follow me, I've something else for you."

Carson led the way out, followed by Skyla and myself bringing up the rear. In front of us was a pair of odd shapes covered with large canvas tarps.

"I heard the soldiers took a cannon with them, and unfortunately I wasn't able to get you another. But I did scrounge up something that may be more useful. Just don't ask where they came from." He yanked one of the tarps off.

A large contraption, mounted on a wooden carriage between a pair of wagon wheels, gleamed in the sunlight. It had five barrels aligned in a circle that rotated with the turn of a crank handle on the side. A large wooden tongue stuck out the back of the carriage and rested on the ground, preventing the weapon from rolling away and was used for hauling the weapon behind a team of horses.

Gatling guns.

"Hell yeah!" I'd used one to good effect on some raiding Mexican bandits once. That'd been a gut wrenching, gruesome slaughter of mangled bodies and horses. But it wiped out the band of miscreants, and that sort of firepower was exactly what we needed now.

"Yes sir, in .45-70. Just like your rifle. If you have ammo and a good team trained in its use, you can fire until the barrels melt," he patted the top of the circular barrels, "which can happen. I also made some minor modifications that make it easier to traverse side to side now."

I checked the feeding trays to make sure they were empty then rotated the hand crank. That rotated the circle of barrels and would fire a single shot every time one of the barrels came in line with the firing pin at the lowest point of the rotation. The gun clanked loudly on empty chambers as I turned the handle. I put some weight against the gun and it slid smoothly to the right, then I moved it to the left. "Excellent. This will help even the playing field against superior numbers. I bet they weren't easy to get," I told him.

"They fell off the back of a wagon," he gave me a conspiratorial look. "Try not to lose them."

"How did those fit on a wagon?" Skyla asked as she looked over the guns.

Carson and I shared a grin.

"That's short for, they've been misplaced. But don't worry, Carson, I'll give them a nice cleaning before I bring them back."

"I'd appreciate that."

I looked around and saw a stack of what had to be wooden crates under another tarp nearby. "Were you able to also scrounge up plenty of ammunition for them?"

"You bet. Enough to start a war," he shrugged. "Or finish one."

"Good."

Carson turned to Skyla. "Miss, let's grab your pistol and go for a ride. I want to make sure you are comfortable with the gun before you need it."

I joined them to get some practice in with my guns as well. Most likely, I'd be killing apes soon and a railroad tycoon afterwards.

***

After Skyla practiced until she could hit the target with her pistol at least half of the time, we parted ways from Liberty Arms heavily laden with weaponry. Carson wished us luck, and promised to supervise the loading of the Gatlings and ammunition, along with the crates of Springfield rifles, onto the train.

We met Wade at the hotel, packed our belongings, and walked to the station several hours later. Fredrick had already boarded the train. He waved to us through a window and shouted that he'd saved us seats. That was a joke considering how deserted the train platform was. It appeared very few people wanted to return to a town about to be attacked.

Mayor Teehorn and Sheriff Johnson were waiting to tell us goodbye. At least the Mayor was. The suspicious lawman stared at me sullenly while working a large wad of tobacco in his jaws. This was probably just another chance for him to size me up and try to figure out who I was.

I thanked them both for their hospitality. Even though the Sheriff was probably going to be a problem and the Mayor didn't do anything but pester me to campaign with him. Still, it was the polite thing to do. More importantly, it was the sort of thing an upstanding, law abiding citizen would do. Respecting the office and his government superiors and such. Not someone guilty of lots of crimes, like me.

The Mayor was polite in return, wishing us a safe trip and luck in the coming 'ape war' as he called it. Johnson simply spat out brown tobacco juice on the floor near my boot.

I was the last of my group to board the short train. With so few people and supplies being sent to Granite Falls there was only six cars after the locomotive and coal car. As I climbed the steps, I noticed Reydan at the far end of the station talking to an attendant. Cato stood beside him, watching everyone who came near suspiciously. Oscar was nowhere to be seen.

Curious as to what they were up to, I paused, one foot in the railcar, watching my nemesis and former friend. With a slow, obvious movement, Cato reached up and tipped the brim of his hat at me.

Curious, I nodded towards him in return, wondering what he meant by it. Was it a sign of respect between opponents, or a sign that he'd not forgotten me after all these years? I scowled as I watched the pair.

Reydan dismissed the train worker and turned back to face the train, his hands clasping the cane before him. I felt his eyes bore into me.

The train's whistle pierced the air. The blast of steam warning everyone to get on, or get off. Either way, the train was about to move. Turning my back on Reydan and Cato, I climbed aboard, silently vowing I'd return and reap my vengeance.

***

Most of the passenger cars were empty, with maybe two dozen other people spread out amongst them. The car we were in was near the center of the train, with five other people. Miners and ranch hands by the looks of them. Most likely returning now that their families were safe, to protect their livelihoods. I hoped my ranch was still standing and that the apes or Otto hadn't eaten all my cattle and burned it to the ground.

A couple cars ahead of us were the Gatling guns. Normally cattle cars were reserved for taking lumber and supplies to town then returning with wool and beef. Now they were empty, which was a good thing since each heavy weapon took up most of a car. With a door on each side of the car for loading and unloading, Carson simply had his horses haul the guns through and stop with the wheel weapons still inside the car. Once the guns were secured with large chock blocks against the wheels, the horses were disconnected, and both doors closed. That would make them easy to unload once we reached town.

I shared a bench with Skyla again.

She was wearing a gun belt now, her new pistol resting in its holster with the long barrel installed. Beautiful and dangerous. Exactly how every woman should be. I was wearing both Colt Peacemakers, and was already uncomfortable with the looks I received from other men. There's a reputation that accompanies men who wear two guns. They were either a gunfighter, or a wannabe. I reckoned I was a little of both. My new Winchester lay on the bench across the aisle in the embossed leather scabbard.

Wade and Fredrick sat in front of us. Both had spoken fondly about swapping stories, but at their first chance to do so, they slept with hats pulled down over their eyes. One of them was snoring softly already. It seemed we were all exhausted, even Skyla had nodded off beside me, her head resting against my shoulder. After staying up late last night, I didn't blame her. I was pretty tuckered out myself.

Our gear was stacked on the bench behind us, except for Fredrick's. He'd brought more equipment than the other three of us combined. It filled several benches in the sparsely populated car. I would've said something teasing about the number of clothing bags he had, except he had an almost equal number of gun cases. And in my experience, the more guns the merrier.

Alone with my thoughts amongst the soft murmur of other passengers' conversations and chugging of the locomotive, I thought back to the confrontation in the Governor's Office. Of all the raiders I found and killed, none knew his name, he was only referred to as 'sir'. His name and origin were always a mystery. That was the only reason he was still on this side of the ground.

And Cato, for all these years, I'd figured he was dead. I didn't know what to think about that.

I closed my eyes and tried to stop thinking vengeful thoughts. There was no telling what we would return to, so I may as well get all the sleep I could during the four-and-a-half-hour train ride home. The last telegram we received before boarding was that another ranch had been attacked, the family slaughtered, one of them sacrificed, and their livestock taken. No sign of an army of apes yet, but plenty of tracks suggested they were still paying lots of attention to the town.

***

It felt like I only had been asleep for a minute before a panicked yell woke me.

Startled, I shot upright, jarring Skyla's head off my shoulder, and looked around in wild-eyed bewilderment, trying to figure out what the hollering was about.

Around us, passengers scrambled for weapons while others rushed to the windows.

"Apes!" Fredrick shouted gleefully. "Look at them! And those great horned beasts they're riding! Magnificent!" He grinned, happy as a kid on Christmas morning. "Let's kill them!"

Wade grabbed his heavy rifle and quickly moved to an open window.

"Oh hell," I said, twisting around to see. "Here we go again."

At least two dozen apes, all colorfully painted with the same swirls and patterns I'd seen at my ranch. Their trikes were painted as well, and they thundered alongside the train, easily keeping pace, their large hooved feet sending up a cloud of dust that trailed behind them.

Then I saw him.

Human skulls dangled from his green and yellow striped dinosaur mount, bouncing with every step the massive broken horned beast took. The leader of the apes rode bare chested and unpainted, a stark contrast to his band of hairy followers. In one hand he held the reins to his trike, in the other he carried an obsidian axe, the glossy black rock glistening in the evening sun.

Beside him rode a female ape. Like the ones I saw in the canyon she was larger than the other males, almost as large as the leader. Dark tanned hides wrapped around her torso and waist. Her face was painted with streaks of green that contrasted sharply with her dark skin. She notched an arrow and drew the bow back, aiming the black tip at us.

Skyla, bless her, already had her pistol pointed out the window to fire. Grabbing a shoulder, I jerked her down as the she-ape's arrow zipped past overhead. It caught a passenger standing in the aisle behind us, punching halfway through his chest. He fell screaming and thrashing. Blood poured from the wound as he tried to pull the shaft from his torso. Another passenger grabbed him, trying to stop the bleeding.

The train began speeding up. I wasn't sure how long the trikes could pace the locomotive's top speed. But it wasn't looking good.

More arrows began thudding against the outside wall, penetrating several inches and leaving sharp points sticking through.

I lunged for my rifle and jerked it from the scabbard, narrowly missing being hit by a three-foot-long arrow that zipped through the window and impaled the bench beside me.

Fredrick ducked and frantically dug through his stack of luggage. Cases were thrown and shoved off the pile, until he found the one he wanted. Popping the brass clasps, he pulled out a rifle and box of cartridges. Kneeling under a window he began loading quickly while peeking at the apes rampaging outside.

Up and down the train a scattering of shots was fired. There weren't many people on the train, but God bless the West, because out here almost everyone is armed.

"Shoot the big, ugly one!" I yelled at the top of my voice.

"They're all big and ugly!" someone screamed back. The voice was high-pitched, panicked, and punctuated with the sharp crack of a rifle being fired.

Wolverine Wade's single shot rifle boomed from the rear of the car. An ape toppled off his trike in a spray of blood as his head exploded from the force of the powerful bullet.

"Good shot, Wade!" Fredrick jammed his muzzle out of the window and began firing quickly. Glancing out the window, I saw he was dumping rounds into the group of riders with little effect.

For such a famous hunter, he could certainly shoot fast, but he couldn't hit the broadside of a barn.

Skyla screamed as a flung spear thunked against the wood siding below a window beside her. A moment later she recovered and fired her pistol in the direction of the thrower.

Pulling the heavy rifle to my shoulder, I searched through the apes for their leader. In the commotion, he'd disappeared amongst the pack and kicked up dust. Picking an ape at random, I fired my new Winchester in anger for the very first time and saw blood splash. Racking the lever to chamber a fresh cartridge, I took a deep breath to steady my aim and fired again. This time, a better hit. The ape left a red smear on the flanks of his mount as he fell and was trampled beneath dozens of heavy trike hooves.

With satisfaction, I racked the lever and picked another target. This time an ape firing arrows. Swinging the rifle after him as his mount surged towards the front of the pack, I chased my moving target and fired as an arrow chipped off the window sill. It zinged by me, knocking my hat off. I flinched, and my shot hit his trike.

Beside me, Skyla was taking careful aim before firing. Her right eye squinted as she focused on the front sight and gently squeezed the trigger as she had been taught.

At that moment, I realized there was nothing more beautiful than a pretty lady shooting guns in the heat of combat.

An ape a mere handful of yards from the train dropped his spear and slumped against the trike's bone shield. The wounded ape struggled to stay mounted. Another shot rang out, striking him in the side with a bloom of red. The ape fell towards our car, dragging on the reins.

"Got him! Did you see that?" Fredrick shouted excitedly while thumbing cartridges into his rifle.

"Look out!" Wade cried, jumping away from the window. Skyla dove after him as Fredrick looked around, confused.

The trike turned with the dragging pressure of its dead rider and rammed into the train at an angle, crushing its dead ape master, splintering boards and puncturing holes in the siding with its horns. Steel wheels shrieked as they protested the sideways pressure. The trike bellowed and thrashed as its head and horns became jammed into the passenger car. Then the dinosaur stumbled on one of the rail ties and fell.

The entangled creature made terrible noises as it was dragged. The train began slowing from the added weight. The animal's hide, and flesh was being ripped away and shredded against the ground and wood ties. Reaching through the shattered boards, I pressed my barrel on the giant beast's forehead and pulled the trigger mercifully. The trike died. As it went limp, its body jammed against a rail tie. With a loud snap, one of its large horns broke off and the mangled body dropped free and tumbled away, leaving a jagged, bloody gash in the side of the rail car.

Rising to peek out the window, I saw our small amount of fire wasn't very effective against the dozens of apes who chased alongside us. They'd spread out now, and were strung all along the train of cars, but blessedly, none appeared to have gone for the locomotive and its engineer. Their ignorance was our gain. But for the most part, we seemed to be the only car killing them, the others were pelting the apes and trikes with bullets to little effect.

"It ain't looking good, Jed!" Wade shouted, crouched in the aisle, tilting his barrel up and working the lever to eject a spent shell. An ape leapt onto a car further down the train, grabbing tight to the siding with his stone axe slung over his back. A brave soul leaned out and tried to dispatch the giant monkey with a pistol, but was jerked out with one arm and flung onto the prairie where he was immediately trampled by the next ape.

We needed more firepower.

Leaning over, I dropped my rifle on the bench beside the wolverine slayer. "You've got four more shots! Make them count!" He looked at me, startled. I turned to run.

"Where are-" Fredrick shouted after me.

"I'll be back!" I called, glancing at Skyla's scared but determined face. Winking reassurance towards her, I slid past and leapt over the dead passenger and sticky puddle of blood. Behind me, I heard Fredrick spraying the apes and trikes again with his rapid and inaccurate firing. Followed by the heavy boom of my Winchester being fired by Wade.

Jerking the narrow door open, I leapt across the steel coupling to the next car. This one was a freight car and didn't have a front and back door, only two sliding doors on the sides. But there was a rusted steel ladder for access to the roof. Shoving my boots into the rugs, I climbed to the top and stood. An arrow zipped by me and I ran. My boots thumped against the wooden roof, and I fought to keep my balance. Bits of tiny burnt coal ash pelted me from the racing locomotive at the front of the train.

Behind me I heard the loud boom of a shotgun firing both barrels. Twisting to look, I saw an ape's body fall off the car and onto the horns of another trike. With a great shake of its head, the corpse was flung into the steel wheels of the rail car and dismembered in the spokes.

Racing to the end, I dropped onto the shaking, rattling coupling, catching the last of the rungs to keep myself from falling under the cars.

I'd reached the cattle car I was looking for. It wasn't built as solidly as the freight or passenger car, this one had gaps between the boards to allow fresh air to get to packed cattle. It was empty of cows now, but what it contained was worth risking my life for.

Jumping up, I grabbed the edge of the roof tightly. Carefully, bracing my boots against the side, I began to work my way around the corner and towards the sliding door. Below, the ground raced by and wind pushed at me.

I was fully exposed to the attacking apes.

An arrow slammed next to my hand, punching through the thin siding and disappeared inside the car.

Startled, I jerked that hand away, losing its grip.

My shoulder screamed in protest as I desperately clung with one hand. I twisted and thrashed, kicking my legs against the car until I found enough purchase to push myself up to get both hands back on the roof edge.

Then I kept moving, hand over hand, until reaching the edge of the door. Bracing my upper body, and holding on with a white knuckled death grip, I used a boot to slide the door away from me. It moved several inches then stopped. I tried again, pushing hard, my grip slipping with the exertion. The door moved about a foot, leaving the opening still too narrow for me to slide into.

More apes were leaping off mounts and onto the passenger cars with howls of murderous rage. One climbed onto a roof, leaned over and dragged a man out through the window. Kicking and screaming, the man clung to the car as gunfire peppered the ape. With a mighty tug, the ape pulled him free and flung him out onto the prairie. His screaming stopped abruptly as his body slammed into the ground and cartwheeled across the prairie like a broken rag doll.

Fredrick, putting himself in obvious danger, leaned out a window and began firing at the apes climbing on the cars behind him. He knocked one off, and wounded another before ducking back in the car.

I kicked at the door in desperation. Our biggest chance of survival was keeping our distance from the apes; if they swarmed the train, we were done for.

On the third kick, it broke free and opened another two feet.

Clutching the edge of the door, I pulled myself into the car. I slammed the door shut and an arrow punched half its length through beside my head. The slotted wood that made up the door and sides of the livestock car wouldn't offer much protection. But I wasn't looking for protection.

Grabbing the canvas sheet, I yanked it off the Gatling gun and gave thanks that it'd been loaded into the car pointing in the right direction. It would have been almost impossible for me to turn around in the narrow confines of the car by myself.

With my Bowie, I pried the top off a crate of ammunition and pushed it next to the gun. Pulling out a twenty-round box filled with large .45-70 cartridges, I slipped them into the gravity fed hopper on the top of the gun. Straddling the gun's wood and steel carriage, I freed the modified traversing and elevation mechanism, grabbed the hand crank and peeked through the gaps in the door.

Without a team to reload, my firing rate would be slowed, but twenty rounds were better than eight in my rifle.

The ape who fired the arrow through the door moved his trike closer to the cattle car. When it was a handful of feet away, the ape dropped the reins, and leapt across the open space. The door buckled and slammed against its rollers as the heavy weight suddenly latched onto it. An eye was pressed against one of the openings in the slats. Spying me inside, the ape growled.

I rotated the handle forward.

Pop-pop-pop-pop...

Gun smoke filled the car as the powerful bullets shredded the door amidst sprays of splintered wood. The weight of the gun made the recoil negligible. Empty shell casings ejected under the gun and the ape was practically cut in half in a spray of red gore and flung off the shot-up door.

The trike he'd been riding tumbled and fell, pierced with over a dozen bullets as the multi-barreled gun went empty.

I stared at the carnage the Gatling created. Blood dripped from shattered boards. The stench of gunpowder filled the air and acrid smoke stung my nostrils.

Screams, roars, and gun shots of the battle snapped me back to reality. I couldn't afford to linger at the destruction wrought with only twenty rounds. Grabbing another cardboard box of ammo, I jammed the cartridges into the hopper as the remains of the cargo door toppled away in the wind.

The locomotive began turning into a curve, blessedly allowing me to see further down the cars strung out behind me. It was a wide-open melee along the back half of the train. Apes on trikes were flinging spears and arrows. Several were crawling over the tops of cars and trying to climb in through windows. Gunfire was coming from over half a dozen cars as the scattered passengers attempted to repel the assault.

Kicking the blocks out from under one of the large wheels, I grunted and strained to tilt the gun carriage upright and rotate it. Ignoring the pain shooting up my legs and back, I managed to turn it slightly before dropping it with a loud boom that cracked the floorboards. I still couldn't shoot down the length of the train, but I had a better field of fire than before.

I searched for the leader of the apes amongst the cloud of dust and dinosaur flesh to no avail. But a pair of apes broke away from harassing my friend's car and headed towards me. Their trikes cut diagonally across the boulder and brush strewn field as the train made the long turn, churning up dust under hooves and further obscuring the other riders and the one I desperately wanted to kill.

As they entered my field of fire, I fired on the trike closest to me and the apes ducked. The bullets shattered its horns, punching holes through its skull and sloped bone shield. The trike dropped, sliding several feet before toppling over, its head a bloodied mess, and its rider sprawled motionless on the ground.

Rotating the gun to the second ape, I fired two shots into the trike's shield before the gun jammed. Ammunition flew as I jerked the feeding tray off and tried to figure out where the jam was. Not seeing anything where the ammo loaded, I shoved my fingers deep into the action from underneath. There was an empty casing stuck inside.

The ape rose behind the bone shield, spear in hand. Now that they were clear of the dust, I saw that the rider was the big she-ape I had seen earlier. She had an empty quiver on her mount and a large club strapped to her back.

A fingernail tore off painfully as the jam broke free and the casing rolled underfoot as I pulled my hand out of the action.

The spear flew at me. Ducking, I fell as it glanced off one of the brass barrels, cutting a groove in the coating before impaling the door behind me. The ape rammed her mount into the side of the freight car. The trike bellowed in pain, and the large gun broke free of the remaining block, its large wheels rolling backwards over me.

Contorting my body, the heavy wheels and carriage tongue narrowly missed crushing my legs as I slid into the gap between them. I tried to squirm out against the rough splintered floorboards and realized I was stuck. Worse, I was twisted up in such a terrible way that I couldn't reach my pistols.

The she-ape leapt into the car as her mount ran away with its face and side gashed open and bleeding heavily from the impact. With a large hairy hand, she lifted one of the wheels on the two-hundred-pound gun off me while reaching for me with the other.

I kicked her painted face and she dropped the wheel as her flat nose sprayed blood and the green paint on her face smeared. The carriage of the gun smacked me across the forehead and I saw stars dance as the wheel broke through the floorboards and sunk lower.

She grabbed me by both legs and dragged me out. My shirt and flesh scraped and tore on the rough sawn floor boards.

Once I was out from under the gun, she flung me out the ruined side of the cattle car.

Wind milling my arms desperately, I caught enough fingers on the bullet punctured siding to stop my fall to certain death. Steel nails screeched as boards began to pry apart under my weight. My feet dangled perilously close to the rail ties speeding past below. Holding tightly to the flimsy siding, I began to move.

As the she-ape looked around the opening, I pulled myself onto the rattling coupling between the cars. Fighting for balance on the swaying steel locks, I climbed the iron ladder.

Once on top of the car, I leaned forward to brace myself against the wind, my torn shirt flapping around me. Thick black coal smoke billowed from the locomotive, choking me, as the engineer desperately tried to outpace the attacking apes.

The battle was still unfolding behind me. Even with my short-lived use of the Gatling, it looked like we'd killed almost half of them so far. But there was no telling how many causalities we'd taken. Cracks and booms of gunfire coming from my friend's rail car reassured me that they were still in the fight. Fewer arrows were being slung now, instead apes were maneuvering their trikes to leap onto the train, where they could fight up close and personal with a size and strength advantage.

Annoyed with the flapping remains of my shirt, I ripped it off my torso. It fluttered away like a red and white checkered flag. The braided black tooth lay exposed on my chest and I felt the cool wind across my scarred back.

Then I saw the leader.

He was clinging to the side of a passenger car, moving towards an arm extended through the window, firing at an ape with a pistol. Powerless, I could only watch as the scar faced ape swung his obsidian axe. The severed limb flew away in a spray of blood, gun still clenched in hand. The high-pitched shrieks of agony faintly reached me as the scar faced ape climbed into the car.

Large, hairy hands slapped the roof edge, and the she-ape climbed the ladder after me. The big monkey snarled, exposing her canines. Blood dribbled from her nose, mingling with the smeared green paint.

"Sorry about your face paint, she-bitch," I snarled, lifting my leg to stomp down on her ugly mug with my entire hundred and eighty pounds.

She grabbed the boot with a large hand and shoved hard.

Stumbling, I fell backwards, swearing as my head bounced onto the rough boards. Disorientated and angry, I struggled to my feet and staggered to the front of the cattle car's roof to gain distance between us as the ape pulled herself over the edge.

Tugging the leather straps free, she jerked the club off her back. The end was formed from a chunk of gray stone bound to a tree limb as thick as my forearm. She easily held it with one hand. It was the perfect size for smashing my skull.

There was thirty feet between us now. I risked a quick glance behind me to see if I could make the jump to the next car. Possible, but difficult in my current position.

I swiveled my head back.

She was barreling towards me. Her heavy stomps shook the roof of the car. Her teeth were bared, club raised, hatred etched across her face.

My hands dropped on their own and grasped the grips on my twin Colt Peacemakers. I drew both and began firing. Just like I'd practiced at Carson's range. Except this time with a three-hundred-pound she-monkey charging at me.

Bullets hammered into her as the revolvers bucked in my hand.

Her hairy body shook and trembled from the impacts of rounds slamming into her muscled chest and torso, punching through the dinosaur hide cloth and black skin. She staggered and slowed, but kept coming, closing the distance between us as I continued to fire.

Organs ruptured, bones shattered, blood sprayed.

The guns went empty.

The ape staggered, swayed side to side, and dropped to a knee. Blood ran down her body in rivets. Her breathing was heavy and labored. The club fell from a limp hand and slid off the roof. She glared defiantly as her strength faded and her eyes dimmed. Her lips curled in a weak snarl.

"Get off my train, you damned dirty ape." Taking one large stride towards her, I kicked her in the chest with the heel of my boot and watched her fall backwards off the roof.

She hit the ground head first, bounced, then snapped a large cactus in half before slamming into an out cropping of rock.

A terrifying roar came from down the train. Spinning, I saw the scar faced ape standing on the roof of a car just past my friends. His body was soaked with blood, his axe dripping gore. He bared his fangs at me. Something round dangled from his hand.

Either I just killed his girlfriend, or he recognized me.

Good.

Let's do this.

Stuffing one of the guns into a holster, I began quickly reloading the other as I walked towards him. There were only two cars between us, and I raced to put fresh cartridges into the Colt before he came after me.

Bellowing something harsh, guttural, and probably insulting, he hurled the round thing at me. As the strange object flew towards me, I jerked the pistol up to fire, but he leapt off the train.

Stunned, I stepped to the edge and leaned over as something thumped against the car roof and rolled towards me.

The scar-faced leader had landed on his massive trike, and turned away from the pursuit, shaking his axe over his head and bellowing guttural commands.

More apes leapt off the train and onto the pacing trikes. One of them, dragging a wounded leg, clambered out a car window and tried to push off the train to compensate for his weakness. He missed the jump and died. The surviving apes peeled off, riding after their leader.

Gun fire slowed, becoming more sporadic before stopping altogether as the apes rode further away.

I kicked myself for missing the opportunity to kill their leader. He was a slippery one, but at least I got his girlfriend. I looked at the trail of splattered blood across the roof from the she-ape.

Hell of a fight.

Somewhere on the train, an ape roared weakly, followed by a single shot.

I was relieved when Skyla stuck her head out of the window, spotted me, and waved. She looked exhausted, but I took the wave to mean that our group was fine. Sadly, I expected the rest of the people on the trains hadn't come out so lucky. My companions had been heavily armed and clumped together, which allowed them to put up a good defense. The others were stretched thin and less armed.

Carefully walking across the roof, I stopped and stared at the object the ape leader had thrown.

It was a man's head. I recognized him from the loading station in Cheyenne. Now his face was twisted in an agonizing grimace, eyes glazed over and unseeing. Scraggly blonde hair was soaked with blood and twisted into a knot. For easy carrying I guessed. The train jarred on the tracks, and the head rolled, revealing the gory hacked end of the neck and severed spine.

I clenched my jaw and picked the head up by the knot before climbing down off the top of the damaged box car.

***

Except for Fredrick, my group was okay. An arrow nicked the hunter's bicep, cutting a nasty furrow through muscle. He simply wrapped his bright red bandana around it and kept fighting.

But the passengers who rode with us hadn't been so lucky. We lost one in the opening moments of the attack, and an ape had burst through the back door and jerked another man out before anyone could react. Bullet holes and blood showed where my companions shot the ape off the car coupling immediately after.

As for me, I was starting to get used to being beaten up and ruining shirts. Everyone in the car saw my scars now. Skyla and Wade already knew, and Fredrick did the math when he remembered my encounter with Reydan back at the Governor's Office. I borrowed one of Wade's shirts to stay covered. He was a bigger man than me, and the light blue shirt was loose around my chest and waist.

We did the best we could to get the wounded bandaged and made as comfortable as possible, then draping blankets over the dead. The severed head I'd left with the Gatling.

By the time we settled back into our seats, we were all smeared with sticky blood of apes and humans. With the excitement long worn off, I was exhausted. Looking at the others' faces, I could tell they felt the same.

"Here." With a grunt, Wade passed my rifle over. "This thing kicks like a mule."

"You hit anything?" I asked, accepting the heavy gun.

He barked a short laugh and scoffed. "Of course."

I ran my hands over the rifle. Figures my first fight with it, and someone else got to shoot it more than I did. But since I got to use the Gatling, I couldn't complain. Much.

The fatigue was hitting Skyla hard, and she rested her head back against my shoulder. Even with a canteen full of water, she had a difficult time cleaning up. Her fingernails were ringed with blood and there were stains of it on her dress. From what I gathered, she'd performed admirably. That made me like her even more.

"So, that's the 1886 Winchester that Carson gave you?" Wade asked.

"Carson Skinner?" Fredrick perked up at the name.

"Yes, and yes," I replied, as I tried to make myself comfortable. My muscles and joints ached from the strain of hanging onto the side of the box car. The torn fingernail throbbed. I carefully shifted myself to a position that didn't hurt too badly.

Fredrick nodded his approval. "Good man. I've bought a few guns from him. But this…" he leaned around Wade to get a better view, "this is magnificent craftsmanship. And in .45-70 no less!"

"That's the second one ever made," Skyla added. She'd already had the opportunity to examine the rifle and shoot it at the range that morning.

The newest addition to our group looked up through his spectacles and grinned beneath his large mustache. "I need one."

"You should give it a name," Skyla said tiredly, her eyes half closed. "All the best guns have names."

Wade nodded, his face serious. "Nothing wrong with that."

"I hadn't thought about it," I admitted, but I liked the notion. This was certainly, by far, the nicest rifle I'd ever own.

"How about The Deuce?" Wade offered. "It goes with the serial number."

"Sounds like a bowel movement," Fredrick laughed to the wolverine slayer's chagrin.

"What about *Eighty-Six*?" Skyla spoke quietly, as she shifted to look up at me.

"*Eighty-Six*, as in 1886…" I repeated, slowly, to myself. "I like it."

Skyla beamed.

"A fine name for a fine weapon," Fredrick said.

Wade swore softly and leaned over to look out the window. "Lookie there."

On a bluff high above the tracks, sat the leader of the apes and the remains of his war party on their dinosaurs, watching our train steam by below. Someone else saw them, because I heard several shots ring out, but no one seemed to connect. The apes seemed unconcerned with being hit at that distance.

"Interesting. They're cutting cross country to follow us." Fredrick shook his head. "These things are smarter than I thought they'd be."

Wade stood. Carrying his heavy single shot rifle in hand, he quickly made his way to the back of the car and settled into one of the seats.

"Can you hit him from here?" Fredrick asked as we realized what he was about to attempt. "That's a far way off."

The wolverine slayer didn't answer. Instead, he cupped the forearm of the long-barreled Ballard in his left hand and rested the pair on the window sill. Peering down the sights, he squatted lower and aimed higher. The distance was great, and the moving train made the shot extremely difficult.

I held my breath, watching the apes and hoping against hope that Wade could pull the shot off. If we cut the head off the snake, we could buy time for more soldiers to arrive. Skyla gripped my hand in hers.

The boom of the rifle filled the car. Skyla's hand tightened reflexively.

For a second, we watched. Waiting. Hoping.

The ape beside the leader toppled off his mount, both hands clutching at his throat. The broken horned trike sidestepped away as the mortally wounded ape crawled onto all fours.

I let my breath out, both pleased that he hit an ape and disappointed that he didn't hit the right one. "Nice try, Wade," I called back to him.

Wade grunted angrily as he pulled the rifle out of the window. "Height was good, just didn't compensate for the train speed enough."

The scar faced leader slid off his trike and stepped over to the dying ape. A shaky hand reached for him and he batted it aside, raised his obsidian club, and brought it crashing down on the wounded ape's head. The other apes watched, unconcerned with their leader killing one of their kind in front of them.

Skyla gasped and raised a hand to her mouth.

"Vicious thing, ain't he?" Wade muttered as he slipped back into his seat.

"Good shooting. We've one less to contend with now," Fredrick said approvingly. "With any luck, that scar faced monkey will kill some more for us."

"Just a couple hundred more to go," I muttered quietly to myself as the apes turned and rode their great beasts down the bluff and out of sight. The leader waited, as if daring us to shoot at him again before mounting his trike. As the train began to pass out of sight, he walked his mount after the others as if he had all the time in the world.

I looked at Skyla as her eyes began to close and wished I'd forced her to stay in Cheyenne.

***

The train rolled into town, shot full of arrows, with pools of dried blood on the floors, and bodies under blankets in almost every passenger car. A pair of soldiers, keeping watch from inside the train station, met us. We unloaded the wounded first, then the dead.

Wade took Skyla to get cleaned up and check on Ashley at the hotel, while I stayed behind to help supervise the unloading of the Gatling guns with Fredrick. Even with the cut across his arm, he seemed to have an endless supply of energy as he moved from helping wounded passengers, to unloading heavy ammunition boxes, to jumping in and directing the placement of supplies and rifle crates as they were carried off the train. He was continually upbeat and cheerful. Even dressed like a leather-bound dandy, he seemed to get along with everyone.

As a team of horses pulled the Gatlings off the train, I noticed a crowd of unruly people shouting on the raised platform near the locomotive. It looked like a bunch of men, with a few families mixed in. Things were getting noisy and angry. I left Fredrick and quickly walked over to see what the commotion was about. The two town deputies stood with the crowd hemming them in on three sides.

"Quiet down! Listen to me!" James shouted to be heard over the ruckus; he raised a hand to silence them, but they weren't listening.

"We're leaving! You can't make us stay." I recognized the miner I'd body slammed in the bar when he pushed forward through the crowd. So much had happened since then, but it still felt like it was just yesterday I was getting my black eyes blackened even further by his sloppy haymakers. His nose was bent from where I had broken it. I dredged his name from the depths of my memory. Timmy. A funny name for such a big man.

"You missed your chance. No one is leaving now until Cheyenne sends more troops. We don't have the manpower to protect both the train and the town," Tom pleaded.

"To hell with the town!" Timmy spat on the ground in front of Tom. The crowd shouted their agreement as the miner thrust out his chest. "Who are you to stop us?" He was playing to the mob, and they were eating it up and shouting their support. The crowd surged in around the deputies as the miner jabbed an accusing finger at them.

I looked for soldiers, but there weren't any in sight.

Tom jerked his pistol out of his belt and fired it into the air. At the crack the crowd shrunk back, then surged forward in anger. "Get back!" he screamed, pointing the pistol at the crowd.

A woman screamed. Men grabbed their wives and kids and began to pull them away, while the rest of the group grew angrier and more belligerent.

James backed his brother's play, drawing his gun as well, but keeping it pointed towards the ground.

"If we stay, we'll be eaten, and these two tin stars can't kill us all!" the miner said, egging others on as he stepped back into the crowd for protection. "I say we grab that engineer and make him take us out of here!"

I'd had enough of this. I shoved my way through the crowd. Broad shoulders came in handy for such things. Stepping in front of the deputies, I hissed at them, "Put your guns away." They both hesitated, looking back and forth between me and the crowd. "Now, dammit!"

James obeyed. Tom didn't, he took a step back and shook his head. His eyes were wide and fearful.

I leaned closer to him. "Do it," I said in as menacing and commanding of a voice as I could muster.

He swallowed hard, then shoved the gun into his holster angrily. But his hand stayed firmly wrapped around the pistol's grip.

I spun to face the mob. They were a bunch of rough and tumble working men, with a few suits looking out of place. The families had disappeared. Fools yanking guns out and firing into the air tended to do that to people who care about their children.

The miner pushed forward through the crowd to confront me. "You!" he hissed through the broken teeth I'd given him. I bet that hurt.

"Yeah, me." I looked him over. He still had a sizeable advantage on me, and this time he was stone cold sober, with a score to settle and instead of a couple drunks backing him, he had a rowdy mob on the verge of violence. I'd have to tread lightly. "Where's your partner?"

A look of disgust crossed the big man's face. "He left town already," he spat at the ground angrily.

"Smart man." I pointed towards the train behind the crowd and shouted, "Take a good look at it!"

The passenger cars were busted to crap. Bullet holes were punched through the sides and roof, blood smeared along the siding from apes being shot off and people dragged through. Horn marks and busted boards where the trike rammed my group's car. And my cattle car, with an entire side riddled with blood splattered bullet holes from where I'd cut the ape in half.

One of the train station attendants was walking down the length of the train, breaking off feathered arrows that had turned the train cars into pin cushions with a long wooden pole. Another man followed with a ladder, leaning it against the train before climbing up and hacking embedded spears off with a small hatchet.

"We lost ten people getting here. The only thing that broke the attack was me kicking the ape leader's lady friend off the roof after opening up on them with a Gatling gun. There's what? Twenty of you? You think you can survive an attack on your own? Especially now that I pissed off the big ape that leads them?"

"We can if you give us one of the Gatlings," Timmy retorted loudly, strutting between the crowd and myself. "Besides," he stopped and looked at me, "like you said. There's twenty of us. And there's only three of you. I bet if we get attacked by your monkeys, we could just throw you to them and they'd leave us alone." He took a threatening step towards me.

Someone whistled sharply and as one, everyone turned to look.

Everyone except me.

I jammed the muzzle of my pistol against the big miner's temple. Surprisingly, it didn't have the effect I intended, as he looked out the corner of his eye at me, then away again. His eyes were wide in fear at something else.

Puzzled, I looked in the direction as the rest as I realized the angry mob had gone silent.

You could have heard a pin drop on the platform.

A hundred feet away, Fredrick grinned wolfishly. His hand rested on the crank of a Gatling that was aimed at the crowd in front of me. "Say when Jed, and I'll cut them down and we can go get some supper."

"Tom, James," I called to the deputies behind me as I holstered my pistol, "Stuff Little Timmy here in a cell. Preferably a damp one with no mattress." I looked over the quiet mob. "As for the rest of you, go home. Forget about this. Clean your guns. Prepare for battle. Soon enough, we'll fight together or die together."

***

The mob dispersed quickly. Nobody wanted to argue with a multi-barreled gun pointed at their belly.

The deputies hauled the wretched miner to jail and I checked on Carbine while Fredrick went to gather the others to meet me at the Sheriff's.

Carbine was excited to see me. He ran to the fence, snorting softly and pawing at the ground. I scratched his neck and along his ears.

"Have you been good, boy?" I looked him over. The stable had taken good care of him in my absence, his coat looked well brushed and his eyes bright. He looked anxious to be out of the pen. "Maybe we can go for a ride tomorrow." I figured I might be able to sneak around a little, try to get a feel for what the apes were up to.

Leaving Carbine, I checked on my saddle and tack. Everything appeared in order and I tipped the stable boy for taking good care of everything. Grabbing a withered apple from an old whiskey barrel turned into a bin, I fed it to my horse and gave him one last scratch before rushing to the hotel to drop off my gear and change from blood stained pants into a fresh set with a shirt that fit.

The Sheriff's Office was crowded when I arrived.

Ashley appeared much better than we had last seen her and stood in the back of the room with Skyla. Judging from their sideways glances at me and giggles, I was being discussed. My ears burned, and I averted my gaze.

Dan sat at his desk with a stern-faced officer standing beside him. The officer was short, with a barrel chest and Lieutenant chevrons on his blue uniform. His brown eyes appeared to measure each person in the room. He was a fighter, his knuckles were busted and scarred, and he had a small white scar that cut through an eyebrow.

I idly wondered if he'd lost rank when they'd tossed him in the brig.

Seated in front of Dan's desk were Wade and Fredrick, discussing hunting grizzlies or something. I wasn't exactly sure.

The two deputies sat on stools near the cells, arguing about how much a horse was worth. Behind them the miner glared in his cell. I was pleased to see it didn't have a mattress on his cot. Wesley stood in his cell, leaning against the metal bars casually.

"Oh... wearing two guns now, eh Jed?" He gave me a sly grin. "I approve."

"Glad to hear it," I told him sarcastically as I stood awkwardly in the center of the room, unsure of what to do with myself.

The officer coughed loudly, and the room went quiet. He spoke with a thick Irish accent. "Ladies, Gentlemen... I am Lieutenant Brandthorn. Governor Hardy sent me here with two objectives. The first is to defend the town against an attack, and the second is to wait for reinforcements then secure the tunnel from any other incursions while the main body of our army meets these apes."

I felt myself twitch at the implications of that. The words of Reydan White ran through the back of my mind, that the government will take my land and give it to him to run a train through. That was a subject to be debated after we survive until reinforcements arrive.

The Lieutenant gestured at the two men sitting before him. "Mr. Mackin and Mr. von Holsack have caught me up to speed on the attack on your train. So, now let me fill you in on what has happened in your absence. Best we know, two ranches and one mining claim have been attacked. The miners were able to fight the apes off, slip away under the cover of darkness, and most made it to town." He sighed and rubbed his temple. "Everyone at the two ranches were killed. Several appear to have been ritually sacrificed with their chests cut open and hearts removed."

"Sons of hairy bitches!" Tom exclaimed angrily, starting to spit on the floor before thinking better of it and swallowing.

"Language!" Dan growled at his nephew, reminding him that women were present. Cowed, the young deputy grunted embarrassingly and studied the floor between his feet.

It shouldn't have been a surprise; I'd already told them of the ritual I'd seen take place in the apes' canyon. But it was unnerving to hear of it happening again, especially to people some of us knew.

I thought back to the skulls draped on the scar faced ape's trike. "Are there any other ranchers or miners who haven't been brought in yet?"

"From what I've gathered, there's such a large scattering of mining claims all around that we can't check them all. All sorts of individuals are out there with secret mines and camps that we have no chance at finding. They're on their own, and God help them. As for ranches, there is just one left. The Claytons. I sent a squad to bring them in."

That was a risky move, I thought. Personally, I'd have sent one ballsy individual on a fast horse to fetch them instead of risking such a large portion of the town's defenders. A dozen soldiers wouldn't stand a chance if they came across a war party of mounted apes in the open. But it wasn't my place to say anything, the decision had been made and the plan already put into action. We'd just have to hope they all came back, and old man Clayton was stubborn as a mule. It would be hard to convince him to abandon his home and run. But he'd be a fool to stay.

The Lieutenant continued in his Irish twang. "We've seen a few apes keeping an eye on the town. Whenever we ride to meet them, they run off. We can't risk the possibility of walking into a trap, so we don't chance a pursuit. Once we posted scouts of our own, they've stayed even further away. But they are keeping tabs on us," his eyes flicked to me, his face suddenly an expressionless mask. "I understand you managed to acquire a pair of Gatling guns. Interesting. Especially since we... lost... two of them several years ago."

"Intriguing coincidence," I responded, carefully keeping my face neutral and ignoring the sudden accusing looks from Wade and Fredrick. I didn't share the knowledge of their acquirement to the others because I'd take forgiveness over permission. Or rather, life over death and we needed these guns to help us stay alive.

The Lieutenant straightened the front of his uniform. "Regardless of where they came from, or how they came to be in your possession, they are much appreciated," he gave me a curt nod with a look of understanding.

"With the Gatlings and crates of Springfield rifles, how are the town's defenses looking?" Wade asked.

Dan answered, "Lieutenant Brandthorn's men are passing the rifles out now to anyone who has a need. We've plenty of firepower. What we lack is manpower." The old Sheriff looked like he had aged ten years in the last week. For a man of his age, that was really cutting down on his remaining life span. He gestured towards the Lieutenant beside him. "They brought a cannon. That will be a big help as well."

"It's a twelve-pound Napoleon. The best cannon there is for all around field service," Brandthorn clarified. "But I've only thirty-eight men with a dozen away collecting the Claytons. Once we are reinforced by the rest of the Alpha Company, we will be sitting pretty. Until then, which might be a week away, we're stretched thin. And without an additional Company to reinforce our own, no offensive can be mounted against the apes."

I took that to mean we'd just be sitting here while they rampaged around the territory. They could even bypass us and move further south. But I suspected they'd want to take the town. We would be a constant thorn in their side and what better way to test their competition than by hitting a small isolated group of locals?

"When do you think they will attack?" Fredrick asked as he cleaned his spectacles carefully with a small piece of cloth pulled from a breast pocket.

"Not a clue. Hopefully, not until the rest of my troops return with the Claytons." The Lieutenant looked around the room at our glum faces. "From what I understand, you gave them a pretty good black eye. I suspect they will lick their wounds before hitting us with everything they've got."

He stepped around the desk, stopped in front of me and looked at the black claw hanging from my neck, partly exposed by the unbuttoned top of my shirt. "I understand you're the one who killed the beast outside the office?"

I nodded.

"Allosaurus," Skyla spoke from behind me.

He smiled at her and corrected himself. "Yes ma'am, that's right, an Allosaurus. That was quite the feat. We saw something similar striding across the plains on our way in."

"Great. We'll need to kill it later," I said. At best, it could run into the apes and kill a few of them. At worst, it'd wander around eating livestock and people until we hunted it down.

"I also understand you have the most experience with the apes."

"Reckon so," I admitted. "I've killed the most of them."

He looked around the room. "With the exception of one of your scientists who didn't return, everyone in this room except the Sheriff and myself have had some run in with the apes. I want your input on our defenses."

193

"When you goin' let me go?" Timmy interrupted belligerently from his cell.

"Shuddup!" Tom shouted and threw a dented metal cup at him. It bounced through the bars and hit the miner in the shoulder.

"Ow!" the big miner feigned injury and rubbed the meat of his shoulder through his filthy shirt.

"Quiet, both of you. The Judge is riding his circuit. He isn't due here for another two weeks. Assuming we are still alive when he gets here, we'll let him handle you," Dan rubbed his gray temples as he spoke. "I've got enough ulcers to deal with, without having you running loose. And Tom, don't abuse the prisoners."

"It was just a cup!" the young deputy protested weakly. His brother snickered and shoved him playfully.

"What about me?" came a low voice from the other cell.

The room went quiet as everyone looked at the infamous gunman.

Dropping his feet to the floor, Wesley sat upright on his cot and adjusted his vest. "Sounds like you could use another gun. In case you haven't heard, I'm pretty good with them. Let me out, and I'll help."

The room suddenly grew loud as the deputies immediately began to protest. He was their money ticket and they had a lot riding on collecting the reward for his capture. Fredrick just leaned back in his chair and stretched, appearing to not care in the least what we did with the man. Wade was an adamant no. Everyone seemed in agreement to not let him out.

I didn't say anything as I looked Wesley over. He had a lot of blood and death on his hands, but so did I. We'd only been acquaintances, but he saved me from being shot gunned in a bar just a week ago. I owed him for that and we could certainly use him. But if I pushed for him to be freed, any future deaths he caused would be on me. Besides, the decision wasn't mine to make.

"No. We'll be fine without you," Dan said firmly. That shut everyone up.

Wesley's eyes met mine and he shrugged. Kicking his feet back up on the cot, he lay down and pulled his hat over his eyes.

The Lieutenant took over the conversation again and turned to Skyla. "Ms. Stratton, do you have any idea why these apes would attack us? Is it simple, barbaric, savagery? Or is there a deeper purpose?"

Skyla looked down at her feet as all eyes turned to her. She took a deep breath and closed her eyes. "I think it's simply resources. Compared to the dangers of the prehistoric side, we are ripe for the plucking. If it wasn't for our technological advancements over them, we wouldn't stand a chance."

"Thank God for gunpowder," I said.

"Amen!" cried Wesley from his cell.

"Shuddup!" Tom kicked his boot against the gunman's iron cell bars.

Brandthorn ignored us. "Makes sense. Thank you." He looked around the room. "Who here has military experience?"

Fredrick, Wade, Dan and myself all raised our hands.

Wade looked at me in surprise. "I didn't know you were in the military."

"Nez Perce War, I served with him," I gestured towards the Sheriff.

Dan confirmed it with a silent nod.

The Lieutenant spread a large roll of paper over Dan's desk as we gathered around. It was a map of town, almost certainly borrowed from the Government Land Office building. I wondered how Tripod was doing without his master. Brandthorn spoke, "I've a plan for our defenses. But I want your input. Let's put our heads together and see how we can keep from being overrun by giant prehistoric monkeys."

***

The majority of town was laid out in a rectangle. Thirteen log and slap board buildings ran north to south along Main Street, effectively splitting town in half. Six on the west side, including the two-story saloon and hotel, and seven on the east, with the extra building being the stables that was distanced from the other buildings by a large fenced corral.

Outside of that lopsided rectangle of buildings were the train station, stock yards, and land office building. The quarter mile between town and the rail station was filled with miscellaneous tents that provided temporary housing and businesses. Scattered around the area were partially completed buildings, none of which we could defend.

"How many people capable of fighting do we have, Lieutenant?" Fredrick asked.

"Including my soldiers, almost a hundred men and women," he replied. "Now's a good time to mention it, with the addition of the Gatlings, I'll need volunteers to help operate them. The cannon, my men will handle."

Dan sucked his teeth. "I know a fella around here who could help," he scratched his beard thoughtfully. "He's an old Confederate, but a good man. I've heard stories of him gunnin' down Yankees by the dozens with a Gatling during the war." He caught himself and looked around the room. "No offense to any of you who might be Yanks."

"That was before my time, so none taken," Skyla assured him.

"I'm from Ohio," Ashley said from the back of the group.

"We'll take him, regardless of which side he fought for. Send anyone else my way," Brandthorn paused as we looked down at the sketched map. "If the apes hit us, they'll have to hit us from the east. With the river to the west and south, they won't be coming at us from those directions." He took a deep breath before continuing. "We can't defend the rail station, locomotive, stockyards, or all those infernal tents between us and the station. We don't have the man power for that. All we can do, is protect this area...." He swirled a pointed finger around the cluster of thirteen buildings in the center of the map. "This is it. This is where we make our stand."

"What if they come at us from the north?" I cut in, already knowing the answer but wanting to make sure everyone else knew as well.

"We're pretty much screwed," Brandthorn straightened and looked around the room. "From the north we have only two buildings to blunt their attack. Our heavy weapons would be exposed and wiped out, there would be little defendable cover to use, and the monkeys would ride down Main Street and split our forces in two. We could pour a lot of fire into them in a crossfire, but we'd also be shooting towards each other. It'd be a bloody mess. I'm hoping, since the terrain is steeper to the north, the apes will take the easy gradual rise to the east."

"Let's hope they don't know much about tactics," Fredrick muttered.

"So, we've a cannon and two Gatlings. Praying they hit us from the right directions, I'm assuming you'll want one of the guns at each end of town?" Wade asked, crossing his arms and craning his neck to look at the map.

"Correct, and the cannon will be placed at the northern entrance. As our most powerful weapon, I want it protected between the blacksmith forge and stables." Brandthorn tapped the corralled area on the map he referred to. "We'll relocate the horses to the stockyards and tear down some of the fences to make room."

I pictured the area in my mind; it'd have a good field of fire up the valley. I looked at the southern end of the row of buildings where the other Gatling would go. That one would be the most vulnerable. I said as much.

"We'll stack rail ties to provide some defensive cover and plenty of men to lay down fire as well," the Lieutenant answered.

"Gonna have to keep an eye on those tents. My deputies can gather some men to tear the closest ones down. If the apes swarm us and come through them, we'll have a hard time keeping that gun defended," Dan said, jabbing a finger at the area the tents were located while looking at his nephews.

Tom and his brother both nodded without voicing their usual complaints. It seemed the threat of destruction had finally sunken in and granted them a sense of seriousness they typically lacked.
There was hope for them yet.

"The biggest issue we have is the main street itself. It's forty feet wide. We've got to keep the apes out," Brandthorn replied, looking concerned as he stared at the map. "That's a large span. We don't have enough rail ties to provide protection for the Gatling teams and block off such a large area at the end of each town. And we don't have the time or men to start ripping rail tracks up to get them."

The room was silent as we studied the problem.

"Chevals de Frise!" Fredrick shouted suddenly, his eyes wide with excitement behind his spectacles.

"Did he just swear in French?" James whispered to his brother.

"No. But that's a grand idea. It'd be effective against both cavalry and infantry," Brandthorn said with his brow furrowed in thought. "How do you know about those, Mr. von Holsak?"

"I've always had an interest in military history," he replied.

"What's a Chisel Fry?" I'd never heard of such a thing. Everyone but the Lieutenant and Fredrick seemed just as baffled as myself.

"Chevals de Frise," Brandthorn corrected me. "An old medieval design. Take a log, drill holes through it, and stick in wooden spikes at crisscrossing angles. Which creates, essentially, an X with the log at the center and the sticks crossing at ninety-degree angles," he showed us by crossing the fingers on both hands. "It rests on the bottom two 'legs' or unsharpened portions of the sticks," he explained.

"Confederates used them pretty often during the war," Fredrick added.

"They're heavy, awkward as hell to move, and mounts don't like running into the sharp points. It also slows down infantry so you can kill them as they struggle to get over the barrier." Brandthorn shifted his weight from one foot to the other, he was getting excited now.

Trikes were larger than horses, with thicker skin and natural armor around their necks, but I doubted they'd be eager to run into things that would poke them. My only concern was that the apes were stronger than men, and more likely to not care about dying crawling over an obstacle to get to us. But I couldn't think of any better options, so I stayed quiet.

He continued, "Best of all, they are quick to build, we have the material, and we can start on them tonight. That takes care of blocking Main Street, now we need to get down to brass tacks and figure out the finer details of our defense."

We were exhausted from the battle on the train, but we pushed through and burned the midnight oil in several lanterns to give us illumination to plan for our survival. There's no telling how many pots of coffee we downed between our large group, but it was an impressive amount.

As we were wrapping up the placement of our group along the defenses, the church bell suddenly began ringing frantically. Grabbing our weapons, we rushed into the dark of night, illuminated only with the few burning lanterns along the street.

Without waiting for the others, I ran towards the shouting and commotion near the northern entrance. Brandthorn easily kept pace beside me as the rest of our party scattered behind us as they followed. Passing groups of armed men and soldiers, we reached the source of the commotion.

A soldier who looked to be fifteen was being carefully pulled off his trembling, froth covered horse. Two large ape arrows jutted from the kid's back. It was a miracle he was still alive, and the horse looked like it'd been run almost to death. As men gently laid him on his side, he moaned faintly. The kid looked delirious from blood loss. The Lieutenant snatched a canteen from a soldier's hand and gently poured it into the boy's mouth. He coughed, and sputtered, red spit dribbling from his lips.

"Gentry," Brandthorn said softly. "It's me. Where are the others? Where's Sergeant Collins?" he asked softly, cupping the wounded soldier's boyish face and leaning in close.

"Dead," the kid coughed, spraying bloody flecks on the Lieutenant's face. "All dead," he trembled, and the feathered shafts shook with him. Tears began to stream down his face, mixing with the blood he'd coughed up and dripping red onto the dirt beneath him. "I think they're all dead," he repeated before coughing again and wincing in terrible pain.

Doc pushed through the crowd, shoving the Lieutenant aside, and taking charge. From a small leather bag, he pulled out a knife and began cutting away the boy's uniform to see the wounds. "One's not too bad. The other is in his lung. He's lost a lot of blood."

Brandthorn stood and stepped back. His face was grim.

The doc pointed at the closest building. "Carry him in there. Bring lanterns and hot water. Now."

A soldier jerked on the reinforced door then kicked it hopelessly. "Locked!" he shouted. A small man in long johns and a night cap with a rifle shoved him aside while producing a ring of keys from his pocket. "It's a bank, dumbass. Of course, it's locked," he said, unlocking then pushing the door open and stepping back to allow the wounded boy to be carried in. "Use the desk in the corner. That's mine and it's the biggest one in here. Toss everything on it into the corner."

The Sheriff followed the doc inside, shouting to make sure everyone heard him. "No one touches any money, or so help me, I'll hang you tonight. Tom, James... unless someone has business with the boy, keep them the hell out." Inside I heard the sound of papers and coins hitting the wall as the desk was hastily cleared off.

Deputies moved to position themselves by the door as I sought Brandthorn out of the dispersing crowd. Fredrick and Wade had moved to take cover, facing the end of the main street where it opened to the valley.

I suspected they were thinking what I was, that it'd be a good time for the apes to attack while we were distracted.

Skyla touched my arm as I passed her, a worried look across her beautiful face. "It'll be okay," I whispered comfortingly, even though I knew full well the chances of our survival just took a significant drop with the loss of the boy's squad.

"Lieutenant?" I asked softly as I approached him from behind.

Before responding, he grabbed the nearest soldier. "Double our guard for the next two hours. Everyone else is to be dressed and armed while they sleep. They may hit us," he shoved the soldier away and the man took off running to relay the message. "Yes, Jed?" he turned to face me. His face was splattered with his soldier's blood.

"Daylight's in five hours. I'm going out to check for survivors and on the Claytons." I knew the rancher and his family vaguely, and we needed men. Desperately. At this point, even a couple would be of immense help.

"If you go, it'll be alone. I can't risk any more men," he said sternly, his face the same expressionless mask I saw before. He was operating on pure professionalism now, emotions tucked away, hidden from his troops. I'd seen men take great losses under their command before and put the same mask on. Often, pushing those feelings down deep was the only way to keep moving forward without succumbing to the crushing pangs of guilt, failure, and defeatism. Facing them would come later, in privacy. Usually with a bottle.

"That's how I'd prefer it."

"Jed, please don't," Skyla warned worriedly as she stepped beside me. I heard the concern in her voice, the borderline panic at the thought of me leaving after most likely an entire squad of soldiers had been killed. But someone needed to go, and I understood the area better than my companions or the soldiers. Alone, I might stand a chance.

"I'm sorry, Skyla. One man less won't make a difference if they attack, but several men more will. If there's anyone alive out there, we need them." Her eyes reddened as she held back tears. "Someone has to," I told her quietly.

"It doesn't have to be you." A single tear escaped, rolling down her cheek. She turned her head and quickly wiped it away.

The Reverend pushed through our group, concern etched across his face and the tattered Bible clutched to his chest. I didn't know he was still here, but it didn't surprise me. He always seemed like the sort to protect his flock. We stood quietly and watched him enter the building with the wounded soldier.

"I'll go with Jed." Ashley hoisted her rifle higher on a shoulder. "He might need some extra firepower."

Brandthorn looked at her, shocked. "Absolutely not." He turned back to me, frowning. He'd made up his mind. "You understand the risk you're taking?"

I kept my eyes on him, unable to look at Skyla. "It's worth it. We need man power. Clayton is a bit long in the tooth, but he's a fighter through and through. His boys are good, capable men as well."

"Then get it done. But don't get killed." Turning his back on us, he entered the bank to check on his man.

I glanced at Skyla. Her face conveyed a mix of emotions. Tears rolled freely down her cheeks as she walked away without a word.

Ashley sighed beside me. "Good luck, and don't worry, she'll still be here when you get back," she grinned. "It's not like she can leave anyways."

***

It was still dark, a solid two hours before the break of dawn, but Wade had already beaten me to the stables and stood waiting with Carbine. I managed to get a few hours of restless sleep, and knocked on Skyla's door several times with no answer. I tried to apologize through the door, reasoning out why I was doing this, but there was no answer. Before I left, I told the locked door to not worry and that I'd return. Because I wanted to feel the press of her lips against mine and the taste of whiskey on her breath. The only answer was a muffled sob that broke my heart.

"Did the boy make it through the night?" Wade asked as he checked the saddle's cinch strap for proper tightness under Carbine's chest.

I shook my head. Doc tried his best, but the young soldier bled out on a banker's desk.

"That's another life they took. They owe us a dozen in return." Wade passed the reins to me. "I hate I'm not going with you."

I swung into the saddle and grinned at him before answering. "You'd just slow me down."

He scoffed and took his hat off, running a hand through his long locks of hair. "I tossed some grub and a couple of apples in your bags for Carbine. Just in case he behaves himself. But I recommend not staying out there too long."

"Thanks, Wade. Listen, if you see Skyla..." I didn't know how to finish that sentence. I gripped the claw she'd given me beneath my shirt.

Wade snorted loudly. "You want me to blow her a kiss too?"

"No! I...wait... what?" I said, baffled at the ruination of my moment.

"Tell her all that emotional crap yourself. I'll see you when you get back." He plopped his hat on, tilted it to his favored stylish angle and strutted away.

"What if I die?" I called after him.

"You won't!" he shouted back confidently.

"But I could..." I whispered to myself. I figured Wade meant for it to be reassuring, but it was a little unnerving with just how unconcerned he was for my wellbeing.

Rolling my eyes after the famous wolverine slayer, I tugged the reins gently, and tapped Carbine's flanks with my heels. As we rode past a pair of posted sentries and onto the darkened valley floor, the half-moon gave off just enough light to orientate ourselves and head in the right direction, but hopefully not enough to be seen by any watching apes.

***

I rode slowly and cautiously, with the *Eighty-Six* laying across the pommel of my saddle. My head stayed on a swivel, constantly looking for threats. This was enemy territory now. Carbine's ears twitched back and forth as he picked up on my nervousness.

I knew where the ranch was, but not how far the soldiers had gone before being attacked. As streaks of red and purple were painted across the sky from the rising sun, I saw buzzards circling and changed course to investigate.

The squad never made it to Clayton's Ranch.

Blue uniformed bodies and dead horses were scattered for a half mile. They'd made a run for it, but were overwhelmed by a superior force.

It'd been a one-sided battle.

Only a few dead apes lay in the tall grass, and a single wounded trike wallowed back and forth on its side, gasping last breaths as blood dripped from its hooked beak.

I left the beast alone to die. The sound of a gunshot putting the mortally wounded creature out of misery might get me put out of mine.

Small green dinosaurs chirped and bounded away from a pair of bodies in shredded uniforms as I approached. Over two dozen of the little scavengers had been ripping and tearing at the corpses. They were three feet long, with yellow stripes running from their head to the blackened tip of their whip-like tails. Their mouths and faces were coated with blood from feasting on the flesh of the dead. They kept their distance from me, dipping and weaving amongst the tall grass cautiously.

The apes had left the soldiers' weapons and the saddle and tack on the horses that wandered nearby. I reckon they'd no need of it. But several of the dead horses had been butchered for meat with the soldiers' equipment tossed aside. More of the chirping dinosaurs hopped around those skeletal remains, tearing off small strips of flesh and gristle, and swallowing with a toss back of their narrow-pointed heads.

These men had dreams, homes, families, loved ones... They were needed. And for them to end up on this desolate patch of prairie, chased down and slaughtered by a bunch of hairy savages infuriated me. Being scavenged afterwards by the tiny dinosaurs was the icing on that horrid cake.

My fist tightened around Carbine's reins. I looked forward to the opportunity to kill more of the apes.

Then I found the Sergeant who'd been tasked with leading the rescue mission.

He'd managed to make it to a small mound of boulders to mount a defense with two others. They'd put up a fight judging by the scattered brass casings. Several more apes lay dead nearby. But in the end, with no rescue coming, the three men died painfully like the rest of them. Beaten with clubs, run through with spears, and hacked apart by stone axes.

The Sergeant's head was smashed to a pulp from repeated blows. He was only recognizable by the brass insignia on his uniform. His sword lay twisted and broken, dried blood covering the length of the blade. The man had fought well, to the bitter end.

With the entire squad accounted for, it was time to go. I hated leaving the bodies unburied. But it would take me days to dig that many holes, and the living have priority over the dead. If the Claytons were alive, we needed them. Now more than ever.

And the ranchers wouldn't stand a chance out here on their own.

The soldiers' weapons and equipment I left behind as well. If the Indians came by, they were going to need it.

***

I didn't approach the ranch from the wagon trail. Instead, I cut across their property. The Claytons raised sheep and I rode through large herds as I moved towards the heavily forested southern side of his ranch. As a cattle man, I hated sheep out of principle. But they were undeniably tasty and every bit as profitable as raising beef, without all the problems an eighteen-hundred-pound critter with horns will give a man.

A few hundred yards away from the clearing around the ranch, I dismounted in the forest and tied Carbine to a tree. Wisps of smoke rose above the tree's canopy, giving me direction to the buildings. Someone was there. I just hoped it wasn't the apes.

"Listen boy," scratching his head, I looked him in the eye, "if you tug that knot loose and leave me, I'll die out here." He nuzzled me in response. I hoped that was him understanding and not wanting an apple. I fished one out of the saddle bags and fed it to him anyways. "Good horse," I patted his head as he crunched on the fruit. "Back soon."

I crept through the trees. Every few steps I paused and listened before taking a few steps more. There were only the usual sounds of the forest, birds chirping, bugs making all sorts of noises, and one startled deer that scared at least a year off my life.

As I snuck through the trees, I thought about how strange it felt to be so heavily armed. I was still trying to get accustomed to wearing two pistols, and felt like I was bumbling through the forest as they caught and pulled at plants and branches. The heavy rifle was hard to shift around as well. But being armed isn't meant to be comfortable, it's meant to be comforting. And my guns certainly did that. I'd get used to it since it was better than dying.

A stick snapped.

I froze.

My heart thudded in my chest as I listened intently for another sound. My eyes flicked back and forth across the murky green of the forest undergrowth. An owl hooted softly. I gripped my rifle tighter, puzzled at an owl hooting during the daytime.

Then I knew.

Indians.

Since they called out to me, I reckoned they were friendly. Which meant it wasn't Otto. He'd have just stabbed me in the back and paraded my hair around his village.

I mimicked the sound back into the woods.

Unseen vegetation rustled softly as someone approached. As they came closer, I realized there were two of them.

Run With Dogs slipped from behind a thicket of junipers followed by another brave. If you could call him that. Thin and gangly, he wasn't much more than a boy. I nodded, and the short one returned it. He was scowling, but didn't look as peeved off as before. Maybe because I wasn't currently a white savage partaking in one of his tribe's sacred rituals.

"Huck Berry," he said in thinly veiled disgust, shifting his rifle from one hand to the other as he crouched beside me. The young man with him carried a traditional Shaynee bow, a decorated quiver strapped around his side full of feathered arrows. He knelt beside us, one knee resting in the rich loam of the forest floor.

"Howdy, fellas."

The Indian gestured at the boy beside him. "This Squatting Bull."

"Hey kid. Wait… did you say Squatting Bull?" I blurted.

The boy glared at me. "Bull strong, berry mushy." He made a squishing motion with his hand.

I squinted at him in annoyance to keep from rolling my eyes. "Right," I turned to Run With Dogs. "What are you doing here? Did the Shaynee get away?" I expected the Chief to have scouts keeping an eye on the apes, but I didn't expect to run into them.

"We get away," Run With Dogs shrugged. "Now we keep eye on hairy men." He pointed in the direction of the Clayton's ranch.

I swallowed hard. It was too late. The apes had already hit the ranch.

"Anyone left alive?"

Squatting Bull shrugged indifferently.

"Did you look?"

"No. No care about white men," Run With Dogs said, casually dusting dirt off his rifle barrel. The blued finish was worn off the metal, and the gun was rusting in places and wrapped with wire. But the stock was decorated with polished brass beads and pretty feathers. Priorities.

"You all die, we get land back," Squatting Bull added happily.

I glared at him. "Well, I don't care about you people either. But I dragged one of you assholes for miles to your village to save their miserable stinking life because I'm a somewhat decent man. What's your excuse?"

The short Indian stared off towards the smoke rising above the trees. I didn't know if he understood all those words, but I figured he got the context of it. After a moment, he looked back at me and shrugged with one shoulder. "White men not worth die over."

That pissed me off, I pointed in the direction of the ranch. "They ain't white men!" I hissed angrily. "But since you aren't going to help," I gestured with my rifle barrel, "go that way. Maybe five miles. You'll see the buzzards. Bunch of dead soldiers. They still have weapons and equipment. Since you people won't join us or help us, you're going to need them. Maybe you can find some cojones while you're at it."

They both looked at me, puzzled. That made me even angrier. An insult is no good if they don't understand they are being insulted.

"Balls." I pointed at the Indian kid's loincloth. "You're both missing them."

Throwing his bow aside, the gangly kid jerked a knife from the belt around his waist. Run With Dogs grabbed his arm and jerked him back.

I watched him struggle against the older brave while I rested a hand on the hilt of my Bowie knife. If I was going to have to kill them, it would need to be done quietly.

"We go. Or you die," Run With Dogs hissed as he pushed the enraged young man away from me.

"Whatever. Good luck breeding, you scrotum-less redskins," I softly called after them.

I watched them slink back into the woods and disappear. After the soft sounds of their movements faded away, I pressed my back against a tree and waited a few minutes to make sure they didn't come back to kill me. One of these days my mouth was bound to make it happen.

***

Satisfied they weren't coming back, I rose and slipped through the forest. As I grew closer to the smoke, the natural noises of the forest faded and I began to hear a familiar rhythmic beating of pounded chests.

A sacrifice. That meant someone was alive, I had to do what I could. No man should suffer through the things those other ranchers did.

Pushing through the brush, I got as close as I dared, finding a gap in the foliage to peer through.

I counted eleven apes standing in the center of the packed dirt of the ranch yard. I suspected they were the same ones that attacked the soldiers. Several were wounded, and many had smears of caked blood across their fur. Those odd purple ferns, the same ones I'd seen in the ape's pouches who attacked me at my ranch, were bound to their wounds with thin strips of leather. Their chests were painted with familiar swirls and patterns.

The apes stood in a semi-circle around the Clayton's outhouse. They chanted, the same haunting deep guttural repetition I heard so many days ago in the ape's canyon. The thumping of their chests pounded in tandem with the chant.

In front of them was Thaddeus Clayton. Stripped to his pants, with hands bound above him by his own rope to the outhouse. A grave indignity to a proud and powerful man. Blood ran down his black face from a large gash across his forehead that exposed a sliver of white skull. A tough old man, he glared fearlessly at the savages gathered around him.

Clayton's sons, big, strapping young men in the prime of their youth, lay stretched out in the dirt between the barns and the ranch house. Judging from the arrows sticking out of their corpses, and the still holstered pistols, they were caught unaware by the attacking apes and killed before they could put up a fight.

The apes' trikes were over a hundred yards away, eating the rich grass of a watered pasture amongst dozens of the Clayton's smaller sheep.

The chanting stopped. Looking back to old man Clayton, I felt a growing sense of dread as I watched a gray-haired ape inhale green smoke from a wooden bowl. Arching his back, he thrust his chest towards the sky and howled with arms outstretched, fists clenched.

The other apes bellowed with him, beating their chests furiously.

Clayton spat at the feet of the ape in front of him. Some of his spittle landing in the smoking bowl and sizzled. He raised his head high, a look of disgust on his face, waiting for death defiantly.

I had to do something.

The gray ape drew a stone knife from the leather sheath at his side.

Raising my rifle, I flipped the Lyman peep sight up. Peering through the small circular sight, I eased the trigger back until it broke and dropped the hammer.

The heavy rifle absorbed a fraction of the recoil, and delivered the rest to my already bruised shoulder. It was painful, but I hardly noticed. My mind shoved it away because it was irrelevant at the moment.

The large 400 grain lead bullet hit the gray ape in the back of the head like a sledge hammer on a water melon. It burst into a red mist as the ape's body toppled over, dropping the knife into the dirt.

Sorry about your ritual, you bastards.

Racking the lever, I ejected the large empty brass cartridge and cycled another into the chamber as the apes stopped beating their chests. They looked around bewildered, uncertain of what just happened to their leader. Clayton's eyes scanned the tree line for the shooter. Spying me, he stared, his lips pressed firmly together.

I had no plan, but I had a lot of bullets. Sometimes, that's enough.

Firing again, I shot the rope that bound Clayton's hands above him and through the outhouse. His hands dropped in a shower of splinters that rained down on the old man's dusky scarred shoulders.

Without missing a beat, the old slave scooped up the stone knife and with a rebel yell, slashed it across the neck of the closest ape with a vicious twist. The ape fell, clutching its savaged throat, blood spurting between its hands. Clayton scrambled towards his closest son's body.

Nine left.

The remaining apes descended into chaos. Several ran towards the trikes. Most went towards the old man. A few came running into the forest, in different directions, uncertain of where I was.

I dropped the ape closest to Thaddeus with a bullet through the big monkey's spine. He dropped, thrashing and roaring as he struggled to make his useless legs work.

Eight left.

Clayton drew a revolver from his dead son's holster, and fired into the nearest ape twice. The others swarmed him as he emptied the pistol into the hairy mob descending upon him. Bellowing and roaring, they circled him, bashing his body to a pulp with clubs and axes, stabbing with spears.

Seven left.

Enraged, I blew the heart out of the ape leading the pack into the woods. The body dropped and tripped the ape running behind him.

Six left.

The apes realized where I was and changed course. My time was up. Thaddeus Clayton was dead. I turned to run.

Then I heard thundering hooves and a loud Indian whoop.

Two Shaynees raced out from between the house and barn on the backs of their small painted ponies. I gave a loud cry of joy when I saw them. Young Squatting Bull loosened arrows at the apes, as Run With Dogs opened up with his battered old rifle. Feathers tied to his decorated stock twirled in the wind as the Indians rode across the beaten dirt yard and amongst the hairy savages.

An ape running towards his trike spun, trying to reach the arrow that suddenly slammed into his shoulder blade, only to catch a bullet in the chest from Run With Dogs. The monkey fell, twitching, as the Indians jumped their mounts over his dying body.

I was wrong. These two Indians were brave as hell. They just hated white men.

That was fair enough.

The chaos was incredible. The timing magnificent. Apes didn't know which way to go, or what direction to attack. Feathered arrows were sent into two others as Squatting Bull used his bow at the group of savage apes still mutilating Clayton's remains.

We just might be able to kill all of them.

Grinning wickedly, I racked the rifle's lever and pulled it into my shoulder, firing and dropping a wounded ape as he ripped a Shaynee arrow out of his thigh.

Five left.

The Indians passed through the scattered group and kept going, rushing through the pasture, leaping a stream, sending terrified sheep running and then riding away across the plains.

I watched in shock as I realized they weren't staying to fight.

Cowardly sons of bitches.

I ran.

The remaining apes gave chase through the woods after me.

My legs felt like lead. My lungs burned as I struggled to suck in enough air to keep from collapsing. I pushed and fought my way through the shrubs and branches. Thorns ripped at my clothes and flesh. Throwing myself over a log, I stumbled to my knees before recovering and pushing myself on. Behind came loud bellows and crashing as I was pursued. The rifle in my hands felt like an anchor that I dare not drop.

Carbine was waiting for me. I could have kissed that horrible horse. Tugging the reins free, I forced my burning legs to hoist me onto my horse's back.

I barely settled into the saddle when Carbine reared and lashed out with his rear feet. A meaty thud sounded as steel shod hooves connected with flesh. An ape went flying, stone axe falling, as Carbine dropped back to all fours and galloped away.

I fell forward onto my horse's neck, clenching my thighs and clutching his black mane to stay seated.

Angry howls followed me as we left the apes behind.

***

I quickly rode towards town, keeping an eye out for the two Indians. But there wasn't hide nor hair of them to be seen. If they were smart, they'd snatch up as many of the soldiers' weapons they could carry and high tail it back to wherever their tribe was hidden and clear out of the territory. Even if they had to push through the Cheyenne or Sioux's land.

An hour later, I crested a knoll and Carbine stopped abruptly on his own. Raising the rifle off my saddle, I moved my finger to the trigger.

Three hundred yards in front of us stood an Allosaurus over a freshly killed buffalo. The rest of its small herd milled around nearby, the shaggy beasts warily keeping plenty of distance between themselves and the terrifying creature that easily slayed a two-thousand-pound bull.

With one clawed foot pinning the corpse in place, the dinosaur ripped a chunk from the buffalo's belly. Tilting its large head to the side, the beast watched me curiously as it chewed.

I wondered if it was the same one Brandthorn saw when they rode in on the train the other day. This one was much larger than the one I killed. It wouldn't have even fit into my barn. The tunnel was the gift that wouldn't stop giving. All manner of beasts was slipping through it.

Behind the feasting predator, I noticed a distant trail of dust rising into the air. I glanced at the mountain where the tunnel was located then in the direction of the town; the trail was between the two.

I knew what it was, but wanted to see for myself. Touching my heels to Carbine's flanks, we made a large and careful arc around the dinosaur, then trotted towards the ape army.

Once I felt we were close enough, I rode Carbine along the bottom of a ridge and dismounted out of sight. With my rifle and collapsible glass, I crawled to the top and slithered forward on my belly in the knee-high grass.

It was the apes alright, and there were so stinking many of them.

I extended the telescope and looked over the army.

When I ruined the ape's evil sacrificial ceremony back in their valley, a lot of them must have still been in the caves. Now they were all out in the open and their full force was on display as they slowly trekked towards my town.

It was a terrifying sight.

The long trail of apes moved in something of a mob, but there was some noticeable structure amongst the army. The scar faced leader rode at the head of the loose column surrounded by mounted apes. Behind them, came apes on foot, making up the bulk of the army. At the end, choking on the dust kicked up by their brethren, were the apes hauling heavily laden two handled carts. Over a dozen of the carts had cages on them, inside each was at least one raptor.

The entire army was stretched out over half a mile, with the trikes lumbering along slowly and the carts struggling to keep up at the rear of the train.

Of the mounted trikes, I counted between fifty and sixty riders. The apes on foot, I guessed two hundred. They moved in such a loose group, it was nigh impossible to count. While most trike riders were male, the infantry appeared split pretty evenly between male and female. And if theses female apes were anything like the one I kicked off the train, they shouldn't be underestimated because of their sex.

I watched the leader through my telescope. It seemed the collection of human skulls draped across his battle-scarred trike had grown since I'd seen him last. Not for the first time, I wondered how he came to lead the army. He appeared to be the largest and strongest, perhaps leadership was based off that alone.

His head turned towards my position, and I saw his scarred face and permanent scowl. I shuddered. It felt as though he was staring right at me.

Maybe he was the leader because he was the ugliest.

He raised an arm and pointed in my direction. His twisted face mouthed words and a pair of apes turned and began moving towards my position to investigate.

Scrambling down the hill at a speed faster than was safe, I leapt into the saddle and kicked Carbine's flanks. I had no desire to get into a battle this close to hundreds of enemy reinforcements. We tore out of there at a sprint. Spying a gulley, I turned Carbine's head and he slid down into it on his haunches. We splashed through the stream at the bottom and onto the other side, dripping water as we ran through small scrub and brush downstream, away from the army and dispatched riders.

Luck was on our side for once, and we easily made our escape without seeing another ape.

As I approached town, the rational part of my mind told me to keep going. To get the hell out of here and that I could make it on my own. It told me if I didn't, I'd die with everyone else. It told me that without an army of soldiers, we were doomed. And the temptation to keep riding was strongest when I thought of Reydan White, and felt the burning desire to put a bullet through his murderous face.

There was also the vision I had in the sweat lodge, of our defeat and slaughter.

But I knew that Skyla and my companions wouldn't tuck tail and run. And truly, it wasn't a real option for me either. I simply couldn't. Running away from a fight wasn't in my blood, even if it was the smart thing to do. My sacred honor, long tarnished, shone brightly now and compelled me onward to town.

Suddenly, I sat upright in the saddle, jerked *Eighty-Six* off the pommel and slapped Carbine's flanks with it.

He leapt into a gallop towards town. Foolishly, I'd let my guard down as I reached the edge of the valley, expecting everything to be as I'd left it.

Instead, the Lieutenant's posted men were gone.

They'd been replaced with several groups of mounted apes patrolling the edge of the valley on their horned dinosaurs.

One band saw me and changed course, running to intercept, but seeing them first gave us the advantage of a head start. They couldn't catch us before we reached the safety of town. We raced down the valley floor, and I turned back in the saddle and watched them slow, then stop, along the wagon trail at the crest of the hill.

We were surrounded.

It was time to circle the wagons.

Because I'd be staying come hell, high water, or an army of bloodthirsty prehistoric sons of bitches.

***

Our defensive plans appeared to be coming together nicely. Already, the corralled fence was pulled down and the cannon and Gatling maneuvered into place between the stables and blacksmith shop amongst the hardpacked dirt and piles of dried and fresh manure. The weapons were manned by a mix of wary looking civilians and bored uniformed soldiers who gave me a friendly wave. Rail ties had been stacked around their positions to give them some protection from arrows or thrown spears. And I hoped the ties would keep them from getting trampled by a charge from the trikes.

Fredrick was helping build Cheval de Frises with several other men. All were wearing gun belts with rifles leaning nearby. At least one of them had been among the mob at the rail station last night; he shot me a dark look before turning back to work. I guess he still held a grudge.

The hunter passed the hand drill off, dusted wood chips off his pants and walked over to me as I stopped Carbine at a half-filled water trough.

Before he could ask, I dismounted and shook my head before summing up the trip. "All dead," I told him sadly. "Did Brandthorn's scouts make it back? There are bands of apes circling the ridge."

He nodded. "They all made it back, safe and sound. The apes chased them off at dawn and have been up there watching us ever since." Beads of sweat rolled down his face and dripped off his mustache. Running a hand drill was tough work, especially when you'd got hundreds of holes to bore through thick logs. He propped a foot on the edge of the trough, leaned forward, and sighed. "You tried. Don't let it get you down. It was a noble attempt, at great risk to yourself."

"I'd feel better if I'd been able to bring back some soldiers or Clayton and his boys." I watched Carbine drink noisily. Some men held horses back from water until they cooled down with the belief that drinking too soon would make them sick. That was a load of bunk. I'd never seen anyone hold a wild mustang back from a river and they did just fine on their own.

I stretched my back and watched a team of horses lean into their harnesses. They pulled a heavily laden wagon, driven by the deputies, and filled with railroad ties to build more emplacements.

The two brothers waved at us and we returned the motion.

"Seen Skyla?" I asked.

He pointed down the street. "Behind the saloon. Wade's teaching her how to shoot a rifle."

"Good. She's going to need one. What about Ashley?"

"She's inside the saloon. Brandthorn's sending groups of soldiers and civilians through a quick rundown about apes and dinosaurs. He even dragged a couple bodies off the train and laid them out on the bar to show off. It takes the mystery out of our enemy, and shoots down all the wild rumors that've been spreading."

"Clever." Fear of the unknown and uncertainty is a dangerous thing, seeing corpses would make them realize they bled red just like us. And if it bleeds, it can be killed.

"Ah well. The battle will be joined shortly, and I've no doubt we will shall emerge triumphant." Pushing his spectacles up his nose, he turned back towards the partially completed Cheval. "Glad you made it back, Jed!"

I walked Carbine to the stable and gave him the last apple in my bags. He'd saved my life several times now and deserved the treat. I scratched his head while he chomped the withered fruit.

"Good boy," I told him as he pushed his muzzle against my shoulder and nibbled at my collar. "You redeemed yourself today."

He pulled back suddenly, my sweat soaked bandana clenched between his teeth. My chest slammed into the fence before Carbine released the fabric. I gasped for air as he snorted and pranced away.

"You rotten-" Scooping up a dirt clod, I hurled it at him angrily and thumped him in the ribs as he walked off tossing his black mane. The stable boy laughed from the darkened shadows of the interior of the large barn. I shot them both a glare before twisting my bandana back to its proper position around my neck and stalking away.

I wanted to check on Skyla first, but decided I should swing by the Sheriff's Office first. Luck was with me, and as I stepped past the decaying Allosaurus head I saw that both Dan and the Lieutenant were inside the now unlocked Mayor's Office.

Brandthorn had large bags under his eyes and his shoulders slumped when I entered the room alone. Dan was staring at the map tacked on the wall as I entered.

"Welcome back Jed," the Sheriff gestured towards the coffee pot on our deceased mayors' desk.

I poured from the pot in silence, knowing that they already surmised that I'd returned alone. I sighed and looked down at the black liquid sloshing in my cup.

"Your men made a run for it. They were chased down and killed. The Sergeant and two others got to an outcropping of rock and made a last stand. They went down fighting."

The Lieutenant took the news as an Irishman should, by swearing and hurling a chair across the room. It slammed into the wall and splintered apart. Dan and I watched in silence as he chased after it, swearing as he stomped the remaining pieces apart under his boot.

Satisfied with the destruction, he pressed his hands against the wall and leaned forward, resting his forehead against the smoothed boards. His voice quaked with grief. "Sergeant Collins was my friend, and a good man. Now I'll have to tell his wife Colleen… and my goddaughter that her daddy won't be coming home this time."

I looked down at my dirty boots, suddenly uninterested in the coffee. I didn't know what to say even though I understood. Losing friends is never easy. I'd lost several before and my father and I'd spent years looking for Cato, only for him to show up decades later with the man who burned our home and mutilated my back.

The twists of fate can be a real bitch.

Dan glanced at me and spoke softly. "The Claytons as well I take it?"

I nodded. "He went out like a warrior. I'm sorry the news is all bad," I sighed regretfully. "Also, we're surrounded by about two dozen apes. They're trying to prevent anyone from leaving. How are the town's defenses?"

"Almost finished," Brandthorn spoke from against the wall, his voice now calmed and even. "Except we lost two more men last night. Deserters. Supposed to be guarding the horses, but they stole a pair and rode off. Damn them both."

I didn't have anything to say about that. Every man we lost reduced our chances of survival, and cowards usually survived while the brave died. I broke the rest of the bad news to him. "The apes will be here tomorrow and there's a lot of them. Two hundred plus on foot, another fifty or sixty mounted. And then, however many raptors they have."

"Any chance the Shaynee will help?" Dan suggested.

"I ran into a couple at the Clayton ranch. They made it real clear that what happens to whites is of no concern to them. Also, they're on the move. It could take days to find them."

Brandthorn grunted and pushed himself away from the wall. Stepping over the wreckage of the broken chair, he walked to the map of the town. He stared at it for a moment in thought.

The map had defensive emplacements carefully sketched on the parchment around the core of the town. Six buildings on one side, seven on the other with a wide street running through the center. Our Alamo.

I waited as the Lieutenant stared at the layout of the town and its defenses in silence.

Finally, he spoke, the words harsh and bitter. "Very well. Let the damned things come. I'm sick of waiting."

"Agreed." I gave them both a nod, downed the last of my coffee and left to go see Skyla like I'd originally planned. I just hoped she wasn't still angry.

***

Gun shots rang from behind the saloon as I walked down the narrow alley. I carefully peeked my head around the corner to make sure it was safe before stepping out of the shadows. There was still the risk of being intentionally shot though.

Wade and Skyla stood side by side, their backs to me as she shot at empty bottles on a log. She was doing well, shattering the brown empty whiskey bottles at least half the time. That was impressive considering she'd never fired a rifle until today.

I waited until she stopped to reload.

"You're turning into a regular cowgirl." I grinned sheepishly from behind her, waiting for the realization to set in.

Her reaction was better than I expected. She spun, unceremoniously shoved the rifle into Wade's unprepared hands and jumped into my arms, pressing her lips firmly against mine. Pleased that I wasn't slapped across the face, I kissed back.

Letting me go, she stepped away, her face flushing a bright crimson. Her brown eyes searched my face. "I'm sorry I didn't answer the door last night. I was torn between being mad, upset, and scared over you volunteering yourself."

"It had to be done," I offered lamely, suddenly overcome with emotion at the realization of how much she cared for me.

"I know," she grabbed my hand and held it tight, as if afraid I'd leave again. "Oh yes, Wade is teaching me to shoot!"

"I see that. That's good. Real good."

Wade looked amused at our interactions. "Fredrick loaned her one of his spare rifles. I figured she may need to use one."

"She will. The apes ought to be here tomorrow and there are a lot more of them than I initially thought."

He leaned Skyla's rifle against a bench covered with ammo and cleaning supplies. "Have faith in gunpowder, Jed. It's the ultimate equalizer."

"Says the man who strangled a wolverine to death with his bare hands," I said wryly.

"And that was the last time I went into the woods to use nature's outhouse without a gun," he laughed at our curious expressions. "There's a part to that story no one knows. Truth is… I was flailing about, wrestling that skunk bear, with my pants around my ankles. Couldn't run and I was too embarrassed to call for help, even though the other outfitters were a few dozen yards away sitting around a fire. That wolverine clawed and gnawed me up good before I managed to choke the life out of it." He grinned in a conspiring manner. "Understandably, I don't tell that part of the story. So, I'd appreciate it if you keep that to yourselves."

We agreed, but Skyla couldn't contain her laughter. I kept my snickering to a minimum as I imagined wrestling a wolverine half naked. It'd be a sight to see, that's for sure.

"That'd make for a great play in the show you and Ashley are trying to put together," I told him once I could keep a straight face without smirking.

"I don't think so," he frowned.

"How'd you know I'd make it back?" I asked him, changing the subject since I was still curious at his callus good bye.

"I didn't." He plucked an empty brass casing off the ground and rolled it between his fingers. "I've simply found that confidence is far more successful than doubt or worry."

I hooked my thumbs in the gun belt and rocked back on my heels. "Well, I appreciate the lack of concern."

"You're welcome. Besides, Skyla was worried enough for all of us."

He handed the rifle out to Skyla. "Now, if you'll excuse us, Jed. You two can get caught up later, right now she needs all the practice she can get."

Skyla gave me a quick peck on my stubbled cheek and relinquished my hand to accept the gun. As she thumbed cartridges into the rifle, I wandered off to find someone to help.

***

First group I ran into looked like they could use a hand flipping wagons.

The process was simple; wheel the wagon into place, flip it onto its side and wedge it in the alleys between the buildings. We wanted the double row of buildings to be our fortress, with nothing slipping through any gaps to kill us from behind.

We begged, borrowed, and stole all the wagons we could find. Many were already abandoned by their owners who'd fled.

By the time the town's defensive preparations were finished the sun was low in the sky. My back and shoulders ached from straining to flip the heavy wagons. We'd managed to scrounge enough of them to block all the gaps between the buildings with a few left over. The remaining wagons were tipped around the Gatling guns to provide cover for defenders to fire behind while still allowing the crew-served weapons to have an open field of fire.

It appeared we were as ready as we could be.

On the way to the hotel, I crossed paths with the Reverend. The man of the faith was struggling to lug a crate of tools down the street.

"Need a hand?" I offered, slinging my rifle over a shoulder and taking one of the rope handles without waiting on a reply.

"Please and thank you, Jedidiah," he breathed heavily from the exertion. His old Bible lay inside the crate amongst hammers, saws, and bags of forged nails.

Between us we carried the heavy box to the blacksmiths forge. He told me they'd been boarding up windows in the buildings, but leaving firing slits for the defenders to shoot through. They'd also secured the church and built ladders onto the roofs of the buildings.

We dropped the heavy tool box in front of the forge and the scarred blacksmith walked out to get it. The large man had a fire scorched leather apron on, filled with tools, and a heavy Colt Dragoon strapped to his hip.

"That's a big gun," I pointed at the hand cannon. The pistol probably weighed five pounds. They were intended to be carried in holsters strapped to the pommel of your saddle, not hauled around on the waist like his was.

"I am a big man," he stated simply, as he looked down at his massive calloused hands and clenched them. I'd shaken hands with him once, it was like sticking my hand into a bear trap. Now I just clasped him on the shoulder when necessary and tried not to make him mad. He had a fearful temper.

"Use your weapon for the good Lord's work, Edward," the Reverend said fondly. He'd spent years looking after the big lug and the blacksmith had become like a son to him. Because while the giant of a man was as strong as an ox and almost artistic in his ability to forge metals into shape, he was more than a little daft.

The Reverend plucked his Bible off the tools before Edward picked up the wooden box effortlessly and carried it inside.

"I'm not surprised to see you here, but I wish you'd left when you had the chance. It's going to get mighty ugly come tomorrow," I told him.

"My place is here, watching over the flock that has been entrusted to me." He knocked dust off his worn book with a thump of his hand then looked at the ridges surrounding our little town. "In the valley of the shadow of death, I will fear no evil, for the Lord is with me. Our

Winchesters and Colts, they comfort me," he grinned mischievously.

I laughed at the changing of the scripture. It was fitting. "What about turning the other cheek?"

He grimaced, "If you'd come to Sunday School, you'd know that's only in regard to small slights, like someone stealing a chicken. It's not about allowing others to murder your loved ones and then offering yourself to be slaughtered as well. When you take the literal interpretation of the Bible, you cheapen God's Word," he took a breath. "Besides, Jesus was the Prince of Peace, not the Prince of Pacifism. Ecclesiastes three, one to eight. There is a time to kill, a time to speak, and a time for war. And not once in the Bible is a soldier, or anyone else who carries weapons, told to lay them down and repent," he caught himself and stopped preaching. "Sorry. This is one of my more popular sermons, as you can probably imagine."

I certainly could.

He patted me on the shoulder, in an almost sympathetic manner. "I've spent many decades worshiping our good Lord. If he calls me home tomorrow, I can't wait to enter the Kingdom of Heaven and do it in person," he gave me a sideways glance. "But you... I think he still has plans for you. Good luck tomorrow, Jedidiah. I'm glad you found something worth fighting for." Smiling, he walked back towards the church.

He may have meant the town, but I thought of Skyla. After a life as miserable as mine, things were finally looking up. While the Reverend might be ready to shuffle off this mortal coil, I was not.

***

When I walked down the boardwalk, I found Fredrick leaning on the hitching post outside the Sheriff's Office. Behind him, the Allosaurus head was starting to stink something terrible and needed to be moved elsewhere.

"That's ripe," I wrinkled my nose. "You waitin' on me?"

"You, Skyla and Ashley."

I propped my foot on the boardwalk beside him and looked both ways down the street. There was no sign of them yet.

"Where's Wade at?"

"Securing the balcony." He pointed at the top of the Bucket O' Blood across the street. Following his finger, I saw Wade resting his forearms on the white rails. Noticing us staring at him, he removed his hat and gave a mock bow. From the ruckus coming from below him, it sounded like everyone was whooping it up at the bar on what might be their last night. I didn't blame them one bit and just hoped no one would be shot or stabbed. We couldn't afford to lose any more defenders.

"And the ladies?"

"Skyla had to fetch something from her hotel room. Ashley went with her. They should be back in a few minutes."

The door opened behind us, and Dan came out of his office with the troublesome miner in tow and flanked by his two deputies. They both looked particularly unhappy.

"What's this?" Fredrick said, surprised and a little angry. Just yesterday, he was about to cut Timmy in half with a Gatling gun, and now we were watching the man being turned loose.

"Reckon the Sheriff figures he does us more good fighting than locked in a cell," I sighed. After two run ins with the trouble maker already, I suspected a third time was inevitable and would most likely be fatal for one of us.

The feeling must have been mutual; Timmy glared and spat on the ground before striding past us. Crossing the street, he pushed through the double doors to the saloon. I hoped he killed lots of apes tomorrow, but I also hoped the apes killed him before I had to. He didn't appear to be the sort to change his ways.

We were even more shocked when Wesley stepped through the darkened doorway with his coat folded over an arm and twin pistols in their holsters. He gave a wily grin before coming over. Now I knew why the two deputies looked so displeased; that was a lot of money they just released.

"They let you out, huh?" I asked the notorious gunman.

"Uncle Dan said we had to." Tom shoved his hands deep into his pockets, looking every bit like a child who had their candy taken away.

"At this point, we need all the guns we can get, regardless of the man carrying them," the Sheriff said with a shake of his balding head. "Besides, you can't spend reward money if you're dead."

Deputy James looked at Wesley with a grimace. "You gonna shoot us once this is all over?"

He smirked. "Probably not you," then he pointed at the deputy's brother. "But maybe that one. He bent a pistol barrel over my head just a few days ago."

Tom's face turned pale and he looked to us for support.

Feeling confident that Wesley was mostly joking, I just raised an eyebrow and shrugged noncommittedly.

"But that doesn't mean you're off the hook," Wesley glared at James. "You helped him. But I may just wing you. Maybe a bullet through the shoulder or calf. Something painful, but not crippling."

The deputy gulped and stuttered. "I was jus-just doin' my job."

"I know," Wesley snorted. "But you need to stay the hell out of my way," he turned his attention to me. "I've been told the chances of riding off into the sunset happily ever after are non-existent, what say you?"

I shrugged again. "If you can out run dozens of mounted apes, be our guest." I pointed my rifle towards the valley ridge. "They're on the other side of that, circling town, waiting on their buddies to arrive."

"That's just lovely," the gunman sighed, resigning himself to his fate. "Well, I was lying about helping you with your monkey problem, but it looks like I'm stuck here. Where do you need me, Sheriff?"

The lawman shrugged. "I knew you were. I figured if you ran, you'd kill some before they rip your heart out. It was win-win. But since you decided to stay, you just get comfortable somewhere and kill every ape you see."

"Clever plan. As for killing monkeys, sure. I can do that." Nodding to Fredrick and myself he strolled across the street towards the bar, whistling Dixie. The man couldn't carry a tune in a bucket.

Fredrick watched the gunman enter the saloon. "If he is as deadly with those guns as his reputation says, he'll be a boon to us, and now he's got no choice but to fight."

"Aye, we need him. Along with that rotten miner. But it doesn't mean I have to like it." The old Sheriff turned to his deputies. "Go home. Get some sleep. I'll be along in a bit."

His nephews bid him goodnight, and wandered down the empty street, walking side by side. Tom said something then playfully shoved James. Their laughter drifted back to us.

I watched them go. They'd handled this situation relatively well. I'd never admit it to them, but I was impressed. They just might turn out alright after all.

"Gentlemen, this is where we part ways as well. I've rounds to make, and dawn will be here all too soon," the Sheriff looked at me. "Just like old times, eh Jed?"

"I hope not. Old times meant chasing Indians across three states, wearing horses out, sleeping on the hard ground, eating tasteless hardtack and beans for months. All while worrying you'll wake up with your scalp missing. This time, we get to sleep in a real bed, eat a decent meal, drink whiskey, and the enemy comes to us while we're in a prepared defensive position. This is almost a luxurious battle in comparison to fighting the Nez Perce."

"Except for the part about giant dinosaurs ridden by prehistoric savages who like to sacrifice people," Fredrick noted.

"That part is a bit depressing." Dan scratched his beard. "Oh well, can't be helped. I'll see you two in the morning."

"Goodnight, Dan."

***

Skyla and Ashley came out of the hotel and we crossed the street to meet them. Our scientist had a small bag slung over one shoulder, and made no mention of what it might contain. Once we were all together, we made our way into the packed saloon.

The Lieutenant was no fool, since the barkeeper had fled with the working girls, he'd posted soldiers inside to keep the peace and serve the booze. They were under strict orders that no man was allowed enough alcohol to become incapacitated the next morning. Even with that order, I fully expected more than a few people would be nursing hangovers tomorrow. Where there is a will, there is a way.

Fredrick led the way through the throng of people towards the stairs followed by Ashley and then myself and Skyla. She slipped her hand into mine. I gave it a gentle squeeze, pulled her through the crowd behind me, and didn't let go until we stepped onto the balcony where Wade was waiting with enough glasses and bottles to go around. To my surprise, Brandthorn had joined us as well.

Once we each had a filled glass, the Lieutenant spoke.

"I won't stay long as I've other duties to attend to," he raised his glass. "But I want to thank you all for your input and hard work. With your help we are as ready as we will ever be. Hopefully, it will have been all for naught. Because with luck, we'll have an entire train full of soldiers and artillery steam in here before dawn to blow these apes to hell without us so much as breakin' a sweat. We'll sit on this balcony, sip this god-awful rot gut whiskey, and watch the show." As we laughed, he nodded at Ashley. "But if you'd like, I'm sure you could shoot a few from here if you want the target practice."

Our sharpshooter laughed and leaned against her business partner. "Think we could work that into our show this winter, Wade?"

"Wait. This winter?" Skyla repeated, voicing all of our confusion.

The wolverine slayer gave a sly grin and pulled a folded telegram from his breast pocket. He wagged the thin paper at us. "As of yesterday, we've secured enough financial backing to put our show together. I've already sent multiple wires to some truly gifted individuals, asking them to join us. If they are willing, and we get some friendly Indians off the reservations, maybe a few gentle buffalo, I do believe we'll be a raging success. Folks want to see the untamed West for what it is, and I intend to show them. Starting this winter in New York," he winked at me. "Told you, confidence is more successful than doubt or worry."

"That's outstanding!" roared Fredrick.

'What are you going to call it?" Brandthorn asked.

Wade scuffed his boots bashfully on the wooden planks. "Well, I was thinking something along the lines of A&W Western Show."

Ashley looked up at her business partner. "Our initials? Absolutely not. Only one name will do," she grinned. "Wolverine Wade's Wild West Show. Anything else wouldn't sound as good."

"Well deserved, and we expect tickets," I told them as I tilted my head towards Skyla. A split second later it occurred to me that I said we, lumping Skyla and myself together. The others didn't seem to notice the slip up, but I felt my face grow hot. I glanced at her. She was beaming from ear to ear. "I'd love to go with you," she whispered in a playfully conspiring tone.

At that moment, reality hit me like a bucket of ice water.

I was a wanted man.

An outlaw in hiding.

For a moment, I stood frozen. A tangled mass of conflicting thoughts and emotions, tumbling through my thoughts, sending me spinning in a hundred different directions. I could feel the anger building, a wrathful rage towards Reydan White, towards my father, towards myself. Towards everything that pushed me to the position I now found myself in: a bad man with a good girl.

"Jed…Jed… are you okay?" Skyla interrupted the insanity running wild in my head. Her black hair was pulled back, with stray strands tucked behind her ears. The brown eyes that'd drawn me into them the first time we met, looked at me with puzzlement. Her lips were parted slightly, the ends dipped down in concern.

It struck me how much she cared for me, and I for her. And just like that, all anger washed away. The self-pity and loathing were replaced with determination. I was going to make whatever we had blossoming between us work. Prehistoric apes and my past be damned.

I unclenched my jaw and smiled. "I am now."

She squinted her eyes at me in confusion, then looked at Fredrick as he raised a glass and spoke. "Jed. This all started with you. Anything you'd like to say?"

I looked at the face of each person standing on the balcony. Like me, they all had doubts as to the chances of us surviving a large-scale attack. But I knew, if we gave into our fears, the battle would be lost before it began.

Taking a deep breath, I began, "When this mess started, I was alone in a burning barn fighting a monster. Now I find myself surrounded by fearsome allies and sincere friends. Each of you know what we are up against, and yet you all refused to walk away when given the chance. Although, to be fair, the Lieutenant was ordered here, and Fredrick was foolish enough to volunteer."

Amidst the laughter, the hunter gave a large grin from under his bushy mustache.

I continued, "We've all got our fears of what will happen tomorrow.

But no one determines if we live or die but us and the choices and actions we make. And since we're determined to live, we will. Tomorrow we're going to slaughter apes by the bushel," I raised my glass. "To us. We may have entered hell, but we're not slowing down or stopping until we're through."

"Here, here!" Wade exclaimed, and we all took a drink. Even Ashley sipped a small amount and blanched, before setting her glass on the white picket railing. Skyla laughed and hugged her. The two girls had grown close during our little adventure. I was glad, because they'd be fighting together in the church steeple tomorrow.

Brandthorn excused himself to check on the men standing post. Judging by what put him in the brig, the Irishman liked to celebrate. But he also seemed to know when to be a professional, and he was all business now.

The mood was cheerful as we sipped whiskey, laughed, and shook our heads at our recent adventures. From the bar below came raucous laughter and the faint melodies of a piano that added to our upbeat moods. We weren't the only ones intent on having a good night.

Fredrick and Wade finally got around to regaling us with their stories. They were a good mixture of hilarious and impressive. I supposed I had stories to tell as well, but I didn't want to ruin the good impression I'd made by telling them of my outlaw days. Instead, I listened and laughed along until my sides were about to burst.

Eventually, Ashley began to tease Fredrick about his famous reputation of being a hunter, while his method of hunting seemed to be emptying his guns at anything that moved. She said for a reasonable fee, she'd teach him how to use his sights.

As he guffawed, I looked around the balcony at my friends. We'd come a long way in a short time. It felt odd to be so happy and at peace right now while knowing that our possible death and destruction was heading our way. I supposed the whiskey helped.

Beside me, Skyla laughed, a bright beautiful sound as she listened to Fredrick attempting to justify his theory of many bullets equaling many hits.

Taking a sip, I watched the best friends I'd had in years enjoying each other's company. The sun was setting behind us, sending red and purple hues streaking across the sky as we enjoyed each other's company.

***

Eventually, only Skyla and myself remained on the balcony. Ashley and Wade had not so mysteriously retired for the evening at the same time. They were soon followed by Fredrick, who was adamant that after this battle he'd beat Wade at being the first man to kill a tyrannosaur.

We sat with our backs against the slap board siding, shoulder to shoulder, listening to the soldiers below clearing out the bar. The Lieutenant had placed a curfew on drinking, and some folks weren't taking it too well. I wasn't sure how much that helped, I'd imagine it'd just drive people to drink faster. But at least they'd be more likely to get some sleep now that the party was over.

Skyla opened the small bag she'd retrieved from her hotel room. She pulled out a chunk of cheese wrapped in cloth and crackers, along with a bottle of Old Grand-Dad's.

I chuckled as she presented the bottle to me with a flourish. "Where did you find this?"

"I bought it in Cheyenne before we left. In case such an occasion as this were to occur." She tossed her dark hair back and grinned playfully. So far, we'd both managed to be respectable in our drinking. But from her giggling, she'd had a bit too much.

"I'm glad you didn't waste this on the riff-raff we had for company earlier!" Breaking the seal, I passed the bottle to her and she took a sip, grimacing at the taste.

She coughed, "Agreed. It's not the fanciest of whiskeys, but it's better than what this town has to offer I'm sure. And we've a history with it now."

I grinned. "Yes, we do." Drawing my Bowie, I wiped the blade on my pant legs to clean it, then carefully sliced several pieces of cheese off and handed her one with a cracker. She passed me the bottle and took a dainty bite then wiped the crumbs from her lips.

Holding the bottle, I stared at her, committing every line and detail of her to memory. She was beautiful, not just on the outside but on the inside as well.

A true rarity.

I blinked, and the vision of her lifeless legs sticking out from behind the bar flashed before me. Her scream as the ape burst through the back of the building, hurling a spear through Wade's back. The horrific sound of Skyla's spine snapping as the ape almost twisted her head off. Her limp body being flung over the bar, crashing into the shelves and falling amongst a rain of broken shards of glass. I recalled gunning the ape down then, in a murderous blind rage, savagely mutilating his corpse with the knife until I couldn't raise my arms.

Blinking, I looked at the knife in my hand. Instead of being coated with blood, it was smeared with cheese. Swallowing, I took a large swig of whiskey to hide my sudden discomfort. The burning sensation did little to ease the agony of the 'maybe soon' that'd I'd seen in the sweat lodge.

"I want you to get on Carbine and ride away," I said quietly. "Follow the train tracks. There's a watering station a half day's ride from here. You can take shelter there before moving on. Keep following the rails, and you'll reach Cheyenne in a couple of days."

Her hand rested on my arm, followed by a gentle squeeze. I felt warmth spread through me at her touch. "No," her soft voice was firm. "I'm not leaving. I'm part of this, and I'll see it through. You and I are in this together. I won't run any more than you will."

I closed my eyes for a moment, resting my emotions in the darkness. The answer was what I expected. "I just want you to be safe," I whispered.

"I know. And I want you to be safe as well, but you foolishly seem bound and determined to be a hero," she shook her head disgustedly. "Besides, I can't ride western style. I don't swear, so I'd fall right out of the saddle."

I barked a short laugh and took a swig from the bottle. A much smaller one this time. Part of me was immensely proud of her and how far she'd come since shooting the ape in the back of the wagon. She was brave, strong, and intelligent. There was no finer woman, anywhere, ever. I was honored to have her affections. The other part of me wanted to tie her up, throw her over my saddle, and slap Carbine's rump so hard he wouldn't stop until he got her to Texas where she'd be safe.

I resisted the urge and resigned myself to accepting our unknown fates tomorrow. Because, barring her being someplace far away and safe... right now, there was nowhere else I'd rather be than sitting with her on a prostitute's balcony, eating cheese and crackers, and drinking expensive whiskey under a clear night sky filled with bright stars.

We were downright classy.

She took the bottle from me and changed the topic. "Enough of that talk, let's not ruin a good night with thoughts of tomorrow. Tell me more about yourself. What happened to your parents?" She took a sip and it went down badly. She coughed, waving a hand at me that she was fine.

"Mother and sister died from scarlet fever. As for my father..." I paused and thought how to answer. "He's still out there somewhere. I haven't seen him in a couple years."

"I'm sorry," she said, sincerely.

I shrugged. "What about you?"

"My parents are... interesting. Father's job and position are everything. I suspect when he hears of Oscar's decision to quit and join that evil rail tycoon..." she shook her head. "He won't be pleased, and he has a temper. I suspect he will try to ruin Oscar. As for mother, well, she's very firm in her belief of what a proper lady does and does not do. Considering how upset she was when I wanted to pursue an education, she'd faint if she knew what I was doing now!" Skyla tapped the pistol resting against her thigh, "Especially something as low brow as carrying a gun!"

Chuckling, I stuffed a cracker in my mouth and chewed. Her parents would certainly disapprove of me.

She borrowed my large knife and awkwardly cut an edge off the chunk of cheese. "After tomorrow, what will you do?"

There was still that old blood debt of Reydan's that needed to be paid, with lots of interest. But that was certainly not the right thing to talk about now. I recalled the Reverend's words from many days ago. "Find something, anything, that is good and worth fighting for." She was certainly that and more. I never wanted anything more than I wanted her and I prayed we had many more years to spend together instead of ending in violence and death.

"Well, I reckon I should check on my cattle. Most likely they've all been eaten by now though," I joked. "But I'd really like to see you more. A lot more. Even if I've got to go all the way east to do it."

Beaming, she swept aside our small meal and placed her hand on the rough stubble of my cheek. "Last night, before you left, you spoke through my door. You said you wanted to feel my lips on yours and the taste of whiskey on my breath again. Well, come here cowboy." She kissed me passionately.

***

The stars shone just brightly enough to illuminate the empty street as I walked alone to the stables. The building was quiet except for the low murmur of the guards posted by the cannon and Gatling. Brandthorn had ordered the horses moved to the stockyards earlier. They would be outside our protected area, and hopefully far enough away from the fighting that they wouldn't go crazy and break down the fences to get away.

Only one horse remained behind.

Carbine trotted over, and pulled his usual stunt of grabbing for my hat. This time, I didn't stop him as he pulled it from my head. He bounced away, happily carrying the Stetson between his teeth before dropping it.

Crawling between the rails, I picked up the bent hat as Carbine pushed his muzzle against me. I scratched behind his ears and opened the gate. He followed me out and when I stopped, he stopped obediently beside me.

I placed my hand on his shoulder, feeling his warmth, smelling the scent of hay and horse.

"Hey boy. I need you to listen to me this one time," I said softly. His ears flicked towards me and he pushed his head against my chest.

I looked at the guards who watched me curiously. If Carbine was wearing a saddle, they probably would've thought I was deserting.

But I wasn't the one leaving.

"I need you to go home," I whispered.

He turned away and began to walk back towards the corral, stubborn to the end.

Grabbing his head, I pulled it around until we were face to face and looked into his brown eyes. "I mean it. Go and don't come back." I said it firmly this time.

I took a step away and pointed in the direction of our ranch.

"Go! Go home!" Whipping my hat off, I slapped his side with it and he started walking away, confused. "GET!" I kicked dirt after him and with a last look over his shoulder, he began to trot, then run.

I watched him disappear into the darkness.

"Best horse I ever had," I whispered to myself.

He may not understand, but at least he'd be alive. Apes ate horses, and I wasn't about to let them eat mine without giving him a fighting chance.

I suddenly felt very much alone.

***

The town was quiet as I walked down Main Street. Peaceful, really. It was hard to think that tomorrow it'd be filled with blood and death. Hopefully the apes and not ours.

"Evening, Jed," a voice came from beneath the balcony. I stopped. A match flared, illuminating Wesley's face as he lit a cigarillo. He shook the small flame out, once again pitching himself into darkness with only a small red ember giving his position away.

"Howdy," I replied, warily watching the gunman as he approached.

He stopped several yards away. The ember flared brightly as he took a drag.

"I know who you are," he said flatly, taking the cigarette from his lips and studying it.

My body tensed. For a moment the urge to gun him down where he stood almost overpowered me. No one would think twice of me killing a killer. But my hands stayed by my sides.

"Easy there. Your secret's safe with me. See, I've known who you were since I first saw you walk into the bar all busted up with double black eyes. We never ran in the same circles, but you were pointed out to me once, and I don't forget a face." The cherry burned hot as he dragged air through the small roll of tobacco. He suddenly flicked the cigarette in disgust and it burst against the ground in a spray of sparks. "I've met killers before. Hell, I am a killer. But you, you're something different."

"No shit. That's why I left that life behind," I snarled.

"Yes," he licked his lips. "But I also know your old outfit ain't too happy with your sudden departure. Rumor has it, you gunned down several of your own gang, then rode off with the loot from a job where some bystander got hurt."

That was true. "I only gunned down two, the third I beat to death with a chunk of firewood. They earned it, they killed a kid and laughed."

He snorted. "You never saw that coming? Your boss was hiring mad dogs. Men who didn't care about nothing but the thrill of the kill. But now… your old crew has a bounty on you." He tilted his head slightly, looking at me thoughtfully. "But only for your location."

My fingers, mere inches away from the butts of my pistols twitched with anticipation. "Then I reckon you're the first asshole I'm going to have to kill, huh?"

He raised both hands slowly, "No. Call it a sense of honor, but bounty hunting doesn't agree with me. Of course, maybe it's because I've a bounty of my own. But I've no intention of telling anyone about your whereabouts. Especially your old gang. They've gotten worse since you left. More risk taking. More casual violence. You've the word of a murderous, blood-thirsty killer outlaw on that," he laughed sarcastically. "Besides a man like you might be able to break free from the past and make good with a fresh start." He stepped closer and waved his hand around the empty street. "But this place, regardless of what happens tomorrow will be in every newspaper across America within the week. If you survive, be prepared to run. You can't stay hid here."

I didn't speak, just stared as I tried to digest the new information. It wasn't a surprise. My gang started with good intentions, just like me. But as they slipped further and further into wrong, I fought to stay in the right. Until that poor kid died. Then I was done with that life.

"See you tomorrow morning… Jedidiah." With that, he walked away and left me standing alone with my thoughts.

***

The next morning, I stood staring at the bed. Grinning broadly, I stretched and felt the tightness of the scar tissue across my bare back. The black dinosaur claw dangled from my neck on its cord, contrasting sharply against my skin.

My rifle and tuned pistols lay freshly cleaned, oiled, and loaded on the sheets. I even prepared the 10-gauge sawed-off shotgun that I'd inherited in the bar downstairs from Timmy's dead buddy. And my Bowie was sharp enough that I shaved with it this morning.

There was something soothing about the ritualistic cleaning of weapons. My life depended on these tools and I wanted them gleaming in the sun as they sent apes off to meet whatever make believe monkey god they worshipped.

The cleaning also helped me not think about Wesley's foreboding words.

A fist pounded against the door.

"Come in."

Fredrick stepped into the small room. He was dressed in his fine leather pants with a fringed, beaded buckskin shirt. His ornately engraved rifle hung from a shoulder on an embossed sling. He noted my weapons on the bed. "Loaded for bear I see," he stopped and sniffed the air. "What's that smell?"

"Gun cleaner."

"It's... sweet, almost tangy. With a little work, it'd make a good cologne," he declared.

I snorted. "You're loco. But it cuts lead and burnt powder like you wouldn't believe." I handed him a small glass bottle from the nightstand.

Adjusting his glasses, he read the brown label. "Hoppe's Number 6." Sniffing the bottle, he coughed at the fumes. "Whew. Potent stuff."

Grabbing a clean shirt from the nightstand, I threw it on and slung the heavy gun belt around my waist. Every loop was filled with cartridges. One by one, I picked the pistols up and dropped them into their respective holsters.

The hunter set the bottle down and picked up my *Eighty-Six*. He threw it to a shoulder and looked down the iron sights. "You ready for today, Jed?"

"Damn right I am."

He grinned at my enthusiasm. "Should be a mighty fine adventure."

"It'll be something alright." I picked up the sawed-off shotgun and with a makeshift sling, slung it crossways around my body. The braided cord was loose enough that I could grab the shortened gun, twist it up and fire from the waist. A handful of shotgun shells were stuffed into my pockets.

Ashley stepped through the open door, waving a hand across her face. "Ugh, it stinks in here." She stopped when she saw Fredrick and looked around the room. "Oh, I thought Skyla would be here."

"Why?" I asked innocently.

She rolled her eyes.

I winked at her mischievously. "By the way, seen Wade? He wasn't in his room this morning."

From the blush that crept across her face as she spun away, I was certain now of where he'd been.

Our sharpshooter couldn't seem to leave the room fast enough. Fredrick laughed as she slammed the door shut behind her. "Just business partners, huh?"

I snickered and slid the Bowie into its sheath on the back of my belt. "That's what they say."

From outside came the frantic clanging of the church bell followed by pounding of hooves and a hoarse, repeated yell. "They're here! They're here! To your positions!"

The ape army must have moved all night to get here so early. Hopefully their eagerness for battle would make them exhausted, slower, more prone to mistakes. With their superior numbers, we'd take all the advantages we could get.

"Good. I didn't feel like waiting in the hot sun all day anyways." Fredrick gave me a toothy grin and strode out the door.

Taking one last look around the room to make sure I hadn't forgotten anything, I slung my saddle bags over a shoulder and followed the hunter.

***

On the eastern ridge of the valley, mounted apes were moving into loose rows. The gods of battle had apparently seen fit for the army to approach from the direction we planned for. Unless they tried to circle around us, they'd run directly into our most heavily fortified portion of the town. Straight into a hailstorm of gunfire and cannon balls.

The streets were filled with heavily armed defenders running to their designated positions. It was barely controlled chaos. You could almost taste panic and fear in the air. Mothers and fathers were rushing their children into the bank. As the most reinforced building in town, as well as across the street from our defended front, they would have the best chance of survival there. They had plenty of food and water. If we lost, they might be able to hole up until reinforcements arrived.

Unless the apes burned them out.

My group stood on the boardwalk in front of the hotel, watching the activity in the street and waiting on me. Everyone was armed to the teeth with as much spare ammunition as they could carry. The .45-70 rounds that fed my rifle were so large and heavy, that my saddle bags were bulging and making my shoulder sore from the leather cutting into the muscle.

It was time for us to say goodbye.

Wade and I would be on the southern end of town, on the roof of the hardware store. Fredrick would be below us, helping defend the Gatling gun. Both ladies would be stationed in the church steeple to the north. This would give Ashley a large field of view so she could put her skill set to best use. Skyla would be beside her, armed with her new pistol and Fredrick's spare rifle.

After the vision in the sweat lodge, I felt immensely better knowing that she'd be in the safest location in town.

Unless we lost, then nowhere would be safe.

Ashley hugged each of us, and lingered in embrace with Wade.

"Don't get killed, partner," she told him.

"You neither," the wolverine slayer said softly back.

Skyla grasped my shirt tightly and pulled in close. "Don't be a hero, and I'll see you in a little while," she said with a confidence that didn't quite reach her eyes. Her entire body trembled with nervousness.

"Never," I pointed at my flat brimmed brown hat. "I'm not the white hat sort." Winking, I gave her my best carefree smile I could summon.

She didn't buy it. "Jed, look... I..." she stammered. Her eyes reddened as she fought back tears.

Without thinking, I grabbed her about the waist, laid her back and kissed her.

Right there. In the middle of the street. In plain view of everyone.

"Whoa there, Cowboy," Fredrick chuckled.

Ashley whooped. "That's romance right there! Wade, take note of how a girl ought to be treated before battle." The famous westerner blushed crimson.

I ignored them all as I stood her up and held her in my arms, my eyes never leaving hers. A single tear escaped, rolling down her cheek. I smeared it away with a rough, calloused hand.

"We're going to be fine," I whispered. "Because you and I ain't done yet. This is just a single day before many other days. We've an entire life ahead of us and we're going to live it."

She sniffed. Her lovely jaw was now set as determination swept away the fear of losing each other.

"Now..." I looked her in the eyes, "I need you to be brave and strong and fierce. Because there's an awful lot of killing that needs to be done, and I can't do that if I'm worried about you. You stay with Ashley, and shoot everything that comes near. Don't worry about me."

She took a deep breath and stepped back, putting space between us. Her shoulders were set and her eyes dry. "Then kill them. And come find me when it's done. Okay?"

I grinned at her giving me orders. "Yes, ma'am. I'll be there shortly."

"You see to it, Jedidiah Huckleberry." Grabbing Ashley's hand, they walked away quickly as we watched them go. Wade's face was a stoic mask. Outside of the church, Skyla turned back, flashed me a smile and disappeared inside.

Dan crossed the street, a scowl across his face. He carried a rifle in each hand and his nephews followed. They looked nervous and were doing a poor job of hiding it.

I raised a hand and gave them the middle finger.

The crude gesture made them laugh before mimicking the offensive gesture back. Their fears momentarily eased, they jogged after the Sheriff to catch up. The three of them would be positioned near the stable, where they would defend the northern Gatling gun and cannon.

Above the ridge the ape version of cavalry was gathered into their rough formation. Apes on foot began to pour over the crest of the hill, moving into position on either side of the mounted trikes.

"Gentlemen, shall we?" Fredrick asked, turning to go to his post.

"We shall indeed." Hefting his heavy Ballard rifle, Wade rested it across a shoulder. We'd tried to get him to take one of Fredrick's spare rifles last night, but he stated that he'd rather die with his favored single shot than with a repeater. Ashley wasn't pleased with that comment and vowed he'd carry something else today, but it seems he never gave into any of her persuasions.

Taking a last, lingering look at the church steeple where Skyla would be, I quickly caught up with the others. We passed the Reverend. Instead of carrying his Bible as usual, he toted a double-barreled shotgun in the crook of his arm.

Surprised, I pointed at the gun. "Where'd you get that street howitzer?"

"From under my pulpit," he said innocently, as though that was the most logical place for it. At my baffled face he spoke quickly, "Jedidiah, there are incredibly powerful forces of evil at work in men's hearts. Sometimes the only way to convince them they are wrong is by sending them to meet their Maker before they do anyone more harm." He hefted the shotgun in his hands and admired it. "But I've never had no call to use old Bessy, not until today."

Something was scratched into the dark wood stock. I leaned forward to read it, but the Reverend turned away before I could make the script out. He took off at a jog for the church, calling over his shoulder. "Good luck today, Jedidiah!"

**

I watched the army through my telescope.

There were so many of them. Hundreds of them. Their ranks swelling as more crossed over the ridge. There was no discipline to the apes on foot. They weren't in any sort of formations. Just a mob of frighteningly strong, hairy savages armed with stone age weapons. Every one of them wore war paint smeared on their bodies or faces. Hues of green, yellow, and red swirls and streaks contrasted brightly against their dark skin. They'd left the carts behind, but hundreds of spears were pointed upright towards the sky, and axes, clubs and bows were held in hand.

The mounted apes though, they had discipline. Their large, naturally armored trikes stood their ground, occasionally shifting in place but staying in relatively neat lines. Just a rippling wave of horns and bone shields. The dinosaurs' bellows echoed to us faintly.

Wade was already on the roof of the hardware store with my spare ammunition and another man, while I stood on the ground with Fredrick. Around us were a dozen defenders resting against stacked rail ties, and a one-legged veteran in a battered Confederate slouch hat. He stood beside the Gatling on his whittled stump, chastising a pair of young soldiers foully for not moving quickly enough in loading the weapon. The Lieutenant, trusting Dan's recommendation, had put the old rebel in charge. Surprisingly, the two soldiers seemed keen on earning the old man's respect rather than bucking his commands. And that was how it should be, with young warriors idolizing the old.

I found myself, of all things, thinking of Carbine and hoping he was safe. It wouldn't surprise me if the stubborn horse returned to the stables in the middle of the night. That would be a very Carbine type thing to do.

The flood of apes turned to a trickle, then stopped entirely as the full force assembled on the sloping hillside. Carts containing the raptors were the last to arrive, pulled over the crest and turned so the back of the cages faced us. The apes dropped the carts in place, then stood beside the cage, awaiting orders to release the vicious feathered dinosaurs. Those would be a problem. As fast and nimble as they were, they could pop up in a lot of places unexpectedly.

Last came the leader of the apes, riding his broken horned trike. He walked the dinosaur around his troops, then stopped in front of the other mounted trikes. Unlike the others, his body was unpainted.

"Is that your scar faced friend in the front?" Fredrick asked as he paced back and forth. The man practically reeked of excitement and energy.

I watched the scar faced ape through the glass as he dismounted with large obsidian axe held in hand. His trike was well trained, staying put as the monkey took several steps forward and stared at our town. "Yes, sir."

"Good. I call dibs."

This was the calm before the storm. I could feel nervousness in the air around me. The excitement and fear before battle, mixed together into an eagerness to begin and the desire to flee. It was an addictive feeling. I realized I didn't know much about the apes. They were foreign invaders. We didn't know what sort of tactics to expect.

"What is it with western towns?" Wade suddenly interrupted my thinking as he called down to us. "It's like they've always got to find a pretty little valley to build a town in instead of on the high ground with a tactical advantage."

"I've thought of that as well!" It was a shame too, charging uphill would have slowed the apes and given us more time to kill them. But now, once they reached us, with their superior speed and strength, the advantage would be theirs.

From where I stood, I couldn't see the church steeple. But I wish I could have looked at Skyla again before the battle was joined. She would do well, I thought. She'd come a long way since she killed the ape in the back of the wagon and saved herself and that wretched cretin Oscar. That was a man I didn't miss one bit.

Four riders moved their trikes forward, two on each side of their leader.

"Jed, what's this?" Fredrick asked.

"No idea." I peered through the telescope.

A pair of soldiers in bloodied and tattered uniforms were pulled through the apes, struggling and screaming as they fought against their captors hopelessly.

Deserters.

Their cries were tiny and pitiful. Apes forced the two men between the pairs of trikes and tied each hand to a cord that was passed to each rider. Their arms were jerked out wide as the trikes side stepped and shuffled apart. The screams intensified as their muscles tore and joints were dislocated.

The ritual chanting and chest beating began.

"We've got to do something!" cried one of the young soldiers. The other looked terrified.

"Shut it, boy. Ain't nothing we can do, so don't let it intimidate you," the old Confederate spat and hobbled to the Gatling gun. He patted the multi-barreled gun fondly. "We'll get our revenge soon enough. You two keep it loaded and I'll do the rest."

A loud boom came from the far end of town, the noise echoing across the valley, startling us.

"What the...! What was that?" Fredrick ducked his head and looked around, startled.

"Cannon," the Confederate grinned. He was missing several front teeth.

One of the deserter's bodies exploded into red chunks of pulverized flesh and pink mist as the twelve-pound solid lead ball burst through his body effortlessly, bounced off the ground and into the mob of infantry. The cannon ball cut a swath through their ranks in a split-second, leaving dead and mutilated apes writhing on the ground and others pushing away, panicked by the sudden carnage that appeared amongst them.

They must have thought they were safe so far away.

Not hardly.

Screams and roars of wounded apes drifted to us. It would have been music to our ears, except we were all shocked at what just happened.

The explosion of meat, clods of dirt and rock from the cannon ball's impact had flung the ape leader to the ground. He staggered back to his feet, blood trickling from his nose and mouth as the mounted dinosaurs pushed and shoved against each other in confusion. His massive trike had bolted, running a dozen paces away before turning and walking back to the leader.

"The Lieutenant ordered the cannon to fire on his own men," Fredrick gasped in awe. The defenders around us shouted their bewilderment and shock.

The Confederate shrugged nonchalantly. "Good for him. Probably aiming for the leader. Really, it's a good shot. At that range, it's rather hard to be accurate. Bad luck for us they didn't hit him."

"What about the man? He just exploded!" shouted one of the young soldiers angrily at the grizzled veteran.

"Listen here, boy," the Confederate twirled nimbly around on his wooden leg and shoved a finger in the soldier's face. "You think that deserting coward would have wanted to have his heart cut out or a quick death as we took out some of his captors with him? I know what I'd want!"

Bellowing, the recovered ape leader raised his obsidian axe with both hands and savagely hacked the surviving soldier from shoulder to hip. The corpse fell apart in two large ragged pieces.

The scar faced ape swung onto the back of his trike and pointed the chipped obsidian weapon towards us while shouting commands. Ape infantry surged forward at a light jog, leaving the mounted trikes behind, and silently charged towards us.

"Alright, you hairy sons of bitches. Come get some," I muttered as we watched the approaching apes move down the valley towards our town.

Fredrick slapped me on the back so hard I staggered. "The battle is about to be joined. Vae victus!" he roared and checked the chamber of his rifle.

"Woe to the conquered," I repeated the Latin phrase. He was right. Be conquerors, or be conquered. If the apes won, no one would be spared.

No one fired as the apes began their approach.

White stones had been painted and placed at intervals around town, giving us an easy way to gauge distance for shooting. They were still at least a hundred yards past the furthest rock and we had our orders to hold fire until they passed designated stones.

***

I climbed to the roof of the trading post quickly, the heavy *Eighty-Six* rifle slung over my back bumping against the sawed-off shotgun. Wade leaned over the edge and grabbed my hand to help me up.

Like most of the buildings, the roof was sloped slightly, with a false front facing Main Street and open behind. We built some waist high rough sawn timbers on all of the roofs to give defenders some measure of protection. They weren't pretty, but they ought to help keep us alive.

A Mexican with a gaudy red and white shirt and a pitiful mustache was stationed on the roof with us. He was one of the few who escaped the ape attack on the mine, and managed to speak passable English with a heavy accent. After seeing his rusted black powder rifle, I loaned him my old Sharps with plenty of ammunition and instructions on its use. He looked nervous. If the rumors of what happened at the mine were even partially true, I didn't blame him. The miners witnessed ritualistic slaughtering of their friends first hand before they could escape.

"Here we go," Wade said, watching the apes approach the first white stone. "Antonio, you ready for this?"

"Si," he set his jaw in determination. "I fight for mas amigos."

"Revenge, eh? I like it." Leaning forward over our hastily constructed defenses, I looked along the row of buildings. Gun barrels jutted from windows and along the tops of overturned wagons jammed in the alleys. More shooters stood on other roofs like us, hiding behind raised edges or similarly built cover, waiting for their turn to open fire.

The big apes trotted past the first pile of white stones.

Sharp cracks of rifles firing simultaneously made me jump, even though I was expecting it. Apes leading the pack, tumbled and fell as marksmen hit their targets, others jerked and twitched as bullets wounded them.

One of the marksmen would be Ashley, using her *One of a Thousand* rifle to drop ape bodies at six hundred yards. Another was Wade; he ejected a large brass casing from his heavy barreled rifle and inserted a fresh cartridge. His Ballard was optimally built for shooting such as this.

The hairy savages broke into a jog as a chorus of bellows and primordial screams filled the valley. Several more apes fell before the infantry passed the second pile of white stones.

We'd intentionally only fired a few shots when they crossed the first stone. We wanted to pick some off, but keep them bunched together.

Because this was the moment that we'd all been waiting on.

Both Gatling guns opened with a steady pop-pop-pop-pop-pop.

Bullets stitched across the grass in front of the apes as the gunners adjusted and shifted the stream of bullets into the attacking infantry.

Blood sprayed as apes were mowed down. Some were practically cut in half, others lost limbs or dropped, writhing in mortal agony with bodies punctured or mangled by the heavy bullets. The rest ran faster, bellows of blood lust mingling amongst the screams of the wounded and dying.

The crew-served guns were chewing them up, but there were still so damned many of them. The Confederate below shouted for the soldiers to load faster as he cranked the handle and spit lead death.

Another thunderous boom came from the cannon. This time with a canister of grape shot.

Dozens of small lead balls burst through the mass of unarmored bodies. It had the effect of a giant shotgun, wiping out an entire swath of apes.

They kept coming, leaving dozens of dead behind. The wounded who could still move, struggled onwards, not giving up. Others crawled, pulling themselves forward as they dragged their bodies over trampled, bloodied grass. Others ran on, clutching wounds and staggering with dribbling blood matted through their hair. The teeming mass of painted hair and weapons began to break apart as the survivors spread out.

Then they crossed the third stack of painted rocks. That was the signal for the rest of us.

I raised the *Eighty-Six* and went to work as a volley of small arms fire erupted from the line of buildings.

The rifle became an extension of my will and I willed the destruction of my enemies with it. The gun stock pounded against my shoulder as I racked the lever and pumped heavy slugs into the approaching apes.

Beside me, Wade fired with the speed and efficiency of a man who'd spent a lot of time mastering a firearm. Antonio fired slower, swearing in Spanish as he fumbled with the loading mechanism on my Sharps repeater.

The crackle of small arms fire and twin Gatling guns, punctuated with roars from the cannon, created a symphony of death and destruction amongst the apes.

Attacking infantry fell across the valley floor. It was a gloriously one-sided blood bath. But they kept coming.

Still the mounted trikes and their scar faced leader sat on the ridge and watched. Waiting for the right moment.

I glanced at the gun crew below me. Sweat poured from the crippled veteran as he relentlessly kept the multiple barrels firing. Brass casings were piling ankle deep beneath the gun and the ends of the barrels were beginning to turn red. Civilians leaned against the stacked rail tie covers, laying heavy fire into the advancing forces. Fredrick was crouched, loading his rifle. His spectacles were gone. In the madness of the moment, I laughed. I doubted it would affect his aim any, and at this range, he'd be hard pressed to miss.

The apes began breaking into several large groups, most of them moving towards both ends of town while those remaining in the center rushed straight at the buildings. Reaching bow distance, they began to stop, fire an arrow, then run again before repeating.

Our rate of fired dropped as rooftop defenders were forced to duck and fire over cobbled together defenses as arrows rained against us with frightening force. Some penetrated the thick boards, driving their sharpened obsidian points through, snagging and cutting us as we fought. Even shooters inside the buildings weren't immune to the arrows; an arrow zipped through one of the narrow firing ports in the shutters below us and a horrific scream sounded from below.

Another scream of agony pierced the air from the roof beside us as a man took an arrow through the shoulder. He staggered upright, clutching the wound. An arrow pierced his skull, snapping his head back and dropping his corpse in a crumpled heap.

Gatling crews shifted their fire into the large groups attacking their positions. Amidst the firing, I could hear the old Confederate below me swearing as his heavy bullets cut apes down in droves.

Our lone cannon fired another mass of grape shot at less than a hundred yards into the attackers. A dozen apes were flung backwards, their bodies taking the full force of lead balls, pulverizing organs and bones, reducing them to mangled clumps of hairy meat.

I dropped one of the leading apes at fifty yards; she fell and was trampled beneath the pounding feet of others.

We'd killed over half of the enemy forces on their approach. Bodies were scattered over the valley floor. The ground was ripped, shredded, and cratered from bullets, and cannon balls. Bright crimson was splashed across the flattened prairie grass.

In return they'd only killed a few of ours.

But it was their turn for retribution now.

Wade pulled a stick of dynamite from his back pocket. The fuse had already been cut short.

"Here they come!" screamed a hoarse, panicked voice.

Heavy painted bodies slammed into the walls. Apes began grabbing siding and pulling themselves up while others reached through windows and shutters. Guns were fired point blank into their faces. Spears were thrust through openings and gaps. Screams of humans mixed among the painful bellows of apes. Others tried tearing the overturned wagons away from the alleys they blocked while men behind them fired into the clawing and grabbing apes.

Below us, the Gatling gun cranked bullets into apes climbing over stacked rail ties. Fredrick dodged the swing of a club and jabbed his rifle barrel into the offending ape's throat. The trigger was pulled, nearly decapitating the savage with the gun blast. Bodies piled as defenders fired their rifles dry then drew pistols.

Striking a match against the rough sawn boards in front of us, Wade touched the small trembling flame to the fuse. It sparked and hissed as the gunpowder filled cord began to burn.

"Dynamite!" Wade screamed the warning then tossed the

nitroglycerine imbued stick in front of our position. It bounced off the mob of apes then fell to the ground between them. We ducked. The explosion rocked our building and sent a gout of shredded flesh and dirt into the air.

For a moment I thought the store was going to collapse and take us with it. But the building held firm as bits of mangled flesh splattered down on us.

I flicked a piece of skull and brain goo off my rifle's butt stock. The torn remains of something squished loudly when it hit Antonio's sombrero and slid off. He gagged and made the sign of the cross over his chest.

We peeked over the edge of our cover. A dozen apes lay sprawled below, most blown apart and twitching while others had been hurled backwards by the force. There was so much red that you couldn't tell who or what was wounded or killed. But the explosion made a gap in their forces, buying ourselves and the big gun some time. With space before them now, the defenders began firing into the remaining apes, wiping them out. Fredrick waved a hand at us in thanks, his face a grim mask of dirt and blood, before turning away to shove a mangled corpse off the rail ties.

More explosions came from along the buildings as others chucked dynamite amidst the attackers. Large groups of apes were wiped out, cutting their number down, but they kept coming, teeth bared, weapons swinging.

A wounded beast grabbed a soldier on the roof next to us. With a great roar, the ape flung him yards away from shelter. The ape was dispatched by a shot from the church steeple and slid off the roof.

A pair of raptors pounced onto the man, clawing and biting. His screams ended abruptly as the dinosaurs savagely tore his body apart.

I dropped one of the raptors; it fell, twisting and biting at its shattered hips. A split-second later Wade killed the other. I let the wounded dinosaur suffer and thumbed a couple more rounds into the *Eighty-Six*. I chanced a glance at Skyla and Ashley. The sharpshooter was picking apes off as they climbed onto the roofs, and Skyla was firing her rifle into the mass of teeming apes. More of them were reaching us, the stragglers, wounded, slow runners.

Mounted trikes that'd been held in reserve now surged forward with a loud roar from their riders. Heavy, thundering hooves echoed throughout the valley.

The ape cavalry seemed to care nothing for the infantry. Some wounded were trampled, others impaled on horns, then flung aside with powerful flicks of the large sloped heads of the dinosaurs.

Swirling dust, kicked up from the charging apes and now the trikes, mingling with the fog of gunpowder drifted over the battlefield.

The mounted apes split into two groups, each one circling around towards the heavily defended town entrances. I lost the leader as a pair of arrows thumped into the roof beside me and I dropped one of the bow wielding monkeys.

An ape pulled himself over our roof's edge. Blood trickled from a bullet wound through his shoulder. He growled at me and I blasted him off the rooftop.

The cannon fired, the cast lead ball bounced through several apes before taking a running trike's leg off. The mutilated trike fell, throwing its rider and bellowing and thrashing in pain.

Flames suddenly sprouted from the tent city between the railroad and us. Apes ran amongst the canvas topped temporary housing, lighting them ablaze with torches. Smoke began billowing across the town and battlefield, adding to the churned dust and smoke of burnt gunpowder. The fog of battle was getting thick.

Antonio fired towards the tents with the Sharps while screaming to warn the men around the Gatling gun.

Defenders turned and began killing the arsonists.

A large female was hit. She tumbled into a tent with her torch and something, a kerosene lantern or jug of whiskey perhaps, exploded in a giant fireball. Screaming, her hair and skin on fire, she crashed into another tent and disappeared amidst the burning canvas.

One of the men below us took a feathered shaft through the chest.

Fredrick blew the top of the ape's head off as the same arrow slinger popped up from a mound of bodies with bow drawn back to fire again.

The two groups of trikes were circling farther out now, riding along the valley edge, moving into position to flank both entrances.

With the attacking infantry slowed on our side, the Confederate and sole remaining soldier rotated the Gatling to face them. It was up to the small arms fire to repel the remaining apes in front of us.

In the building next to us, a pair of hairy feet slipped inside through an open shutter. A shotgun roared, followed by a bellow of pain and human screaming before a burst of gunfire silenced the beast's roars.

Wade glanced over, then jerked his rifle towards my face. Instinctively, I ducked as the barrel blasted, stinging me with bits of unburnt powder. A meaty thump came from behind as the bullet pounded into something.

Spinning, I saw a painted ape on its knees, blood pouring from the hole in its chest. He snarled, exposing large canines amidst the bright green handprint that painted his face. A stone club lay fallen on the shingles. Another step closer and he'd have smashed the life out of me.

Drawing my pistol, I executed the hairy savage with a bullet through his eye.

The Gatling below opened on the ape riders to devastating effect. The group fractured apart, veering off as apes and mounts began to die. The remaining riders split around the town; the trike charge broken.

The northern entrance was struggling. Ape infantry was tying up their Gatling and cannon, leaving only small arms fire to combat the riders. They couldn't stop them.

Taking only a few casualties, apes leapt off their mounts and rushed forward to leap over make-shift defenses, swinging clubs and thrusting spears. I lost sight of them behind the buildings as the crew-served weapons went silent, and the defenders were hit between the main force and the flanking party. The crackle of gunfire intensified as they fought for survival at close range.

Men raced down the street towards the opening. I looked at Wade, tempted to follow.

"Go!" he shouted, and I sprinted across the roof. Rushing past Antonio, I leapt over the narrow alley with rifle in hand and onto the Sheriff's roof. The shotgun slung over my back slammed into me painfully and I staggered.

A man defending the roof rose from behind cover, sighting down his rifle. A spear slammed through his chest, leaving the bloodied obsidian tip jutting from his back. He fell, screaming hoarsely. As a companion reached for him, I kept moving. There was nothing I could do.

As I jumped across the space between the two buildings and onto the Mayor's roof, a trike rammed through the wagon blocking the alley below with a crash of flesh and shattering wood. Surprised, I tripped and fell on the landing. The *Eighty-Six* flew from my grasp and skittered across the roof.

Rolling onto my side, I drew one of the Colts and fired into the back of the ape as the wounded trike pushed the broken wagon through the alley and onto Main Street. The ape fell and began dragging himself out of the street. His trike stopped, standing confused and bleeding, his horns entangled in the twisted boards between the wheels. He shook his head, rattling his long horns, trying to break free.

Amidst the roar of battle, I never heard the shot. But the ape spasmed and dropped, twitching in the throes of death.

Across the street, Wesley sat in a chair in the shade of the saloon. He held a gun in one hand and a bottle in the other. With his pistol, he gave a mocking salute that I ignored as I scrambled to my rifle.

A trio of apes rushed through the open alley below me. Leaping to his feet, in one deft move the gunman dropped the bottle, drew his second pistol, and began firing into the attacking apes.

The church was the next building along our front. Glancing at the steeple, I saw Skyla and our sharpshooter spreading death amongst the attackers below who were breaking the defenses at the northern entrance.

I reached the edge of the roof as a severely wounded trike barreled into one of the spiked log Chevals at a full run. The beast, its upper horns and bone shield shattered from the heavy bullets from a Gatling, was blinded with blood, pain, and rage. The mangled dinosaur impaled itself onto the sharpened stakes with such force that the defensive structure gouged deep rivets into the packed dirt as it shifted over a dozen feet backwards. Apes began running through the opening and onto Main Street.

More apes poured through the opened alleyway, effectively surrounding the men who'd moved to reinforce our cannon and Gatling gun. They scattered, taking what cover they could as they faced attackers from the front and rear.

Wesley lit into the apes coming through the alley, both pistols blazing fire and gun smoke as he backed through the bat wing doors into the protection of the saloon.

Apes were coming from multiple directions now. Our solid front was gone. Men were shooting in every direction as each building was turned into an isolated fort. Apes began knocking doors down with clubs, ripping windows open, rushing into buildings. Screams came from everywhere as the apes took advantage of their size at close range.

The hairy bastards trying to get into the bar were gunned down at the door. Wesley piled the bodies until his guns went silent and apes rushed through. I hoped he was as fast at reloading as he was shooting.

The blacksmith Edward came bellowing madly down the street, impaled on the long horn of a trike, and slamming his large blacksmith hammer repeatedly against the dinosaur's skull. Blood poured from his mouth and as his body went limp, the trike stumbled and crashed into the boardwalk, collapsing a porch roof onto the dead blacksmith.

Glancing at the steeple, I locked eyes with Skyla. She had a brave face on. But we'd discussed this possibility last night. Once the apes broke through our defenses, we were doomed. She knew to save a bullet for herself.

It looked like the maybe-future was coming true after all, except my friends would be killed scattered all over town, instead of being slaughtered inside the bar.

I quickly looked for the scar faced leader. He'd been strangely absent. We were going to die, but I'd be damned if he was going to survive.

Amidst the smoke from the burning tents, lingering gun smoke and churned dust, I couldn't find him.

Growling in disgust, I jerked the *Eighty-Six* into my shoulder and began dumping rounds into the apes rushing through the northern entrance. Arrows dropped around me. Uncaring, I ignored them. One cut through my shirt, slicing flesh along my ribs before embedding itself into the shingles of the roof beside me.

The church was putting up a magnificent defense, apes were dying by the bushel as they fought to gain entrance. I could hear the Reverend's Old Bessy reaping souls for the Lord. If these murderous apes even had them.

The few defenders from the north entrance who survived had holed up in the stables and blacksmith shop. Gunfire was still coming from the blacksmith shop, but the guns in the stable were falling silent.

Another trike slammed into the other Cheval, this one unwounded and intentionally ridden into it by an ape who was promptly shot off the dying mount. Now the entrance was wide open for trikes.

They charged down the street, heavy bodies the size of wagons swinging their heads as apes loosened arrows, or leapt off to attack on foot. Apes in the street dove out of the way, taking to the sidewalks to fire their arrows through open windows.

A raptor climbed our building unseen and tackled a defender behind me. Amidst painful screams the pair bowled off the roof and into the street. A rider-less trike ran into them, hooking the feathered dinosaurs on its horns and trampling the man under hooves. With a shake of its head, the trike flung the raptor off its horns and through a window of the saloon.

An ape loomed in front of me as it clambered over the side of the building. Before I could react, the ape's head deflated. Bits of brain and gore splattered across my face and shirt. Looking up, I saw Ashley swing her *One of a Thousand* away and fire again.

Another ape pulled herself over the edge. She had almost perfect swirls of red smeared around her eyes and a double streak of yellow down her chin. The war paint was rather well done.

I smashed the buttstock of my rifle against her ugly face and knocked her back down into the alley. Streaks of ape paint were left smeared across the wood grain of my gun.

At that moment, our saviors raced over the grassy peaks of the valley in a flurry of pounding hooves, war cries, and war paint.

At the head of dozens of Shaynee, rode Chief and Otto, leading the charge with the unbridled fury that only an angry Indian out for blood could possess.

God bless the heathens.

A ragged cheer came from the remaining defenders.

The Indians shook war clubs and spears, battered, abused rifles and decorated bows as they rushed down the corpse strewn killing field.

Mounted apes charged to meet them.

The great white ape led the way. Without slowing his mount, he hurled a spear through the chest of a brave, flinging him off the back of his painted pony and impaling his body to the ground.

Arrows were loosened back and forth as they barreled towards each other, punctuated with rifle fire.

Then they were amongst each other in a churning of dirt, gun smoke, and screams of wounded and dying.

Man against ape, swinging stone clubs and lances, tomahawks and spears. Nimble ponies and slower, but naturally armored dinosaurs shifted around each other, each rider trying to get the upper hand.

Other apes renewed their attack against the fortified buildings, climbing roofs, running through alleys, or trying to rip the building apart with their bare hands and clubs to get inside.

Hearing the Gatling from the southern entrance go quiet, I turned back and saw they were now in danger of being overrun. There was no sign of Antonio, but Wade was standing on the edge of the roof, shooting his heavy black powder revolver one handed. He cut a dashing figure as he disappeared in the swirling smoke from the burning tents.

Torn between running to both entrances, I dropped onto the porch overhang of the merchant store to climb down. A trike clipped the corner post, knocking it from its foundation and collapsing the porch roof. I fell with it, and the *Eighty-Six* slipped from my hands.

Gasping for breath, I saw another mounted ape rushing down the street towards me. Drawing both pistols, I emptied them into the face of the trike. It bellowed, shaking its horns. Blinded by bullets and pain, it missed me and ran head first into the side of the building I'd just fallen from. There were screams of terror as it plowed through the wall in a shrieking of boards and beams snapping. The roof gave way, collapsing onto the ape rider, trike, and anyone else inside.

I ducked behind a water trough as an ape loosened an arrow at me from the back of its trike. Water splashed at its impact into the wood container. I began emptying shells and reloading my pistols, one at a time, while peeking over the top. The ape lost interest in me, and rushed his trike towards the southern entrance.

Another ape was climbing the side of the church, intent on getting the ladies in the tower. The church steeple was hit with so many arrows it looked like a pin cushion. The ape was using the thick shafts as handholds to help pull himself upwards. Skyla leaned out and fired her pistol into the ape. He slipped, falling several feet, before latching onto the siding with one hand. She fired again, and the ape fell and tumbled out of sight.

I glanced around for my rifle as the partially collapsed building heaved and trembled from the wounded trike trying to free itself. I didn't see it anywhere.

A decapitated body in a hideous red and white shirt landed in the middle of the street with a sickly thud of flesh and breaking bones. Antonio. The poor man survived the attack on the mining camp only to die in town.

Twisting about, I spied the scar faced leader on one of the roofs across the street.

He stood with obsidian axe in one hand and the Mexican's severed head gripped by the hair in the other. Blood was splattered on his chest and arms. The single canine exposed by the hideous scarring across his face showed his perpetual snarl.

He hadn't seen me yet.

Thumbing the hammer back, I raised my pistol.

Time to die, you bastard.

A bullet clipped the wood siding of the fallen building, sending out a spray of splinters. I flinched and jerked back. My eyes watered from the stinging dust and wood chips. The scar faced leader leapt off the roof to the next building and out of sight.

Growling in rage at the lost opportunity, I spun to see what idiot almost hit me. From inside the school house across the street, the wretched miner Timmy was aiming down a rifle.

I ducked as it blossomed fire and a bullet whizzed by overhead. Dashing across the street, I tried not to trip on corpses or the numerous arrows sticking from the ground while firing my pistols in his general direction. The sawed-off shotgun thumped against my back.

He ducked out of sight and I managed to reach the other side without dying.

Squatting Bull raced down the street on his pony, loosening an arrow at the ape emerging from the alley beside the Mayor's office. The arrow pinned the ape's foot to the boardwalk and the savage roared painfully.

After the Indian came a charging mounted ape, hurling a spear and narrowly missing the young brave.

Sprinting along the boardwalk with pistols in hand, I saw the rifle barrel resting on a window sill. The gun swung back and forth as Timmy tried to find me. Raising a boot, I kicked the barrel with the flat of my heel, knocking the gun from his grasp.

Leaping in front of the window, I pointed both pistols at him.

The would-be murderer's face paled, and his hands began to rise in surrender. He stammered, trying to find the words to stop my wrath.

I shot him through the forehead.

My vengeance dealt, I turned and took a step away.

The movement saved my life as an ape's stone axe barely missed splitting my skull. Stumbling off the boardwalk in surprise, I tripped and fell. The ape roared, showing yellowed canines amidst a blood splattered face. He raised the axe above his head. I jerked the pistols up, thumbing the hammers back.

Spurts of blood erupted from the ape's chest. The axe fell to the ground, and the hairy savage dropped to a knee. He touched one of the bullet holes in his chest in surprise. The big monkey looked puzzled as his eyes began to glaze over.

Wesley kicked the dying ape over and grinned. The gunman's face and clothes were smeared with dirt and blood oozed from a lacerated scalp. But the dual Colt Lightnings that filled his hands were still unwavering.

An Indian whooped from behind us and hurled a lance through the back of an unsuspecting ape trying to rip a shutter off the Sheriff's Office. The ape staggered, grabbing at the spear sticking from her back before falling. We jumped aside as the Indian raced past us with a savage grin amidst his war paint.

I rolled to my feet. Wesley nodded towards the school house and the miner's corpse. "Took you long enough." Grinning, he strode away. As he passed the wounded ape pulling the lance through her chest, he shot her through the skull before continuing towards the northern entrance.

Holstering one Peacemaker, I thumbed cartridges into the other and ran towards the Blacksmith shop. The few remaining defenders manning the cannon and Gatling appeared to be holed up there. Sporadic gunfire came from the building. Bodies of apes and several trikes were piling up outside. They'd drawn a lot of attention from the attackers.

Apes were climbing on top of the building and were ripping planks and shingles off the roof as they tried to dig inside. Bullets peppered through the roof as the defenders fired upwards. I fired at them, wounding several before ducking into an alley to reload as large green and yellow fletched arrows were loosened in my direction.

A handful of Shaynee braves, led by Otto, burst through the smoke and rushed past me. Using scavenged soldier rifles from the doomed rescue squad, they unloaded on the apes on the roof. Several dropped and others howled in pain before the Indians twisted their ponies around and sped back towards the southern end of town.

One of the braves took an arrow through the shoulder and fell from his horse. Rising, he took two staggered steps before a pair of arrows hit him and he fell dead.

I took stock of our increasingly hopeless looking situation.

The Shaynee certainly helped, but they were being wiped out with us. It was only a matter of time before they decided whites weren't worth the lives of their braves and withdrew. Corpses were everywhere, in the streets, alleyways, and roof tops. Our crew-served weapons had been out of the fight for some time now, our defenses were overwhelmed, and we were barely holding onto the street and our buildings. The school house and some outlying partially constructed buildings had caught fire as well, adding more smoke to the confusion of gun shots, screams, and roars of rage.

My eyes flicked at the bank; the shutters were still closed and nailed in place. So far, the building hadn't drawn any apes to it yet. For now, the children and women were still safe inside.

I thumbed the hammers back on the pistols. It was time to fight my way to the church and Skyla. The end was here.

I hoped she was still alive.

A loud, sharp train whistle cut through the air.

Peeking around the alley, I glanced south. Amidst the billowing smoke of burning tents, there was a thick black column of smoke moving towards us.

I grinned wickedly. With the soldier reinforcements, our chances of survival just increased drastically.

A white hairy hand grabbed me by the shirt and flung me into the street. I lost my grip on the pistols and they fell away as my body tumbled across the arrow filled street.

Several feathered shafts snapped under my weight before I slammed into the mangled remains of a broken wagon.

A single moment of excruciating pain came from my back as the shotgun was sandwiched between my body and the boards, then my head slammed into a wheel.

For a moment everything went dark, then bright bits of light sparked across my vision. I blinked.

Remembering the danger, I fought to stand. My hands fumbled at the shotgun slung to my back. My body was responding sluggishly.

The great ape, his solid white hair now smeared pink with blood, drew the spear back to thrust.

My eyes flicked to the church steeple. I didn't see Skyla.

Otto appeared out of nowhere, his painted pony pierced with arrows but still gamely holding on. The scarred Indian leapt off his horse, tackling the white ape and sending the spear flying.

Otto's bullet pierced tomahawk flashed overhead.

The ape fought to defend himself, raising hands and arms to stop the weapon. Blood sprayed as Otto hacked savagely through them. A white hand flew away, the jagged bone sticking out.

As the great ape weakened, the scarred Indian brought the tomahawk down with an animalistic scream of victory, driving the blade deep into its white blood smeared chest.

Otto drew his knife. Grabbing the dead ape's head by the hair, he scalped him with a vicious swipe of the blade.

Whooping, he raised the bloodied flap of skin high and shook it at me. Wrenching the tomahawk from the ape's chest, he ran towards his wounded pony and leapt onto its back. The painted animal staggered under his weight, and ran stumbling into the smoke with the Indian screaming Shaynee insults.

I reckoned by saving my life, his honor had been restored.

Guess I wouldn't have to kill him after all.

Through the thick smoke of burning tents and buildings, I couldn't see the train pull into the station. But I heard the barrage of gunfire that came before the squeal of train brakes. Judging by the number of guns firing, it was the company of soldiers Governor Hardy promised to send.

Apes began to retreat under the onslaught of fresh reinforcements. They ran between alleys and leapt off rooftops to make their way out of the valley. Those on trikes thundered away, leaving their infantry behind. Survival of the fittest.

I pushed away from the broken wagon and picked my pistols off the ground.

From down the street came the loud bellow of a trike.

Spinning, I saw the scar faced leader sitting on his massive trike in the middle of the street. The big ape was splattered with blood across his face and chest. His mount stomped its feet, then rose on its hind legs, shaking its head and horns with a loud bellow before landing with a heavy thud. Antonio's head and several others hung from the beast with the other skulls.

The ape pointed his obsidian axe at me and roared something angry and guttural.

Gritting my teeth, I began stalking forward.

Let's do this.

The ape leader slammed the flat of his axe against the side of the trike and it lunged forward.

Behind them, Fredrick limped out of the trading post and began firing as fast as he could work the lever. Bullets missed the pair and cracked as they passed by me. But some found their mark, and the trike stumbled and slowed.

Then came the loud boom of a single shot Ballard rifle. A chunk of the dinosaur's bone shield shattered off. The ape stayed standing in full view, axe raised high.

I knew my pistols were almost empty. I hoped it'd be enough.

Raising the Peacemakers, I emptied them at the leader.

Several rounds chipped off the top of the trike's shield, but a couple hit the ape in the chest before the guns went empty. He dropped the axe and fell out of sight behind the bone shield.

I calmly pulled the sawed-off shotgun from my back and thumbed the dual hammers back, knowing double loads of buckshot wouldn't do much against the giant charging dinosaur. But it was all I had left.

The trike was almost upon me.

Another loud boom came from Wade's rifle.

A large hole appeared between the trike's narrow eyes as the heavy bullet punched through thick skull and into the dinosaur's brain.

The trike slowed, staggering side to side several more paces before dropping a scant six feet in front of me. With one big heave, the giant animal gave its final breath.

Raising the shotgun, I moved around the trike to find the wounded leader. He was nowhere to be found. I spun around in confusion.

The scarred ape tackled me, knocking the shotgun from my hands.

We grappled. I futilely fought to get the upper hand before he pinned me under his crushing weight. Even wounded, he had incredible strength. Dark eyes in his hideously scarred face were full of savagery. I twisted my head away as canines snapped inches from my face. Bloody saliva dripped on my face.

My Bowie was pinned against the small of my back. But the shotgun lay nearby. I stretched my hand towards it, my fingers mere inches away. With one hand fighting to keep the ape's mouth at bay, I heaved myself to the side as far as possible

My fingers flicked on the buttstock, shifting the gun further from my reach.

He wrapped his hands around my throat. Like bands of iron, they closed my windpipe.

I squirmed and punched hopelessly at his sides. My fist connected with something tucked in his belt. Grasping at the object, my hand closed on the hilt of his sacrificial knife.

Ripping it from his belt, I stabbed the chipped obsidian blade deep into the ape's side. He roared and rolled away, ripping the knife from my hand.

I scrambled on all fours for the shotgun.

Scooping it off the ground, I shoved my fingers onto the double triggers and contorted my body around.

The ape, blood pouring from his wounds, rushed forward with the sacrificial knife held in hand.

Without aiming, I pulled the triggers.

Twin loads of buckshot burst through the ape's legs, severing one and badly mangling the other.

Shrieking, the leader toppled over and thrashed.

The roars, screams of pain, pounding hooves and gunshots turned to background noise, barely noticeable amidst the pounding in my ears and righteous rage that filled my vision.

Snarling, I crawled on top of his mangled body and drew my Bowie.

The large blade flashed as I stabbed it down with both hands into his chest and jerked it down to his waist. His brief roar of pain turned into a gurgle as he thrashed weakly. Blood pulsated out from severed organs and arteries. The stench of slashed intestines must have been foul, but I didn't notice or care.

I shoved my hand into the large gash. Pushing aside organs, I reached deep inside of his ruined body until I found what I desired.

Clenching my fingers, I felt it beat weakly.

I stared into the ape's eyes and saw them begin to dim.

Refusing to let him die on his own, I jerked hard with every ounce of remaining strength and ripped the heart from his chest. The ape died.

I bit into the large organ savagely. Blood squirted, running down my face and chin as I ground my teeth through the raw muscle.

With a twist of my head, I ripped a mouthful free and spat it in the scar faced leader's face.

Screaming, I raised the mangled lump of flesh overhead for all to see.

Otto stood on a new, unwounded pony, a handful of freshly cut ape scalps hanging from his belt. The look on his face was one of approval.

Kicking the horse's flanks, he raced away, bounding over corpses in the street.

***

I dropped the worthless organ in the dirt and stood over the leader's corpse.

The apes were gone, and the street was filled with silence amidst the crackle of flames from burning buildings and moans of the wounded.

Soldiers walked down the street from the train station in uniforms fresh and unbloodied. With rifles held warily, they looked at the carnage in disbelief. Defenders, wide eyed and bloodied, began emerging from buildings.

Bodies were everywhere. White man, red man, apes, trikes, and raptors. Everywhere. Arrows stuck from the ground, buildings, and corpses.

From the church steeple, Skyla and Ashley waved and began to climb down. My lovely scientist looked exhausted, but alive.

That's all that mattered.

Ignoring the other survivors, I walked to the partially collapsed building. The trike managed to free itself and only a pile of broken boards and timbers lay where the dinosaur had been. I kicked some fallen porch boards around until the familiar shape of my *Eighty-Six* was exposed.

I picked the rifle up. There were smears of red and yellow ape face paint on the buttstock, a few dings in the wood, and some bluing scratched. But the Winchester 1886 seemed fully operational.

Skyla and Ashley came out from around the church. Brandthorn limped beside them, his uniform ripped and torn, with blood oozing from a broken arrow shaft embedded in his leg. His bent and bloodied officer's sword was clenched tight in his hand. I was pleased to see the Irishman had survived.

Seeing my bloodied face, Skyla rushed forward. Her face was pale and her eyes searching as she rubbed hands across my mouth and jaw, looking for a wound. Not finding one, she threw herself against me, wrapping my body in her arms.

I held her tightly while keeping a look out for any more apes that might be lingering behind.

"I knew we'd both make it." She pushed away and curled her fingers around the large black claw on my necklace she'd given me for luck. "Our story is just beginning."

"Yes, it is. And it's off to a wild start," I grinned down at her, knowing I looked hideous with my blood smeared mouth and grimy face. Even my teeth were probably red with bits of ape heart stuck between them. My mouth still had the tangy taste of iron from the blood.

Wade came up behind us, his rifle slung over a shoulder, the single shot Ballard rifle deserving every bit of praise the wolverine slayer had heaped upon it. The front of the man's body looked like he'd been dipped in blood and rolled in dirt. His black powder revolver had what looked like ape hair and brains stuck to the butt of the gun. He shrugged at me sheepishly. "Sorry Jed, would have shot that big ape off you, but a couple jumped me. Figured you could handle one while I handled two."

I rolled my eyes in disgust and reminded him, "Mine was bigger."

Ashley slammed into Wade with such force that the man almost toppled over. But he managed to stay upright, and with complete and utter disregard for those of us standing in front of them, they locked lips.

"Yeah, just business partners, huh?" I teased with a smirk. Skyla elbowed me in the stomach not so gently. I grunted in pain. My entire body felt like one large bruise.

They pulled apart as Brandthorn hobbled to us. He painfully leaned against a hitching post and looked at the corpses around us. "We won, I suppose. But at great cost. I should know within an hour how many men we lost. But I suspect well over half of us," he nodded towards the fresh soldiers helping wounded defenders. "If it hadn't been for them, we'd all be dead."

"Sheriff Dan and his nephews make it?" Skyla asked hopefully. They'd been stationed with him at the northern entrance, helping to defend the crew-served weapons.

He gave a heavy sigh. "Raptor got the Sheriff. Dragged him out of our defenses before we could react. Both deputies went after him…. Then the trikes charged," he grimaced and shook his head. "Neither made it."

"Oh no, no, no," Skyla stammered, her voice quivering. I swallowed hard. The deputies had been pains in the ass, but the boys proved their courage in the end.

"Wade... what about Fredrick?" I was afraid to ask about the famed hunter. He'd volunteered to come, and I felt responsible for whatever may have happened to him.

"Alive and unwounded. Or was a few minutes ago." He jerked a thumb towards the rail station. "He's helping put out the tent fires."

I barked a short laugh, thankful he was alive, "If I had an ounce of that man's energy-"

Hooves thundered behind us. We all spun and raised guns, but didn't fire as Wesley rode through the smoke. He gave a solemn nod as his horse trotted past us. Several papers blew from saddle bags strapped to the back of his mount.

Reaching out, I caught one. Rubbing the dollar bill between my fingers for a moment, I released it and watched it drift away.

Apparently, the gunman robbed the saloon before leaving.

I guess most outlaws aren't meant to be heroes. I wished him luck, and hoped that this battle changed him for the better. But I doubted it. Some of us have a casualness towards human life that will never make us pure of heart, but it makes us hell on wheels in a fight.

Heavy doors to the bank opened, and women and children poured outside looking for loved ones. They stopped abruptly on the boardwalk in shock, looking at the death and destruction surrounding our once peaceful town. Some of the smaller kids started to cry and were quickly ushered back inside the building. Others ran frantically down the street, calling out the names of loved ones they hoped were still alive.

From the dusky haze strode Reydan and Cato. The gunman had both pistols in hand and his head on a swivel as he watched for threats. Oscar hurried along behind them, a handkerchief pressed to his lips and nose.

The tycoon was dressed sharply, not a wrinkle or smudge of battle showing on his clothing or person. His cane was tucked underneath his arm and he casually stepped over bodies and pools of blood in the dirt. Knowing his history, it was no surprise to me that the corpses surrounding us didn't bother him any.

"Ah, the valiant defenders of Granite Falls," he flashed a fake smile. His eyes darted towards me, "I see you survived."

The black gunman ignored us, still looking around as he holstered one pistol and began dumping empty shells out of the other. Oscar stared wide eyed in disbelief at a scalped ape several feet away.

"We did, sir. But a lot of good people died," Brandthorn told him evenly.

"Glad I arrived in time to save the day," the tycoon chortled. He snapped his fingers at Oscar to get his attention. "Make sure the newspapers know that," he smirked and turned back to us. "Never waste the opportunity to make your mark."

Shifting the rifle to my left hand, I punched him in the face.

With a flick of his wrist, Cato snapped the cylinder shut on the pistol and jammed the muzzle against the side of my temple so hard a burst of pain shot through my skull.

The tycoon dropped the ivory handled cane and staggered backwards, holding his face. Blood oozed between his fingers and onto his immaculate white shirt.

"You little bastard!" he bellowed and pointed a blood smeared finger at me. "Cato, kill him!"

"No!" Brandthorn raised his blood smeared sword at the gunman in warning. "Do it, and I'll have you hanged." He shifted the tip of the sword towards Reydan. "No one shoots a man for throwing a punch, and only cowards have others do their killing for them."

Skyla drew her pistol and cocked the hammer back. Wade placed his hand on the grisly butt of his revolver. Ashley's rifle was already pointed at the tycoon's midsection. She winked at him with a sly smile.

Turning my head slowly, I looked down the barrel at Cato. His face was expressionless. Not for the first time, I wondered if anything remained of my friend inside the cold-hearted killer.

The gunman calmly holstered his pistol before pulling out a bandana for Reydan. The tycoon jerked the cloth from his hand and clenched it against his nose. "Worthless. As for you," he glared at me over the black handkerchief, "your land is already mine. And your day of reckoning is coming."

The temptation to loan him one of my guns to duel was strong. But it was too quick a death for the old union raider. His crimes would require a slow, painful death.

Turning his back on us, Reydan began walking toward the rail station. The gunman picked up the cane and followed. Oscar waddled behind them.

"I do believe he's going to have you killed," the Lieutenant said as he sagged against the rail.

"Maybe, but he ain't so proud now."

Skyla grabbed Brandthorn around the waist to help him up. "Jed doesn't seem to kill easy. And you, sir, need some help." She glanced over her shoulder. "Come find me later, Jedidiah Huckleberry."

"Yes, ma'am."

From the alley, Chief Toko swaggered out proudly followed by Squatting Bull. Both of their painted faces were splashed with blood. The Shaynee Chief carried a soldier's rifle and pointed the barrel at the black smoke billowing over us. The fires were beginning to burn out and chain gangs of fresh soldiers were heaving buckets of water on anything that appeared worth saving. "You white men send smoke signals like shit."

Ashley leaned against Wade as he barked a short laugh.

"Glad you lived, Chief. Thanks for saving us white folks. If there is anything we can do in return, let me know."

"You can get hell off our land," Squatting Bull growled angrily. I was glad to see he didn't hold grudges.

"Maybe next spring, pooping cow," I smirked at the hot-headed Indian.

He started towards me, but the Chief stopped him with an outstretched arm. Ignoring the banter between his young brave and myself, the old Indian chuckled. "I see Otto no kill you."

"Saved me actually," I admitted ruefully. "Reckon we are even now."

"We see. Come Squatting Bull," he shot a glare towards the soldiers by the train. "We go regain strength before push white man off land for good."

Reaching out, he clasped my hand firmly in his.

"Huck Berry, you ate hairy man heart. Make you strong now," he winked and walked down the alley where a brave on horseback held the reins to two other ponies. The young Indian sullenly followed.

"Now what?" Ashley asked.

"I reckon I need to find Carbine." I wondered what my terrible horse had been up to. Hopefully not being eaten. I looked first in the direction Reydan and Cato went, then up the street where Skyla was helping a pair of soldiers hold Brandthorn down while another removed the broken arrow shaft from his leg. Even with stringy dark hair draped over her gun smoke and dust smeared face, she was beautiful. I stretched my back, feeling the familiar scar tissue tugging at my skin. Revenge could wait a little while longer. Reydan White was a walking dead man.

Soldiers pointed towards the direction the apes attacked from and began shouting. Racking a round into my rifle, we rushed down an alley and climbed onto the battered remains of an overturned wagon to see.

A flock of pterosaurs were descending upon the battle field. At least two dozen, identical to the one that splattered Oscar days ago. With piercing shrieks, they began feasting on dead apes scattered across the valley floor.

***

I found the Reverend reading his Bible on a rough sawn pew inside the church. His clothes were torn and stained with blood, but he appeared well enough. He nodded at me silently as I shifted his shotgun aside and sat.

"Care for a drink?" he asked, pulling a bottle out from under our bench.

I accepted and took a sip. It burned wonderfully down my parched throat. "I reckon the good Lord wasn't ready for you yet." He didn't appear interested in a drink, so I set the bottle on the floor between us and leaned back.

He shrugged. "That's alright, His plans for me continue."

I picked Old Bessy up. The shotgun was caked with blood and dirt. Snapping it open, I checked the chambers. It was loaded. "So, you finally got to smite evil. How do you feel about that, Reverend?" I felt like it was my turn to check in on him for once.

"Surprisingly, satisfied," he smiled sadly. "Maybe I should've been a lawman instead of a preacher?"

I looked around the room. It was a mess. Dozens of brass cartridges were scattered across the floor, mixed with plenty of fired shotgun shells. "Maybe, but I think you answered the right calling."

The man of faith nodded quietly beside me and closed the Bible. We sat in silence.

Remembering there had been an inscription carved into the shotgun's stock, I used the ragged end of my shirt to wipe off the grime and read the words aloud, "The Lord keeps all who love Him, but all the wicked He will destroy." I swallowed hard. "Reckon I got lucky then. For a while I was certainly wicked."

The Reverend gently took the shotgun from my hands. He leaned close to me and whispered conspiringly, "I told you, He's got plans for you as well."

***

It'd been several days since the battle.

Thirty-five people died, including all but six of Brandthorn's soldiers. The one-legged confederate died well, his teeth buried in an ape's throat even with a spear jammed through his guts. He death was a testimony to the perseverance of the South.

When the school house burned, Timmy's body burned with it. There was a bullet hole through his blackened skull, but no one knew who put it there. His crispy remains were dumped into an unmarked grave.

There were a lot of funerals. I only attended Dan's and his nephews'.

The town was rebuilding as folks returned to their damaged or destroyed homes, businesses, mines. Journalists and photographers appeared almost overnight to take pictures and write articles about the 'Battle of the Apes' as they called it.

Even President Cleveland came to town.

On a hastily built platform standing beside Governor Hardy, he announced Wyoming Territory had been formerly accepted into Union and was now the State of Wyoming. Also on the stage was Reydan White, beaming with his broken nose as he accepted much praise for his daring rescue of our doomed town.

I skipped the entire dog and pony show, preferring the company of Skyla and Carbine at my ranch. Surprisingly, the place hadn't been burned by Otto or vengeful apes. But it'd been rifled through and several things were missing. I wasn't sure who to blame.

Skyla still didn't know about my past and I wasn't sure how to tell her. In the meantime, I kept as low of a profile as possible. But stories got out about me. Those kept me up at night wondering when my past would come calling.

Wade and Ashley were in Cheyenne, getting things moving on their western show and trying to figure out if dinosaurs had a part to play in it. They promised to visit, and come running should we need them. It's good to have friends like that.

The day after the President's announcement, I led Brandthorn, now a Captain, through the tunnel with a company of soldiers and four Gatling guns hauled behind teams of horses. Even freshly wounded, the Irishman was adamant that he led the expedition to the other side.

The grand questions were, if this was an army of apes, where was the supporting civilization that raised them? We knew there were people on this side, the Shaynee's history and my witnessing of the Indian sacrifice confirmed that. But where were they?

There were too many questions with no answers.

Skyla and Fredrick rode with us as well. Our scientist was now a regular westerner, complete with pistol and rifle, even though she struggled to ride western style on her borrowed appaloosa horse. As usual, our famous hunter was sharply dressed in fringed clothing, and armed to the teeth. He had a rifle in scabbard strapped to each side of his horse, and twin pistols wrapped around his waist. He was adamant to be the first to kill a Tyrannosaurus.

It was slow going, especially pulling the Gatlings. But our party was large enough that everything seemed to avoid us. The scouts we sent ahead to find us a route through the forest weren't so lucky. We lost one, and when we searched all we found was a large splatter of blood and pieces of shredded uniform amongst trampled brush. After that we pulled the other soldiers in and made it to the ape's canyon without trouble.

It'd been abandoned.

There were no hairy savages, but all manner of weapons and equipment had been left behind. The large black obsidian altar had days old blood smeared across it. No doubt a sacrifice in exchange for victory over us.

I guess that meant we kicked their evil monkey god's butt as well.

We lit lanterns and entered the ape's caves with weapons drawn. Natural tunnels had been chiseled into shape with numerous rooms cut into the rock. Burnt out torches lined the walls. We found paintings drawn on the rock depicting scenes of battle, of apes, humans, beasts, and creatures we hoped weren't real.

After finding no sign of life, we broke apart in small groups to explore.

At the end of a dead-end tunnel, Skyla, Fredrick and I found a sheet of thick, pebbled leather hanging from across a carved doorway. Cautiously pushing the hide aside with the shotgun, I walked into a room filled with junk. All manner of hides, pouches, broken weapons, along with chipped bits of obsidian were strewn across the floor in piles.

Skyla, always the scientist, dug through several of them.

Seeing a glint reflected from our dancing light in the corner, I kicked through a pile of broken spear shafts and cracked clubs.

Among them was an old metal breastplate. Rusted, dented, with a large hole through the side... just large enough for a spear. Surprised, I shoved the lantern at Fredrick and dug deeper into the pile as he and Skyla watched. At the bottom, I found a strange pistol. It was huge, almost two feet long. The wood was cracked and splintered, the end of the grip had a round engraved metal knob covered in a thin film of rust. It appeared to be an ancient flint lock pistol, with a strange rotating hammer on the outside. The mechanism was loose; whatever strange contraption worked it had rusted away or been lost long ago.

Puzzled, I passed the gun to Skyla. She took it in both hands and examined it in the torch light while I dug for more old stuff. Not finding anything else, we made our way back outside for a better look at our loot.

While my friends discussed the possibilities of how the old weapon and plate armor ended up in an ape cave with Captain Brandthorn, I slung the shotgun over my saddle pommel and pulled the *Eighty-Six* from its scabbard to go for a walk.

I intended to look at the raptor cage, but a group of soldiers were already over there, inspecting the construction and area. Not feeling particularly social, I walked to the small hill where I'd seen the ape leader's broken horn trike before. Walking through the knee-high grass, I heard a soft mewing noise and the rustle of shifting grass. Tucking the rifle stock into my shoulder, I moved slowly, searching for the maker of the noise.

I found a nest.

It was six feet across, made of matted grass, and contained numerous broken shells from what must have been eggs the size of melons. Amongst them lay a pitifully small female trike, tan and yellow streaked, and about a foot long from beak to tail. She appeared to have been left behind during the ape's retreat. Most likely too young to survive their journey to go piss someone else off.

Upon seeing me, she rose on all fours and shook her underdeveloped horns at me.

Squatting, I slowly pulled a piece of hardtack out from a pocket and held it out.

With a tentative step, watching me curiously, the little dinosaur moved forward. Then another step, and another. She mewed again and cautiously took the piece of dense bread from my fingers with her beak.

I gently ran my hands along her top horns and the developing bone shield as she ate. The little trike seemed to like that, and moved closer, pushing against my hand like a cat.

"You look like you could use a new home. And a name."

She playfully nipped at my fingertips with her beak.

"How about Sara?"

The End

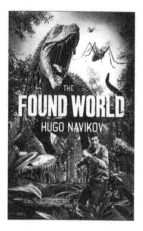

CHECK OUT OTHER GREAT DINOSAUR BOOKS

FLIPSIDE
by JAKE BIBLE

The year is 2046 and dinosaurs are real.

Time bubbles across the world, many as large as one hundred square miles, turn like clockwork, revealing prehistoric landscapes from the Cretaceous Period.

They reveal the Flipside.

Now, thirty years after the first Turn, the clockwork is breaking down as one of the world's powers has decided to exploit the phenomenon for their own gain, possibly destroying everything then and now in the process.

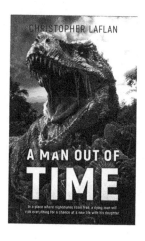

A MAN OUT OF TIME
by Christopher Laflan

Five years after the Chinese Axis detonated an unknown weapon of mass destruction off the southern coast of the United States, Special Ops Sergeant John Crider and the members of Shadow Company have finally captured what they all hope will lead to the end of the war. Unfortunately, the population within the United States is no longer sustainable. In an effort to stabilize the economy, the government enacts the Cryonics Act. One hundred years in suspended animation, all debt forgiven, and a chance at a less crowded future are too good to pass up for John and his young daughter.

Except not everything always goes as planned as Sergeant John Crider finds himself pitted against a land of prehistoric monsters genetically resurrected from the fossil record, murderous inhabitants, and a future he never wanted.

Made in United States
Orlando, FL
14 December 2022